Elizabeth Falconer lives in Gloucestershire and spends part of the year in the south of France. *Tiger Fitzgerald* is her seventh novel; her first six novels, *The Golden Year*, *The Love of Women*, *The Counter-Tenor's Daughter*, *Wings of the Morning*, *A Barefoot Wedding* and *Frost at Midnight*, are also published by Black Swan.

www.booksattransworld.co.uk

TIGER FITZGERALD

Elizabeth Falconer

BLACK SWAN

TIGER FITZGERALD
A BLACK SWAN BOOK : 0 552 99840 0

First publication in Great Britain

PRINTING HISTORY
Black Swan edition published 2001

1 3 5 7 9 10 8 6 4 2

Set in 11pt Melior by
County Typesetters, Margate, Kent.

Black Swan Books are published by Transworld Publishers,
61–63 Uxbridge Road, London W5 5SA,
a division of The Random House Group Ltd,
in Australia by Random House Australia (Pty) Ltd,
20 Alfred Street, Milsons Point, Sydney, NSW 2061, Australia,
in New Zealand by Random House New Zealand Ltd,
18 Poland Road, Glenfield, Auckland 10, New Zealand
and in South Africa by Random House (Pty) Ltd,
Endulini, 5a Jubilee Road, Parktown 2193, South Africa.

Printed and bound in Great Britain by
Clays Ltd, St Ives plc.

To Ursula

CHAPTER ONE

As she usually did, Alice Fitzgerald woke just after dawn in the vast mahogany four-poster in which her parents had slept throughout their married life. In this bed they had conceived their only child, continued to make passionate love into old age and finally died within a few short weeks of each other. Their last rites of passage had taken place ten years previously, and since that sad time Alice herself had been the sole occupant of their beautiful bed.

Lying indolently against the piles of lace-edged Irish linen pillows, her eyes half closed against the dust-laden beams of early sunlight that streamed through the uncurtained windows, one thin hand resting on her bony chest, Alice allowed her unreliable memory to drift, like a homing pigeon, back into the distant and adored territory of her childhood. Without conscious effort, she invoked the image of her father Daniel O'Neill cantering along the lake shore below the house, pursued by his bold, beautiful and resolute wife, Tara.

Dan had been the fortunate and proud owner of Neill's Court, a Georgian house of singular beauty, built on the south-facing shore of a large freshwater lake in the west of Ireland. He was a fair-haired, handsome man with clear hazel eyes, a florid complexion and the loud, insistent voice of one accustomed to being obeyed. He had inherited the property from his father, an Anglo-Irishman who had made a great deal of money by dubious and unspecified means during the First World War. It had been at Neill's Court that Alice had spent a childhood of virtually unalloyed bliss, more often than not mounted on a succession of much loved ponies, her innocent happiness untrammelled by the boring interruptions of education. Dan had not believed in education, especially where girls were concerned.

In fact, Alice had learned to read, out of sheer curiosity, by means of deciphering the labels on the bottles containing various equine medicaments in the tack room, the instructions printed on tins of Harpic in the lavatory, and the reading material obtained from cereal packets and jam jars on the breakfast table. In bad weather, when it was impossible to be out of doors, she gradually advanced her reading skills by laboriously perusing the books to be found, uncut, in her father's library.

Liam Dainty, Alice's lifelong companion and devoted servant, now entered the bedroom bringing early morning tea. 'Sit up, me darling girl,' he said cheerfully, 'and drink it while it's hot.'

'Angel,' whispered Alice, dragging her mind back to the present, and sitting up.

Liam had lived at Neill's Court all his life. Raised in an unemotional way by the groom's wife, he had been fifteen years old at the time of Alice's birth. From the very beginning, he had adored the baby girl in an entirely uncharacteristic way, for he was ordinarily a youth of formidable attitude, despising most of his acquaintance, resentful of authority, and quite incapable of gratitude in the face of kindness. It was obvious to all concerned that it was only his skill with horses and his devotion to the little Alice that had saved him from the sack years ago.

The years passed, and the strange pair rode out every day, spent hours together roaming the hills, or lying in the sweet-smelling long grass, watching the bees and butterflies flit from blue scabious to fragile scarlet poppy. In due season, they gathered sloes from the hedgerows and packed them into bottles of gin, stolen from Daniel's cellar, for secret consumption at Christmastime in Liam's room over the stables.

Then, on Alice's eighteenth birthday, everything changed. Tara had been so preoccupied with her own delightful life with Dan that she had scarcely noticed the passage of time, and it was quite a shock for her to take on board the fact that her daughter was now on the brink of womanhood. With characteristic enthusiasm, she engaged a local dressmaker to make Alice a decent suit, for lunch parties, as well as three suitably frilly and youthful-looking ball gowns. Within a month, these clothes hung in Alice's wardrobe, and invitations had been sent out to 'the county' to celebrate Alice's coming out, in the shape of a dance at Neill's Court. Although in itself modestly spectacular, this occasion failed to impress its heroine, and she spent the latter part of it in the stables with Liam. Greatly encouraged by the rapid consumption of the bottle of non-vintage champagne Alice had had the foresight to bring with her, the two friends lost little time in engaging in highly enjoyable sex. This activity did nothing to improve the appearance of Alice's pretty dress, and they decided that it would be a mistake for her to return to the house until the last of the guests had departed, at half past two.

The fallout from this ill-mannered behaviour was predictable, and when Liam explained that Alice had just slipped out for a breath of air, having a headache from all the music and dancing, and that they had gone for a brief walk, during which Alice had had the misfortune to fall into a ditch, Dan cut him short with a roar of rage and threatened Liam with instant dismissal for allowing such a thing to happen. This catastrophe was prevented by the hysterical screams and tears of Alice, who went so far as to issue dire warnings of her

9

certain suicide if Liam got the sack on her account. Fortunately, neither Dan nor Tara suspected for a second that the episode had been anything more than the gauche behaviour of an immature young girl, unwittingly encouraged by a servant in whose basic trustworthiness they had good reason to believe.

So, for the time being, Liam Dainty remained at Neill's Court, and Tara told her bemused husband to go to London, and find out whether any of his old college friends had eligible sons, and if so, to invite them for a weekend's fishing. It was as a result of one of these forays that Con Fitzgerald first came to Neill's Court, and was introduced to the lukewarm debutante, Alice O'Neill.

At eighteen, Alice was small and slight, deceptively frail-looking. She had a lot of fine curly fair hair and the wide-apart, slightly staring hazel eyes of her father. Unused to any kind of society other than that provided by Liam Dainty, she treated the newcomer with the condescension and lack of interest of an absent-minded child. Since he was not even a horseman, she lost little time in dumping him, and, with vaguely muttered excuses, took the horses out, as usual, with Liam.

Con Fitzgerald was, at that time, twenty-one years old and just down from Cambridge, where he had obtained a second class degree in English. He was a personable young man, more than ordinarily good-looking, a fact of which he was quite aware. He was tall, and his hair was very dark, almost black, in the Irish manner. His eyes, under straight black brows, were an intense violet-blue. The only feature that he would have wished to change, had the option been available to him, was his nose, which was large and hooked, like a hawk. If Con had had the funds, as well as the confidence to risk the ridicule of his friends, he would certainly have had a nose job.

While at university, he had distinguished himself by contributing some pretty sharp pieces of criticism to various undergraduate publications, as well as a few anonymous verses. His mind was now firmly set on a literary career, and since he had no means of support other than any money he could earn himself, or cadge from his widowed mother, Con saw at once that marriage to Alice O'Neill might at least have the advantage of providing him with a roof over his head, a quiet place to work, and regular meals. He therefore set about courting the reluctant Alice, and made it plain to her parents that he was a serious applicant for her hand.

For more than a year, during which Con was a frequent visitor to Neill's Court, Alice refused his oft-repeated proposals. She continued to ride over the hills with Liam, and was an eager participant in their frequent and energetic lovemaking. This enjoyable activity sometimes took place, rather poetically, under the wide blue sky, or, occasionally, behind the potting-shed in the walled kitchen garden, illuminated by the brilliance of a midsummer moon. At other times, very late at night, Alice would seek Liam out in his lair over the tack-room, and there she would slowly undress and lie down in the truckle bed that smelt of horse and Sloan's liniment. Liam, bedazzled by her beauty, and scarcely able to believe his luck, would dowse the lantern, take off his own clothes and lie down with Alice, covering her nakedness with his own body.

Eventually, Alice, after several false alarms, began to realize that it could only be a matter of time before she conceived. She was also dimly aware that her desire for joyful sex with Liam Dainty had nothing to do with her birthright as Miss O'Neill of Neill's Court. Quailing at the very idea of finding herself in the awkward position of having to inform her parents that she was pregnant by the stable-lad, she therefore sought out her father and told him that she was ready to marry Con Fitzgerald.

Daniel O'Neill remortgaged the house, in order to give his only daughter an impressive wedding, and pay for the honeymoon in Sri Lanka. Neither bride nor groom particularly enjoyed this once-in-a-lifetime trip, finding the climate too humid and hot, and the sea far from refreshing. Alice, in a sulky mood, openly pined for the mists and green hills of Ireland. It did not take her very long to begin comparing Con's skills as a lover extremely unfavourably with those of Liam Dainty, though, it goes without saying, she kept these thoughts to herself.

At Neill's Court, Liam Dainty, although heartbroken at the turn of events, was none the less determined not to allow anyone to guess at his private humiliation and distress. He suspected that if the slightest hint of his relationship with Alice, other than that of trusted servant and bodyguard, were to reach the ears of the O'Neills via the malicious tongues of the other servants, or from village gossip, all hell would break loose and he would be dismissed, turned out of his room and sent packing without a reference.

After giving the matter some thought, he decided that the smart plan would be to start building himself a reputation as a local womanizer, and not one who was too fussy, either. He began by flashing at the schoolteacher, a middle-aged spinster, waylaying her in the dark lane that connected her cottage to the village school. Rather flattered by these attentions, the good woman did not at once scream for help, and thus provoke the little scandal Liam had in mind. Instead, she advanced upon him with enthusiasm, causing him to button his breeches immediately and beat a hasty retreat.

A few days later, in the pub, he leered suggestively at a group of young girls, who stared back at him in collective astonishment, and then removed themselves from his vicinity amid gales of laughter.

Depressed by this lack of success, he visited a pub in the next village, but failed entirely to catch the eye of any girl. At last, as a final desperate throw, he tried to chat up a couple of stable-lads from a neighbouring estate, whom he knew to be gay. He insisted on buying them drinks, and did his best to imply that he was one of them. Later, outside the door of the shed that housed the pub's earth-closets, he overheard the lads discussing him. 'He'd fuck a stoat if he could get his hands on one,' said one, with a snort of derision. 'Dirty little wanker.'

Cringing at these words, but satisfied that he had done enough for the locals to embroider and enlarge upon, Liam continued to visit the pub twice a week, and knew, from the watchful eye kept on him by the landlord, that not one of them would ever guess that, far from fucking a stoat, he had been fucking O'Neill's daughter for years.

Liam Dainty was not a man of great physical appeal. Thirty-four years old at the time of Alice's marriage to Con Fitzgerald, he had bandy legs as a result of his long association with horses, a pock-marked weather-beaten face like a walnut, sparse brown hair that needed cutting, and small, rather cold blue eyes. Having made himself the butt of local hilarity and obscene jokes, he was now painfully aware that he had acted in a crass and foolish manner, in a pathetic attempt to cover his tracks. A wiser man would have left the area, and sought work elsewhere, as far away as possible. Lying miserably alone in his smelly little bed, Liam also knew that he was utterly incapable of leaving Neill's Court of his own volition, so abject and intense was his devotion to Alice, and so desperate his desire to see her.

Alice and Con returned from their honeymoon, and moved into the east wing of the house. For three months, they seemed quite content, Con working away in his study every morning, and fishing every afternoon after tea, sometimes with Alice dutifully at his side. However, it was not very long before Con began to find himself increasingly unwilling to endure the monotony of his life at Neill's Court. Forced by lack of funds to dine with his in-laws each evening, and having to listen to the incredibly boring conversation of their occasional guests, he decided that he must find a way of supplementing his income, and went to London in search of work. What he found turned out to be entirely suitable for someone with his qualifications, though unfortunately not as well paid as he would have wished. By means of a little networking he established himself as a reliable copy-editor, and this employment gave him the excuse to make frequent trips to London, as well as the funds to enjoy the company of his own friends once more.

Alice, completely unruffled by her husband's increasingly long absences, slipped back seamlessly into her former role as daughter of the house, and, to his joy, resumed her relationship with Liam, in every sense of the word.

On Alice's twentieth birthday, she gave birth to a daughter, Orla, and seven years later to another daughter, Niamh. Their father, whose time was now spent largely in London, took little interest in their upbringing, and they grew up at Neill's Court, adored by their grandparents, and looked after with absent-minded affection but little competence by their mother, aided by Edna, a beefy young nursery-maid from the village. The indefatigable Liam Dainty had both girls up on ponies before they could walk, and became a major presence in their young lives.

Things drifted on in this haphazard way for ten more years, with little change except the slow passage from spring to summer, autumn to winter, and back again to spring. Orla was now seventeen, and, at her own insistence, was receiving a good education at an English boarding school. She was a confident girl, top of her form, and aiming for university. Of medium height, and slim, she had her mother's fair curly hair, though her eyes were green, like unripe gooseberries. The younger sister, Niamh, now ten, had the same O'Neill curly hair, but quite dark, and her eyes were blue-grey, like the wet pebbles on the lake shore. She looked extremely like her mother, but did not share Alice's love of horses.

Then, to everyone's astonishment, and to her own dismay and consternation, Alice gave premature birth to a third daughter. At thirty-seven years old, she had assumed that another pregnancy was not at all on the cards. She had completely ignored the warning signs and her thickening waistline, putting it all down to middle age and wind. The unlooked-for event took place in her bed, in the early hours of the morning.

Tara O'Neill, awakened by the sound of urgent voices in the corridor outside, went to investigate and found Liam Dainty hurrying towards Alice's door, carrying a bucket of hot water. 'What the hell are you up to, Dainty?' she demanded.

'It's Miss Alice, ma'am. She's brought to bed again, so it seems. Another girl, so it is, ma'am.'

'Good heavens! Are you sure?'

'So I believe, ma'am.' He knocked on Alice's door.

Edna, the nursery-maid, appeared, and took the bucket from him. 'It's towels we need now, Liam, and be quick!' she ordered briskly, then turned to Tara. 'Will you be coming in, ma'am? It's a fine girl, so it is, a real little beauty!'

Liam departed at the double in search of towels, and Tara hastened into Alice's room to view her grand-child. She was far from impressed by the little scrap of red flesh and realized immediately that the baby was unlikely to weigh more than a couple of packs of butter. It occurred to her that the infant might easily die without the benefit of Christian baptism, so she rushed downstairs to the telephone and, after calling the midwife, sent the jaunting-car to bring the Anglican priest from the nearby town.

The midwife was the first to arrive. After cutting the cord, she took the baby and went to the bathroom, where she bathed her in the washbasin. Tara fetched her best pink bath-towel and wrapped it tightly round the tiny girl, then carried her down to the drawing-room, where she found Daniel, a glass of brandy in his hand to steady his nerves, watching the shabby little priest preparing the necessary paraphernalia for the christening ceremony. Alice, supported by Liam Dainty and the nursery-maid, was half-carried into the room and installed on the chintz-covered sofa.

The priest indicated that he was ready, and Tara, carrying her granddaughter, went and stood before him. The ceremony began. At such short notice, the unfortunate man had not had time to perform his usual ablutions, and the smell that emanated from his body was overwhelming. Tara took a step backwards, and then another, treading on Daniel's toes as she did so, bringing tears to the poor man's eyes.

The priest gabbled through the service, as fast as he decently could. He lifted his eyes to Tara's. 'Name this child,' he said.

Taken aback, Tara O'Neill turned to her daughter. 'What's her name, darling? Have you thought?'

Alice's eyes fell on the moth-eaten tiger-skin rug that lay before the fireplace, its huge stuffed head display-ing open snarling jaws and gleaming yellow glass eyes. She looked thoughtfully at the rug and then at her mother. 'Tiger,' she said.

'Tiger?'

'Yes. Tiger O'Neill Fitzgerald. That's her name,' said Alice firmly, in case there should be any doubt about it.

Two weeks later, Con Fitzgerald returned from London, and found himself to be the father of yet another daughter, with the offensive name of Tiger. No amount of pleading, ranting or bullying could make Alice change her mind, and Tiger the little girl remained.

Humiliated, completely sidelined by the O'Neills,

and treated as of little consequence by Orla, his eldest daughter, Con packed his bags and went to stay with an old friend in southern Italy. A month later, Alice received a curt note from him, giving his new address and undertaking to continue paying for the education of their daughters. She did not bother to reply, merely passing Con's letter to her lawyer.

Tiger Fitzgerald, like her siblings, grew up at Neill's Court, and by the time she was five years old it was clear that she would become the beauty of the family. Tall for her age, and slender, she had the beautiful violet-blue eyes of her father Con, as well as his straight black hair. Orla, at twenty-two, was already married and living in London. Niamh, at fifteen, was in the throes of a spotty and monosyllabic adolescence, and it was understandable that the enchanting little Tiger should have become the darling of the household, and the apple of her grandparents' eyes. These sentiments were not shared by her older sisters, who regarded her as a spoiled brat, and an unnecessary drain on the already precarious O'Neill finances.

Soon after Tiger's eighth birthday, a series of very sad events took place. Tara, on one of her regular visits to offer carrots and peppermints to the horses in the stables, had, in her fearless way, gone alone into the loose-box of a nervous young horse that the lads were bringing on as a potential racing prospect, and had paid for her folly by being viciously kicked and then trampled on. Her cries for help had brought three lads running, and she had been swiftly rescued, but her internal injuries were too severe for a woman of seventy to survive, and she died three days later in the arms of her distraught husband. Daniel was utterly heartbroken, becoming even more dependent on alcohol than usual, and six weeks after Tara's death, he got up in the night and went for a swim in the cold grey waters of the lake. His body was found on the shore the following morning.

After the funeral the will was read, and Alice, at the age of forty-five, found herself to be the sole heiress of Neill's Court. The house and land turned out to be even more heavily mortgaged than had been supposed. The income from the estate was practically non-existent, comprising the small amount of interest on the remaining capital fund, and the erratic earnings from the buying, training and selling-on of horses that had been her father's only other source of revenue.

To the dismay of her two older daughters, Alice seemed unmoved by the implications revealed by her father's will, and Orla, in particular, lost no time in pointing out to her mother that in all probability there would come a point when she would have to sell up, dispose of the horses, dismiss the servants, and retire to a small house more suited to her new circumstances. Then, tight-lipped, she returned to London.

Alice's willingness to pay any attention to the financial vagaries of day-to-day existence had always been somewhat tenuous, and, far from being unduly disturbed by Orla's dire prophecies, she moved calmly into her parents' big, comfortable bedroom, and life continued much as it had always done.

Tiger was now a pupil at her sisters' school in England, with slightly reduced fees, on account of being the third sister to grace the establishment with her presence.

Niamh, having taken her A-levels with very disappointing results, decided that her education was complete, and, since she had never harboured any ambition to go to university anyway, looked forward to spending the rest of her life in Ireland, and, perhaps, marrying some pleasant and suitable man in due course.

Wishing to give her sister a taste of city life, Orla invited her to stay with her in London, and Niamh was happy to accept. Islington, where Orla lived, she thought a pleasant enough place, but was appalled by the traffic, the dirt and noise of London. Equally, she was surprised at Orla's evident pride in her small terraced house, with its poky little rooms, no garage and scarcely any garden. After the shabby spaciousness of Neill's Court, it seemed to Niamh rather like a doll's house.

Orla's husband, Matthew Cleobury, a barrister by profession, was an unexceptionable young man of impeccable background. Niamh observed without surprise that he appeared to be completely under Orla's thumb, rarely disagreeing with her in any way. Curiously, far from giving pleasure to Orla, this seemed to irritate her, and this Niamh found somewhat depressing. It will be better when they have children, she thought. He'll be a perfect father, I'm sure, and she'll realize her luck.

After a week of sightseeing, shopping and visits to the theatre, Orla decided to tackle her sister on the subject of their family home and its uncertain future. The interview took place in Orla's custom-built kitchen, at the breakfast table, after the departure of Matthew to his chambers, and before the arrival of the cleaning lady.

Orla poured each of them another cup of coffee, and lit a cigarette. 'I have to tell you, darling,' she said, 'that I am quite worried about you. If you're not very careful, you'll find yourself stuck at home, housekeeping for Mother and Tiger, as well as looking after that ghastly great pile of a house.'

Niamh blinked. 'What makes you think that?' she asked.

'It's obvious, isn't it? Mother can't run that place on her own, you must realize that. She's like a child; she looks straight through you; doesn't want to listen, if you try to pin her down. At Grandfather's wake, her eyes were darting everywhere, as if she wanted to escape from something. Didn't you notice?'

'That's just her manner, Orla. She's always got upset and fidgety about things she doesn't want to take on board, hasn't she?'

'Hysteric is the word I'd use, Niamh, as a matter of fact. You're too close to her to see what's happening, that's the trouble. If you'd been away for a few years, as I have, you'd see at once how much she's deteriorated. I'm going to check it out with a psychiatrist friend of mine, but I'm pretty sure Mother's suffering from premature senility. Probably, the kindest thing would be to have her put away, for her own good.'

'You can't be serious?'

'I am.'

'I can't believe that you can even *think* such wicked thoughts, Orla. It's a load of garbage, and I'm going home tomorrow. And if necessary, I *will* look after the place; and Mother, too, whatever you say.'

On the journey home, Niamh had plenty of time to think, and plenty of time to formulate a plan of action. Not wishing to alarm her mother in any way, she decided to consult Liam Dainty privately and, after Alice had gone to bed, summoned him to the library. For several hours, they went carefully through the various legal documents and bank statements, until Liam was entirely au fait with the situation. His shoulders drooped, and he sighed. 'I suppose she'll just have to sell, poor lady, and there's an end of it.'

'Well, not necessarily, Liam. I've got an idea.'

'Oh? And what idea would that be, miss?'

'I thought we might turn the place into a fishing hotel. You know, a sort of guest-house.'

'A guest-house? You mean, *strangers* sleeping in the place?'

'That's exactly what I mean, Liam.'

'What about the cooking and that?'

'I'd do it.'

'What about your mother? Don't you think she'd mind seeing the house full of people she doesn't know?'

'She needn't see them, if she doesn't want to. Her bit of the house could be quite separate; she could even have her own garden. Not a big one, of course, but quite private.'

'What about the horses, Miss Niamh?'

'They'll have to go, of course. The lads, too, I'm afraid, Liam.'

'And the indoor staff, miss?'

'We'll keep Edna, of course, and I'll need some help in the kitchen.'

'And what about me, miss? Will you be letting me go, too?'

'*You*, Liam? Of course not! My mother depends on you for everything, you know that.' She smiled. 'It's your own fault. You've spoiled her for years, haven't you?'

Liam looked gratified, but said nothing.

Niamh frowned, and looked at him, choosing her words carefully. 'Liam,' she said quietly, 'my sister is worried about Mother's health. She seems to think that Mother has become rather vague and forgetful. What do you think?'

Liam stared at Niamh for a long moment, then lowered his eyes. 'If that's so, Miss Niamh, isn't it our Christian duty to take the best care of her we can?'

Niamh went to the glass-fronted bookcase, and took a bottle of whisky and two glasses from their secret hiding place. She poured two large tots, then handed a glass to Liam. 'You're a loyal friend, Liam,' she said. 'I won't be able to pay you much to start with, you understand?'

'Money's not uppermost in my mind, just at present, miss.'

'I know that, Liam. Thank you.'

Much later, as the hard-working months went by, Niamh was to ask herself many times whether it had been her love for her mother or her passion for Neill's Court that had been the motivation for hanging such a millstone round her own young neck. As she toiled in the kitchen garden, hoeing the endless rows of organically grown vegetables and herbs that formed the basis of her increasingly admired cooking, she was unable to decide what it was that had provoked her into making such a sacrifice. Although for the present the scheme seemed to be working fairly well, at least well enough to keep their heads above water, Niamh was not without intelligence and she was uneasily aware that, in the long term, both she and Neill's Court were probably on a hiding to nothing.

From time to time, as she had always done, Niamh recalled with pain and bitterness the departure of her father, after the birth of Tiger. She had, as a girl, rather worshipped Con, and had missed him cruelly, though she had never mentioned this to anyone. At ten years old, it had been too difficult to articulate the sense of loss and anguish she had suffered at her father's rejection of her.

Now, in a confused way, she was trying to convince herself that the burden she had undertaken was her way of proving to Con that she was quite capable of assuming what should have been his responsibility: looking after Alice, protecting his children and keeping the roof over all their heads. The fact that Con was entirely unaware of the current situation at Neill's Court never seemed to occur to her.

In fact, there was an additional element in her narrow world that prevented Niamh from throwing in the towel: she had a lover. Like her mother before her, she had become sexually involved with a man much older than herself, and equally unsuitable in many other ways. The headmaster of the local primary school, Michael Keen was already married, with two children and a bored and unhappy wife, who had rapidly come to the conclusion that she had married beneath her. She longed to go back to Dublin, and return to work and a more interesting social life, as she never ceased to remind her husband.

Niamh and Michael were very discreet in the matter of their illicit relationship, meeting infrequently, and always at night. The old potting-shed, the former scene of such meetings between Alice and Liam, provided the pile of old sacks on which their brief and fairly perfunctory couplings took place. It was this unlikely liaison with a man practically old enough to be her father that somehow convinced Niamh that there was some kind of point to her life, other than the gardening, cooking and waiting at table that kept her busy for ten long years. Her twenty-eighth birthday passed with little to show for it except a card from Tiger. The former friends of the O'Neills had long since ceased to regard the family as of any consequence, and her own mother, of course, was simply not aware of the date. Liam had forgotten things like birthdays long ago.

Orla deliberately chose not to wish Niamh many happy returns, for she considered that her sister's determination to keep Neill's Court going at all costs was an act of incredible folly, and constantly harangued her long-suffering husband on the subject. By now, Matthew had provided Orla with two sons, Edward and Charles, eight and six years old respectively. These little boys were down for Winchester, and it was Orla's waking nightmare that when the time came, Matthew would not be able to afford the enormous fees required for such an education. Both children were fairly bright, but neither of them was clever enough to be scholarship material, and Orla often reminded Matthew of this distressing fact. 'Of course,' she said bitterly, 'if bloody Niamh had had the common sense to agree with me, and make Mother sell that ruin, and divide the money between us, all this need never have arisen.'

Matthew was climbing the legal ladder with some success, and saw no reason why, in the fullness of time, his income should not be equal to Orla's expectations. He was, however, burdened with an enormous mortgage and they lived wildly beyond their means, a fact frequently pointed out to him by his bank

23

manager. He quite saw Orla's point that forcing the sale of her family home would ameliorate their financial situation, but was not very happy about the methods proposed by his wife in achieving this end. 'Even if your family could be persuaded that selling up would be in their best interest,' he said in his reasonable way, 'surely it would cost a great deal to settle your mother in a new home, with the appropriate staff and nursing care.'

'That shouldn't be a problem, Matthew. Ghastly old Liam Dainty does everything for her, you know that perfectly well. It's disgusting. He even baths her, and takes her to the loo, all that.'

'If that's what she wants, darling, then she's lucky to have him.'

'You're talking utter rot, as usual; you're as bad as Niamh. I can't understand why she hasn't kicked the repulsive old brute out years ago, and put Mother in a home.'

'Darling Orla, do try to be reasonable. I'm pretty sure that nursing homes in Ireland cost a small fortune, just as they do here.'

'OK, then,' said Orla sulkily. 'Perhaps we'd better get her certified. Maybe the loony-bin would cost less?'

Matthew closed his eyes, and his mind. 'In any case,' he said quietly, after a pause, 'even if Niamh would agree to such a plan, which I doubt, I think it's more than probable that Neill's Court wouldn't fetch enough these days to realize more than a few thousand each for you three girls, at the end of the day.'

'It might, if it was sold as a fishing hotel; a going concern. At least, there'd be no harm in looking into it, Matthew.'

Matthew sighed, and reluctantly agreed to speak to a friend who dealt in country estates, and get an opinion from him. He then drove to his chambers, applied himself thankfully to the brief waiting on his desk, and managed to put the entire distasteful affair out of his mind. That night, at dinner, Orla eagerly asked what

24

progress Matthew had made, and, very smoothly, he replied that Piers was unfortunately in the West Indies at the moment, but that his secretary had promised to get him to call Matthew on his return.

Fortunately for the residents of Neill's Court, they remained in blissful ignorance of Orla's intentions for their future, and life continued much as before.

It was true that Alice's memory had become seriously unreliable, and quite frequently she even had difficulty in remembering her own name. Sometimes Niamh stole enough time from her labours to pay her mother a visit. Usually, she found her sitting submissively in a cane chair in the orangery, gazing disinterestedly through the dirty glass of the windows, wondering vaguely what all those people were doing down there, fishing in her father's lake. On these occasions, Alice sometimes failed to recognize her own daughter straight away, which Niamh found extremely hurtful, in view of the fact that Alice never forgot who Liam Dainty was.

It was in the orangery that Alice spent most of her waking hours, waiting for Liam to bring her a drink, or her meals, until, finally, at six o'clock, it was time for him to take her up to bed again. Uneasily aware that there was something not entirely proper about Liam's all-encompassing physical care of her mother, Niamh had from time to time suggested that they try to find a trained nurse to undertake these duties, thus releasing Liam to give Niamh herself more help in the kitchen garden. Such attempts to prise him from Alice's side were, however, quickly rejected by Liam himself. 'In any case, Miss Niamh,' he said sardonically, but with perfect truth, 'you couldn't afford it.'

So it was that Liam Dainty continued to care for the woman he loved, year after year. He got her up and dressed her in the mornings, brushing her greying blond curls, and applying a little eye-shadow from an ancient pot to the lids of her vacant hazel eyes.

Throughout the day, as she sat in the orangery, he brought her cups of tea, glasses of watered wine, her lunch and supper. If necessary, he sat beside her, and fed her with a spoon. After lunch, he read the paper to her. He did not think that she really understood anything, but the attention seemed to please her, and she smiled and laughed, nodding her head.

The happiest time of the day, for them both, was after Alice's early supper, when Liam would take her upstairs and give her a bath. As she lay in the warm scented water, he would gently soap her withered breasts, her wasted arms and legs, and Alice would respond to these caresses with little moans of pleasure. Sometimes her eyes would blaze with remembered passion, and she would wind her bony dripping arms round Liam's neck and drag his willing mouth down to hers.

Very occasionally, if Liam, listening at her door, heard her muttering distractedly to herself in the darkness, he would enter her room silently, and slip into bed with her, taking her in his reassuring arms, comforting her with soothing whispered words. From time to time, if she seemed more than usually anxious, he would make love to her, knowing that its effect on her would be better than a sleeping pill.

If Niamh was aware that parts of Liam Dainty's care of her mother were of an intensely personal nature, she chose to ignore it. In any case, as she reminded herself philosophically, there was not a lot she could do about it, without stirring up a hornets' nest, and depriving Alice of the little happiness at her disposal.

CHAPTER TWO

Tiger Fitzgerald's schooldays passed without her displaying a particular aptitude for any subject except drawing, at which she excelled. She left just before her eighteenth birthday, with little to show for her education except the good opinion of the art mistress.

Still tall for her age, and with the glossy black hair and violet-blue eyes of her father, Tiger's early promise of unusual beauty had proved to be a false dawn, since, at the age of fifteen, her nose had grown too big for her small white face. Worse was to follow, for this same nose had developed an unmistakable bump below the bridge. Tiger had not only inherited her father's beautiful hair and eyes; she had inherited his unfortunate hooked nose. Her resemblance to Con was absolute, and whenever she went to sit with her mother, Alice would become quite agitated, even abusive, making it very plain that Tiger's presence was extremely unwelcome. In the end, it seemed better not to confuse her, and Tiger kept out of her way as much as possible.

For the rest of the summer, she helped Niamh in the kitchen, and, rather unwillingly, made the beds for the guests and waited at table. Niamh could see that it was hardly fair to her younger sister to expect her unquestioning co-operation in the running of Neill's Court on a permanent basis, and she cast around in her mind for some way of helping Tiger expand her horizons, without taking on the added burden of having to pay for her to do so. She racked her brains, trying to think of something, but could not, and had no idea where to begin.

In the middle of October, diffidently, she wrote to Orla for guidance in the matter. Orla replied by telephone, assuring Niamh that she would do her best for Tiger, and would be in touch shortly. She was as good as her word, and a week later she wrote to Niamh with the news that she had procured a job for Tiger, in Paris. She was to be an au pair to a noble family, friends of Matthew's head of chambers, with a house in rue Monsieur as well as a château in the country somewhere.

At the very least, Orla wrote, *Tiger will learn to speak French properly, and will hopefully meet the right kind of people. She might even find herself a rich husband, who knows? The Martel-Cluny family are extremely cultivated, and tremendous patrons of the arts. Tiger could hardly fail to profit by the experience, and I'm quite sure she will.*

Although slightly surprised at these decisions regarding her future, taken without consulting her in any way, Tiger was quick to appreciate that a year in Paris would be infinitely preferable to her current occupation as unpaid skivvy to a load of red-faced elderly fly-fishermen, and she readily agreed to the plan. Orla invited her little sister to spend a couple of days with her on her way to Paris, and this Tiger did. One look at Tiger's shabby school raincoat and down-at-heel Doc Martens convinced Orla that her sister needed more suitable clothes. She took her to Harrods, and there she spent more money than she cared to think about on a pleated grey skirt, a cashmere twinset, and a pair of flat-heeled loafers. They proceeded by taxi to another shop, and there Orla bought Tiger a beige raincoat, with a plaid lining. 'The French are mad about the English look,' she assured Tiger. 'It's a really good investment, you'll see.'

'Thank you so much, Orla,' said Tiger, as cheerfully as she could. 'It's terribly kind of you.'

'Don't you think it might be wise to get some of that hair cut, darling?' suggested Orla, as they ate a sandwich at lunchtime, looking with disfavour at the river of black hair that cascaded down either side of her sister's small face, tending to find its way into whatever she was eating.

'No, I don't,' said Tiger firmly, extracting a long hair from her mouth. It was her habit to allow as much of her hair as possible to cover her face, in the belief that this distracted from the gross imperfection of her nose.

Orla did not press the point, and the next day, dressed in her dreary new clothes, Tiger took the Eurostar to Paris.

On the train she sat next to a French girl of her own age, who spoke excellent English. When they arrived at Gare du Nord, her new friend suggested that to spend money on a taxi to rue Monsieur was quite unnecessary. She herself was going by Métro to St-Germain, and advised Tiger to accompany her, and get off at Odéon, the stop before her own. 'You'll find rue Monsieur quite close to the Métro station,' she said. 'It's not at all difficult.'

The afternoon rush hour was just beginning, and Tiger found the Métro quite alarming, particularly as she was lugging her heavy suitcase with her. However, everything proceeded fairly smoothly, and three quarters of an hour later she found herself at the concierge's little gate-house in rue Monsieur, asking for Mme de Martel-Cluny.

The concierge, after demanding identification, picked up Tiger's heavy suitcase and escorted her across the empty paved courtyard which was surrounded by the cliff-like grey stone walls of the house, an elegant eighteenth-century *hôtel particulier*. Wheezing, the old woman dumped Tiger's case beside a tall glazed door. '*Vous-y-êtes, mademoiselle,*' she announced. '*Sonnez!*' Then, without waiting for a reply, she hurried back to her lair.

For a moment or two, Tiger remained where she was, looking around her at the details of the beautiful building; its carved cornices and tall, mostly shuttered windows. It was incredibly quiet, considering that it was in the centre of a busy capital city. There was no sound of voices, or music, or laughter, and no sign whatsoever of children. There were no abandoned bicycles to be seen, not even an old tennis ball, and the atmosphere of the place was heavy, silent and subdued.

Tiger was not especially awed by the grandeur of the house, since in some respects it resembled her own home, but she found the tidiness and quietness unnerving. She turned back to the door, and, half expecting that no response would be forthcoming, rang the bell. She stood back and waited, assuming that it was likely that the maid, if such a person existed, would probably be at some distance from the door.

In fact, it was opened almost immediately by an exquisitely dressed woman with impeccably styled grey hair, and the peach-perfect skin of the seriously rich and leisured city-dwelling lady. She wore black, and three strings of the most enormous pearls Tiger had ever seen.

'Madame de Martel-Cluny?' Tiger stammered, confronted with such elegance.

'*Oui*. And you are Miss Fitzgerald, of course. Do come in, my dear. You must be tired, after the journey.'

'Oh,' said Tiger. 'Do please call me Tiger, won't you? And no, I'm not tired at all, thank you.' She picked up her bag and humped it into the hall.

'Leave it there, Tiger,' said Mme de Martel-Cluny. 'You'll want to hang up your coat, and maybe wash your hands and so. Then come and have some tea.' She opened a secret door to a small *vestiaire*, cunningly concealed in the painted panelling that lined the entrance hall. 'In here,' she said, and then pointed across the pale marble floor to a half-open door. 'I'll be waiting for you in the salon.'

Tiger hung up her coat as instructed, and, rather thankfully, used the loo. Washing her hands in the tiny basin, she was surprised at the amount of dirt they had accumulated during the journey from London. Then, taking a small wire brush from her bag, she swiftly restored her long hair to respectability. The little room was scarcely bigger than a broom cupboard, and was so poorly illuminated by the single wall-light with its frilled green glass shade that there seemed little point in giving herself more than a cursory glance in the spotty mirror that hung above the basin. After a slightly panicky struggle with the door latch, she emerged once more into the hall, and made her way carefully across the highly polished marble floor towards the salon. Through the half-open door she could see that the room was full of light, its *boiseries* painted a very pale shade of pearly grey. The marble flooring of the hall continued into the salon, making the room seem even more light and airy, though the coolness of the marble was softened by several large rugs, worked in brilliant shades of vermilion, pink, sand and cinnamon, which Tiger subsequently discovered were English Regency needlepoint.

Against the walls stood red-lacquered and gilded console tables, and each of these carried a large wrought-iron lamp with a scarlet shade. Groups of eighteenth-century gilded *bergère* chairs stood around the room. These were upholstered in ivory satin, and embellished with cushions of needlepoint, echoing the vibrant colours of the rugs. From the door, Tiger could see right across the room and through open glass doors into a park-like garden, with manicured grass and graceful mature trees. Since it was the end of October, there was little in the way of flowers, but a few white-painted Versailles boxes held balls of clipped box.

For the first time, she began to feel seriously impressed, and to wonder how such pristine

31

surroundings could be maintained in a house with children. She drew a slightly nervous breath and entered the salon.

Mme de Martel-Cluny was sitting on one of her amazingly clean white chairs, before a small log fire that burned cheerfully in the iron basket of the fireplace. A large swagger portrait of a bewigged man in pale blue velvet hung above the chimneypiece, and many prints and drawings in gilded frames adorned the pale panelled walls. The room smelt deliciously of freesias, which stood, packed tightly into silver bowls, on every available surface. Her hostess smiled and extended a hand. 'Come and sit down, Tiger, and tell me all about yourself.'

Tiger installed herself in the chair facing her hostess, accepting a cup of tea and a madeleine, which was crisp and delicious, and tasted faintly of limes. 'There's not a lot to tell, really,' she said.

Mme de Martel-Cluny, by dint of gentle probing, extracted from Tiger the information that one of her sisters ran Neill's Court as a fishing hotel, on account of financial necessity, and that her father, Con Fitzgerald, was living in Italy with a sculptor friend, having been there for all of Tiger's lifetime, eighteen years.

'Is he gay, my dear?'

Startled, Tiger said, 'Er, no, I don't think so.' She added, rather primly: 'It never occurred to me, actually.' Then, seeking to change the subject, she asked: 'When will I get to meet the children?'

'Children? What children?'

'Isn't that why I'm here? To help with the children, with time off to attend French classes?'

Mme de Martel-Cluny laughed, an amused silvery tinkling sound. 'French classes, yes, of course, but we have no children, unfortunately. You are here to be a companion to my husband's elderly mother, Tiger.'

'*Really?*' Tiger's beautiful violet-blue eyes widened, and, though she tried, she was unable to disguise her dismay at this news. 'Nobody told me,' she said quietly. 'So, what would my duties be?'

'Your *duties*, my dear, will not be very onerous. It will be a question of reading aloud the English newspapers to my mother-in-law every morning, and taking her little dog for walks in the Jardin du Luxembourg, twice a day.'

'Oh. I see.' Tiger looked relieved. 'Which newspapers?' she asked, for something to say, rather than any real desire to know.

'*The Times*, and the *Telegraph*, I believe. *Ça vous va?*'

Tiger grinned. 'What about Sundays? Does she take an English Sunday paper, too?'

'She does. It's called the *News of the World*.'

Tiger laughed. 'Your mother-in-law sounds like fun, I think.'

Mme de Martel-Cluny glanced at her watch. 'Nearly five thirty. She will soon be up from her rest, and ready for her evening cocktail. I will take you to your room now, Tiger. Of course you'll want to unpack, and have some time to yourself. Shall we meet down here at seven fifteen?'

They returned to the hall, and as they did so the front door opened and a harassed-looking young man entered. He had dark hair and a very red face, and was energetically hauling on a lead attached to a small dog. It was a blond black-faced pug, evidently unwilling to obey orders and return to its home, for its four short legs were stiff and its feet firmly planted on the ground, so that the young man was forced to drag it along on its bottom.

Mme de Martel-Cluny hurried forward. 'Oh, poor Gaston, have you been having trouble with Fanny again? Never mind, after today, here is Miss Fitzgerald, who is going to take the naughty thing for her little walks.'

Gaston, who, Tiger quickly guessed, was a man-servant, to judge by his striped waistcoat and black trousers, seemed glad to hear this, and handed the dog's lead to his employer. He bowed stiffly towards Tiger, and ran a hot hand through his heavily gelled hair. '*Enchanté, mademoiselle,*' he murmured, since his small amount of English did not seem to him to be adequate to the occasion.

'Gaston,' said Mme de Martel-Cluny, 'could you carry Miss Fitzgerald's bag upstairs for her, please, and show her to her room?'

Tiger followed Gaston up the gracefully curved stair-case to the first-floor landing. He led the way along a short, dark corridor and opened the door to her room. He placed the heavy suitcase on the bench at the foot of the bed.

'*Merci*,' said Tiger, feeling unable to manage a more elaborate way of thanking him.

He hesitated for a moment, then gave her a shy smile and departed, closing the door quietly behind him.

Tiger had never before stayed in a grand house with servants, and uneasily she wondered whether she should have given Gaston something for his trouble. On reflection, she rather thought not; it would probably be more appropriate to give him a worthwhile present at the conclusion of her stay. In any case, she said to herself, opening the lid of her suitcase, I'm a sort of servant here myself, so maybe he wouldn't expect anything. I'd better ask Orla, she'll know.

The bedroom in which she found herself was un-believably comfortable, pretty and romantic. Practically everything in the room – walls, curtains, bed-hangings and the upholstery of two small eighteenth-century armchairs – was covered in a printed fabric; a glowing reddish-pink *toile de Jouy* on a cream ground. The whole effect was warm, cheerful, welcoming and friendly, and Tiger's response to its atmosphere was immediate. Feeling relaxed and con-fident, she opened the white-painted casement that

34

overlooked the garden. Kneeling on the cushioned window seat, she leaned over the sill and looked down at the paved terrace immediately below. She recognized the tubs of clipped box balls, and the grass and trees beyond, and guessed that her room must be over the salon.

As she watched, a tall, grey-haired man came out onto the terrace. He wore formal city clothes and was smoking a cigarette. The smell of the cigarette was at once acrid and aromatic, and not at all like the tobacco smoked by Liam Dainty at home. The thought of mad old Liam induced in Tiger a sharp pang of homesickness, and she quickly withdrew from the window and began to put away her clothes. I must send them all a card, she thought, as she hung her few things on the padded hangers in the capacious wardrobe, though I don't suppose anyone's actually missing me at all. Poor old Niamh is too busy, and Mother can't stand the sight of me, anyway. I'd better write to Orla, and tell her that I got here safely, and how lovely it is. As she arranged her shirts and sweaters in the chest of drawers, Tiger told herself firmly how lucky she was to be here, to have escaped from the weird set-up at Neill's Court. This beautiful bedroom was, in itself, a huge improvement on the mouse-infested night-nursery that had been her room since her birth, she thought, recalling the lumpy banana-shaped mattress of the bed, the peeling Edwardian floral wallpaper and the bare elm floorboards. Luxury, or even simple comfort, had never been a feature of life at Neill's Court; the priorities had always been the horses and the dogs, when any question of spending money arose.

Equally, the food at home had never been at all ambitious, but was of the schoolroom variety: pork and apple sauce, rice pudding, and rabbit pie with onions appearing on the menu with monotonous regularity. Nowadays, of course, since Niamh had her guests to cater for, the general standard had improved, though the basic simplicity of the cooking had remained.

Luckily, the fishing fraternity seemed almost to prefer it to more elaborate fare.

Tiger sighed, and closed the drawer, then looked critically at herself in the pier-glass, wondering whether she ought to have a bath and change into something else for dinner. Since she was already wearing the only decent new things she possessed, changing her clothes was probably a bad idea, but she decided that there was plenty of time for a bath. She took her sponge bag and opened the door to her bathroom, which was, predictably, everything the heart could wish for, with steaming hot water and every kind of luxury in the shape of bath essences, soaps and thick white towels.

As she lay in the hot fragrant water, with her long hair knotted on top of her head, Tiger smiled, thinking how kind it was of Mme de Martel-Cluny to treat her as a proper guest, and how sad it must be for her not to have a daughter of her own, when she would clearly have made a really brilliant mother.

Reluctantly, she got out of the bath, dried herself, using three of the beautiful towels, then got dressed. She brushed her hair, and put on an invisible smudge of the lipstick Orla had given her. She checked the time, and went downstairs.

In the salon, she found the man she had seen smoking on the terrace, seated on a needlework pouffe with a drink in his hand, and talking to an extremely old lady. She, too, was enjoying a glass of something, and was installed on the gilded settee that faced the small log fire. Fleetingly, Tiger observed that the logs had not altered at all since she was last in the room, and realized with a feeling of surprise that they were bogus logs, concealing a gas fire. She advanced shyly into the room, and M. de Martel-Cluny rose politely to greet her. 'Miss Fitzgerald? How nice to meet you.'

'How do you do?'

'Maman, may I present Miss Fitzgerald? My mother, the Comtesse de Martel-Cluny, mademoiselle.'

Tiger stepped forward and took the claw-like hand extended by the old lady, and shook it gently. 'Hello,' she said, though even to her own ears this sounded pretty inadequate.

The comtesse smiled, and Tiger saw how pretty were her faded grey eyes in her wrinkled face, and how beautiful were her clothes. She wore a long loose robe of a silky amethyst-coloured material, with quantities of frilly white lace at the neck, secured by a large sapphire brooch. Like her daughter-in-law, she was evidently the possessor of many lustrous pearls, and her freckled and veined hands were loaded with glittering diamond rings. 'Hello,' she replied, in a husky voice.

'A glass of champagne, mademoiselle?' her host suggested.

'Thank you, that would be lovely.'

The comtesse held out her hand. 'Come and sit beside me,' she said. 'I am a little deaf, you understand.'

Tiger sat as instructed, Monsieur gave her her champagne, and they chatted rather formally, talking of this and that, waiting for Madame to appear. Tiger, mindful that it was part of her job to converse in a civilized manner, and emboldened by the consumption of half a glass of champagne, turned to the comtesse. 'I saw your little dog coming home with Gaston,' she said. 'She seems quite a character.'

'*Character* is not a word I would choose to describe Fanny, Miss Fitzgerald, except in the very worst sense. She is a very wicked little creature, stubborn and *maligne. Mais alors*, one loves 'er, unfortunately. The only person she does not 'ate is me.' She looked at Tiger, her eyes alight with mischief. 'She will bite you many times, I feel very sure, Miss Fitzgerald.'

'Tiger.'

'Tiger?'

'It's my name, madame. If Fanny is thinking of biting me, it is better she knows I am called Tiger, don't you think?'

Gravely, the old lady considered this. 'Yes,' she allowed. 'I can see the logic of your argument.' She looked quizzically at the young woman sitting straight-backed beside her in her unfashionable clothes. 'So 'ow was it that so curious a name was bestow upon you, Tiger?'

Half laughing, half perfectly seriously, Tiger gave them a detailed account of the circumstances of her birth, but could tell by the expressions on the faces of her aristocratic audience that they thought the entire history bizarre in the extreme. Losing confidence, she ran out of words. 'I'm sorry,' she said, rather lamely. 'The Irish are a bit like that, I'm afraid. You know: quite unconventional, really.'

M. de Martel-Cluny, sensing Tiger's slight discomfiture, rose gallantly to the defence of the Irish. 'They are also a gifted, highly articulate and extremely cultivated people. Look at Shaw, Wilde, Joyce, and Brendan Behan, for example.'

Tiger looked at him, her eyes shining. 'That's true, of course, but it has to be said that three of those writers didn't hang around in Ireland for very long, did they?'

M. de Martel-Cluny laughed, and at that moment his wife made her apologetic entrance, explaining that she had been speaking on the telephone to her sister, and had found it difficult to terminate the conversation.

'*Comme d'habitude*,' murmured Monsieur, just as Gaston entered the salon and announced that dinner was served.

The meal, served in a small sage-green-painted panelled dining-room off the hall, was absolutely delicious, though unexpectedly simple and unfussy. They sat at an informal round table covered in a white damask cloth, the four chairs high-backed in the Swedish style, their seats upholstered in dark blue and cream *toile de Jouy*, evidently a fabric close to Madame's heart. In the centre of the table was a large bowl of ripe purple figs, and tallow candles in tall glass photophores augmented the light from the crystal chandelier suspended over the table. Each place was laid with elaborately chased though rather dull-looking family silver, beautiful old glasses and dark blue napkins.

'Since my husband is so often detained on important government business, we do not entertain here very frequently,' remarked Madame, as if some explanation were required for the modesty of their dining-room, with its small table and comparatively few chairs. 'Occasionally, when it is necessary to offer hospitality, we take our guests to a restaurant.'

They sat down, and Gaston brought the first course, a chilled soup of courgette, tomato and basil. This was followed by a roast chicken, which, to Tiger's surprise, was placed before M. de Martel-Cluny. He stood up and carved the bird, exactly as they did at home, and Gaston handed the plates, offering vegetables at the same time. After the not-very-filling soup, Tiger still felt extremely hungry, and attacked her dinner with an enthusiasm bordering on greed. The chicken had a delicious and unusual flavour, and Tiger turned to her hostess to enquire what it was that made it taste so good.

'Lemon balm and garlic,' Madame replied. 'I grow lots of herbs in pots in the garden.' She laughed. 'Unfortunately it is not a perfect world, as the cooks of the tenants have the *tendance* to steal my favourites, from time to time.'

'The tenants?' asked Tiger, who had assumed that the family occupied the whole house.

'Yes,' said Monsieur. 'The tenants. They are a necessary evil, in order to maintain the fabric of the house. *Sinon*, it is like pouring money into a hole, you understand?'

'Absolutely,' said Tiger, suddenly feeling much less of a second-class citizen. 'It's just like us at Neill's Court – lovely house; not enough money?'

'Exactly.'

The comtesse had taken almost no part in the conversation at table, but had switched off her deaf-aid and devoted her full attention to her dinner. Now, however, the words 'tenants' penetrated the profound silence of her ear, and she put down her fork and switched on her microphone. She looked at her son accusingly. 'Are you speaking of the tenants, Antoine?'

'*Si, Maman. Pourquoi pas?*'

'That is not a subject that can give me pleasure, Antoine, especially during dinner.' The old lady turned to Tiger, her grey eyes glinting. 'I wish you 'ad been able to visit us 'ere at the beautiful time of my marriage, Tiger. *Then*, it was a *real* 'ouse, built for a large family with many servants. *Now*, there are no children, very few servants, nothing. Even my only son refuse to use his familial title, for reason of political convenience. This old 'ouse is merely an *anachronisme, comme moi.*'

After a short, embarrassed silence, Tiger ventured to speak. 'I know how you feel,' she said sadly. 'It's exactly the same at my home, and why my sister is trying to save the house by running it as a hotel, but it's not exactly what you'd call a brilliant success story. The difference is that, here, at least you're able to mend the roof and all that. Compared with this place, Neill's Court is on its last legs, believe me.' Suddenly, tears of tension and tiredness filled her eyes, and she hung her head, not daring to speak. Two fat tears rolled down her nose and fell with a plop onto her plate.

Mme de Martel-Cluny put down her napkin and covered Tiger's hand with her own. 'You are very tired, poor girl. You need a good night's rest. Don't be upset, *mignonne*. It's all right, really.'

Tiger mopped her tears with her napkin. 'How stupid of me. I'm so sorry,' she said, and tried to smile. The comtesse, looking guilty, switched off her hearing-aid and finished her dinner.

'Silly old bat,' said Monsieur very quietly, and

smiled reassuringly at Tiger. 'She likes to wind one up, isn't that the expression? The trick is to ignore her.'

When Tiger woke the following morning, early, and to the sound of rooks quarrelling in the trees outside her window, it took her a moment to recognize her new surroundings. Since at least an hour would have to pass before she could go down to breakfast, she decided to write to Orla. This she did at the small writing-desk, equipped with headed paper, stamps and even a pen. It's amazing, she told herself, you could fall out of the sky with nothing at all except your clothes, and you'd be OK here.

Dear Orla, she wrote in her large clear schoolgirl's handwriting, *You would love it here, it is very lush and comfortable, and the Martel-Clunys are very kind and nice. The old lady, Monsieur's mum, is a bit of a case, but I expect I can handle that OK. You didn't tell me that I was going to have to read the English newspapers to her every day and – guess what? – the NOTW on Sundays! What do you think of that? Madame has not yet told me about the arrangements for the French lessons, but I expect she will today. Could you be a real saint and phone Niamh to tell her I'm OK? It's so far from Ireland here that I think it would be a bit cheeky to ask to phone home, don't you?*

Love to Matthew and the boys, and you too. Tiger.

P.S. I can tell they are dead impressed with my clothes! T.

At eight o'clock she went downstairs, put her stamped letter on the hall table along with two others, then went to the dining-room. Here, she found Monsieur alone, reading *Le Monde*, with a very large cup of coffee on the table in front of him.

'Good morning, Tiger,' he said amiably, slightly lowering the paper. 'Help yourself to something, won't you?' He waved a hand vaguely at the sideboard, then retreated behind his paper.

'Yes, OK, thanks,' said Tiger, and poured herself some coffee and a glass of orange juice. She took a warm croissant from a covered silver dish, put it on a plate, then carried everything to her place at the table. Doing her best not to make slurping noises as she did so, she consumed her breakfast, then sat silently, her hands folded on her lap, waiting for Madame to appear.

At eight thirty, Gaston entered the dining-room and announced that the car was waiting. Folding his paper, Monsieur thanked him, and wished Tiger a pleasant day. 'My wife is never very early up,' he said, with a small ironic smile. 'It may be necessary for you to go by yourself, to find my mother.'

'Oh, I see. Yes, of course. Thank you.' She stood up hastily and followed Monsieur to the hall.

'If you go along the terrace to the right, you will find her door. It's the third one, you can't miss it, and in any case Fanny will announce your arrival.'

'Oh, right. Thank you.' She said goodbye yet again, then went through the salon and out onto the terrace. It was quite warm and pleasant in the late October sunshine, and the neatly maintained garden looked elegant and inviting in the way that a public park might before the arrival of its visitors. Tiger walked along the terrace to the third door, and, peering through the glass, saw the comtesse, wrapped in a Paisley dressing gown and with her hair covered by a net mob-cap. She was sitting on a sofa, feeding chocolate buttons to her repulsive little dog.

After a moment's hesitation, Tiger tapped timidly on the glass. The reaction of Fanny was instantaneous: she hurled herself towards the door with unbelievable violence, her huge bug eyes starting from her head, as she barked hysterically, her pink tongue and black lips dripping with manic white foam. Tiger waved at the old lady through the glass, but did not feel brave enough to open the door.

The comtesse thumped her stick on the carpet and

yelled at Fanny to desist, at once, and come here, so that eventually the little animal obeyed her instructions, and returned to the old woman's side, still quivering with rage. 'Come in, Tiger, the door is open. Don't be afraid, my dear!'

Tiger opened the door a crack and stuck her head round it. 'I *am* quite afraid,' she said. 'I must say, she's a very good guard dog.'

'Come in! Come in! She won't bite you, now she 'as seen we are speaking together.'

Nervously, Tiger entered the room, and advanced towards the sofa. Fanny, softly growling, lay down on the floor. 'What about her walk, madame? Shall I take her out before I read the papers to you?'

'No, it's all right. I 'ave already let 'er do pipi in the garden, though I entreat you, please do not mention that to my daughter-in-law. She is angered if the grass becomes burned because of Fanny's necessary functions.' She laughed mockingly, then pointed to a hard chair beside a magnificently inlaid ebony table, on which the newspapers were laid out tidily. 'First, we read the papers. And after, you can take Fanny for 'er proper walk.'

The comtesse's sitting-room was nothing like as large as the salon, and since she had been from girlhood an ardent Anglophile, it was decorated in warm shades of apricot and rose, and furnished with comfortable easy chairs and squashy sofas, with loose covers of faded, flowery chintz. It was, in fact, a Parisian decorator's interpretation of the English country-house style, but on a miniature scale. It reminded Tiger of Orla's Islington house, where a lot of too-big furniture had been crammed into too-few, and too-small rooms.

'*Alors, Tiger, on commence?*'

By eleven o'clock, Tiger's voice was beginning to give out, and her throat felt extremely dry. She was relieved when a knock on the door heralded the arrival of

Gaston, carrying a tray of tea things. Fanny, thinking that he had come to take her for a walk, ran eagerly to his side and attempted to climb up his leg, to his red-faced embarrassment.

'Fanny! *Imbécile!*' The comtesse gave Fanny a hard whack with her stick, and the little dog, with a yelp of pain, released the unfortunate Gaston, who lost no time in making his escape from the room.

'A cup of tea, Tiger?'

'Thank you, I'd love one.'

They sipped their tea in silence, and then the comtesse turned her speculative gaze onto Tiger's clothes. 'Are those all the clothes you 'ave, my dear?' she asked bluntly.

Taken aback, but not really hurt by the old woman's curiosity, Tiger answered quite truthfully. 'Yes, pretty much, madame,' she said.

'I see. And do you take pleasure in these garments, Tiger?'

'No, I don't. I find them boring. My sister bought them for me, in London, at Harrods. It was very kind of her.'

'Indeed, kind, but not your style, I think?'

'Well, you could say that, I suppose. Though quite what is my style, I don't really know, yet. In any case, I can't afford to buy more clothes, at least until I've earned some money.'

'I believe that nowadays it is the fashion for all the young students in Paris to buy their things at *les puces*, in the stands called *friperies*, for very little money.'

'Really? You mean like Oxfam shops at home?'

'Yes, but much better I think. Very often it is possible to find beautiful old things, and much more suitable for you than this banal style of the English young lady. With such dark hair, and those strong features, you should not try to look like a *gouvernante*, Tiger, but like a *gitane*.'

'What does that mean, *gitane*?'

'A Romany, or you say gypsy, perhaps?'

44

Tiger laughed, rather amused as well as touched by the interest displayed in her appearance. 'Are there such places quite near here?' she asked. 'I should certainly like to have a look, at least.'

'There is one at Porte de Vanves, I understand. It is quite easy to arrive there, by Métro, from St-Sulpice.'

'How is it that you know about these places, madame?'

'Oh, they are *très snob* with the young, my dear. I read all about the trends, in *Vogue*, naturally.'

'I see.' Tiger looked at her watch. 'Shall I take Fanny out now, do you think?'

'Yes. It is the hour for my massage, and then I will dress for lunch, so now is good time to take 'er. If you go in the Jardin du Luxembourg, don't remove 'er lead, or she will quickly make 'erself lost. The lead is 'ere. *Tenez!*'

'Right, I understand,' said Tiger, getting to her feet, and taking the lead.

She found the Jardin du Luxembourg without difficulty, aided by the little dog's determined pulling on the lead in the direction of her favourite park.

After the pressures of the morning and the previous day, Tiger was delighted to be alone for a while, and she ran as fast as she could through the gardens, exercising her own legs as well as those of her small charge. As they sped past each of her favourite trees, Fanny, denied her customary pause for the purpose of sniffing its trunk and adding her own contribution, cast baleful and reproachful looks at her tormentor, who appeared entirely unconcerned by her distress. By the time they arrived back in rue Monsieur, the little dog was in a state of near-collapse, and utter dejection. Tiger rang the bell, and when Gaston answered the door, Fanny crawled through it without a murmur of dissent, and allowed the astonished Gaston to take her to the kitchen for her lunch.

CHAPTER THREE

A few days later, Tiger, having been provided with a small guide-book to Paris by Mme de Martel-Cluny, made her way to rue St-Sulpice to attend her first French lesson. The class took place on three afternoons a week in a large empty room, situated over a shop which sold ecclesiastical articles of every description, including church candles in many different sizes. The staircase that led up to the classroom was dark and narrow, and at the top was a glass-partitioned landing, with several doors leading off it, in various directions. Pausing uncertainly for a moment, Tiger looked through the glass of the first door on her right, and saw an elderly man, grey-haired and goatee-bearded, wearing gold-rimmed pince-nez spectacles, standing before a blackboard and addressing a group of girls. Deciding that she must have found the right place, she opened the door as quietly as she could, and, rather nervously, sidled through it.

At her entrance, the professor peered myopically over his spectacles in her direction, and a dozen curious faces turned and stared at her. 'I beg your pardon,' Tiger stammered. 'I'm late. I'm sorry.'

'*Mademoiselle Fitzgerald, n'est-ce pas?*'

'Um, yes. Er, *oui, monsieur.*'

'*Alors, entrez, mademoiselle. Asseyez-vous, s'il vous plaît.*'

Tiger found an empty place at the end of the second row of seats, and sat down.

'*Eh bien, on recommence.*'

Since the course in which Tiger had been enrolled was already in its sixth month, she found the first lesson very nearly incomprehensible, and the level of competence displayed by the other students depressingly high in comparison with her own.

At four thirty, the class broke up. The other girls, who seemed to be of many nationalities including Vietnamese and Chinese, as well as German and Italian, with few, if any, English speakers, left the room chattering to each other in loud and fluent French. I'm out of my depth here, said Tiger to herself. It's a waste of my time. I'd better say so, straight away.

She marched up to the professor's desk, and waited while he finished cleaning his blackboard. Eventually, he shook his chalky duster, and turned towards her, his eyebrows raised enquiringly.

Tiger cleared her throat. '*Je suis désolée,*' she said. '*Mais je n'ai compris aucun mot, monsieur.*'

'Well,' the man replied in English, his small dark eyes sparkling with malice, 'that is not altogether surprising, is it? The English are not famous for their command of foreign tongues, I believe?'

'Irish,' said Tiger.

'*Pardon?*'

'Not English. I'm Irish. *Je suis irlandaise.*'

'Ah! And this makes a difference, mademoiselle?'

Refusing to be intimidated by a man she perceived as decrepit, seedy and quite unattractive in every respect, Tiger held her ground. 'Since this language course must be costing my hosts a good deal of money, it seems to me dishonest to continue, when I shall clearly fail to benefit from it, monsieur.'

The professor, alarmed at the prospect of a disappearing student, climbed down with gratifying speed, and set about overcoming Tiger's objections. In five minutes he had produced a textbook and notes for the course, together with a small box of cassette tapes. 'I am confident that you will find these helpful, mademoiselle. Let us continue for two or three weeks, and if, after that, you still find the work too difficult, you could, if you wish, transfer to my beginners' class, which takes place on Tuesdays and Thursdays, in the morning.'

'I can't do mornings,' said Tiger. 'I am an au pair. In the mornings, I work for the Comtesse de Martel-Cluny.'

'*Ah, bon?*' The professor, sensing the possible benefits to be derived from such a connection, could barely restrain himself from rubbing his horny old hands together. 'In that case, *chère mademoiselle*, we must do our very best for you in the time available to us, must we not?'

'Yes. Right. OK.' Feeling that she had managed to manipulate the cynical old man with some degree of success, Tiger put the books and tapes into her bag, and smiled kindly upon him. '*Au revoir, monsieur*,' she said. '*A vendredi.*'

'*A vendredi, mademoiselle.*'

Thoughtfully, Tiger walked back to rue Monsieur. It was not only the fluency in French of her fellow students that had seemed to her so dauntingly discouraging, but also their incredibly chic and sophisticated appearance. Few of the girls had long loose hair like herself, and all of them wore the sort of clothes that Tiger had seen only in glossy magazines, or, fleetingly, in the windows of London boutiques. Equally, their faces were skilfully made up, and the air around them was heady with the mingled scents that she guessed came from Saint Laurent, Dior and Chanel. They appeared to Tiger alarmingly worldly, and she felt herself to be entirely incapable of existing on equal terms with them, much less competing in any way at all.

Not that I bloody want to, she told herself crossly, as

she knocked on the concierge's door. She recalled the comtesse's recent advice to her: 'You should not try to look like a *gouvernante*, Tiger, but like a *gitane*.' Very well, she thought, I'll suss out this fleamarket place at the weekend and see what I can find. If I can't join the smart set on their terms, the least I can do is try to be noticed on my own account, and the hell with Orla.

On Friday evening Tiger received her first pay packet, an envelope containing five hundred francs. Saturday was her day off, and immediately after breakfast, armed with her guide-book, she took the Métro from St-Sulpice to Porte de Vanves, in search of retro heaven.

The market, when she got there, was packed. Clutching her bag firmly to her chest, she followed the slow-moving hordes of bargain-hunters through the avenues of stalls filled with every conceivable object of desire, from beautiful though shabby seventeenth-century chairs to grotty army-surplus greatcoats. She saw pre-1914 street-signs, nineteenth-century dolls, a little shop entirely filled with empty birdcages of every size and complexity of structure, and stalls selling old books, gramophone records and sheet music.

On the pavement were baskets containing silk scarves, feather boas, and the elaborately decorated hats of the Thirties. On seeing these, Tiger sharpened her concentration and looked keenly around, in search of her goal. Almost immediately, she found it, in the shape of a narrow stall hung with silks and velvets; dresses, coats and shawls, crammed together on long steel rails. The clothes were guarded by a bored-looking young woman, who sat on a bentwood chair, smoking a cigarette. She was wearing a high-necked white lace blouse, a long dark green velvet skirt and a black shovel hat, of the clerical type worn by priests in Ireland.

Tiger wished the young woman good morning, and worked her way slowly through the merchandise, noting the prices, looking for the best bargains. Since winter would soon be approaching, she decided that a coat of some kind would be a sensible buy, and chose a black *fin de siècle* gabardine jacket, three-quarter length, with a high waist and tight leg-of-mutton sleeves. It was lined with satin and slipped on easily, fitting her perfectly.

'*Formidable!*' remarked the bored young woman, and blew a delicate blue smoke ring. Much encouraged by this early success, Tiger bought a pair of men's pin-striped grey trousers with a matching waistcoat, a plain white shirt and a black silk knitted tie. She tried on the trousers and waistcoat behind a makeshift curtain, peering at herself in a cracked narrow mirror propped against a pile of cardboard boxes. Even in such unflattering circumstances, Tiger could see that she had metamorphosed into an entirely different person, and she grinned at herself, delighted at the transformation. She decided to wear her new things, so she slipped on the long black jacket and knotted the silky tie loosely under the collar of her shirt. Rather guiltily, she stuffed Orla's expensive London clothes into her bag.

Altogether, the new wardrobe cost three hundred and fifteen francs, which, taking into account the high quality of the materials and workmanship, she considered excellent value. She handed over the cash, making no attempt at haggling over the price. The girl took the money without rising from her seat, and gave Tiger a lopsided smile. '*Merci*,' she said.

'*Je reviens*,' responded Tiger, hesitantly. '*La semaine prochain.*'

'*Prochaine*,' said the girl.

'*Oui*,' said Tiger.

Before returning to rue Monsieur, she installed herself at a café table on the pavement, and ordered a bowl of mussels and a glass of wine. The waiter brought a basket of crisp fresh bread with the seafood, and Tiger ate her lunch as slowly as possible, savouring every delicious mouthful, basking in the autumnal sunshine, enjoying the chilled white wine. She felt relaxed and happy, even fairly confident, and enchanted to be in Paris with the Martel-Clunys and the repulsive Fanny, rather than waiting on Niamh's ghastly old guests at home. At a distance, even the smart creatures at her French class seemed much less intimidating, and she quite looked forward to their reaction when she appeared in the class on Monday, wearing her new clothes.

Looking down at her feet, Tiger suddenly thought that Orla's flat-heeled loafers looked completely wrong with her new gear, and since she had plenty of time at her disposal she decided to look for more appropriate footwear. Plain black lace-ups, with a bit of a heel, is what I want, she thought. Finding them took a very long time, and she was beginning to think of giving up when she saw exactly what she had in mind on a stall selling army-surplus stuff, and old nurses' uniforms. The shoes were piled up in a basket, in a jumble of mixed pairs, black, brown and white, their laces tied together in knots.

An elderly man appeared to be in charge of the stall, and Tiger approached him. '*Je voudrais acheter les chaussures noires, monsieur*,' she ventured, pointing at the basket of shoes.

'*Vous chaussez du combien?*'

'Er, *pardon? Je ne comprends pas, monsieur.*'

'What size you are 'aving, mademoiselle?'

'Oh,' said Tiger. 'Six, I think.'

'*Six?*' The man frowned, and studied Tiger's feet. '*Non. Quarante, je crois*,' he muttered, and extracted a pair of shoes from the basket. The shoes were not exactly the right size, but after a couple of attempts, a satisfactory pair was found. Tiger parted with fifty francs, and the old man produced a plastic bag in which to carry her loafers. She looked at her watch, and remembering her promise to take Fanny for her

51

evening walk, she thanked the man and hurried to the Métro station, hobbling a little in the stiff new shoes.

It was after six o'clock when she arrived in rue Monsieur. Gaston opened the door to her, and told her that Monsieur and Madame were preparing to go out for the evening, that Madame la Comtesse was engaged with her hairdresser, and that Fanny had been fed and was waiting in the kitchen until Tiger should arrive to take her out. She had half expected that he might make some comment about her altered appearance, but he did not, merely hurried away to fetch the dog. While he was gone, Tiger took her bag to the little *vestiaire* and hung it on a peg beside her raincoat. Once again, she looked at her reflection in the mirror, although it was too small to show much more than her head and shoulders. It was, however, enough to reassure her that she had chosen wisely; that the clothes were a definite success.

Gaston was waiting in the hall, with Fanny on a tight lead. Silently, he handed over his charge, and equally silently, opened the front door, for Tiger to pass through. 'Thank you, Gaston,' she said.

'*Il est trop tard, mademoiselle.*' Gaston spoke in a low voice, urgently. '*Elle a déjà fait ses ordures!*'

'*Où?*'

'*Dans la cuisine, mademoiselle.*'

'Oh, dear. Sorry, Gaston. *Je suis vraiment désolée.*'

The young man gave her a wintry smile, cast a look of loathing at the little dog, and closed the door very quietly.

'Oh, really, Fanny,' said Tiger severely, 'you are the bloody end.' She tugged on the lead. 'Come on!'

Fanny, having already dealt with her urgent need to evacuate her bowels, ran along beside Tiger in quite a sensible manner, and did not wind her lead around lamp-posts, or attempt to eat undesirable objects in the gutter, her usual preferred mode of travel to the park.

Once inside the Jardin du Luxembourg, Tiger, as usual, began to run, and was enchanted at the freedom her new trousers gave her, though this was somewhat diminished by the slight discomfort of her shoes. It's OK, she thought, I'll soon break them in. She slowed down to a brisk walk, and was presently aware of one or two heads turning to look at her as she passed. Such attentions had never before come her way, at least not since she had become an adolescent, and she found the experience slightly embarrassing, but none the less extremely pleasurable.

Dinner was a little late, on account of the comtesse's hair taking longer than expected, and Tiger waited for her, alone in the salon, along with the exhausted Fanny. The drinks tray was waiting on its usual table, and she poured herself a small glass of *Pineau de Charente*, curious to know what a drink with such a pretty name tasted like. Hm, she thought, taking a sip, it's no big deal really. She helped herself to a handful of pistachio nuts from a silver bowl, and returned to the sofa, taking care not to step on the slumbering Fanny.

Presently, the door to the terrace opened and the comtesse, accompanied by Gaston, came into the salon, leaning on a black cane with a silver knob. She was, as usual, formally dressed; this time in rustling black taffeta, with a white satin scarf tied loosely round her neck. As Tiger stood up to greet her, a curious vision flashed before her inner eye, of the comtesse wearing baggy blue jeans and a black leather biker's jacket, an eccentric but strangely appealing manifestation.

'Tiger! You 'ave been to Vanves, *n'est-ce pas*?'

'Yes,' said Tiger, smiling. 'I have.'

The old lady settled herself on the sofa, and Gaston brought her a cocktail, a lethal concoction of gin, gin and fresh lime juice, in a glass with the dampened rim dipped in salt. He then departed, with instructions to serve dinner in ten minutes.

The comtesse turned to Tiger, smiling, her eyes bright with pleasure. '*Félicitations*, my dear. This is a good style for you; elegant and amusing.' She took a sip of her drink. 'You no longer look like a *gouvernante*, Tiger, but also you do not look like a *gitane*, isn't it?' She shook her head, reprovingly.

'What do I look like, madame?'

'Like a suffragette, absolutely!'

Tiger laughed. 'Is that so bad, do you think?'

'*Pas du tout, c'est très bon chic.* I like it.'

'Maybe next week I will go again, and do *gitane*, but if I go on like this I will be spending all my salary on clothes. Not a very serious thing to do with one's money, is it?'

'My dear Tiger,' said the comtesse, 'style is not a frivolous subject, though its importance is little understood.'

Gaston came silently into the salon and announced that dinner was ready. The comtesse drained her glass, and smiled at Tiger, her sharp grey eyes alight. 'Do not forget that empires 'ave been won and lost for the love of beautiful and clever women, my child.'

'Oh, right,' said Tiger, trying to look suitably impressed. She rose to her feet and offered the old lady her arm. 'I'll try not to.'

They went slowly in to dinner together, leaving the snoring Fanny asleep in the salon, her short legs twitching as she dreamed of running down an endless avenue of deliciously fragrant trees, and stopping at every one.

By the time she had been in Paris for a month, Tiger's life had settled into a pleasant routine, her French had improved quite a bit, and her relationship with her fellow students had become much more positive. One or two of the girls had become fairly friendly, and occasionally she had had a coffee with them after the class. All of them spoke quite good English, and Tiger suspected that their friendliness probably had an ulterior motive: that of practising their skills on a native speaker, herself. Sometimes, she allowed them to manipulate her in this way, but more often, in her own interest, she resisted, and insisted on speaking French.

Twice more, she had made a Saturday morning trip to Vanves, and her wardrobe was now enhanced by the addition of two long velvet skirts, a pair of soft black leather boots, knee-high and with small Louis heels, several Edwardian white pin-tucked blouses with big sleeves, and a hooded cranberry-coloured felt cloak. Tiger was especially fond of the cloak, which, although quite heavy to wear, was exceptionally warm, and had been a terrific bargain at seventy-five francs.

One evening, as she left the French class, she saw a dark-haired, shabbily dressed man pinning a notice to the board in the entrance lobby. Curious, she went and stood behind him, trying to read the notice over his shoulder. He turned, smiled at her briefly, and ran down the stairs. Slowly, Tiger read the notice, which appeared to be advertising a class of some description.

'*Qu'est-ce que ça veut dire: "peindre d'après nature"?*' she asked one of her new friends, who stood beside her.

'Painting from the life, I think.'

'Ah, I get it. It's a life class.'

Passing the board several times a week, Tiger began to think that it might be fun, as well as interesting, to join such a class. After all, art had been far and away her best subject at school, and sitting alone in her room after dinner watching French TV was beginning to be a little boring. Carefully she read the notice again, and garnered the information that the class was held on two evenings a week, in an atelier several doors further down rue St-Sulpice. The classes lasted for two hours and the price of each session was twenty-five francs, plus the cost of materials. Very reasonable, she thought; I wonder if the teacher is any good?

55

That evening, rather shyly, she asked Mme de Martel-Cluny whether she would be permitted to attend such a class.

'But *of course*, Tiger. You must go out whenever you wish, my dear. You are not a prisoner here.' As an afterthought she added: 'Naturally, you will be sure that Fanny has had her little walk before you go?'

As it turned out, the studio was quite difficult to access, since it was in a courtyard behind yet another shop full of ecclesiastical paraphernalia. If the shop was closed, a special bell had to be rung to gain admittance. On her first visit, the shop was still open and the man behind the counter showed her to a door at the rear of the showroom, which led to a large walled courtyard, completely covered by a glass roof, like an old-fashioned greenhouse. In the centre of the cobbled yard was a raised wooden dais, beside a rusty iron Godin stove, whose chimney rose straight up through the glass roof. Close to the stove, a nude model sat on a hard wooden chair, with her hands hooked behind her head, gazing up at the darkening evening sky, the stars clearly visible through the glass. Several students were at work, each standing before an easel at a different position in the studio.

The dark-haired man whom Tiger had seen pinning up the notice was evidently the instructor, for he was not working, but looking over the shoulder of one of the students, and apparently giving her advice. Seeing Tiger as she came through the door, he approached and introduced himself. He led her to a small desk, took her details, and asked her for two hundred and fifty francs, to cover a course of ten sessions. If Tiger was surprised at being required to hand over the full fee before she had even had a trial lesson, she decided not to show it, but took the notes from her wallet and laid them on the table. He thanked her, counted the money and put it into a cash box in a drawer of his desk. 'Do you wish to begin painting straight away, Miss

Fitzgerald?' he asked, in perfect English. 'Or would you prefer to draw first?'

'Draw first, I think.'

'Pencil or charcoal?'

'Charcoal, perhaps?'

'OK.'

By the third session, Tiger had got into her stride and her first timid efforts, having been severely trashed by Mr Marylski, had developed into a much bolder and relaxed style of drawing. She began to understand the structure of the female body, and took pleasure in observing the musculature of the model's long back, her broad hips, the tilt of her neck and the heaviness of her large and beautiful breasts.

On the following Thursday, she arrived at the studio, fully expecting to finish the drawing she had half completed, and received a slight shock. The familiar Olga had gone, and had been replaced by an old man, bald, with silver hair sprouting on his sagging chest, and wasted, scarecrow-thin arms and legs. Tiger's heart sank, and she frowned. Poor old creature, she thought. What an indignity for him, to sit there, naked, in front of a group of students.

Still frowning, avoiding the old man's eye, she hung up her cloak, put on her apron, and went to her easel. She took a can of fixative from her bag, and carefully sprayed her unfinished work. After waiting for a few minutes to make sure that it was dry, she unpinned the drawing of Olga, rolled it up and secured it with a rubber band. Then she approached Marylski's desk and asked for a fresh piece of paper.

'I think, mademoiselle,' he said, 'that this would be an appropriate moment for you to begin using paint. It is not possible to do justice to such an exceptional model in charcoal, don't you agree?'

'Um, yes, I suppose so,' said Tiger uncertainly, for she had no opinion at all on the subject, other than an intense desire to be anywhere but here, staring at the collapsing naked body of this pathetic old man.

Marylski gave her a medium-sized, already primed canvas; half a dozen partially used tubes of paint; some small bottles of oil and turpentine; an old, scraped palette and a handful of brushes.

'Do I draw first? Or what?'

'If you wish, you can lightly sketch in the framework of your composition. Use a fine brush, and very diluted paint, sienna for preference.'

'Oh, right.'

Tiger fixed the canvas to her easel, arranged the rest of her equipment carefully on the small table beside her, and sat down on her stool. Only then did she raise her eyes and look at the model. The old man was staring straight ahead, his rheumy old eyes glazed, fixed on a distant point, far beyond the walls of the studio. How weird, said Tiger to herself, and blinked incredulously. He doesn't give a damn, does he? It's not a problem, for him, not at all, so why should it be for me, for heaven's sake?

She removed the cap of a tube of sienna, and squeezed a small amount onto her palette. Then, not at all sure that what she was doing was the right thing, she mixed a little oil and turpentine together in the little tin clipped to the edge of the palette. Choosing a fine brush, she added the medium to the reddish pigment until she had a transparent consistency, then, after staring for a long concentrated moment at the model, began to draw on the bare white canvas.

The hours that followed were a revelation to Tiger. The rough sketch finished, she began to block in the long planes of the old man's limbs with Naples yellow. Then, wiping her brush clean on her apron, and staring hard at the model's flesh, she realized that the skin was not a uniform colour, but had blue, green and grey tones as well, and that the whole body seemed encased in a web of purple veins, some of them fine and delicate, some startlingly engorged and standing out like ropes on the withered arms and legs. Suddenly, the battered old man appeared to Tiger to be incredibly beautiful, though his face bore the ravages of a lifetime's drinking, and his body had become merely a testimony to the human capacity for survival. For a second, his eyes, sharply focused, met hers with total indifference, then he looked away again, refixing his gaze on the original spot.

By the end of the session, Tiger had managed to put some of her perceptions onto the canvas, in the shape of the model's head, and one of his legs. Marylski, making his tour of the students, came to Tiger last, and sat down beside her. He examined her work in silence, for what Tiger felt was an inordinately long time. She grew increasingly nervous, and at last could bear it no longer. 'What's the matter?' she asked, in a small voice. 'Is it as bad as all that?'

'You have never used oil paint before, mademoiselle?'

Tiger shook her head. 'No, I haven't.'

'Did you enjoy the experience?'

'Yes, I did, very much.'

He looked at her and smiled. 'Yes, one can tell. Next time, mademoiselle, we will start again, and I will show you a few techniques; for example, how to put a glaze of colour over another to achieve a specific effect. If you go to the Louvre and study the work of the Italian Renaissance masters, you will be able to see exactly what I mean.'

'Oh. Well, thank you. I'll do that.' She hesitated, then looked at him candidly. 'So you don't think it's complete rubbish, then?'

'What? Your work? No, I don't. Your painting shows unusual promise, in my opinion. You should be studying full time, mademoiselle.'

'*Really?*'

He laughed. 'Yes, really!' He looked at her speculatively. 'I must pay the model, and say goodnight to the other students, but after that I am free, mademoiselle.

Perhaps you would care to have a drink with me? That is, of course, if you are not otherwise engaged.'

'No,' said Tiger, truthfully, 'I'm never otherwise engaged. I'd love to have a drink, Monsieur Marylski. Thank you.'

When they had installed themselves at a small marble-topped table in a nearby café, evidently Marylski's local, he ordered a carafe of the house wine. Then he turned towards Tiger, putting his elbows on the table and giving her his undivided attention. 'OK,' he said. 'Tell me, why are you not a full-time art student?'

'Because no-one ever suggested it, and it never entered my head that I would be good enough to try. It was never exactly a passion with me, you know.'

'And now you have tried it a little, do you think it could become a passion?'

Tiger considered this, then she said, 'Actually, yes, I think it easily could.' She laughed. 'Only since this evening though. I really loved the paint, the feel of it under the brush, and the *smell*, too. I'd like to live in a house that was always full of that lovely smell.'

'So, what is a little English girl doing in Paris, if she is not a student, mademoiselle?'

'Irish,' said Tiger.

'Irish, English, is there a difference?'

'Huge.'

The wine arrived, with a dish of olives. Marylski filled their glasses, and Tiger took a sip of her drink, then ate an olive. 'In any case,' she said, 'I *am* a student of sorts. I am here to learn French, as a matter of fact. It's a good job you speak such good English, Monsieur Marylski, or I'd have lost the plot ages ago.' She looked at him curiously. 'How is it that you have a Russian-sounding name, live in Paris, and speak English as well as you speak French?'

'Do you really want to know?'

'Certainly, I do.'

'It's a long story.'

'I don't mind that.'

'My family is Polish, and my parents left Cracow as a result of the anti-Semitic campaign in 1968. Many Jewish intellectuals felt forced to leave the country at that time, my father and mother among them.'

'How awful for them.' Tiger frowned, puzzled. 'But if they were Polish, how could the anti-Semitic campaign affect them?'

'My mother is Jewish. She came originally from a town called Rzeszów, which had a large Jewish population before the war, though most of them were liquidated by the Nazis during the occupation.'

'I see.'

'They met at Cracow, at the university. My father read chemistry, and my mother English. After he qualified, my father stayed on to do research, and my mother taught English. They were married in 1966, when she was twenty-two and he twenty-five. They lived in a tiny flat in Cracow, and at weekends they drove out to Przywnica, in their little car.'

'Przywnica?'

'It's my family's home. Once it was a large estate, and the land all around as far as the eye could see belonged to the Marylskis. They were good landlords; they treated their peasants fairly, as far as I know. But after the war, in '45, Poland had become a Communist state and all our land was confiscated, and redistributed among the hundreds of peasants who had formerly worked for my grandparents. We were fortunate to be allowed to keep the main house, and a small garden. I think it was the fact that my grandmother was a young war widow, with a baby son to look after, that tipped the scales in her favour.'

'So the baby boy was your father?'

'Yes, he was.'

'What was his name?'

'Milosz.' He smiled. 'Still is.'

'And your mother?'

'Renata.'

'Lovely name, Renata.' She took another sip of wine. 'And your name?'

'Tadeusz. Yours?'

'Tiger.'

Solemnly, they shook hands across the table, and Tiger was pleased that he did not ask her to explain the reason for her unusual name. 'So they came to Paris,' she said, 'and you were born here?'

'Yes, in 1970.' Then, guessing that Tiger was doing a rapid mental calculation, he laughed. 'I am a great deal older than you, Tiger. Twenty-eight, I'm afraid. Getting a bit past it, from your point of view.'

'Don't exaggerate, Tadeusz,' said Tiger, and grinned. 'You're scarcely eligible for a bus pass, are you? Tell me, is your grandmother still at Przyw . . . ? What's the place called?'

'Przywnica. Yes, she is. My parents did their best to persuade her to come to Paris with them, but she was determined to stay in her own home, and she's still there, battling on.'

'Do you ever get to see her?'

'Yes, we do. Every two months or so. We drive over to Poland with a furniture van, and my father buys old household goods, and furniture, from anyone who wants to sell things, and plenty of people do, because sadly the younger generation prefer to buy modern plastic stuff, and new gas cookers, and so on.'

'You mean they're flogging off their heirlooms, cheap?'

'Yes, that's exactly what I mean, Tiger. My mum and dad live at Barbizon, where they've got a farmhouse with some outbuildings, and that's where my mum restores the furniture, and they sell it to *antiquaires*, at a pretty obscene profit. They've got a thriving business there, and a good reputation.'

'Why couldn't they carry on with their original careers? It seems an awful waste, to be doing this sort of thing, for highly qualified people like them.'

'To have continued with their professions would

have been very difficult for them, if not impossible. For a start, it took them for ever to get work permits, even longer to get residential status, because they were pretty well penniless refugees when they arrived in France, and the language was a problem, too. Neither of them spoke much French. Mum would have probably been able to teach English, but first she had to have fluent French.'

'Yes, of course, I understand. Poor them.' Tiger ate another olive. 'Tell me more about your granny. How old was she when your grandfather was killed?'

'Very young, poor girl. Twenty-three, I think. It was in 1944, when my father was only three.'

'So it was only a year after that that she lost all the land?'

'That's right. She was left virtually penniless, for the family income came entirely from the land, of course. Fortunately, she did have the house.'

'God, how frightening for her. How did she manage to survive, and bring up her little boy?'

'Actually, and typically, she made a first-class job of it. She grew vegetables in the little garden, and kept chickens and rabbits, so they never went hungry. Once a week, she took surplus eggs and vegetables and herbs into Cracow, and sold them at the market there.'

'That must have made things easier for her. Did she have a car?'

Tadeusz laughed. 'No way! She had a little horse-drawn cart, except it wasn't a horse, it was a mule. She stabled it in my great-grandfather's library, in the east wing of the house.'

'East wing?' Visions of a vast mansion rose before Tiger's inner eye. 'Sounds very grand.'

'The old country houses in that part of Poland were built for large extended families. They were simple buildings, often made largely of wood, but spacious and frequently very beautiful. The landowners who lived in them were a bit like the characters in Chekhov plays: educated, well read, but doomed to live in a

63

rural paradise with few intellectual diversions to speak of. The high point of their day was a trip to inspect the estate, either on horseback or driven by a liveried coachman, in an open carriage.'

'So you must have had stables and coach-houses at Przywnica?'

'Yes, indeed, but the Communists burned them down, after they'd confiscated the horses, of course.'

'How awful.' Thoughtfully, Tiger twisted the stem of her glass between her fingers. 'How did she manage your father's schooling, things like that, Tadeusz?'

'She taught him herself, at first. Then he went to school in Cracow, and stayed with a cousin during the week. Granny fetched him home for the weekends, in the cart.'

'It must have been a hard life for her.'

'Yes, but it's her choice. She loves Przywnica; she'll never leave, except in her box.' Tadeusz sighed, and looked at his watch. 'It's getting late, Tiger. I'll walk you home. Is it far?'

'No, it's quite near. It's rue Monsieur. But don't worry, I can manage on my own, really.'

'I'll take you, OK?'

'OK. Thanks.'

At the concierge's gate, they said good night. 'On Saturday, I will be working in the morning,' said Tadeusz, 'but if you would like to meet me at the Louvre in the afternoon, we could look at the Italian paintings together. Would you like that?'

'Yes,' said Tiger. 'But I'll have to be back in good time to take the dog for a walk in the park.'

He looked at her, his dark eyes amused. 'Why do you have to take the dog for a walk?'

'It's my job. I'm paid to do it.'

Without replying, Tadeusz took her in his arms and kissed her, in an extremely uninhibited manner, so that Tiger felt almost as though she were being eaten. Then, quite abruptly, and with an air of detachment, he released her. 'I'll see you on Saturday, at two thirty, outside the Pyramid in the Cour Napoléon of the Louvre, OK?'

'OK,' said Tiger faintly, and slipped through the concierge's door.

Safe in her bed, Tiger lay in a glow of amazed happiness, astonished by the turn of events. At Neill's Court the opportunity for any kind of sexual contact had never presented itself, so that this was the very first time anyone had actually kissed her on the mouth, or, more accurately, *in* the mouth. Although she had watched a few fairly explicit movies, she had never really taken seriously the possibility that a kiss of that nature could release such a flood of delightfully urgent sensations within her body, and she had never consciously hankered after them. If this is what sex is all about, she said to herself, smiling, I can hardly wait for the next instalment. She did not realize it, but she was already on the way to emulating the youthful indiscretions of her mother.

CHAPTER FOUR

Tadeusz stood in the street, staring at the small door of the concierge's gatehouse, through which Tiger had disappeared, like a rabbit bolting into its hole. That was a bloody silly thing to do, he said to himself, frowning with annoyance at the recollection of his impulsive behaviour towards his student. She's just a kid, after all, a stranger in a foreign land, and now I've scared the hell out of her. Quite probably she won't show up at all at the Louvre; she might cancel the rest of her lessons; even ask for her money back.

His narrow shoulders drooped, and he turned on his heel and began to walk back to rue St-Sulpice. Without surprise, he felt the familiar waves of black depression and self-pity rise within him, as he trudged heavily along the lamplit streets, his cold hands deep in the pockets of his threadbare overcoat, his eyes fixed on the pavement beneath his feet. A constant sense of disappointment and failure was a feature of his life that Tadeusz felt quite unable to overcome, however much he wished to do so. Not that he tried terribly hard, he admitted to himself, smiling wryly; pessimism seemed inbuilt in him, and was, he assumed, a fundamental part of being Polish.

The studio was cold, for the stove had gone out. Tadeusz considered relighting the fire, then decided against it. Instead, he plugged in his electric kettle, and took off his coat. The corner of the studio in which he slept and prepared his meals was hidden behind a tall folding leather screen, cracked and peeling but still functional. On its panels were depicted nostalgic scenes of the beautiful Polish countryside, badly painted but nevertheless a source of comfort to the exiled Tadeusz, for that was how he chose to see himself. The screen had been purchased by Milosz, some years ago, on one of his buying trips to Cracow, and given to his son as a birthday present. Behind the screen was a divan covered in a purple fake-fur rug, a small round metal folding table, painted green, and two slatted chairs. A shallow stone sink, with a single cold tap, stood against the wall. Beside it, balanced on a precariously constructed set of wooden shelves, was a microwave oven, a gift forced upon him by his mother. The shelves were supported by piles of layered loose bricks, and also housed Tadeusz's inadequate collection of cooking pots, crockery and cutlery.

The kettle boiled and he made tea, pouring the water straight onto a tea bag in a glass. He cut a slice from a half-used lemon and added it to the strong black brew, then sat down on the divan to drink it. On the wall behind the bed were pinned many black-and-white photographs, taken by himself during his many visits to Przywnica, and, as he usually did before going to bed, Tadeusz gazed at them with adoration and an anguished longing, and asked himself for the thousandth time why he found it impossible to attempt what he would have wished to do more than anything in the world: to go back to Przywnica, to repair the house that meant so much to him, and to look after his grandmother.

Miserably, he shook his head. It's a question of money, of course, he said to himself, sipping the scalding tea. Lack of a proper means of livelihood, not really knowing anyone in Cracow, and especially not even speaking Polish particularly well seemed to him to present unsurmountable obstacles to the fulfilment of his dreams.

Tadeusz's childhood, spent first in a run-down northern suburb of Paris, where he had been born, and later in the village of Barbizon, near Fontainebleau, had been a happy one, and he had rarely been aware of the terrifying struggle to remain solvent that had dogged the early years of the refugee Marylskis. Once settled in their rented farmhouse in Barbizon, their business as *brocanteurs* at last providing a modest but secure income, Milosz and Renata had become doubly intent on giving their only child all the educational support and encouragement he might need to achieve his own ambitions, whatever they might be. If they were surprised, or even dismayed, when Tadeusz announced his intentions of becoming a painter, they took care to conceal their feelings. In their nice middle-class way, they had thought that a career in accountancy would have been both reassuring and appropriate.

Tadeusz had managed to gain admission to the *Beaux-Arts*, and during his time there, his parents, in spite of their reservations, had provided for him in every way, tending to spoil him, and never suggesting that he should obtain work in the vacations to help with the expenses, as most students did. Their pride in him was unswerving, and they encouraged Tadeusz's own belief that he was a seriously gifted painter, with a glittering future before him.

At the end of the course, the students prepared for their diploma show, and Tadeusz hung his enormous paintings in the exhibition space allocated to him. They were mostly executed with a palette knife, in broad sweeps of heavy green and brown *impasto*. Seeing his huge canvases properly hung for the first time, he felt full of excitement; entirely confident that his work would create a stir among the critics, and that the best galleries would be falling over themselves to sign him. It was a bitter blow when he received not a single approach. It was galling to note that the students who did receive offers were those whose work Tadeusz had been inclined to despise, for their canvases were tiny by comparison with his, and their style restrained and derivative, or so he privately thought.

Characteristically, Tadeusz had at once retreated into a mood of deep depression, even despair, at this early rejection of his talent, and he had spent that summer at Barbizon, helping Renata with her work of stripping and restoring furniture in a half-hearted way, but drinking every evening in a local bar and sleeping late every morning. In October, he had returned to Paris, found the cold and inexpensive studio for rent in rue St-Sulpice, and begun pinning up his *petites annonces* wherever a suitable notice-board presented itself in the district. Still subsidized by his parents when the going got really tough, Tadeusz had lived, taught and worked there for seven years, occasionally selling one of the very small paintings that were now his trademark. When his clean laundry ran out, or he felt desperately in need of a good nourishing meal, he stuffed his dirty clothes into a rucksack and rode out to Barbizon on his ancient two-stroke motorbike, to spend a weekend with his parents.

Tadeusz finished his tea, put the empty glass on the floor beside the bed, and lay down on the fake-fur rug, not bothering to take off his clothes. After a while he realized that he had not even removed his boots, and, crossly, he sat up and tugged at the laces impatiently. Suddenly, making him jump, the doorbell rang. Frowning, he looked at the luminous dial of his watch: one twenty-two. Who the hell could it be at this time of night?

He crossed the studio in his stockinged feet, then picked his way carefully through the darkened shop, taking care not to bang into the numerous plaster saints balanced on pedestals that stood among the glass cabinets of religious books, candles and incense burners. A faint light from a street-lamp filtered through the grille that protected the window, and Tadeusz saw a shadowy female figure, a hand shading her brow, peering through the glass. The lamplight shone on the woman's frizzy red hair, and he recognized the model, Olga. Oh, shit, he thought. What now, for Christ's sake? For a second, Tadeusz toyed with the idea of not answering the door. Then he sighed, and opened it.

Olga stood on the pavement, looking pathetic, with a large battered suitcase beside her. 'Sorry to be a nuisance, Tad,' she said humbly, and coughed painfully. 'He's slung me out again, the shit. I've nowhere else to go.'

'It's OK,' said Tadeusz. 'You'd better come in.'

Olga had been an occasional item in Tadeusz's life since his student days. He had painted her voluptuous nude body many times, and had spent many sexually gratifying nights in her strong arms, his dark head cradled between her large, maternal breasts. Since Tadeusz himself was short, slightly built and permanently undernourished, Olga had no objection to his using her body as a mattress and her breasts as a pillow, after their respective sexual frustrations had been relieved. Fifty years old, and married to an alcoholic and abusive fishmonger, Olga's nights with her handsome young artist friend seemed to her inexpressibly romantic. As for Tadeusz, he did not even particularly object to the fact that Olga always smelled faintly of fish.

He dumped her suitcase behind the screen. She took off her coat, and her thin highheeled shoes. 'Are you hungry, darling?' she asked.

'Are you? I'm afraid there's nothing here, except a bit of cheese or something.'

'I brought the supper. The old brute didn't eat it, so we might as well.'

Quite familiar with Tadeusz's domestic arrangements, she put the carton of ready-cooked stew into his microwave oven, and set the timer. She got plates, knives and forks from the shelf, and Tadeusz, suddenly feeling pretty hungry himself, uncorked the partly drunk bottle of wine and poured two glasses.

Predictably, their little supper party ended as it usually did: with a tot of cognac, a swift undressing and an even swifter dive under the fake-fur rug. Their coupling was brief and mutually satisfactory, and afterwards both of them slept very well indeed. In the morning, since it seemed likely that Olga would be staying for a few days, Tadeusz began work on a new portrait of her, reclining against a heap of cushions, in the manner of Manet's *Olympia*, wearing only her high-heeled shoes.

On Saturday, Tiger spent the morning trying to make up her mind about what to wear for her visit to the Louvre with Tadeusz; how best to present herself as a serious art student, and at the same time look as attractive as possible, given the handicap of her nose. Actually, she thought, he didn't seem to bump into my nose when he kissed me, did he? She sat for a long time at the dressing-table in her bedroom, combing her hair this way and that, trying to decide whether she looked better with it flopping around her face as usual, in black curtains, or brushed firmly back and secured with a rubber band. Finally, she came to the conclusion that her instinct to conceal as much of her face as possible was the right one, and then enlarged on this theory by wetting her front hair and cutting a thick fringe, long enough to cover her eyebrows, at the same time shading her eyes. Critically, Tiger stared at her altered reflection, and was pleased to see that the fringe not only diminished the prominence of her nose, especially in profile, but emphasized the size and beauty of her violet-blue eyes.

She decided to wear her long black velvet skirt, a white shirt, and her soft leather boots. Since the weather was cold, she added the pinstriped waistcoat and tied the silky black tie round her neck. Good, she thought, I look quite *intello*; older, too. Since rain seemed likely, she considered briefly wearing the despised and expensive trenchcoat that Orla had forced upon her, and immediately rejected the idea. Instead, she wrapped herself in her cranberry-coloured cloak, picked up her bag, left the house, walked quickly to the Métro, and bought a ticket to Louvre.

A light rain had begun to fall, but the weather failed to spoil Tiger's surprise and pleasure at her first sight of the great glass Pyramid in the Cour Napoléon. The powerful jets of the fountains that stood like sentinels around the spectacular edifice sent tall white columns of water high into the air, shimmering against the threatening November sky. Reflected in its ornamental pools, the glittering translucent sloping sides of the beautiful glass construction allowed the eye to pass through and travel around the surrounding elaborately decorated façades of the Louvre Museum, and Tiger thought it magical.

She stood near the entrance, in case Tadeusz should miss her when he arrived, but did not join the queue of people waiting for admission. At ten past three, since she was beginning to feel a little bored with waiting, and cold as well, she decided to walk right round the Pyramid, and enjoy the views from every side. The lights inside the ethereal structure twinkled in the fading light, giving it an air of mystery and improbability, as if it might decide to float up into the sky at any moment.

At half past three, Tiger began to feel distinctly annoyed as well as pretty foolish. Clearly, she had been stood up, or at best, Tadeusz had forgotten all about their appointment. In an hour, she would have to think about returning to rue Monsieur, in order to take Fanny for her walk. If the afternoon were not to be a complete write-off, she couldn't hang about any longer. The queue had by now shrunk to a matter of half a dozen people, and she decided to go in and take a look.

72

Once inside the Pyramid, she paused for a moment, and looked around her, unable to make up her mind whether to descend the wide spiral staircase that led to the impressive marble-clad entrance hall below, or to take the shiny high-tech lift instead. She chose the staircase, and walked over to the central information desk, where she picked up a leaflet explaining the layout of the museum. She soon realized that the place was vast, the collections having been divided into separate 'regions', and thereafter into smaller sub-divisions. After a little time deciphering the method of colour-coding employed, she bought a ticket and made her way without mishap to the Italian collection.

Tiger looked very carefully at the Titians and Raphaels, but the painting that really enchanted her was by an artist she had never heard of: Giorgione. The picture was called *Fête Champêtre*, and depicted four figures apparently chilling out in a stunning pastoral Tuscan landscape, the whole scene bathed in intense golden light. Two of the figures were women, one standing beside a well, apparently drawing water with an exquisitely painted glass jug, and the other seated on the ground, with her back to the audience, a flute in her hand. Both were naked in the presence of the two fully clothed males, though neither woman seemed in the least concerned at this circumstance, but appeared perfectly relaxed.

Between these two golden sunlit creatures, two young men sat on the ground, heads close together, evidently a good deal more interested in each other than in the girls. One of them was playing a lute, and so brilliantly had the artist conveyed the tranquillity and happiness of the occasion that Tiger almost believed she could hear the mellow notes plucked from the instrument by the long supple fingers of the musician. The youth in question had long black hair very like her own, and wore a scarlet velvet cap that seemed to be in the very centre of the picture, its colour dazzling against the background of a golden scorched hillside. The young man's hair parted to reveal a bare sunlit neck and a glimpse of white linen chemise, like a T-shirt, under a square-necked black doublet, but his main garment was a cranberry-coloured robe with generous folds of cloth and enormous ballooning sleeves. Tiger smiled a small secret smile, for it was the exact colour of her own cloak, though the musician's robe looked as if it were made of a stiff heavy silk, rather than wool.

His companion, young like himself, wore a buff-coloured jacket, quite dull-looking, but a subtle foil for the gorgeous colours of the central figure. His hair was brown, a mass of untidy curls, and his gentle ruddy face, the eyes fixed on the moving fingers of the lute-player, was full of a kind of rapt admiration. Those two guys are in love, one can tell, said Tiger to herself.

She looked again at the composition of the picture; at the trees, in full summer leaf, dark and mysterious, languorously heavy; at the tiny distant figure of a shepherd with his flock, half hidden under the trees; at the *castello* perched on the sunlit hill in the middle distance; then again at the two beautiful nude girls. They're just there to balance the composition, she said to herself; they're acting as a counterpoint to the real subjects of the picture. That's why they're naked, too, though as far as they're concerned it's not an erotic occasion at all. Those two girls are perfectly safe, they could just as easily be on their own. How beautiful, she thought, and how clever.

She read the short biographical note about Giorgione, and learned that he died of the plague, caught from his mistress, in 1510 at the age of thirty-two. Very little seemed to be known about him, except that he was an exceptionally fine lute-player. His output as a painter was not huge, since only fifteen of his works were identified in the records of paintings in Venetian houses, but in spite of this, many experts considered him to have been a major influence on the more famous Titian, who subsequently developed Giorgione's style for himself.

Tiger looked again at the painting, long and hard, promising herself to come again soon, to delight in its glorious innocence, and uncomplicated sensuality. She sighed, and turned away. On the way out, she bought a coloured postcard of her Giorgione, and put it carefully into her bag.

Hurrying back to rue Monsieur, she remembered that the purpose of the visit to the Louvre had been to study the use of transparent glazes of pigments, layered one upon another, in order to create luminosity in a painting. It doesn't matter, she said to herself. The techniques are important, and I must learn them, of course, but the really important thing has to be the heart and soul of a work, surely? If it doesn't speak to you, have something to teach you, then all the technique in the world is a waste of time.

The rain was still falling when she took Fanny to the Jardin du Luxembourg for her walk, and Tiger felt curiously tired, not in the mood to run with the little dog. It was almost as if her encounter with the wonderful Giorgione had sapped all her youthful energy, leaving her emotionally drained, strangely quiet, and feeling as if she had taken a surprising step into another world, and one for which her simple and narrow upbringing had not prepared her.

She spent the evening with the comtesse, doing her best to master the intricacies of bridge, which the old lady was determined to teach her, in spite of the fact that Madame was spending the evening with her sister, and Monsieur had refused point-blank to join them, so that they had to try to play with two dummies. Tiger found it impossible to concentrate, and at ten o'clock she excused herself, pleading a headache, and went to bed.

After she had left the room, the comtesse turned to

her son, who was dozing quietly in front of the fire, his finger trapped between the pages of a book he was pretending to read. 'The little one is not 'erself, Antoine. She seems rather sad tonight, *n'est-ce pas*?'

'Mm?'

'Don't you think so?'

'*Quoi, Maman?*'

Irritated, the comtesse glared at her son. '*Ce n'est pas grave*,' she muttered crossly. She gathered up the cards, then rose shakily to her feet, leaning heavily on her stick. 'Come, Fanny!' she ordered, and headed for the terrace door.

Antoine opened his eyes, shook his head at the departing figure of his cantankerous old mother, got swiftly to his feet and quickly caught her up. 'I'll walk you to your door, darling,' he said gently.

In bed, tired but unable to sleep, Tiger thought about her day. She thought about all the time she had taken, fussing over her appearance, worrying about her nose and her hair, in order to look her best, presumably trying to impress Tadeusz Marylski. It had been humiliating, as well as a gross waste of her precious free time, to be stood up, or at the very least forgotten about, by him. She acknowledged that her feelings were hurt, and that she was angry with him, but none the less admitted to herself that she had probably expected too much out of what was, after all, only a visit to a museum. She would take extremely good care not to fall into such a trap again, she promised herself grimly.

She looked across the room at her dressing-table, and to the postcard of the Giorgione *Fête Champêtre* propped against the looking-glass. The afternoon had not, in fact, been a total waste of time; she was aware that something interesting and valuable had happened to her. Perhaps, even the fact that she had been alone was no bad thing, if it meant that her entire attention had been focused on the painting. Taking a kind of comfort from this philosophical thought, Tiger switched off her light and was very soon asleep.

On the following Tuesday evening, as usual, she went to the studio for her painting class. As soon as she entered the room, she saw that the decrepit old man of the previous week was no longer seated on the rostrum. In his place was the over-endowed Olga, reclining languorously on a chaise-longue, wearing a black ribbon round her neck, and high-heeled shoes. The assembled company, including Tadeusz himself, had taken up positions in a semicircle around her and were hard at work at their easels.

Tiger hung up her cloak, then fetched her equipment from the cupboard where such things were stored. Carefully, she set out her paints on the work-table beside her easel, then, critically, studied the canvas she had been working on last week. Tadeusz left his work and came to her side.

Tiger folded her arms and looked at him severely. 'Am I to understand that we won't be working from the other model any longer?' she asked quietly. 'This is getting to be quite confusing, Tadeusz. I don't see how one can be expected to make progress if there is all this chopping and changing.'

'Don't get uptight about it, Tiger. He'll be back in a few days. At present, it's more convenient to use Olga, since she is staying with me.'

'Oh, I see.' To her extreme annoyance, Tiger felt herself blushing. 'I suppose that's why you failed to meet me at the Louvre on Saturday?'

'What?' He stared at her blankly, then comprehension dawned. 'Oh, shit! I completely forgot! Olga turned up, so I started a painting.'

'It didn't matter at all,' said Tiger stiffly. 'There's no need to apologize.'

'I didn't apologize.' He looked at her, and smiled gently. 'You've cut your hair, haven't you? It suits you like that. Come on, let's find you a new canvas, shall we?'

*   *   *

In the end, Olga stayed for two weeks. Tiger grew very bored with painting what she regarded as little more than a pastiche of a famous masterpiece, and felt she had learned very little from the experience. She still felt annoyed with Tadeusz, only speaking to him when absolutely necessary, and then briefly. He could hardly fail to notice her cool attitude towards him, but was not unduly disturbed by it.

It was now the middle of December, and becoming too cold for Tadeusz to wash and dry his laundry in the studio. Since his tiny income precluded the use of the local launderette, the alternative was to take a large bundle out to Barbizon, and let his mother take care of it for him.

The old man had been reinstated on the model's rostrum, and Tiger's mood improved as she settled once more to the congenial task of conveying her responses to his collapsing flesh through the medium of paint.

Tadeusz, as he had promised, demonstrated to her the technique of glazing pigments, and she proved an apt pupil, quick to learn, deft in execution. 'Brilliant!' she exclaimed. 'It's magic, isn't it?' Pleased with her swift progress, and glad that the cloud of disapproval engendered by Olga's temporary residence had now evaporated, Tadeusz did an impulsive thing: he invited Tiger to come with him, and spend a weekend with his parents in Barbizon. 'It will be interesting for you to see a genuine Polish interior, and study the techniques my mother uses, transforming old country furniture into desirable collectables.'

'Oh, thank you!' said Tiger, delighted at the invitation. 'I'd love to come, of course.' Then she frowned, and shook her head. 'But I would have to get permission from Madame first. It's a question of walking the dog, more than anything. They rely on me, absolutely.'

'What nonsense!' said Tadeusz briskly. 'Just tell

them you're going away for the weekend, Tiger. They'll have to make other arrangements for the stupid dog. You must have some proper time off, for heaven's sake.'

Madame de Martel-Cluny was perfectly content to give Tiger leave to go to Barbizon, merely delegating the dog-walking to the long-suffering Gaston during her absence. The old comtesse's reaction was not quite as amiable, and she expressed her disappointment at the prospect of two days without her English sessions with some vigour. 'I 'ave become accustom to you, Tiger, and so 'as poor Fanny. She will *suffer*, it goes without saying.'

'Well, it's only for two days,' said Tiger. 'I'll be back on Monday, don't worry.'

'*Quand même!*' The old lady turned her face away, refusing to be comforted.

The journey to Barbizon was slower than usual on a motorbike, since, in addition to the saddlebags crammed to bursting with dirty clothes and bedlinen, Tiger had to wedge herself between Tadeusz and his bulky backpack, which was strapped behind the pillion.

They arrived at lunchtime, and as they drove slowly through the village Tiger got a fleeting impression of comfortable-looking houses in well-tended gardens; a street filled with shops and hotels; high walls; brown-tiled roofs and a general air of prosperity.

The Marylski house was on the outskirts of the village, and hidden behind a high, pebble-dashed wall. On the grey-painted gate was a small metal plaque: *Attention! Chien méchant.* Beside the gate, a bronze bell was suspended from a coiled spring, and when Tadeusz pulled its string it uttered a surprisingly loud clang. In a moment, they heard footsteps behind the gate, and it opened to reveal a pink-cheeked, smiling man in his fifties, accompanied by a huge black mountain dog. Father and son greeted each other with affection. Tiger was introduced, and Milosz bent and kissed her hand with charming formality. The dog seemed entirely unmoved by the family reunion, and retired immediately to his kennel.

They entered the yard, for garden was an inappropriate term for the strictly utilitarian area that fronted the house, as well as the long outbuilding at right angles to it. Tadeusz parked his bike alongside a large and shabby horsebox, used by the Marylskis to convey the bric-a-brac and old furniture from Poland to France.

Milosz opened the front door, and Tiger and Tadeusz followed him into the house, which was filled with a deliciously warm and spicy smell of cooking, redolent of hearty winter comfort food.

'Renata! They are here!'

There was a clatter that sounded like a metal pan being dropped, then a door was flung open and Renata, wrapped in a long butcher's apron with floury streaks down the front, hurried to meet them, wiping her hands on a tea towel as she came. 'Tadeusz!' she cried joyfully, throwing her arms round her son, and Tiger stood by and watched as Renata murmured incomprehensible, presumably Polish words of endearment into his ear.

'Mother,' said Tadeusz patiently, releasing himself from his mother's arms. 'This is Miss Fitzgerald, one of my students.'

'Tiger,' said Tiger, smiling, and held out her hand.

Renata took her hand, and smiled. 'You must forgive me; it is not too often that we have the happiness to see Tadeusz, here in Barbizon.'

'It's very kind of you to let me come,' said Tiger.

'No, no, the kindness is all yours, my dear, especially as it gives me the rare chance to speak English.'

'And also,' added Milosz, rubbing his hands together, 'it allows us the opportunity to celebrate, and have a small vodka before lunch, isn't it?'

He led the way into a salon, small and rather dark. French windows with thick brown glazing bars over-looked the yard, and allowed a small amount of wintry natural light to illuminate the room. The walls were painted grey, and the parquet floor was also grey, of a slightly deeper shade. A black upright piano, open, stood against one wall, and on its top was a large Jewish seven-branched brass candlestick. A cut-glass vase stood beside it, containing some bronze chrysan-themums. On the wall behind the piano were several large glazed reproductions of paintings of historic events, in ornate gilded frames. Beside these was a small oil painting, also in a gilded frame. Its subject was an extremely beautiful girl, apparently in her early twenties, with long curly dark hair and lustrous dark eyes. Tiger recognized at once the features of the young Renata, but felt too shy to make any kind of comment.

Centrally placed on the parquet floor was a round mahogany table, highly polished and surrounded by a set of six matching mahogany chairs with dark red leather seats. On the table was a square, white, crocheted table cloth, and on it was a tall glass vase containing a bunch of Parma violets. Beside it stood several very small crystal glasses.

'Sit down, sit down,' urged Milosz, and took two bottles from a mahogany sideboard. They all sat down and he placed the bottles on the table. 'We have a choice,' he said expansively. 'Russian vodka, or Polish. Which would you prefer, my dear Miss Tiger?'

'Polish, of course, thank you,' said Tiger politely, and they all laughed, as if she had said something extraordinarily clever.

They drank one glass of vodka only, to Tiger's con-siderable relief. Then Renata showed her the bathroom and took her to her room. 'It is very brave of you to travel on that terrible old bike of Tadeusz's, especially in such horrible weather,' she remarked, sitting down on the bed.

'Oh,' replied Tiger, opening her satchel and taking from it the gift-wrapped box of *marrons glacés* she had bought for her hostess, 'I don't mind the cold. It's rain I really hate.' She held out the pretty parcel. 'This is for you,' she said.

'How very kind of you! But really, you shouldn't have gone to the expense, my dear.' She looked at Tiger, her dark eyes sparkling. 'Students are always broke, aren't they? And not only students, do you not agree?'

Tiger grinned. 'You mean Tadeusz, I suppose?'

'Yes, of course. He is darling, one adores him, naturally. But like all young men, he only comes home when he is hungry or needs his washing done.'

'But I thought he always goes with you on your trips to Poland, to help with the driving?'

'Only when he needs money, Tiger.'

'But he loves the place – what's it called? Przywnica? – doesn't he?'

'Oh, yes, absolutely! Of course he does! But he wishes it was as it used to be, long ago, before the war changed everything.'

'But isn't that what you all wish for?'

Renata looked at Tiger, and shook her head. 'No, not any more. You must go where life takes you, Tiger. In my experience, that's the best way. To be always looking over your shoulder is a disaster waiting to happen.'

Tiger studied the grave face of Renata, and saw how beautiful she still was, in spite of the marks of time around her eyes, and on her neck; in spite of her work-stained hands, thickened and coarsened by repeated contact with Nitromors and the other chemicals she used in her work. She would have liked to explain to Renata that Tadeusz had told her the history of the sufferings of the Jewish population in Poland, but felt that it would be better for Renata herself to raise the subject, if she should wish to do so. 'So you don't feel homesick for Poland, yourself, any more?'

Renata laughed, and stood up. 'I didn't say that,' she said. 'Lunch is ready. Let's join the others, shall we?'

The meal was eaten in the kitchen, an informal and much less gloomy room than the salon, in Tiger's private opinion. In the first place, it was a great deal warmer, on account of the oven, and in the second place, its walls and ceiling were lined with narrow cedar planks, which gave it a cosy, welcoming atmosphere. From a hook in the ceiling hung a very large steel lamp, in the art nouveau style. It had originally burned oil, but was now converted to electricity, its light bulb concealed by the white milk-glass shade that rested on its circular steel gallery. Lavishly decorated with panels of what appeared to be blue butterflies' wings, the heavy lamp was a pretty imposing affair, and dominated the cedar-clad room.

On the walls were displayed many framed family photographs, some a soft faded brown and obviously very old, and, rather to Tiger's surprise, an icon of the Blessed Virgin, encased in what looked like a cuckoo clock, though minus the mechanism. A long wooden counter ran along the wall under the single window, and on it were arranged piles of plates, cooking pots and pans, an egg-timer and a massive green fern. Built into this worktop was a modern stainless steel sink, and beneath it was a full complement of contemporary domestic equipment, including an impressive state of the art electric cooker.

Beneath the lamp was a long table, covered in brightly coloured patterned oilcloth, and already laid for lunch. Surrounding the table was the most beautiful set of traditional Polish country chairs, their solid wooden backs pierced and carved to represent three-headed eagles, interspersed with hearts. They had been polished with beeswax until they shone like stars.

Milosz, Tadeusz and Tiger sat down, and Renata took from the oven a shallow black casserole and placed it in the centre of the table, followed by a dish of boiled potatoes, sprinkled with finely chopped onion and parsley. She, too, sat down and Milosz lifted the lid of the steaming pot.

'Bravo!' exclaimed Tadeusz, clapping his hands like a child. '*Bigós*, my absolute favourite! *Dziekuje*, Mum.'

'I should think so, my boy,' said Milosz. 'The crazy woman's been up since six, making it for you.'

Renata said nothing, but smiled, and Tiger knew from her expression that she was enchanted by her son's words of praise and gratitude.

After lunch Tadeusz took Tiger out to the yard, to have a look at the workshop. The long building, originally a coach-house and stables, was divided into three sections, each one entered through its own double doors.

The first room, measuring about sixty square metres, was stacked to the high rafters with furniture. Some of it looked quite ordinary, plain wooden settles and chairs, tables and chests of drawers, but the bulk of the collection was painted with flowers of every description, in brilliant primary colours, and covering every available inch. In addition to the furniture decorated in this naive style, there were kettles, buckets, cache-pots and even a small dog kennel, all smothered in colourful blooms.

Tiger had never seen work of this kind before, and was struck by its exuberance and simple charm, as well as by the patience and dedication that must have gone into its creation. 'Is this sort of thing still being done in Poland, Tadeusz?' she asked.

'Yes, but not so much, nowadays. There are a few villages where even the houses themselves are lime-washed inside and out, and the walls are then painted with garlands of flowers in the traditional way, exactly like this.'

'Presumably there's quite a lot of interest in such things, here in France?'

'No, there's very little indeed. Come, I'll show you.'

Tadeusz led the way to the next room, and Tiger followed him. Inside, an unpleasantly acrid smell filled the air and Tadeusz opened all the windows and doors to the yard, letting a draught blow through. In the centre of the room was a deep tank, covered with a series of thick wooden lids. Tadeusz put on a pair of rubber gloves, and, carefully, lifted one of the covers. 'Hold your breath, Tiger, and take a look. Don't inhale the fumes.'

Nervously, Tiger peered into the tank and saw three or four pieces of furniture, in the process of having their paint stripped down to the bare wood in the acid bath. Swiftly, she drew back, and Tadeusz replaced the lid. He pulled off his gloves and they went out into the fresh air. Frowning, she said, 'Isn't it awfully dangerous, that stuff?'

'Yes, it is, bloody dangerous, and personally, I hate the whole business. It seems to me a kind of vandalism, even though it's a means of livelihood for us, of course.'

'Yes, I see that. I think it very courageous of your mother to take it on. Does she ever get burned?'

'Occasionally, she does, but so far, not too seriously. If that stuff touches you, you know about it.'

'I bet!' Tiger smiled at Tadeusz, anxious that he should not think her critical of his parents in any way. 'So, what happens after the acid bath? Show me.'

He unlocked the door to the third workshop, and switched on the light. Inside, and arranged in the form of room-settings, complete with lamps, cushions and books, was displayed the most beautifully restored furniture. The wooden pieces, stripped of all or practically all of their original paint, had been carefully rinsed and air-dried. They had then been sanded down, and given a patinating coat of flat grey or sage-green oil-wash. When the oil-wash was almost dry, Renata, with astonishing delicacy and skill, had rubbed away virtually invisible sections of the paint with fine wire wool, to suggest the natural wear of centuries of use. Finally, she had given each piece three waxings, followed by hand-buffing to produce a gentle gleam.

Against a wall stood a small pine chest of drawers, with a bay tree growing in a terracotta pot on either side. On the top of the chest stood a bronze head of a child, a pair of twisted brass candlesticks, and a basket containing a set of china carpet-bowls. The drawers of the little chest had graceful brass handles, and Tiger observed that around each handle were dirty finger-marks, clearly the result of many years of repeated opening and closing. She lifted one of the handles and let it drop with a small click. 'Did your mum put those marks there, after she'd finished the restoration?'

'I expect so. It's the kind of detail she likes.'

They looked at a pair of box beds, each dressed with linen sheets and white stitched quilts, then at a marble-topped console table, with fragments of gilt still adhering to the base. On its top was arranged a nostalgic still-life: a bundle of dried lavender; a pile of leather-bound books and a red lacquer tea caddy. Tiger raised her eyebrows. 'I bet this didn't come from a peasant's house?'

'No, it didn't,' said Tadeusz, stiffly. 'It came from Przywnica. My grandmother needs money to rewire part of the house.'

'Oh, I'm sorry, Tadeusz! I didn't mean to pry!'

'Of course you didn't. I know that.' He took her in his arms and kissed her, slowly and languorously, as before. The same rush of sensations raced through Tiger's veins as on that first occasion, which now seemed a long time ago, and she wound her eager arms round Tadeusz's neck, responding passionately to his embrace.

Too soon, he released her, laughing. 'I can't help feeling that your name is quite appropriate, dear little Tiger. It suits you very well, or will do, in time.'

'What do you mean, *in time*? You're very insulting, Tadeusz!'

'And you are just a child, Tiger!'

'I am *not*!'

'You are, my darling, and none that worse for it, I assure you. Come on, let's go in. My mother will doubtless be making tea, and heaven knows what else, to make absolutely certain that we don't starve.'

They returned to Paris on Sunday afternoon, with the saddlebags neatly packed with Tadeusz's clean laundry, and his backpack stuffed with enough food to last him for a week. Throughout the journey, Tiger, her arms wound tightly round Tadeusz's body, her nose pressed to his leather-clad back, fantasized about the romantic attachment with him that she felt sure was to be her destiny, bringing with it a swift release from the tiresome burden of her persistent virginal state. Sadly, nothing as dramatic or exciting was to occur for the present. He dropped her off at rue Monsieur, giving her a chaste kiss on each cheek. 'See you on Tuesday,' he said.

CHAPTER FIVE

Christmas was approaching, and Tiger's French classes were suspended until January. In rue Monsieur, the family was preparing to go south, where their many cousins, nephews and nieces would be gathering to celebrate Christmas and the New Year in the traditional Provençal manner.

Reluctantly, Tiger made arrangements to fly home for the holiday. She left it until the last moment, still hoping against hope that Tadeusz would invite her to spend a romantic bohemian Christmas alone with him at rue St-Sulpice, but this he failed to do. Disappointed, she booked her flight to Dublin, and bought some small presents for her mother, Niamh and Liam, assuming that Orla and her family would not wish to come to Ireland in winter.

Her flight, unsurprisingly, was delayed, which meant a long wait for the next coach to her local town. She got to Neill's Court, finally, at nine thirty the following morning, having hitched a lift in the postman's van. Wearily, clutching the mail in one hand and her small suitcase in the other, she left the empty stable-yard, walked along the path to the front of the house, climbed the stone steps and opened the garden door.

Wearing her winter coat and boots, for the house was extremely cold, Niamh was seated at the hall table, talking on the telephone. She looked up as Tiger came in, and raised a finger, acknowledging her presence. After her months away from home, Tiger was surprised to see how incredibly like their mother Niamh looked, with the same wispy curly hair, albeit darker than Alice's, and the same wide-apart eyes, though hers were blue-grey rather than the true hazel of her mother. She looked tired, and a good deal older than her twenty-eight years. 'Yes, yes, I understand,' she said impatiently, into the telephone, 'but please tell him to come at the earliest possible moment. I'm sure he could manage it if he tried hard enough.'

Very quietly, controlling herself, Niamh replaced the phone, and turned towards her sister, who stood waiting, wrapped in her long cranberry-coloured cloak, her black hair tumbling over her shoulders, the long fringe framing her beautiful violet-blue eyes. In the grey morning light of that bleakly cold room, Tiger looked to her exhausted older sister like a vision of youthful perfection, but equally an undeniably frivolous one. Clearly, Tiger was no longer the sister's little helper that Niamh had hoped she would be. 'You've cut your hair,' she said accusingly.

'Only the fringe,' said Tiger, frowning.

'You won't be much use to me, tarted up like that, will you?'

Tiger swallowed. 'What did you have in mind, Niamh? I thought you hadn't any guests at the moment?'

Niamh stood up, and raised a hand to her eyes. 'I'm sorry, Tiger, I didn't mean to pick on you. It's just that everything's got a bit on top of me.'

'Oh, dear. What happened?'

'Well, for a start, the effing wind blew part of the roof off the other night, and I can't get anyone to come out and patch it up.' Niamh looked at Tiger, and her face was grim. 'They make excuses about it being Christmas and all that, but actually, it's because I haven't been able to pay the last bill.'

'Is the roof leaking, then?'

'Yes, of course it bloody is! It's pouring into the bed-rooms in the east wing, whenever it rains. We've got buckets everywhere, but it's no good. It's not a few drips and leaks, Tiger, it's a sodding flood. Thank God it didn't happen in the fishing season.'

'What about Liam? Can't he do something?'

'I expect he could, but you know what Mother's like. If he's out of her sight for more than a few minutes, she runs around like a banshee, wailing for him, daft old bat.'

'Why don't we take her up to the attic, so that she can see him while he's working?'

'You're not serious?'

'Certainly I am. But first, Niamh, I'm starving. I haven't had anything to eat since yesterday, on the flight from Paris.'

'Oh, God, I'm sorry, Tiger. Come to the kitchen at once, I'll boil you an egg or something.'

It was a good deal warmer in the kitchen, and Tiger sat in the creaky old rocking chair, cradling a mug of tea in her cold hands, while Niamh boiled eggs and made toast for them both. The long kitchen table of Tiger's childhood had now vanished, and in its place was a spectacular marble-topped fitting, occupying the central part of the room. For the purposes of informal family meals, a small folding card table with a green baize top had been erected close to the stove, with two garden chairs. 'What happened to the old table, Niamh? Did you sell it?'

'No. It's in one of the stables. I needed something more efficient, and hygienic.'

'Oh, I see.'

With professional competence and speed, breakfast was prepared. Niamh sat down at the card table her-self, and the two sisters attacked the food hungrily.

Niamh swallowed the last piece of her toast, and poured another mug of tea for them both. 'How was

Paris?' she asked, doing her best to sound as though she really wanted to know.

'OK, I suppose,' replied Tiger, deciding that to enthuse about her good fortune in living in Paris would be guaranteed to make Niamh feel even more negative about her own somewhat difficult circumstances. 'It's quite tricky being a sort of servant to a spoilt old lady, as a matter of fact. Even worse, having to take her foul little dog for endless walks.'

'I thought you were an au pair?'

Tiger laughed. 'So did I! The "children" turned out to be the old comtesse and dread Fanny, the pug. I wrote to Orla, and told her about it. Didn't she tell you?'

'Oh, yes, come to think of it, I believe she did say something about it.' Niamh's eyes glazed over with lack of interest, as though she regarded Tiger's problems as minimal compared with her own. She put down her empty mug, and stared at her sister's long skirt and pretty white shirt, looking worried. 'I hope you've got something a bit more practical to wear, if you're going to give me a hand while you're here, Tiger. You've grown quite a bit since the summer, haven't you? Do you think your old jeans will still fit you?'

'I don't suppose it matters if they're a bit short, or tight, do you? There's no-one here to notice, is there?'

'There's Liam.'

'Oh, *him*! He doesn't count, Niamh, does he? He must be well over seventy now?'

Niamh laughed, shortly. 'Whatever gives you the idea that men cease to look at girls when they get old, Tiger? If anything, they get worse, in my opinion, dirty old sods.'

Up in her old room, Tiger gazed about her with considerable distaste, as well as dismay. In her absence, the mice had lost no time in taking over completely, and the low-ceilinged room not only smelt disgustingly of rodents, but their little black droppings were everywhere. Her room was exactly as she had left it, for Niamh had found neither the time nor the inclination to think about changing the sheets on the bed, or even getting the floor swept. The thin old eiderdown folded over the ottoman at the foot of the bed had been attacked by the mice, and quantities of wadding had been pulled through the large holes made by their sharp little teeth. It was easy to see where this valuable nesting material had been taken, for a trail of evidence lay on the floor and led to a hole in the wainscoting.

Tiger went to the small dormer window and opened it, letting in a blast of arctic air. Quickly, she shut it again. She sat on the window seat and looked around the dreary little room, and thought about her warm and welcoming room in rue Monsieur, with its comfortable bed, and its own bathroom. 'Sod it!' she said. 'I'm not sleeping in this dump any more, and Niamh can't make me.'

She opened her clothes cupboard, and took from it her old jeans, a beaten-up pair of trainers, two thick sweaters and her grandfather's old flannel hunting shirt. Then she left the room, carrying her unopened suitcase, as well as the clothes. She went down to the first floor, and opened the doors of all the guest rooms, until she found one which appeared to be ready for occupation. It seemed curiously familiar, and after looking carefully round, she came to the conclusion that it was the bedroom always spoken of as 'Con's Room' during her childhood. Good, she said to herself, this will be fine for the ten days I have to be here. After all, no-one else will be needing it, will they? She turned down the quilt on the bed, to make sure that it was made, then unpacked her case, and changed into jeans and trainers, and a black polo-necked sweater. She brushed her hair and plaited it into a thick braid to keep it out of the way. Then she went downstairs, in search of her sister.

*   *   *

Niamh was in the library, in earnest discussion with Liam Dainty. On seeing Tiger, he got to his feet, and spread his arms wide in astonishment, his wrinkled face splitting into a pleased grin. 'Miss Tiger, as ever is! Mother of God, 'tis as tall as a young giraffe you are, me darlin' girl!'

Tiger laughed, and submitted to Liam's rib-cracking hug. 'It seems the roof needs mending, Liam. Is it possible at all, do you think?' Unconsciously, Tiger slipped back into the rhythms of speech of her childhood. She turned to her sister. 'By the way, Niamh, I can't sleep in that foul old attic; it's overrun with mice. It's disgusting. I've put myself in Dad's old room; it's the only one I could find that's ready.'

Niamh flushed angrily. 'You should have asked me first, Tiger.'

'Why?'

'Why? Because I try to run this place efficiently, and that room is always ready, in case a visitor turns up out of the blue.'

'You weren't seriously expecting me to sleep in that freezing garret, like a servant, Niamh?' Tiger glared at her sister. 'You bloody were, weren't you?'

Niamh looked guilty, and kept her eyes lowered. 'You never minded your old room before, Tiger.'

'Well, now I bloody do! You forget, I've been living in a *civilized* house for some time now, and there I have a really lovely room, and my own bathroom. Even if I am a sort of servant, they're far too nice to treat me like one. This is *my* home as much as yours, and I'm certainly not going to allow you to insult me while I'm here.' Pink-cheeked, and bright-eyed with indignation, Tiger turned to Liam. 'Right, Liam, where's this stupid roof, then?'

'What about Mother?' asked Niamh, in a subdued tone. 'Aren't you going to say hello to her, Tiger?'

'Oh, really! Do I have to? She'll only kick up hell if I go and see her. She always thinks I'm Dad, doesn't she, Liam?'

93

'Sure an' she does, poor lady. You're the spitting image of your daddy, darlin', and that's the gospel truth.'

'Right,' said Tiger. 'So, let's not rock the boat, shall we? Come on, let's go and inspect the damage, and see what we can do.'

After they had gone, Niamh sat at her desk and stared moodily at her neatly written lists, spread out before her. She made lists for every conceivable activity to be carried out during her long working day, and now, feeling somewhat flattened by the combination of aggression and assertiveness exhibited by her younger sister during the last few minutes, she asked herself whether it might not have been better if Tiger had stayed in France, or gone to visit Orla.

On a purely personal level, she felt herself to be obscurely threatened by this striking-looking, bizarrely-dressed creature, so recently her mild-mannered little schoolgirl sister. Or if not exactly *threatened*, then she felt her authority to be seriously eclipsed, by Tiger's complete disregard of her wishes. I suppose it was a bit rotten of me not to see to her room, she said to herself. That's what this is all about, isn't it? She's angry about that, I suppose, silly girl. Can't she see how bloody tired I am, chasing after everything, getting nowhere, not even managing to pay the bloody bills on time? Nobody ever puts clean sheets on my bloody bed, do they? So why should they expect me to do it for *them*, I'd like to know. Tears of exhaustion and self-pity filled Niamh's eyes, and she brushed them away angrily.

She got up, and went to the kitchen to make tea for her mother. While the kettle came slowly to the boil, she went out to the yard, caught a chicken, and wrung its neck. Holding its twitching corpse over her knee, she ripped out handfuls of its feathers from its still-warm flesh, with the unconcerned skill of long practice. Then she went inside and put it on a platter

94

on her magnificent, though still unpaid-for counter, ready for cooking.

She washed her red, rough hands under the cold tap, then took the tea tray to the orangery, where Alice, wrapped in plaid rugs and wearing Tara's old fox-fur hat, sat in a Lloyd Loom chair, staring through the steamed-up windows at the grey waters of the lake. At the sight of Niamh, she smiled her sweet and vacant smile, a slight trickle of saliva hovering at the corner of her mouth. 'Hello, dear,' she said. 'Where's Liam? He hasn't died, or gone away, has he?'

'No, Mum, he's here, darling. He's just doing a little job for me. He'll be here in a minute, don't worry.'

Up in the roof, Liam and Tiger surveyed the damage. It was a question of three or four square metres of missing slates, ripped from their rotting battens by the ferocity of the gales. Some of the slates were still intact, though scattered about, precariously clinging to the undamaged surfaces of the roof, or piled up behind the stone parapet that ran along the eaves. 'God,' said Tiger, 'what a mess! How many new slates will we be needing, Liam?'

'Thirty or forty, I shouldn't wonder, miss.'

'So, what's the problem? We'd better go and buy some, then nail them all back on.'

Liam wiped his nose with a horny, arthritic finger, looking thoughtful. 'It's the bank, Miss Tiger. They've cut up rough about the overdraft. Miss Niamh's up to the wire, for sure.'

Tiger stared at him. 'What the hell do you mean? I thought she had the place full all summer long? What happened to the cash that the fishing brought in?'

'Spent.'

'*Spent*? What on?'

'What she calls the battery for the new kitchen. She needs a dozen of everything to make sense, she says, so she's ordered it and paid for it in advance, to get a discount.'

'Liam, what the hell are you on about? What new kitchen?'

'For the cooking school, miss.'

'The *cooking school*?' Tiger sounded incredulous.

'Yes, miss. Miss Niamh read in the paper about an Irish country house that runs a cooking school. They grow all their own fruit and veg, just like us, and people come and stay at the house, and learn how to do all the cooking, and then they eat it, which is to kill two birds with one stone, in a manner of speaking. Money for old rope, Miss Niamh says, and a good way of keeping going in the closed season.'

'Actually,' said Tiger slowly, 'it's a bloody *good* idea, Liam.' She frowned, and shook her head. 'It looks as though she's gone about it the wrong way, though, doesn't it, if she's got up the bank's nose? What possessed her not to talk to them first, and sort out the money thing?'

'It's my belief she got carried away with all the lovely catalogues that she sent for, from London. She just ordered everything she needed, and sent them a cheque.'

'Did the cheque bounce?'

'No, but the carpenter's did.'

'The carpenter, Liam? What carpenter?'

'Have you never seen the lovely new fitting in the kitchen, miss? Young Lonnie from the village made it, and a fine job he's done of it, to be sure.'

'And he's not been paid?'

Liam shook his head, and looked past Tiger, out over the bare twiggy tops of the ash trees, towards the blue hills beyond. 'He'll not be the only one, neither, miss.'

'Oh, Liam! Do you mean *you*?'

'Doesn't matter. I'm still being fed. It's only the pub of an evening, and the fags that I miss.' He turned towards Tiger, and smiled doubtfully. 'It'll be all right, at the end of the day. Miss Niamh advertised in the *Lady*, and the first two lots are coming in January, and four lots in February, and she says that'll make everything OK again, God willing.'

Tiger put her hand on Liam's sleeve. 'In the meantime, I suppose I'd better stump up for the new slates. Luckily I'm quite well paid, and I've saved a bit. You'd better take me into town after lunch, Liam. How *weird* to have to use plastic to get Irish punts out of my French bank account!'

In the kitchen, Tiger found Niamh preparing lunch, which smelt as though it was fish. Niamh turned from the stove. 'Where's Liam?' she asked, looking worried.

'He's gone to see to Mum.'

'Oh, good. She's been making a fuss, as usual. You know how she is about him.'

Tiger got herself a glass of water at the sink. 'It must make things difficult for you, Niamh, if she wants him for herself all the time?'

'Yes, it does. It makes things bloody difficult, and it's getting worse. It means that when we have people in the house, he has to stay with her all the time, and make sure she's kept out of sight.' Niamh took a dish from the warming drawer, and slid the poached fish onto it. She turned her head, and frowned at Tiger. 'Imagine being a paying guest here, and bumping into this senile old woman on the stairs, demanding to know whether you're hiding Liam in your bedroom! It's grotesque!'

'Mother's not old,' said Tiger. 'She's only fifty-five, isn't she?'

'What the hell difference does her actual *age* make, Tiger? She's got bloody Alzheimer's, don't you realize that? Orla thinks she should be put in a home, and I'm beginning to think she may be right.'

'Do you really, Niamh?'

'Oh, *shit*! No, of course I don't, and in any case, we couldn't possibly afford it.' Niamh picked up a tea towel, and carefully wiped the rim of the dish she was holding. 'It's just that I have to do so much, and that

97

imbecile Sorcha isn't much of a help, really.' She looked at her sister, and sketched a small bitter smile. 'I need a holiday, Tiger; I'm fucking knackered, actually.'

If Tiger was surprised to hear such crude words, she took care not to show it. 'Here,' she said. 'Give me Mum's tray. I'll take it to her. Sit down. Give yourself a drink, and I'll get the lunch, Niamh.'

'OK, but don't hang about, will you? We don't want her winding herself up, thinking Dad's here, for Christ's sake!'

Tiger picked up the tray and took it to the orangery. She tapped on the glass door, and called softly, 'Liam?'

He came at once and took the heavy tray from her, with a conspiratorial smile. 'I'll settle her for her rest, darlin', and then we'll take the trap and go into town, right?'

'Right.'

Buying the new slates, as well as new nails, took longer than expected, and it was four o'clock and already dark when Tiger and Liam returned to Neill's Court, so the repairs to the roof had to be postponed until the next day.

The evening passed slowly. Niamh did not light a fire in the sitting-room, and the two sisters sat in the kitchen, finding very little to say to each other. Having seen the new slates stacked in the hall, Niamh was forced to conclude that Tiger must have paid for them, Liam having doubtless told her about their temporary insolvency. She felt irritated and humiliated at the thought of her younger sister coming to her rescue, and wondered how much money, exactly, Tiger had at her disposal. After all, she thought, if she's got it, she might as well cough up for her bed and board while she's here. Niamh opened her mouth, intending to suggest this, then changed her mind, got to her feet and began to prepare the evening meal.

The chicken she had killed that morning was quite

young, although scrawny, so she decided to roast it. She cut off its head and pulled out its entrails, then stuffed the cavity with an apple, a head of garlic, a bunch of sage and a cup of cold cooked rice from the fridge. She rubbed it all over with butter, gave it a good grinding of salt and black pepper and put it into the oven.

'Can I do anything, Niamh?'

'No, it's all right. I'll just do colcannon with some leftover spuds and sprouts, and a chicory salad. In any case, you've done enough, don't you think?'

'I haven't done anything, have I?'

'You went out with Liam. I presume it was you bought the new slates for the roof?'

'You didn't mind me doing that, surely?'

'I didn't *mind*, Tiger, but at least you could've had the common courtesy to consult me about it, couldn't you?'

'Why? Just so that you could have ordered me to do it, and made me feel that it was my *duty* to do it, Niamh? As it is, it's my *pleasure* to give you the bloody slates, and to help Liam fix the sodding things tomorrow. Of course, if you're incapable of accepting a gift from me, I can always take them back, can't I?'

'That won't be necessary.' Tight-lipped, silent, Niamh opened the oven door and basted her chicken.

Tiger stared at her sister's stiff back, at the greasy fronds of curly, unwashed hair that clung round her neck, and felt a stab of pity, and remorse. 'Sorry, Niamh,' she said quietly. 'I didn't come home for Christmas just to upset you; I know you've been having a rotten time.'

'I don't know why you did come, really. It won't be much of a Christmas, Tiger. I won't have any money until the dividends come in next month, and I daren't even ask for credit at the village shop any more.'

'But I think it's a very good idea about the cookery school, Niamh. It was brilliant of you to think of it, it really was.'

Niamh closed the oven door, and fetched some cold potatoes from the fridge, spread them out on a floured board and began to chop them with sprouts and onions. 'Well, yes,' she said, sounding a little mollified, 'it is quite a good idea, and I know I could make a success of it, but I realize now that I simply don't have the cash I need to get it off the ground properly. I need *help* in the kitchen, Tiger, and not just that useless peasant Sorcha. I need two girls that I could train properly, to work in the house as well as in the kitchen, and another man for the kitchen garden, too. It's hopeless relying on Liam, poor man. He's at his wits' end trying to keep Mum happy, and out of my hair.' Niamh got a frying pan, greased it, and spread the potato mixture carefully over the base, pressing it down with a fork. 'Frankly, I feel as if I'm already staring defeat in the face,' she said, with a sad little laugh. 'I probably won't be able to buy the fucking food for the first guests, as things are.'

The supper was excellent, and although she did her best not to appear greedy, Tiger ate ravenously of everything on offer. 'No question, Niamh,' she said, 'you're a terrific cook.'

'Thanks,' said Niamh, looking at the wrecked carcase of her chicken, and casting round in her mind for something less exotic to make tomorrow. Spaghetti, she thought, with a cream and herb sauce.

After supper, Tiger ran upstairs to fetch her mother's tray, for Liam had taken her up at six o'clock, and given her her supper in bed. The tray was now on the floor outside Alice's door. There was no sign of Liam, but through the door Tiger could hear the faint sound of voices and a throaty laugh. Thoughtfully, she carried the tray down to the kitchen, and helped with the washing-up.

'Do you never get out, Niamh?' she asked. 'It's not much of a life, stuck in here, is it? What about your bloke, Michael? Don't you ever see him?'

'No, I don't,' said Niamh shortly, and the plate she was wiping slipped through her fingers, smashing itself on the stone floor. 'Bloody shitting thing!' she screamed, threw down her cloth and ran from the room, slamming the door behind her.

Tiger picked up Niamh's cloth, cleared away the broken china, wiped out the sink, and took herself to bed. There seemed little point in doing anything else, in that grim and sorrowful house.

The following day dawned cold and crisp, with a blue sky, and Liam and Tiger lost no time in starting work on the roof. All day long they laboured in the cold wind, with frequent breaks for Liam to run down and reassure Alice that he was still there for her. By four o'clock the job was very nearly done, and Tiger held the Hunter lantern while Liam nailed the last few slates in place.

Niamh, having recovered her composure, and relying on her sister's sensitivity in avoiding the subject of the philandering bastard Michael Keen, made a special effort to jazz up the spaghetti dish she had prepared for supper, by defrosting a large packet of Dublin Bay prawns she had kept in the freezer for several months. She also produced a bottle of red wine, and all four members of the household enjoyed their dinner very much indeed, including Alice, tucked up in her lacy bed, and fed by Liam.

After such an unusually pleasant evening, it was all the more unfortunate that Alice should be taken violently ill in the night, and vomited her prawns all over her counterpane. Hearing the ensuing commotion, Tiger slipped out of her father's warm bed, and went to help the frantic Liam, running to the bathroom, getting towels and buckets of water for him, and afterwards rinsing all the soiled towels in the bath.

'I should never have let her take the prawns, Miss Tiger; I knew it was asking for trouble.' Carefully, he folded a wet towel, and hung it in the airing cupboard

101

to dry. 'But she gets so few treats, poor lady, and she does so love the shellfish.'

'It's not your fault, Liam. And since Niamh's slept through the whole thing, best keep stum, don't you think?'

'My lips are sealed, Miss Tiger. Never give it another thought, darlin'.'

Too wide awake to go quickly to sleep again, Tiger lay in bed and stared into the darkness, wondering how Niamh would manage to work through her problems, and make her scheme work. It's a question of money, nothing more or less, she told herself, and frowned. I wonder, should I talk to Orla, she thought, and instantly dismissed the idea, knowing that Orla would jump at the chance of selling Neill's Court and putting Alice in a home, or worse, the loony-bin. Suddenly, the very idea of the family losing the house, and having no real home to call their own, filled her with a cold fear, and a deep uneasiness. Equally, the thought of her mother, frail and frightened, bewildered and panicky without the constant comfort and support of Liam at her side, locked up for the twenty or thirty years that probably still remained to her, seemed to Tiger a situation to be resisted at all costs. Poor Mum, she thought, she'd be better dead than dumped in a home for the senile, in totally strange surroundings, looked after by hard-faced impatient nurses, and worst of all, without Liam.

Christmas Day was grey and gloomy, and rooks cawed restlessly in the woods all day long. Niamh and Tiger discussed the possibility of having their festive lunch with Alice and Liam in the orangery, but wisely decided against this plan, so the day passed in exactly the same way as any other. Not at all sure that she was doing the right thing, Tiger produced her small gifts of French soap and bath-salts for her mother and sister, and a carton of Gauloises for Liam. The cigarettes were accepted with a joyful hug, but Niamh's thanks were perfunctory, even resentful, and Tiger wished she had not bothered to bring the presents in the first place.

'In any case,' Niamh said, 'Mum won't know who this is from, so it's rather a waste, isn't it?'

'Why don't you give it to her, yourself?'

'What, *me* give her a present that's really from *you*?'

'Do whatever you like, Niamh, it really doesn't matter.'

'OK, I'll give it to her, then, if you really want me to.'

At eight o'clock in the evening, Orla telephoned to wish them all a happy Christmas. She spoke to her mother, to Liam, and to Niamh. Finally, she asked to speak to Tiger. 'How's it going, Tiger? Are you having a good time, or is it hell, like always?'

'It's just the same, thanks, Orla,' she said quietly, feeling somehow disloyal to Niamh, but unable to pretend that she was enjoying her brief homecoming. She glanced guiltily in the direction of her sister, but she had gone back to the orangery with their mother. Only Liam remained, his little blue eyes gleaming, bright with comprehension.

'How would you like to spend a few days with us, Tiger, before you go back to Paris? We might go to the theatre, or the opera, perhaps. The boys would love to see you again, I know.'

'That would be great, Orla. Thanks, I'd love to come. When would you want me?'

'Let's see, what about Wednesday? You'll have to check the flights and let me know, OK?'

'Yes, of course, I'll do that.'

'Good. We'll look forward to seeing you, then.'

'Me, too, Orla. Love to Matthew and the boys.'

Tiger replaced the phone. She looked at Liam, who hovered at a little distance, grinning, his wispy white halo of hair transparent against the lamplight. 'I'll not pretend I'm surprised at you, Miss Tiger, darlin'. It's not what you'd call a barrel of laughs here at present, is it?'

'Do you think Niamh will mind?'

'Indeed she won't; she'll be glad to see the back of yous.'

That night, as she lay in bed, and during the rest of her stay at Neill's Court, Tiger racked her brains to think of a way to help solve Niamh's cash-flow problem. She toured the house, looking at all the mediocre paintings of horses and gun dogs that hung in a depressed fashion on the shabby walls, wondering if it would be possible to flog one or two of them, and reaching the gloomy conclusion that a) they wouldn't fetch much, and b) there wasn't enough time to organize such a sale, if it were to have an instant effect on her sister's bank balance.

On her last night, her little suitcase packed, all ready for an early departure, she stood at the window of her father's room, wrapped in a moth-eaten old shawl, and gazed at the wind-ruffled waters of the lake, shimmering in the light of a watery moon. She thought about her grandfather Dan O'Neill, and her grandmother, Tara. He must have loved her a terrible lot, Tiger said to herself, to have walked into the water and drowned himself, like that. Although she had been only eight years old at the time of their deaths, Tiger remembered her grandparents perfectly clearly, for in some respects they had acted as surrogates for the absent-minded Alice and the physically absent Con Fitzgerald. Tara, especially, remained a vivid image in Tiger's recollections of childhood, with her fading beauty, wild curly greying hair, and long legs. In her memory Tiger saw Tara, still magnificent, booted and spurred for hunting, astride her quivering chestnut mare, alongside her still handsome, though ageing and somewhat slower-witted husband, Dan. Equally, Tiger remembered Tara standing in the hall, tall and slender, ready to go to some grand affair, wearing a loose, floaty thing of silvery gauze, with her blazing emeralds encircling her wrinkled neck.

'I wonder what happened to all her things?' said Tiger softly, wrapping the shawl round herself more tightly. She closed the curtain, and got into the high bed, thrusting her legs between the cold sheets. As she lay, her eyes closed, waiting for her feet to get warm and allow her to sleep, insubstantial memories flitted through her head, of things she had not thought about for years, and especially the personal possessions of Dan and Tara: a heavy gold watch; a gold signet ring; a cigarette case; a necklace of black pearls; a baby's teething rattle made of coral and gold; a set of jangly silver bracelets; and, of course, the amazing emeralds.

Tiger opened her eyes and stared at the dark ceiling. Those emeralds must be worth a lot, she thought. If Mum's still got them, and if she wasn't ill, I bet she'd sell them in a minute to help Niamh out, wouldn't she?

She waited until half past two, sitting on the edge of the bed, wrapped in the shawl, her jaw stiff with yawning, then crossed the room, and opened the door to the corridor. Quietly, she made her way on silent bare feet to Alice's room, slowly turned the shiny brass knob and slipped through the door. A dim electric lamp spread a soft circle of light on the pink cloth that covered the night table, and gradually Tiger's eyes accustomed themselves to the remembered features of the shadowy room.

Her cheek illuminated by the lamp, Alice lay on her pillows, fast asleep and making a noise between snoring and snuffling, like a child with a cold. Looking carefully around, Tiger found what she was looking for: the serpentine-fronted chest in which Tara had kept her nicest things; her beautiful underwear, her cashmere pullovers and silk scarves. In the deep bottom drawer were her hats, including her silk topper and the red fox-fur bonnet. On top of the chest was a much smaller chest, a set of tiny drawers, and it was in these drawers that Tiger hoped to find Tara's jewels.

She glanced anxiously at her slumbering mother, then very slowly advanced across the carpet towards the chest. Her pulses racing, Tiger pulled out one drawer, and then another, but found nothing. Hell, she thought, they must have been sold long ago. She took another quick look at Alice, then carefully slid open another drawer, without much hope of finding anything. To her surprise, and excitement, she saw that it contained a package that looked exactly like a rolled-up yellow duster, tied with tape. Swiftly, she took the package in her hand, and closed the drawer. Then, resisting the urge to run, she crept back to the door and slid through it, her heart hammering in her breast. For a second, she leaned against the wall of the corridor, eyes closed, willing herself to be calm, then she walked swiftly back to her father's room, and leaped into bed.

Under the sheet, Tiger undid the tapes and unrolled the soft package. Inside, in another wrapping of tissue paper, was the emerald necklace, sparkling with green fire, exactly as she remembered it.

In the morning, she got dressed in the clothes she had been wearing when she arrived at Neill's Court. Then, in case her suitcase or handbag were to be searched going through customs, she fastened the necklace carefully round her own neck, under the frilly white shirt, and then, to be doubly sure, pulled the black polo-necked sweater on as well. In fact, it looked pretty good with the long black skirt, the black boots and the cranberry-coloured cloak. Eat your heart out, gross old Olga, she said to herself, and laughed.

After breakfast, the two sisters hugged each other, and promised to write. 'Safe journey,' said Niamh. 'See you at Easter, darling. We'll be busy then, I'll be glad of your help.' They could hear Alice, in the orangery, wailing in her high-pitched complaining mode. 'Go on, Liam, drive Tiger to the coach station. I'll take care of Mum, don't fret about her.'

'If you're sure, Miss Niamh?' Liam sounded anxious.
'I'm sure. Go on.'

The flight to London was smooth, and would have been enjoyable, had Tiger not been worrying about the best way of setting about selling the emeralds, now that she had actually stolen them from her mother. She went through customs without being challenged, carrying her little suitcase, and followed the signs to Arrivals. At the barrier, she saw Matthew waiting to meet her, alone, and at once she saw that here was the answer to prayer. Without question, he would know *exactly* how to set about the disposal of the jewels, she felt quite sure.

'Hello, Tiger,' said the unsuspecting Matthew, taking her suitcase. 'Good flight?'

'Darling Matthew,' said Tiger, and kissed him with unusual warmth. 'How lovely to see you.'

CHAPTER SIX

In the car park, Tiger lost no time in broaching the subject of the emeralds. As briefly as possible, she outlined the situation at Neill's Court, and Niamh's problem with her bank. She described the predicament in which her sister now found herself, having ordered all the necessary new equipment for her cooking school, as well as accepting advance bookings from some sixty people. 'So you see, Matthew, something has to be done, and quickly, don't you agree?'

Matthew sat in his seat, frowning, alert, taking in this worrying piece of news. 'Yes, I see that, Tiger,' he said quietly. 'But what exactly did you have in mind?'

'This.' Tiger undid her cloak, then slid her hands inside the collar of her polo-necked sweater. After a brief struggle with the clasp, she undid the necklace, and, holding it in the palm of her hand, showed it to Matthew. 'I thought we might flog Granny's emeralds to help Niamh deal with her cash-flow problem, Matthew. I thought you'd know how to set about it.'

Matthew stared at the handful of gleaming green stones with disbelief, followed by horror. 'Tiger! Where the hell did you get these?'

'I went to Mum's room in the middle of the night, when everyone was asleep, and took them from the little chest where Granny kept all her bits and pieces.'

'You do realize that this is a question of *theft*, my dear girl?'

'Well, I suppose you could put it that way, but what's the alternative? Let Orla bully everyone into selling the house, and put poor old Mum into a home?' Tiger stared implacably at Matthew, her mouth hard, obstinate. 'She wouldn't last five minutes, in a place like that, without Liam to look after her, you know that, don't you?' Her hand closed round the emeralds, protectively, as though they represented her mother's last chance of a quiet old age. 'Let's be clear about this, Matthew,' she said, sternly. 'If we just stood by and allowed that to happen, it wouldn't be a case of petty larceny, it'd be a question of *murder*, wouldn't it?'

Matthew stared sightlessly through the windscreen, his mind working furiously. 'What kind of sum are we talking about, Tiger? How much money does Niamh need, have you any idea?'

'Well, she's already paid for the *batterie de cuisine*, as she calls it – pots and pans to you and me – so that's all right. But she owes Lonnie from the village for the huge great kitchen fitting he's built for her, and I guess that must be a couple of thousand at least, what with its marble top and everything. Then she had to get new sheets and stuff for the guest rooms, and she needs at least two women to work in the house, as well as a bloke for the kitchen garden. Poor old Liam can't be much help in that way, because of Mum. He's more or less shackled to her all day long. Half the night, too.'

Tiger turned and looked at Matthew, meeting his troubled, sympathetic brown eyes. 'It's ghastly, you know. I'm afraid Mum's going downhill faster than we all thought. Do you know what she does sometimes, Matthew, if Liam isn't watching over her? She runs around the house at night in her nightie, and bursts into people's rooms, swearing like a trooper and accusing them of having Liam in their beds! It's a nightmare, for Niamh as well as Liam.'

'My God, it must be,' said Matthew quietly. 'Poor

Niamh, it sounds to me as though she needs at least five thousand to get things on an even keel. I should imagine that the emeralds are worth a lot more than that. If I arranged to sell them for you, and Orla found out, she'd never forgive me, and rightly so, since it's probable that when your mother dies, the emeralds will come to her, as the eldest daughter. Therefore, on balance, selling them seems a non-starter.'

Tiger's face fell. 'So, what do you suggest?'

'I don't know. I need to think about it for a day or two. In the meantime, give me the necklace, and I'll put it in the safe, tonight, when everyone's gone to bed.' Matthew shook his head, looking embarrassed and guilty. 'You're putting me in a very awkward position, Tiger; I can't say I'm at all happy about it. For one thing, I don't like being manipulated into behaving in an underhand way towards Orla.'

Tiger handed over the necklace. 'What if she looks in the safe, and finds the emeralds?'

'She wouldn't have any reason to look. We don't usually conceal things from each other, you know.' Matthew made a strange sort of noise, between a sigh and a groan, switched on the ignition and drove out of the car park.

The street in which the Cleoburys lived looked cheerful and festive, its pavements shining moistly under the lamplight, and through the windows of the tall narrow houses Tiger saw comfortable sitting-rooms bright with twinkling lights, coloured paper chains and elaborately lit and decorated Christmas trees. It was like looking into the windows of an old-fashioned Advent calender, and Tiger felt a twinge of sadness, remembering the cold and dismal non-Christmas she had just shared with her sister in Ireland. Poor old Niamh, she thought, is that really all that life holds for her?

A large round holly wreath, embellished with red ribbon and shiny glass balls, hung on the front door, but before Tiger had time to take a really good look at it, the door was wrenched open and her two young nephews flung themselves upon her with enthusiasm, and tried to drag her upstairs to their room. 'Come and see what we got for Christmas,' said Edward. 'It's brilliant, and I'm ace at it.'

'It's a computer,' said Charles, thrusting a sticky little hand into Tiger's, 'but it's wasted on me, 'cos I haven't started learning it yet, at school. It's a swick.'

'Never mind, Charlie.' Matthew took Tiger's cloak, and hung it in the coat cupboard. 'I'll start teaching you tomorrow.'

'It's really great, Tiger. We can do e-mail, and I'll be able to e-mail you in Paris, probably.' Edward grabbed a handful of Tiger's skirt and gave it a peremptory tug. 'Come *on*! Come and *see*!'

'Hang on, Ed,' she exclaimed, laughing. 'I must go and say hello to your mum first, then I'll come, I promise.'

'OK, but don't hang about!' The two small boys thundered up the stairs and disappeared into their room, slamming the door behind them.

Matthew gazed after his sons, his brown eyes soft, his smile tender and resigned. 'The wonderful thing is, Tiger, it keeps them occupied for hours, absolutely. Very non-PC, I know, but it makes Orla's life more bearable in the holidays, and that's the main thing.'

In the kitchen, Orla was preparing supper, which was to be a cold fillet of beef stuffed with ceps, preceded by a most exquisite soup, adapted from a recipe she had found in *The River Café Cookbook*. It was Orla's current culinary showpiece, and although strictly a summer dish, she was substituting frozen broad beans, green beans and peas, and using fresh asparagus from Thailand combined with chicken stock, cream and pesto to make this masterpiece, and producing in the process the most delicious smell.

'Wow, that smells wonderful, Orla. I hope you haven't gone to an awful lot of trouble?'

'No, not at all,' replied Orla, who had actually taken great pains with the soup. She lowered the heat under the pan, turned from the stove and looked at her little sister. 'Good heavens, darling, how tall you've grown!'

'I know,' said Tiger, slyly. 'It's awful, I've even grown out of the lovely clothes you gave me. It's such a shame. I had to buy myself some more things at the fleamarket.' She reached across the table, and kissed her sister's cheek. 'Hi,' she said. 'It's lovely of you to let me come, Orla, it really is, when I know how busy you are, with the boys and everything.'

Orla returned the kiss, and stood back, taking in Tiger's transformed appearance. To her surprise, she found that on the whole she actually approved of the way her sister looked, and especially, the change of hairstyle. 'Your hair looks very nice,' she said. 'Did you go to a proper hairdresser?'

'Oh, of course,' Tiger lied. 'The comtesse insisted. She paid for it, too. Wasn't it nice of her?'

Orla looked pleased. 'They must quite like you, then,' she said, and smiled.

'Yes, I think they do,' Tiger agreed. 'And I like them, a lot. They're really kind to me, and let me go to my art classes twice a week, as well as my French lessons. I think I told you, they don't have children, so in a way I'm a bit like a daughter to them.' She laughed. 'Not everyone likes me, though. I don't think Fanny does, *la pauvre*! I make her run in the park, and she hates that, pampered brute.'

'Fanny's the old lady's dog, right?' Orla turned back to the stove. 'What about your social life, Tiger? Have they introduced you to lots of nice people? You know, the right sort?'

'Um, not really. They don't entertain very much, actually, at least not at home. They take people out to a restaurant, rather than invite them home.'

'They don't take you with them?'

'No. If they go out, I have to babysit the comtesse.'

Orla frowned, and gave her soup a gentle stir. 'I see.

112

Not a lot of fun for you, is it, not meeting amusing young people?'

Tiger smiled, knowing that by 'young people', Orla meant eligible young men of good family. 'I don't mind at all. The comtesse can be very amusing when she wants to be.'

There was a crash of feet and bodies descending the stairs and the two boys burst into the kitchen. '*Tiger!* What are you *doing*? Come *on*! You *promised*!'

Tiger looked at Orla, smiling. 'Do you need a hand, Orla? Shall I set the table, or something?'

'No, it's OK. Go on, I can manage, really.'

Matthew came into the room and silently offered his wife a large gin and tonic. 'What about you, Tiger?' he asked.

'Thanks, but I'll wait,' she replied. 'I'd better go and inspect this brilliant computer first.'

Orla was happy to be in Islington again, and in her own kitchen, after spending two days with her in-laws in Herefordshire, and having to endure the agony of watching her mother-in-law wreck by overcooking the delicious free-range turkey she had brought with her for the festive lunch.

Matthew's father was the rector of a tiny country parish, and he and his wife Dorothy had lived there for forty years, in uncomplaining and unambitious fashion, perfectly content with their lot. Christmas, like Easter, was an unusually busy time for the elderly parson, for his flock expected to attend Midnight Mass, as well as the Family Eucharist and the Carol Service, though during the rest of the year they were conspicuous by their absence, and Francis Cleobury was accustomed to saying his daily Mass, as well as the weekly Matins and Evensong, to an empty church. Empty, that is to say, except for Dorothy, who attended the services regularly, wearing a straw hat in summer, and a tartan tam-o'-shanter in winter. She also did the flowers, took the collection, and played the organ.

Orla had almost nothing in common with her parents-in-law, finding them incredibly dull. Mrs Cleobury – Dorothy, as Orla tried to remember to call her – always fussed over the two little boys, forcing them to look at old photograph albums, depicting Matthew at his prep school, Matthew at his public school, and Matthew at university. 'You both look exactly like him,' she told them, over and over again, and they squirmed and looked embarrassed.

Matthew was quite aware that Orla found the visits to his parents tedious beyond belief, but could do little to inject any enjoyment into their stay. Their bed was cold, and, she asserted, damp, and the stone hot-water bottle that Dorothy kindly provided did little to improve their comfort. When Matthew attempted to warm her up by taking her in his arms and making love to her, Orla had pushed him away quite violently. 'Not *here*, Matthew! What the hell do you think you're playing at?'

Matthew had sighed. 'They are not entirely unaware of the facts of life, darling,' he had said plaintively, for he could have done with a cuddle himself. 'Please yourself, though, of course.'

Now, the annual ordeal over, and back in her own kitchen, making something elegant and *civilized* for dinner, to impress her younger sister, Orla smiled at Matthew, took a deep swig of her gin, and allowed him to kiss her.

At dinner, which was delicious, Tiger, encouraged by a couple of glasses of wine, did her best to be amusing. Wisely, she had decided to keep off the subject of Niamh and Neill's Court, in case she might inadvertently let something slip about the emeralds. To satisfy Orla's extreme curiosity about the Martel-Cluny family, she described the house in rue Monsieur, and its residents, especially the sparky old comtesse and her wonderful clothes. 'You'd love her, Orla. She pretends to be in a towering rage all the time, but she's really

114

adorable, and terribly kind. She must have been absolutely beautiful once, poor old thing.'

'Why "poor old thing"?' asked Orla. 'She sounds like an extremely lucky and rather spoilt old woman, to me.'

'Don't you think it's rather sad when someone who must have been quite perfect when they were young, finds themselves all wrinkly and decaying, and pretty ugly, in the end?'

Irritated by her sister's sentimental attitude, Orla frowned, and Matthew interrupted quickly. 'I expect it's quite likely that people like your comtesse aren't actually aware of their decline, Tiger.'

'Oh, well, maybe you're right,' said Tiger, sensing herself to be on dodgy ground, for some reason. She changed the subject, quite abruptly. 'Did I tell you about my art classes, and Tadeusz?'

'Yes, you did. He sounds like a bit of a layabout.'

'He thinks I should be studying painting full time, actually, and not waste my time being nanny to a dog!'

'Does he really?' said Orla sarcastically. 'And what end does he have in mind for you, darling?'

'End?'

'You know what I mean, Tiger. What end, career-wise?'

'Oh. I hadn't really thought.'

'Perhaps you should, darling.'

Making yet another swift change of subject, Tiger told them about Liam and herself repairing the roof at Neill's Court. Both little boys, whose table manners were normally impeccable, having been taught never to interrupt the conversation of grown-ups during meals in which they were allowed to participate, put down their forks, and stared at their aunt with open-mouthed admiration. 'Oh, *Tiger*! You are *lucky*! All the really brilliant things happen to you!' Edward sounded deeply impressed, and filled with envy. 'It's so unfair, Dad! Why couldn't we have gone to Ireland with Tiger, instead of going to boring old Grandpa's? Then *we* could've climbed up onto the roof, too, couldn't we?'

'Ho!' said Tiger. 'I bet you wouldn't have dared!'

'Would!'

'Wouldn't!'

'WOULD! WOULD! WOULD!'

'That's quite enough, children,' said Orla firmly. She looked round the table. 'Cheese, anyone? Or have you all had enough?'

'I'm still a bit hungry, Mum,' said Charles. 'Is there any more of that left-over Christmas pudding?'

'You *can't* have room for any more, Charlie, I don't believe you!'

'I believe him,' said Edward. 'I want some, too, please.'

Orla turned to Matthew. 'What about you, darling?'

Matthew shook his head. After a week of too much food and booze, and two days and nights of his mother's indigestible fare, his stomach was in revolt. 'I think I'll just have a small medicinal brandy,' he said, getting up from the table.

'Tell you what, Orla,' said Tiger. 'You go and have a brandy with Matthew, and I'll bring you some coffee. Then I'll make a Christmas pud soufflé omelette for the boys and me.'

'That sounds disgusting, Tiger.'

'No, it's lovely, especially if we can have half a glass of brandy to flame it with?'

'*Please*, Mum?' Edward and Charlie spoke as one, enchanted at the prospect of a taste of brandy.

'OK,' said Orla wearily. 'I suppose so. As long as you promise to help Tiger clean up afterwards, boys.'

The next morning Orla woke with a splitting headache and a sore throat, and croakily informed her husband that she thought she had flu. Matthew was privately of the opinion that she was suffering not so much from flu as from the stress induced by Christmas and the school holidays. Nevertheless he suggested that she should stay in bed, while he organized hot lemon and

116

paracetamol for her, followed by a cup of tea. 'Angel,' whispered Orla thankfully, closed her eyes and drifted off to sleep again.

Downstairs, Matthew found Tiger and the boys already up, and eating breakfast in the kitchen. 'Your mother's not feeling too brilliant,' he said. 'She's going to stay in bed today.'

'Poor old thing, what a shame,' said Tiger.

'Yes, poor old thing,' repeated the boys, munching cereal.

Matthew put on the kettle, then sat down at the table. 'I was intending to go to my chambers today, Tiger, and deal with a few things. Do you think you can cope with the boys on your own?'

'Yes, of course, why ever not? Charlie and Ed and me thought we might go to the park and fly their plane, that is, unless you'd rather we stayed here to look after Orla?'

'No, I think the best thing for her would be peace and quiet, and in any case I'll be home by lunchtime. Stay out as long as you like; enjoy yourselves; have lunch somewhere, why don't you?'

'Brilliant, Dad, can we really?'

The kettle boiled and Matthew got up and prepared a tray of tea and medicaments for the invalid, then took it upstairs.

Tiger guessed that Matthew's trip to his chambers was for the purpose of transferring the emeralds to his safe deposit box, and for the first time felt a pang of unease at involving him in her hare-brained scheme to save Niamh's bacon. Guiltily, she made fresh toast and another pot of coffee for him, then told the boys to stop mucking about and go and wash their hands and get ready to go out.

'Are we going *now*?'

'Yes, as soon as you're both ready. And don't forget the plane.'

The boys departed with their usual quarrelsome pushing and shoving, and collided with Matthew as he

117

came back into the kitchen. 'Watch it!' he exclaimed. 'And don't make a racket on the stairs. Your mother's got a rotten headache.' He turned to Tiger and smiled wryly. 'Are you sure you can handle them, Tiger? They are quite a handful, you know.'

'Don't worry, they'll be fine. Here, I've made you some breakfast.' She looked at him timidly. 'I'm sorry I've put you to all this trouble, Matthew.'

'Don't worry about it.' He buttered a piece of toast, and ate it silently, then drank his coffee.

'Well, if you don't need anything, we'd better be off, then,' said Tiger uncertainly, hovering by the door.

'Yes, fine. See you later. Have a good time.'

'OK. See you later, Matthew.'

He looked up then, frowning. 'What about money, Tiger? Do you have enough for the day?'

'Oh! I don't know. How much do I need?'

'Here.' He took two twenty-pound notes from his wallet, and handed them to her. 'This should be enough.'

'Gosh, isn't this rather a lot?'

'I think you'll find you need most of it, for a whole day out.'

'Well, thanks, it's very kind of you.'

Charles had been given a remote-control aeroplane for Christmas, and they spent a happy morning flying the noisy little machine in Regent's Park. At half past twelve, ignoring the protests of both children, Tiger packed the plane carefully into her bag, and they went in search of lunch. At the boys' request, this consisted of hot dogs and a Coke, bought at a refreshment stall. Then, since it was only two o'clock and far too soon to go home, Edward suggested that they visit the Planetarium.

The queue to get in was very long, since half the junior residents of London had evidently had the same idea, but once inside, the boredom and irritation induced by the long, cold wait in the street vanished, and both children were immediately transfixed; drawn into a special kind of astronomic heaven.

When they came out, it was already dark and raining slightly. They took the Underground to the Angel, and then waited at a bus stop for a bus to Islington. After a few minutes, Tiger looked at her watch: five twenty. 'I don't know about you two,' she said, 'but I could do with some fresh air and exercise, couldn't you? Let's walk home, shall we?'

It was nearly six when they reached the house, and Matthew let them in.

'How's Orla?' asked Tiger.

'Better,' said Matthew. 'She might get up for supper.'

'Oh, good. Come on, you guys, let's go quietly up and see her, shall we?'

They found Orla lying comfortably in bed, on a pile of pillows, looking pink-cheeked and rested. She hugged her little boys affectionately, and smiled at her sister with genuine gratitude. 'What a star you are, Tiger,' she said. 'You can be my au pair any time.'

Matthew set about cooking dinner, while Tiger supervised the boys' bath and gave them baked beans on toast for their supper. After their long day out, both boys seemed prepared to go early to bed without a fight, so that it was with considerable relief that she descended the stairs to the kitchen, sat down at the table and accepted a glass of wine from the bottle that Matthew had just opened. 'Pwoah!' she said. 'It must be knackering being a full-time mum, Matthew!'

He laughed. 'It's pretty knackering being a part-time dad, as a matter of fact.'

Tiger took a sip of her wine. 'They're great kids, all the same, aren't they? They're good crack, as Liam would say, and up to anything.' She looked at Matthew, a little wistfully. 'It's strange, there's nothing of the Fitzgeralds in them at all, is there? You can see a bit of Orla in them, but really they're exactly like you.'

'Do you really think so?' Matthew transferred his casserole from the hob to the oven, closing the door gently. 'Physically, I suppose you're right, but characteristically, they're far more assertive and confident than I ever was as a child.' He picked up his glass and sat down at the table, a self-deprecating smile on his face. 'I was a pretty good wimp, Tiger, as a matter of fact, as well as being the ultimate unforgivable thing for a boy, a swot.'

'I don't think you're a wimp, Matthew, not at all.' Tiger lowered her voice. 'Look how bravely you agreed to look after Granny's necklace for me.'

'More accurately, the decision was *forced* upon me, Tiger, you wicked creature! Have you no shame?' He laughed, then suddenly grew deadly serious. 'I've thought it over carefully, and I've come to the conclusion that the best plan would be to send a certified cheque to Niamh immediately. In Orla's long-term interest, I'll hold on to the emeralds for the time being; no-one but you needs to know that they're here. I'll write to Niamh, explaining that you've told me in confidence about her problems, and tell her that I'm lending her five thousand pounds, on the strict understanding that she agrees not to tell anyone about it, that she discusses it with no-one, not even you, Tiger. That way, she won't be able to censure you for your part in this clandestine business.' Matthew looked stern, his brown eyes unsmiling. 'Because that's what it is, Tiger, and I can't say I'm at all happy about being put on the spot like this. Apart from everything else, stealing your family's jewels is strictly against the law, and now you've made me a receiver of stolen goods, and compounded the injury.'

'Shit!' exclaimed Tiger. 'You make me sound like a thief!'

'It's what you are, my dear girl.'

'God, how awful! Can we send them back, do you think?'

'How the hell would you propose doing that? In any

case, it's too risky, and too likely to cause a major row between you all. One does rather quail at the thought, I must say.'

'Are you angry with me, Matthew?' Tiger's voice shook slightly. 'I was only trying to find a way of saving Mum from the home for geriatrics, you know.'

Matthew smiled kindly, and covered Tiger's hand with his own. 'I know you were. Don't worry. We'll find a way of smuggling them back, somehow.'

Tears filled Tiger's eyes. 'You are a saint, Matthew. You're more like a real brother than a brother-in-law. I do love you.'

Matthew said nothing, but raised Tiger's hand to his lips and kissed it gently. I wish, he said to himself silently.

After supper, Matthew was let off the dishwashing, since Orla was of the opinion that by cooking the meal he had done his fair share of the household chores already. 'You go and put your feet up, darling,' she said. 'Watch telly or something, and we'll bring you some coffee later, OK?'

Matthew, realizing instantly that Orla wished to be left alone with Tiger for some reason, and knowing that any kind of protest from him would be overruled, smiled politely at the sisters and left the kitchen without comment.

'I was thinking about you, darling, while you were out with the boys,' said Orla, after a slight pause to be sure that Matthew was out of earshot. 'This artist chap, what's his name, Tadeusz? Is he just a friend, or is the relationship something more than that?'

Quite unprepared for this unlooked-for intrusion into her private feelings, Tiger felt her face grow hot, while her hands felt suddenly like blocks of ice, and a strong rapid pulse started beating in her neck. She stared at her hands, blinking nervously, her mind a chaos of indecision, as she searched unsuccessfully for a cool way of telling Orla to mind her own business.

'Well?' said Orla, smiling knowingly. 'Is he your lover, Tiger? You can tell me, can't you?'

'There's nothing to tell.'

Orla laughed. 'Oh, come on, there must be.'

'There isn't.'

'Pull the other one, Tiger. I can tell by your face; you're having an affair. Or if you're not, you're thinking about it, aren't you?'

Tiger continued to stare blindly at her hands, praying that Orla would shut up, change the subject, leave her alone. Since that first disturbing kiss in rue Monsieur, it was true that Tadeusz had occupied a great deal of her thoughts, in spite of the extremely casual way in which he so often treated her. At night, her dreams, in which he figured prominently, were of an extremely explicit sexual nature, at the same time thrilling and alarming, and she was quite aware that, given the opportunity, going to bed with Tadeusz was still at the top of her secret wish-list.

At Neill's Court, she had become so preoccupied with Niamh's problems that her life in Paris had begun to seem to her unreal, distanced, and curiously alien, as though she had failed in her duty to her family by having such an interesting and exciting time, while both her mother and her home hovered on the brink of disaster. In such circumstances, her emotions in respect of Tadeusz had become blurred, and pushed to the back of her mind.

'Well?' said Orla again, quite gently. 'It's not a big deal, Tiger, is it? Everyone has a few flings before they settle down and get married, you know.'

'Oh?' Surprised, Tiger looked up, meeting her sister's eyes. 'Did you have affairs, before you married Matthew?' She found it difficult to imagine Orla throwing caution to the winds in such a reckless way, before a ring was firmly on her finger.

Orla laughed. 'Of course I did. Whatever do you think happens at university, darling? It's not all boring lectures and stuff, I can tell you.'

'I see.' Tiger lowered her eyes again, unwilling to discuss her non-relationship with Tadeusz with a sister nearly twice her own age, and clearly much more experienced than herself.

Orla got up from the table, sensing Tiger's embarrassment and reluctance to confide in her. Thoughtfully, she began to stack the dishwasher.

'I'll do that, Orla!' Tiger got up hastily. 'Please sit down, won't you, and let me help?'

'It's OK, it won't take more than a couple of minutes. Put on the kettle for me, if you like, and I'll make some coffee.'

Tiger did as she was asked, then turned to Orla. 'I know you're trying to tell me something, and mean to be kind. It's just that I'm not sure what it is exactly that you're interested in knowing.'

'Contraception, Tiger, that's what I've been trying to get around to. Are you on the pill, darling?'

'No.'

'You should be, just in case. And you should have the morning-after pill, too, in case of accidents.'

'Oh, I *see*!' Tiger gave a snort of laughter. 'I thought you wanted a blow-by-blow account of my sex life!'

'Certainly not,' said Orla primly, though in fact she had been hoping for a sisterly chat on precisely that subject. 'I just want to be sure you're properly equipped, that's all.'

'Well, I'm not, and you're quite right, I should be. How do I set about it?'

'I'll take you to my GP, tomorrow.'

'Thanks, Orla, that'd be great.' Impulsively, Tiger put her arms round her sister, and gave her a kiss. 'I'm sorry I was so prickly. It's very kind of you to bother about me, at all.'

Orla returned the hug. 'I wouldn't have to, would I, if our mother wasn't so bloody useless?'

A few days later, Niamh received a letter from Matthew, enclosing a certified cheque for five thousand pounds. The letter was short, extremely formal and quite impersonal, or so she chose to believe. Angry and humiliated, for two pins she would have sent the cheque straight back to Matthew and told him to get stuffed. In a very short time, however, common sense prevailed and Niamh lost no time in driving into town, paying the cheque into her account and withdrawing Liam's overdue wages, as well as half the cash she owed Lonnie for the kitchen fitting. In her experience, it was always a good idea with Lonnie to withhold part of his money, to make sure that he turned up to finish the works still in progress.

Since Matthew had firmly stipulated that she was forbidden to discuss the loan with anyone, she spent a frustrating afternoon in the vegetable garden, furiously digging holes for the six young apple trees that had been heeled-in in the potato patch, until she found the time to plant them.

At lunchtime, when she had given Liam his pay, with a bit extra as a Christmas bonus, he had expressed surprise and delight. 'How the devil did you manage to pull the wool over the old fart's eyes?' he had asked, presumably referring to the bank manager.

'I have my methods, Liam,' she had replied crisply. 'Go on, take Mother's tray to her, before it gets cold.'

Casting a reproachful look in Niamh's direction, Liam had picked up the tray, and left the kitchen without another word. After lunch, as he sat beside Alice, reading the *Sporting Life* to her, he turned over in his mind the likely reasons for the sudden improvement in their finances. It did not take him very long to work his way back to Tiger, for he had not spoken of Niamh's problems to anyone else. It'll not be Miss Orla that's the fairy godmother, that's for certain, he said to himself, remembering the falling-out between the sisters after the death of their grandfather. Tiger will have told Mr Cleobury about the trouble, that'll be it, and he's come to the rescue, like the good man he is. Well, he thought, he's able to afford it, no doubt; I never heard of a poor lawyer yet.

'Liam?' Alice stretched out a small bony hand and clasped his wrist in a surprisingly strong grip. She looked up at him, her greying curly hair untidy, her beautiful hazel eyes full of animation.

'Yes, darling?'

'Should we take the horses out now, do you think? It'll be dark soon, won't it?'

'Good idea.' Gently, he unhooked Alice's hand from his wrist, and folded the paper. 'Let's go upstairs, then. You'll need to change first, won't you?'

Niamh looked at the darkening sky and decided that she had enough time to bring a couple of barrowloads of muck to put in the holes for the apple trees, but the planting itself would have to wait until tomorrow. As she laboured, lifting shovelfuls of the heavy wet manure from muckheap to barrow, she promised herself that tomorrow she would set about finding a good strong man to take over the work in the vegetable garden, and to do the mowing when the grass started to grow again. The bloody place looks like a tip, she thought; there's a lot needs seeing to before my cooking courses start, and not just in the house. Pushing the heavy barrow along the rough paths to the other end of the garden, her arms and back stiff and sore, she asked herself for the thousandth time what on earth she thought she was trying to achieve, when it was obvious that absolutely everything was stacked against her. With a groan of relief, she lowered the barrow to the ground, and began to fill the planting holes. It was lovely of Matthew to send the money, she thought, but in a way I quite wish he hadn't. Then I could've packed the whole thing in, and let someone else pick up the pieces for a bloody change.

'Niamh?' Startled, she swung round. Michael Keen had come into the garden without her noticing his presence, and was standing on the path a few feet away.

'What the hell do *you* want?' she asked belligerently.

'I miss you, Niamh. I came to say I'm sorry. I'd like us to be friends again.'

Niamh stared at her former lover with disbelief. 'After what your *wife* told me about your activities, Michael, I'm astonished that you have the brass neck to show your face here again. You're nothing but a serial adulterer, and I've no wish to have anything to do with you, ever again.'

'There's no need to get uptight about it, Niamh. They're just girls, after all. They don't mean a thing, to be sure.'

Niamh took a firm grip on her pitchfork, and raised it in a threatening manner. 'Get out of here, you bastard! Go back to your miserable wife, where you belong, you rotten little shit!'

'OK, OK, I'm going.' He raised his hands, backing off, then turned and hurried away down the path. At the gate he looked back, with a last attempt at bravado. 'You're nothing but a whore yourself, so there's no call to go calling me names, woman!'

'Fuck off!'

Upstairs, in her bedroom, it had slipped Alice's mind that her intention had been to change into her riding things. Instead, she was standing in front of her open wardrobe, wearing only her vest and knickers, obsessively snatching old dresses from their hangers, one after the other. Holding them up in front of herself to study her reflection in the tall pier-glass, she repeated the same question, over and over again. 'Where are we going, Liam? Will this one do, or should I wear the black lace, do you think, darling?'

Liam followed her, picking up the discarded frocks, doing his best not to become irritated. 'This one is lovely, it suits your eyes, sweetheart. You wore it to the hunt ball, remember?'

Alice frowned, shook her head violently, angrily throwing the dress onto the floor, and Liam could have cut his tongue out, for he knew that to ask Alice whether she remembered anything at all inevitably led to confusion and panic. Now, she stood clasping her stick-like arms round her shivering body, her mouth twisted, while childish tears ran down her face.

At once he took her in his arms, and spoke to her, the sort of words of comfort a mother might say to a little child, patting her back and kissing her wet cheeks, smoothing the wispy hair from her forehead. Quite soon, the tears ceased and Alice smiled radiantly, suddenly looking as beautiful and as desirable as she had ever been to him.

'Better now?' he said softly.

'Better now,' she replied.

'Let's get you dressed then, my darling. You'll be catching your death of cold, else.'

'Is it time for tea, Liam?'

'Yes, it's time for tea.'

On Tiger's last evening in London, she telephoned Niamh to say goodbye, trying to bear in mind her promise to Matthew not to bring up the subject of the loan. Slightly apprehensively, she dialled the number. There was the usual long wait before Niamh heard the phone, and when she answered it she sounded out of breath, as if she had been running. 'Hello?'

'Hi, Niamh, it's me, Tiger. I just rang to say goodbye for the present, and thanks for a lovely Christmas.'

'It's nice of you to say that, Tiger, because in my opinion it was a bloody awful Christmas. Thank goodness the year's finished and done with, and things will get better.'

Tiger laughed. 'I suppose there were a few problems, weren't there? How's the roof? No more leaks, I hope?'

'No, thanks be to God.'

'Well, I hope the cooking school goes well, Niamh. Best of luck with it, and maybe I'll see you at Easter.'

'Yes, I'll be flat out then. I've already got two new

girls lined up, but an extra pair of hands is always useful.'

'OK, fine, I'll see what I can do. I'd better say goodbye now; you know how expensive it is to call Ireland.'

'Tiger?'

'Yes?'

'Thanks.'

'OK. See you soon, Niamh,' said Tiger. 'Bye.'

In the sitting-room, Orla and Matthew were watching the late news, and her sister looked up as Tiger came back into the room. 'Everything OK?' she asked. 'Mum's behaving herself?'

'Yeah,' said Tiger. 'They're all fine. Niamh's got a couple of girls in, to help in the house. That's good, isn't it?' She glanced at Matthew, her expression bland. Fleetingly, their eyes met, then he returned his gaze to the television screen.

'I suppose it is,' said Orla. 'Poor old Niamh, she's such a bad organizer. Don't you think so, darling?'

'Think what?' Matthew's eyes remained glued to the screen.

'Honestly, Matthew, you are rotten! Aren't you at all interested in poor Niamh's project?'

'Can't say she's at the forefront of my mind, darling.'

Orla turned to her youngest sister. 'Men!' she said, with a complacent smile, and Tiger laughed.

CHAPTER SEVEN

Tiger returned to Paris, relieved and happy to be back in rue Monsieur, and the comparatively stress-free orderliness of her life in the Martel-Cluny household. She arrived in time to have tea with the comtesse, who regaled her with wildly exaggerated accounts of the boredom of French country life, as well as delicious Earl Grey tea and little almond cakes.

'And how was Fanny?' asked Tiger. 'Did she behave herself, madame?'

'But of course she did not, *la petite merdeuse*! I 'ave to tell you, Tiger, 'er *comportement* was 'orrible!'

'Oh, dear!' Tiger laughed. 'So, what did she do that was so awful?'

'First, it's necessary to explain that all the curtains at the château are very old and very beautiful, although naturally very, very *fragile. Qu'est-ce que ça veut dire, ma chère?*'

'Fragile,' said Tiger, anticipating what was coming next, and doing her best not to smile.

'*Alors*, fragile.' The comtesse flicked cake crumbs from her elegant long tweed skirt onto the carpet, and looked at Tiger, her malicious old eyes bright. 'I expect you can guess what this terrible Fanny is doing?'

'*Pipi?*'

'Not just *pipi*, my dear, but much worse, and in

every room.' She laughed. 'Antoine is not please with 'er, you understand?'

'I can imagine! Was there nobody to take her out for walks?'

'*Personne*. Not Gaston and not you, Tiger. Antoine was all the time pushing 'er out of the door, onto the terrace, but that does not please 'er, not at all. She is standing outside the door, looking through the glass, and making *gemissements*. So 'e 'as to let 'er come in again.'

'Poor Fanny!'

'Poor Antoine! 'e is not loving *les animaux*, except to shoot them.'

'We used to have lots of dogs at Neill's Court, when I was a child,' said Tiger. 'They're all dead now, or put down. All we've got these days are some chickens and a funny old skewbald pony, but he's rather on his last legs, Liam says.'

'Liam? Who is this Liam?'

'He used to be a stable-lad, but now he mainly looks after my mother, and makes sure that she doesn't bother the paying guests. I think I told you about her, madame. She is ill; she has Alzheimer's disease.'

The comtesse frowned, for she feared both illness and death, and did not allow herself to dwell too much on these things. 'That is sad,' she said briskly. 'I think Fanny would like a little promenade, Tiger, if you would be kind and take 'er.'

'Of course.' Tiger replaced her cup and saucer on the table, and woke the slumbering dog. 'Come on, Fanny, *allons-y*!'

Running in the park with the anarchic Fanny, Tiger was reminded of their first outings to the Luxembourg Gardens, and their early battles of will. After the Christmas break, curiously, the incorrigible little animal actually seemed pleased to see her, casting her bug-eyes in Tiger's direction from time to time, her pink tongue lolling out of the side of her mouth, as she bounced along beside her minder like a small wheezy tennis ball.

Darkness was falling as they returned to the house, and Tiger let herself in with the latch-key that Madame had given her. She delivered Fanny to the kitchen for her supper, then returned to the hall. She was on the point of going upstairs to her room, when the front door opened, and Monsieur entered the hall, followed by a tall, extremely good-looking young man. In the brief moment that Tiger allowed herself to notice him, she observed that he had short fair hair, and wore delicate gold-rimmed spectacles.

'Tiger! How nice to see you again.' Monsieur crossed the hall and gave Tiger a swift peck on each cheek, then turned to introduce the newcomer. 'May I present Monsieur Marcassin who is staying with us for a few weeks. Luc, this is Mademoiselle Fitzgerald, Tiger, who has the misfortune to be the custodian of my mother's perfidious little dog.'

'How do you do,' murmured Tiger coolly, trying to acknowledge the introduction in the manner specified by Orla, though regretting that Monsieur should have chosen to mention the less than dignified aspects of her employment to the newcomer.

'*Enchanté, mademoiselle.*' The blond young man gave a slight bow in her direction, then, taking off his coat, looked enquiringly at Monsieur.

'In the cloakroom, I'll show you.'

'I was just on my way upstairs,' interrupted Tiger. 'I need to unpack my bag, and change for dinner. If that's OK?'

'Fanny has had her walk, I take it?'

'Yes, she has.'

'Well, good. Thank you, Tiger.'

'Don't worry, monsieur, I don't think she'll be making any *bêtises* this evening. She's too tired to bother, I think.'

'My mother told you about her wickedness, then?' He laughed, and shook his head.

Tiger joined in the laughter. 'Dogs are a nightmare, aren't they? No self-control at all!' Taking two steps at a time, she ran up the stairs to her room, and turned on the taps for her bath. Gaston had placed her overnight bag on the bench at the foot of her bed, and she unpacked it swiftly. In the bathroom, she poured a generous dollop of Penhaligon's *Bluebell* bath essence under the running tap, then stripped off her clothes, got into the bath and lay down, draping her long hair carefully over the curved rim of the tub.

Caressed by the warm scented water, she closed her eyes and allowed her mind to float, feeling all the tensions drifting away from her muscles. How strange, she thought, that this soft, luxurious way of life should have come to mean so much to me, that I missed it so badly when I was at home in Ireland. After all, I lived at Neill's Court for eighteen years, and I can't remember thinking that the place was dirty and uncomfortable as well as horribly cold until now.

She opened her eyes, and stared up at the ceiling, imagining Niamh preparing supper in the dark kitchen, while Liam and Alice watched the flickering old telly in the sitting-room. I wonder if they've bothered to light the fire, she asked herself, or are they just sitting there, with Mum wrapped in coats and mufflers, and Granny's fox-fur hat? When she compared them with the Martel-Clunys, downstairs, having their pre-dinner drinks in centrally heated splendour, the alarming thought struck Tiger that perhaps Niamh's paying guests would be unable to endure the torments of Neill's Court in winter, and would leave, demanding their money back? My God, she thought, we'd really be in the shit if that happened. I must write to Niamh and tell her how cold I found it, and advise her to get the central heating going, however much it costs. I'll do it tomorrow, before breakfast. 'There's not much else I can do,' she said aloud, and got out of the bath. 'At least she's got some money now, thank heaven.' She wrapped herself in a warm towel, sat down at her dressing-table, looked critically at her reflection and wiped her face with a cleansing pad.

Only then did she turn her attention to the new arrival, the young blond stranger Luc Marcassin, no doubt enjoying an aperitif with the family at this very moment. To her surprise, and annoyance, she felt a slight twinge of disquiet at this unexpected addition to the household, feeling the young man's presence to be an intrusion, and, possibly, even an obscure threat to her own popularity within the family. Don't be ridiculous, she said to herself, he's probably just an inexperienced boy, barely out of school. Nevertheless, she chose to wear the prettiest of her *gitane* outfits, and brushed her black hair until it gleamed like a raven's wing, before going downstairs to the salon.

In the event, it turned out that Luc was a nephew of Madame's, and a graduate of the *Grande Ecole*, a circumstance which seemed to be a matter of some pride to his relations, to judge by the smug expressions on all their faces. He had recently been appointed to his first job, in some ministry, and had bought his first apartment, now in the process of refurbishment. This was the reason for his temporary lodging in rue Monsieur.

Luc was not a stupid man, and he was well versed in the art of pleasing others, as well as amusing himself. At dinner, he listened attentively to the reminiscences of the chronically irritable comtesse, responding to her sometimes acid complaints with a dry dead-pan wit, disarming her completely, and causing her to dissolve into peals of delighted laughter. It was a very long time since anyone had had the temerity to pull the rug from under the old lady, and she revelled in the young man's audacity.

Monsieur and Madame seemed equally under his spell and, rather against her better judgement, Tiger, too, soon found herself seduced by his charm and wit. It was the first time in her life that she had attended a dinner party in which the food, the excellent wine and the sparkling conversation all combined to make everyone present appear clever, funny and beautiful, and she found the experience intoxicating.

At eleven o'clock, the party broke up. Monsieur took his mother to her room, Madame told the young people to help themselves to anything they wanted, said goodnight and went to bed.

'Are you tired, Tiger?' asked Luc. 'Would you like to go out for a drink, or to a club, perhaps?'

Exhilarated by the evening, and not at all tired, Tiger agreed that it would be fun to go out. 'But I'd quite like just to walk, if you wouldn't find that too boring?' she said.

'Excellent idea,' he replied. 'Let's go.'

They walked briskly along rue Monsieur until they reached the carrefour de l'Odéon, where it began to rain.

'What a pain!' Luc stepped into the street and hailed a passing cab. '*Place St-Germain-des-Prés, s'il vous plaît,*' he said to the driver, and they got into the taxi.

Apart from her visits to the fleamarkets, Tiger had so far not felt the need to venture further than the area around rue Monsieur, the Luxembourg Gardens or St-Sulpice, so the busy, crowded Boulevard St-Germain took her by surprise. It took a few minutes for the cabbie to negotiate the heavy traffic in order to deliver his passengers to their destination. While Luc paid the fare, Tiger admired the one remaining spire of the great abbey church of St-Germain. Floodlit, it soared into the darkness of the rain-lashed night, dominating the lively square lined with brightly lit cafés, brasseries and bookshops, and crowded with people, most of whom appeared to be young.

Luc took Tiger's hand, and they ran through the rain

to a café immediately opposite the church, the *Deux-Magots*.

'Why the Chinese mandarins?' asked Tiger, her curiosity roused by the two large wooden effigies that adorned the café, and stared inscrutably down at the passers-by.

'*Magot* means a pile of money in French, so it's quite likely that those two old boys were usurers or something of that description.'

'Oh,' said Tiger, feeling none the wiser.

There were no tables on the pavement, since it was far too early in the year, and they went inside the crowded café. By a fortunate chance a couple rose from a table near the door and they were able to sit down at once.

'As a matter of fact,' said Luc, taking off his dripping coat and hanging it over the back of his chair, 'this is a particularly touristy area these days, and really cool people don't come here much, so I'm reliably informed. But since I have no personal ambition to be cool I rather adore it, largely on account of Rimbaud.'

'Who's Rimbaud?' Tiger let her cloak fall over the back of her chair, and looked enquiringly at Luc.

'Do you really not know?'

'I don't. Should I?'

Luc laughed. 'Yes, of course you should. I know a great deal about English-speaking authors – Shakespeare, James Joyce, Auden, Eliot, Virginia Woolf, Tom Stoppard; the least you can do is know about poor little Rimbaud!'

A waiter appeared, ready to take their order. 'What would you like, Tiger? A cognac? Some wine? A coffee?'

'Coffee, please.'

Luc turned to the waiter. '*Un café, un armagnac et une carafe d'eau, s'il vous plaît.*'

'*M'sieur, 'dame.*' The waiter scribbled the order, and took himself off.

'OK,' said Tiger, not at all offended by Luc's poor

135

opinion of her knowledge of French literature, 'tell me about Rimbaud.'

Luc took off his rain-spattered spectacles, wiped them on his handkerchief and replaced them. He put his elbows on the table and locked his long white fingers together, looking serious. 'He was born in 1854 and died in 1891, so he didn't have a very long life, by present-day standards, poor guy. He had a very stormy relationship with the poet Verlaine, and when he was only twenty, he wrote *A Season in Hell*, a record of his emotional sufferings, and their final resolution.'

'Do you mean he was in love with Verlaine?'

'But, of course. Why not?'

'No reason, I just wondered, that's all.' Tiger gazed speculatively at Luc's long, pale fingers, recalled his amusing behaviour with the comtesse at dinner, then looked at his beautiful blond hair, and told herself that it probably came out of a bottle.

Luc caught her eye, and burst out laughing. 'You're wondering if I'm gay, aren't you, Tiger?'

She blushed hotly. 'Certainly not!'

'You are!'

'I'm not!' She dropped her eyes, as the waiter arrived with their order. When he had gone, she said, 'Well, I suppose I was a bit. Sorry, I didn't mean to be offensive.'

'You weren't offensive, not in the least.' He took a sip of his drink. 'Seriously, would you mind if I was?'

Tiger put a lump of sugar into her coffee, and stirred it thoughtfully before replying. 'Seriously,' she said slowly, 'I don't really know. You probably won't believe this, Luc, but I've only known about half a dozen men in my whole life so far, and most of them are to do with my family. The only non-family men I know are Monsieur de Martel-Cluny; the rather odious old *prof* who teaches me French with a bunch of other girls, and Tadeusz Marylski, whose art classes I go to twice a week. As far as I can guess, I don't think that any of them are gay.'

'My God, where have you been all this time?'

'Locked up in a girls' boarding school, I'm afraid.'

'A fate worse than death?'

Tiger laughed. 'Something like that, yes.' She took a sip of the hot, strong coffee, suddenly very happy to be in the touristy *Deux-Magots* with the delightful, beautiful and enigmatic Luc, and realizing that she didn't give a fig for his sexual inclinations, one way or the other. 'Is it because of Verlaine and Rimbaud, that you like this place so much?' she asked.

'Yes, I like to imagine them drinking here, discussing their work and their sex life, and because the ghosts of more recent literary greats are here, too; or in the *Flore*, a few doors away. In the Fifties, Sartre, de Beauvoir and the other Existentialists, like Camus and Duras, came here all the time; some of them even worked here. Before them, in the Thirties, the place was a Mecca for expat Americans like Gertrude Stein, Hemingway and Scott Fitzgerald.' Luc emptied his glass. 'God,' he said quietly, 'it must have been absolutely brilliant to be alive in those days, Tiger.'

'Don't you think it's great to be alive now?'

'No, not particularly.'

'Why?'

'Why?' Luc poured himself a glass of water. 'I suppose because I would have given a lot to have lived my life as those guys did, doing their own thing; sitting in cafés all day long, writing; not worrying about paying the bills or climbing the career ladder, all that crap.'

'And is that what you're doing? Climbing the career ladder?'

He smiled ruefully. 'I'm afraid it is, yes. And the worst of it is, I've brought it all on myself.'

'Tell me about it.'

'Well, first you need to know a little about my background. My parents live in a small town in the Gers, in south-west France. My father is a local *notaire*, and my mother keeps house for him, and looked after me and my younger sister, until I left home to study at the

137

Grande Ecole. It's a quiet, dull life down there, with few amusements or distractions, and as a boy my one idea was to escape as soon as possible, which is how I came to work my fingers to the bone in order to get into the *Ecole Polytechnique*, an establishment widely believed to be the gateway to a brilliant career in the civil service or politics.'

'Is that why it's called the *Grande Ecole*?'

'Yes, it is.'

'So, what's the problem? Isn't it good that you've got a job already, and an apartment in Paris?'

'On the face of it, it's what I've worked for. Trouble is, it's only now that I'm having doubts. Suddenly, the thought of three or four decades as a career civil servant, and then retirement on a pension seems to me to be a ghastly mistake, a ridiculous trap I've set for myself. It probably sounds silly, but I have the feeling that I've already achieved all that's required of me; all I have to do now is keep my nose clean and work out my time, until I get the gold watch and the bus pass.'

Tiger laughed. 'It does sound a bit dire, put like that, but most people would give a lot to be in your shoes, wouldn't they?'

'Would you?'

'I wouldn't have the brains for it.'

'You'd be surprised! The students are not all the geniuses you might assume them to be. In fact, some of them struck me as pretty thick in some respects.'

'*Really?* And what became of *them*, Luc?'

He laughed. 'They became statisticians, Tiger, and very worthy members of society, I'm sure.' He looked at his watch. 'Come on, it's time I took you home. We don't want a fuss with the oldies, do we?'

The following afternoon, Monday, Tiger resumed her French lessons, and after the class broke up she walked along rue St-Sulpice to see if Tadeusz had returned from his holiday with his parents, and whether his life class had recommenced. As she approached the door through which it was necessary to go in order to gain access to the studio, it opened and Olga stepped into the street and put up her umbrella. She passed very close to Tiger, suffusing the moist air with her heavy odour, a combination of musk and alcohol. Tiger opened her mouth to say something, then saw that Olga's face was ravaged with grief, or perhaps anger. Her cheeks were tear-stained and streaked with black mascara. Tiger decided that a greeting from herself would not be well received.

After she judged that Olga had now covered a little distance, Tiger turned and watched her go, observing the dirty hem of her bedraggled black coat, her tangled flame-coloured hair and her broken-down high-heeled shoes. She was carrying a battered brown suitcase, held together with string, and Tiger guessed that she must have been staying with Tadeusz. Clearly, there had been a quarrel and Olga had left, or been slung out. Poor old bag, Tiger thought, she's a pain in the neck, but you can't help feeling a bit sorry for her.

Suddenly, Olga's suitcase burst open and its contents spewed all over the pavement. With a scream of rage, Olga spun round and saw Tiger, standing like a statue outside Tadeusz's door, staring at her. Furiously, she stamped her foot and shook her umbrella in Tiger's general direction. '*Vas-y, putain!*' she screamed, and Tiger lost no time in entering the shop.

She found Tadeusz in his studio, working. In spite of the damp and wintry weather, the stove was not lit, and the place was terribly cold. Tadeusz was wearing his overcoat, several knitted mufflers and a pair of grey woollen fingerless gloves. 'Hello,' he said, casually, as though she had not been away for nearly two weeks. 'Put the kettle on, if you like.'

'I came to see when the life classes begin, Tadeusz. Is it this week, or next?'

'I don't know. I'll have to find a model. Bloody Olga's fucked off, just when she's needed, the cow.'

'Yes,' said Tiger. 'I saw her in the street, just now.

She looked pretty upset, as a matter of fact.'

'It's her own stupid fault. The bloody woman's mental. She'll find herself in the *asile de folles* if she's not careful, daft bitch.' Tadeusz looked at Tiger, his dark eyes moody. 'Where's this tea, then?' he said. 'It's cold in here, or hadn't you noticed?'

'Yes, I've noticed. Why haven't you got the stove on?'

'No money. No fuel.'

Tiger said nothing, but went behind the screen and put the kettle on. She was relieved to see that the gas bottle appeared to be quite full. She washed two dirty mugs under the cold tap, looked in vain for milk, made the tea and carried the tray to Tadeusz's side, putting it on the floor beside him. She poured two mugs and handed one to him. 'Did you have a nice Christmas?' she asked.

'No, did you?'

'Yes, lovely. I stayed with my mother, and one of my sisters, in Ireland, and then I spent a few days with my other sister in London. It was fun.' Sitting on the floor beside Tadeusz, the hot mug warming her freezing hands, Neill's Court and its eccentric inhabitants seemed a million miles away and quite unreal, like a dream. Orla and Matthew and their little boys, on the other hand, were still fresh in Tiger's consciousness, and comfortingly familiar.

'It must be nice to have so many posh houses to stay in when you feel like it,' said Tadeusz sarcastically. 'You must take me with you next time, Tiger.'

'Of course I will, if you'd like to come,' she replied quietly, and smiled at him. 'I'm sure they'd love to meet you.'

He glanced at her, suspecting irony, then looked away, feeling oddly confused. 'Well, anyway, and more urgently, what the hell am I going to do about a model? I need to earn some money, and fast.'

'What about the old man, Tadeusz? Couldn't he take Olga's place till she comes back?'

'He's dead, worse luck. Had a stroke on Christmas Eve, so I heard.'

'God, how awful!' said Tiger, shocked.

'Yes, well. These things happen, don't they? Poor old sod, I don't suppose he minded; it wasn't much of a life for him, was it, taking his kit off in front of a bunch of kids, to earn a living?'

They drank the tea without speaking, in silent tribute to the old man's passing. Tiger put her mug on the tray. 'If you like, I can let you have an advance on my fees, so that you can get some charcoal for the stove,' she said. 'At least, then, the place would be a bit warmer.'

She got up, and took her purse from her bag. She extracted a hundred-franc note and offered it to Tadeusz. He took it without thanks, frowning resentfully. 'Still doesn't solve the problem of a model, does it?' he muttered, sounding childish and defeated.

'Why not do it yourself? At least that way it wouldn't cost you anything, until you get things sorted out. I must go now, or I'll be late for dinner. I'll come on Thursday, and see how things are, OK?'

On Wednesday evening, returning from her French lesson, Tiger arrived at the concierge's door just as a taxi drew up, and Luc got out, carrying a briefcase.

'Hi,' said Tiger.

'Hi.' Luc paid the fare, and they entered the courtyard together. 'I was just thinking about you,' he said. 'Are you busy this evening, or would you like to come and see my apartment? It's still a shambles, but I think you'll like it. I need to see how the builders are getting on, and I'd like to take you there, anyway, if it would amuse you?'

'I'd love to see it,' said Tiger, gratified that he had asked her. 'But first, I'll have to take Fanny for her walk. Would after dinner be OK? I don't want to upset Madame in any way, you understand, or be rude.'

'I'll speak to her, ask her to excuse us this evening

– I'm sure she wouldn't mind if I took you out to supper.'

'OK, if you're sure?'

Luc smiled. 'I'm sure.'

The front door opened and Gaston appeared, holding Fanny on a tight lead. Tiger gave him her pile of books and files, and took the lead. 'See you later, Luc,' she said, then ran across the courtyard, into rue Monsieur, and kept on running until she reached the Jardin du Luxembourg, suddenly full of energy, excited at the prospect of a visit to Luc's apartment. Is he planning to seduce me? she asked herself, rather hoping that that was indeed his intention. Just as well I've been taking Orla's pills, she thought. I certainly wouldn't want to get pregnant, or anything as stupid as that.

On her return to the house, she took Fanny to the kitchen as usual, then went straight to the salon. In earnest conversation with a smartly dressed, grey-haired woman of her own age, Madame was seated on one of her white satin sofas. She looked up as Tiger entered the room, and smiled, holding out her hand. Briefly, she introduced her friend. 'I understand that you are going out this evening, with Luc, my dear?'

'Is that all right, madame? Madame la Comtesse won't mind?'

'She probably will, but she can't expect to have you all to herself. Of course you must go, and enjoy yourself. You are only young once, after all.'

'Well, thank you,' said Tiger. 'I'll just go up and change.'

On the stairs she met Luc, coming down. He was wearing corduroy trousers and a dark blue sweater, and looked quite unlike the formally dressed man she had become accustomed to.

'Don't bother to change,' he said. 'The apartment is filthy; I wouldn't want you to spoil your nice clothes.'

It was a still, fine evening, although cold, and they

walked briskly to the carrefour de l'Odéon, then up rue Mazarine, and turned into rue de Buci. Here, the stall-holders of the street market were just beginning to pack up for the night, so Luc lost no time in buying the things he needed for their supper. Swiftly and efficiently, he bought a dozen oysters, a small pack of butter, two kinds of cheese, an onion tart, some tangerines, and finally, in a boulangerie, two long freshly baked baguettes. 'I hope you like oysters, Tiger?'

'Yes, I do.'

'Well, that's a relief. We don't want to have to start all over again, do we?'

'I could have just eaten the onion tart.'

'That's true.'

The shopping completed, they retraced their steps, crossed rue Mazarine and entered rue St-André-des-Arts, a traffic-free street lined with fashion boutiques, bookshops and cafés. Carrying their shopping bags, they turned into an arcade under a glass roof, the passage du Commerce-St-André. Luc led the way along a cobbled alleyway, and through an iron gateway that led to a series of small linked courtyards. As they entered Cour de Poitiers, secluded and peaceful, sheltered by high ivy-clad walls, Tiger stood stock still and gazed about her, admiring the exquisite Renaissance town houses that lined the tiny square. It seemed to her astonishing that this quiet, tranquil place should exist, only a stone's throw from the bustle of the busy rue St-André. 'Luc,' she said, sounding awed at the thought, 'you don't mean to tell me that your apartment is here?'

'Don't be too impressed,' he replied. 'It's only a very small basement.'

Stone steps led up to the front doors of the houses, and some much less grand wooden ones went down to their nether regions. A handcart full of builders' rubbish stood in front of one of the houses, and Luc stopped beside it, frowning. 'I do wish they'd come and remove this eyesore,' he said crossly. 'The people upstairs are getting pissed off with the disruption and mess, and I can't say I blame them.'

Silently, Tiger followed him down the steps. Inside, he closed the door and switched on the light. The heating was turned on and the place felt pleasantly warm, so Tiger took off her cloak, and Luc hung it on a hook behind the entrance, pulling off his own sweater at the same time.

She looked around and saw that they were standing in a large square stone-walled and vaulted cellar, without windows but with the back wall completely removed and replaced with sliding plate-glass doors. Luc crossed the room and pressed another switch, and immediately the space outside the glass doors sprang into life, revealing a small courtyard, apparently hewn out of the living rock. He turned to Tiger. 'What do you think?'

She smiled. 'It's lovely,' she said. 'Or it will be, when you've finished the work.'

'As a matter of fact, I intend to leave it pretty much as it is, apart from a few bits of necessary furniture.'

'Really? What about a kitchen? And a bathroom?'

To the left of the sliding doors was a rough stone archway, through which Tiger could see a narrow dark passage.

'In here,' Luc said, and she followed him into the tiniest imaginable kitchen. It was simple to the point of austerity, with extremely basic equipment, and was just large enough for two people to stand in.

'This used to be the coal-hole.' He pointed to a brick-lined chute in the ceiling, its metal cover now replaced with a glass skylight. 'Great, isn't it?'

'OK if you're a midget,' Tiger said, dumping the shopping bags on the stainless steel work surface. She turned towards him. 'A bit of a squash for two tallish specimens like us, though, wouldn't you say?'

'It's my secret weapon with women, Tiger. A perfect excuse for close proximity.' He slid his hands round her waist and drew her against his body.

144

Her heart beating a little faster, Tiger did not resist, but gazed at him, her violet eyes wide with curiosity. She put her arms round his neck and waited for the hoped-for kiss, which was soft, gentle and exploratory, and not at all like the rapacious, hungry embrace of Tadeusz.

After a moment, Luc released her. 'Do you want to see the rest of the apartment?' he asked, in a matter-of-fact manner. 'Or shall we have supper?'

'Um, see the rest first, and then have supper?'

The bathroom was hidden behind what Tiger took to be a cupboard door in the kitchen, down a short flight of stone steps, and like the kitchen had formerly been a small cellar for coal or wine. Cell-like and bleak, its walls roughly limewashed, it was equipped with an old-fashioned overhead shower, a contemporary lavatory, and a plain white basin with lime-encrusted chrome taps. Above this basin was a glass shelf, holding shaving things, an antique adjustable mirror, a tall glass jar containing several tablets of soap and a matching jar filled with colourfully decorated packets of condoms. Tiger tried not to stare at this riveting object, but turned her attention to the extremely unusual bath. It stood in the middle of the little room, tall and forbidding, its stained white enamel tub encased in a patinated gunmetal surround, with a rolled rim.

'Wow!' she exclaimed. 'It's just like the bath Marat was in when Charlotte Corday stabbed him, isn't it?'

'Bravo, Tiger! You're not as badly educated as I thought.'

She laughed. 'There was a picture of it, in a book in my grandfather's library, at home. The staff at my school wouldn't have let us see anything like that, Luc. You know? A naked man, too rude.'

He smiled. 'Haven't you ever seen a naked man, Tiger?'

'Yes, at my life class.'

'Apart from the life class?'

'Actually, no.' Tiger felt herself blushing.

145

'Would you like to?'

'As a matter of fact, yes, I probably would.' She looked at him, and grinned. 'Specially if he was young, and not like the wrinkly old bloke I used to draw. He's dead now, poor thing.'

Luc did not react to this sad piece of news. Instead, he turned out the light and led the way back to the kitchen. He took plates from a rough wooden shelf containing crockery, cutlery and several cooking pots, and unpacked the food they had bought in the Marché Buci.

'Is that it?' asked Tiger.

'Is what it?'

'Is that all there is of your apartment? Don't you have a bedroom?'

'I shall sleep in the studio, as I rather pretentiously refer to it, Tiger, since it's not exactly a sitting-room. Studio makes me feel a bit less like a civil servant.'

'And a bit more like what?'

'A writer, perhaps, who knows?'

Luc arranged the seafood on one plate, the onion tart on another, and the butter, cheese and fruit on a third. He put the dishes on a black tin Russian tray decorated with yellow roses, took knives, forks and glasses from the shelf, told Tiger to bring the bread and led the way back to the studio.

The big room was sparsely furnished, the floor a pale uneven stone. Hanging against one wall was a large and anatomically correct painting of a camel, in a plain gilded frame. Beneath it stood a daybed, a simple black iron base with curved ends, fitted with a blue-and-white striped cotton mattress, and two bolsters, one at each end.

'I'm still looking for a table,' said Luc, putting the tray on the floor in front of the daybed. He pulled up the only chair in the studio, a worm-eaten eighteenth-century *bergère*, its gilding practically worn away, its upholstery faded and threadbare. 'Sit here, Tiger, and I'll sit on the bed.'

146

Tiger sat down, stretching out her legs and caressing the carved scrolls of the chair's armrests with gentle fingers. 'It's beautiful,' she said, 'and comfortable, too. Isn't that supposed to be the criterion of good design?'

'Beautiful and *functional*, I think.' Luc brought a bottle of wine from a deep niche in the wall, and pulled the cork.

'I'd rather have comfortable.'

'So would I.' He poured a pale golden wine into two glasses, handing her one of them. 'See how you like this, while I open the oysters.'

Tiger kicked off her boots, and sitting cross-legged in the capacious old armchair, took a sip of her drink. It was cold, delicious, powerfully scented and mouth-filling. She held the glass against the light, admiring the colour of the wine. 'Is this something special, Luc? It's lovely.'

'It's a white Châteauneuf, Château Rayas. I thought you'd like it. It's good with seafood.' Frowning, he opened the last oyster, picking out the stray bits of shell. 'There,' he said. 'Now we're in business. *Bel appetit!*' He handed a plate of prepared oysters to Tiger, with a lump of butter and a hunk of crusty bread.

Beside the sliding glass doors to the courtyard was a large lemon tree in a terracotta pot. 'In the spring,' Luc said, shovelling an oyster down his throat, 'I shall put that tree in the garden outside, and with any luck it might even grow a few lemons in time for autumn, so it won't matter if I forget to buy some when we have oysters. I'm looking for an old metal table and chairs, too, so that we can eat out there when the weather's fine.'

'Can't wait,' said Tiger. 'Sounds wonderful.'

They ate every scrap of the food and drank the wine, with all the spontaneous hunger of youth, finishing with the tangerines, their sharp juice delicious with the last glass of wine. 'God,' said Tiger. 'What a mess! My hands are all sticky, Luc. I daren't touch anything!'

'Hang on.' He went to the kitchen and returned with

147

a tea towel wrung out in cold water. 'There you are, you scruffy creature.'

'Thanks.' Tiger wiped her hands, folded the towel and put it on the tray, and he took it to the kitchen. Presently the smell of coffee floated into the studio, followed almost immediately by Luc, with a cafetière and two small white cups.

Tiger, feeling sleepy, soothed by the food and wine, delightfully spoiled, smiled at him affectionately as he put the tray down. 'You'll have to pour the coffee,' she said lazily. 'I think my head's stuck in the lotus position, as well as my legs.'

They drank the coffee in a relaxed silence, happy to be together in that peaceful, uncluttered space.

'What are your plans, Tiger?' Luc asked quietly, after a while.

'Plans?'

'What do you intend to do with your life? Get married; have lots of kids, all that?'

'No, I don't think so. What about you? Will you marry, Luc?'

'I suppose I shall have to, eventually, in the interests of my career; it's expected, the normal thing.' He looked at Tiger, his pale blue eyes very bright, mocking, cynical, behind the gold-rimmed spectacles. 'When I have the misfortune to reach the age of thirty-something, I shall propose to a woman of twenty-something. The chosen one has to be of good family; preferably rich; certainly a virgin. This hypothetical young lady is therefore fourteen at present, and at school, of course. She has no idea of my existence, and the poor girl would doubtless object violently to the very idea of an arranged marriage with me. In the meantime, and probably after the event as well, I shall expect to have many attachments, it goes without saying.'

Tiger laughed, and so did he. 'You've got the whole thing mapped out, haven't you?' she said.

'Not really. It's the system, that's all. So, what are

your plans? Tell me.' Luc lay down on the daybed and closed his eyes, waiting for Tiger to speak.

'I don't have any plans, really. Except, maybe, trying to be a full-time art student. The problem would be money, though. My family is stony broke, Luc. My oldest sister, Orla, would like me to marry someone rich, so as not to be a financial liability. That's why she arranged this job for me, in Paris. I'm supposed to be on the prowl for a suitable husband, right now.' Tiger looked speculatively at Luc, as he lay with closed eyes, his hands linked beneath his fair head, a faint smile on his lips, listening. 'It's a shame I don't fit in with your requirements. We could have had fun; you in your ministry, me at art school, and living here together, couldn't we?'

'We could have even more fun without the doubtful sanctity of a marriage licence, Tiger.'

'Could we?'

'Of course we could.' He opened his eyes, and smiled. 'Come here, darling.'

Tiger uncurled her legs, and, stepping carefully over the coffee tray, perched on the edge of the daybed.

'That's better,' said Luc, softly. 'Now, why don't you kiss me?'

Tiger hesitated for a moment, for it had never occurred to her that in the preliminary skirmishes of love, it might be appropriate for the woman to initiate the process. Then, slowly and deliberately, she un-buttoned Luc's shirt, and began to kiss the smooth bare skin above his navel, working upwards until she reached the hollow at the base of his throat. Suddenly, his arms closed tightly around her and his mouth sought hers, urgent and demanding, and not at all like their first gentle embrace.

'Wait!' said Tiger, tearing herself from Luc's arms. Swiftly, she stripped off her clothes, until she stood, radiant with desire, beautiful and completely naked, beside the daybed.

'Tiger! Are you sure?'

'Don't you want to sleep with me, Luc?'

'Yes, of course I do.' In a moment, his clothes, too, were in a heap on the floor, and he lay down again, making room for Tiger at his side. Tiger stared at him, then, trembling, got into the bed and folded her body against his, folding her arms around him.

'Darling Tiger, you're shivering. Are you cold?'

'No, I'm boiling hot, I promise.'

They woke after midnight, still clasped tightly in each other's arms, face to face, warm where their bodies touched, their backs rather chilled. Luc kissed Tiger, very tenderly. 'Am I talking nonsense, Tiger, or are you a virgin?'

'Not now, thanks to you, darling Luc. I've been desperate not to be one for ages.'

'I'm sorry. I had no idea.'

'Don't be. I'm not. I think I must take after my mother. She was married when she was nineteen and had her first child on her twentieth birthday.'

Luc looked alarmed. 'You're not planning to do that, are you?'

'Certainly not!' A note of pride crept into Tiger's voice. 'I'm on the pill, of course, what else?'

'Well, good. One can't be too careful.'

'Are *you* careful, Luc?'

'Yes, I am. Obsessively so, as a matter of fact.'

They took a hot shower together, then walked slowly back to rue Monsieur, let themselves silently into the sleeping house, and crept up the stairs to their respective rooms.

CHAPTER EIGHT

On Thursday evening Tiger, accompanied by Luc, went to her life class in rue St-Sulpice. Luc had arranged to meet a friend, so he left Tiger at the shop door, promising to pick her up at ten thirty and take her for a drink.

She found the class already in progress, with Tadeusz himself standing on the model's podium, naked except for a small and grubby-looking leather pouch. She got her drawing materials from the cupboard, and pinned a sheet of paper to the drawing-board already waiting on her easel. She was amused to see that Tadeusz had allocated her a position with a view of his back. She put on her overall, took a stick of sanguine from her box and began to mark the points of her composition.

Tadeusz was not a good model. He seemed unable to hold the pose for very long without swaying in a distracting manner, and shifting the position of his feet. As she blocked in his thin, rather fragile-looking legs, pallid from lack of sunshine, Tiger was concerned to observe how extremely underweight he looked, how prominent were his ribs and the bones of his vertebrae. Poor thing, she thought, he must be half starved. Further evidence of his unhealthy condition were the angry-looking spots that disfigured his shoulders and buttocks. Oh well, at least his classes have started

151

again, she said to herself. He'll get a bit of money from the fees. Let's hope it's enough to hire a new model, too.

When she had got her eye in, and had begun to look more objectively at the naked body before her, she was soon able to dissociate herself from any personal feelings she might have concerning Tadeusz, and discovered interesting and subtle aspects of the cold and unhealthy flesh so cruelly exposed to anyone prepared to pay for the privilege of drawing it. Nevertheless, there was something about the droop of his shoulders, and later, when the class had changed positions after the break, the sullen expression on his face, that induced a stab of unease, even pity, in Tiger's heart, and she quite longed for the session to be over.

At ten thirty, Tadeusz stepped down from the podium and the class broke up. Tiger sprayed her drawings, and unpinned them from the board. Turning from her easel, she saw Luc standing just inside the door to the shop, and went to speak to him. 'I have to pay the balance of my tuition fees, Luc. Then I'll be right with you, OK?'

'Fine, there's no hurry.'

Tadeusz, wearing his old black coat and very little else, not even his boots, was standing at his desk, extracting money from the dozen or so students who had signed up for the life classes. When Tiger reached the head of the queue, she took the crisp new bank notes from her wallet and handed them to Tadeusz. He took the money, but looked at her rather coldly, his eyebrows raised. 'Do you really want to do the whole course, Tiger?' He shot a malicious glance in Luc's direction. 'I see you have a new friend now. Are you sure you'll have enough time for your studies?'

'Of course I'm sure, Tadeusz. Don't be ridiculous.' She touched his hand gently. 'You're tired, that's all. Go out and buy yourself a decent meal. You'll feel better afterwards, I promise.'

'Come with me, Tiger.'

'I can't. Another time, perhaps. Good night.'

'Good night.'

She turned and saw that Luc had taken her cloak from its hook, and was standing by the door, holding it. She hurried to join him, and they went out through the shop, and into the dark night.

'What was all that about, Tiger? Is the model the *prof* as well, or what? He seemed pretty uptight about something. Or is that just how he is?'

'It's just how he is, poor chap. He's perpetually broke, can't sell his work, all that. He's twenty-eight, and still fairly dependent on his parents, which must be pretty humiliating for him, I expect. One of his models died recently, and the other's a rather ghastly creature, and totally unreliable. She just pitches up when her old man slings her out, moves in with Tadeusz, and does the business. You know? A roof over her head in exchange for sex and modelling.' Tiger glanced at Luc, with a disapproving sniff. 'And she's not even *pretty*, silly old bat!'

Luc laughed. 'The classic *vie de Bohème* bit? Brilliant young artist starves in garret, genius unrecognized by cruel world?'

'You got it,' said Tiger, laughing too. 'Trouble is, he's not young any more and not terribly talented, at least *I* don't think so, anyway. Not that I'm qualified to judge, I hasten to add.'

'But your gut reaction tells you so?'

'Yeah.'

Now began a happy time for Tiger. The weather in January and February was cold and blustery, but she hardly noticed it, so full and exciting had her life suddenly become. On one or two evenings each week, and sometimes at weekends, she accompanied Luc on his shopping expeditions as he searched for the perfect lamp, the perfect garden furniture, the perfect oriental rugs for the apartment in Cour de Poitiers. The quests were long and exhaustive, for he had extremely clear ideas about the age, provenance and colour of the things he planned to acquire, and was unwilling to make any kind of compromise.

As a reward for her patience and occasional useful advice, Luc took Tiger to dine in his favourite restaurants in the *quartier*, and the one she liked best was the *Café Procope*, in rue de l'Ancienne Comédie and close to the carrefour de l'Odéon. It was a lively, fashionable place, decorated to demonstrate its historic significance during the Revolutionary era. A portrait of Rousseau hung on the wall, and prominently displayed was a desk said to have been given to Voltaire by Frederick the Great. Glass-fronted cabinets exhibited Phrygian bonnets, tricorne hats and other powerful symbols of the period.

'It wasn't always like this,' said Luc, as he ate his way through an enormous platter of spider crabs, sucking the tender flesh from their dismembered legs before embarking on the body. He washed his fingers in the bowl of water provided, and raised his glass to his lips. 'It was opened in 1686 by a Sicilian ice-cream merchant called Francesco Procopio dei Coltelli, who seems to have been pretty good at making coffee as well as *gelati*, because it soon became the buzz place, not only with the actors from across the road, but also with all the stars of the Enlightenment: Beaumarchais; Voltaire and Rousseau of course. Danton, Robespierre and Marat were all habitués too, no doubt plotting away as they drank their coffee, and probably a few glasses of something a good deal stronger.'

Tiger, although only mildly interested in these historic associations, felt none the less flattered that Luc should take the trouble to broaden her knowledge, and listened attentively, doing her best to commit to memory the salient points of his little lecture.

'Francesco Procopio?' she asked. 'I suppose that accounts for the place's name?'

'One imagines so.'

'It must have been quite an adventure, leaving Sicily

154

and opening a café so far from home, in 1686? How do you suppose he made the journey? On foot?'

Luc renewed his attack on the crabs, and smiled. 'You're much more interested in the mechanics of people's lives than in their politics, aren't you, Tiger?'

Tiger took a sip of her wine and looked at him seriously. 'If you mean that I'm more interested in old Signor Procopio than in Robespierre and his chums, then you're probably right. You obviously know every single thing there is to know about them; it's all documented, isn't it? On the other hand, the immigrant Sicilian is quite an enigma, and I'd like to know more about him, that's all.'

Luc laughed. 'Am I boring you, Tiger?'

'No, not at all. Go on, and tell me what happened, after the Revolution.'

'Right. It became the meeting place for all the luminaries of the Romantic era, especially writers. Alfred de Musset and Georges Sand came here, and so did Balzac and Victor Hugo. After them came Verlaine and Mallarmé, and later, in the Fifties and Sixties, Sartre and de Beauvoir.'

'Crikey,' said Tiger. 'What a pedigree! No wonder it's a place of pilgrimage for you.'

'Indeed. It used to be fairly run-down, romantically shabby and full of historical associations and atmosphere, but not a lot to recommend it otherwise. Then, in 1988, just before the bicentenary of the Revolution, it was given a complete overhaul, and its appearance restored to what it might have been in 1789. As you can see, it's been going like a bomb ever since.'

'Did Rimbaud come here, too?'

'Tiger! You're not listening, are you?'

'I am, I am! I just *wondered*, that's all.'

'You're adorable. I think I love you. Let's go home, shall we?'

'Do you mean to rue Monsieur?'

'No. My place, of course. Unless you really like creeping about the house, playing Russian roulette?'

*   *   *

It was less than five minutes' walk from the *Café Procope* to the apartment, and on the way there Luc bought an armful of scented white lilies from a cold-looking woman still selling her wares on the pavement, in spite of the lateness of the hour. In the cobbled passageway leading to Cour de Poitiers, he turned towards Tiger, took her in his arms and kissed her, then gave her the flowers. 'I can't imagine how I endured the boredom of my life before you came into it, Tiger. Thank you for a lovely evening.'

Tiger took the flowers, inhaling their scented waxy fragrance. She did not try to conceal the sexual chemistry that flickered between them like an electrical charge, but laid a hand against Luc's cheek, her violet eyes luminous in the lamplight, and dark with passion. 'It's not over yet, is it?' she said.

Much later, as they lay quietly together, under the beautiful stitched quilt they had bought that morning, Luc ran a finger down Tiger's face, following the contours of her cheekbones and her neck. 'You're a beautiful woman, Tiger,' he said softly. 'I'm glad I had the privilege of being your first lover.'

'My nose is too big, everyone says so.'

'Who says so?'

'Oh, everyone; especially my sisters.'

'It's a load of old bollocks. Your nose is part of the magic of your face, and divine, like the rest of you. You should never listen to sisters, Tiger. They sound like a pair of frustrated bitches.'

Tiger laughed. 'No, they're not, really. But it's nice of you to think so, *quand même*.'

On the way back to rue Monsieur, walking through the frosty silent pre-dawn streets, they stopped frequently to embrace each other, reigniting the special enchantment of being both young and in love. Almost at their destination, they drew apart reluctantly, and walked silently, with a discreet distance between them.

Suddenly, Luc said, 'Yes, of course he would have been there.'

'Who would have been where?'

'Rimbaud. At the *Procope*, with Verlaine.'

Tadeusz, trapped in his impoverished world, barely able to sustain himself and pay the wages of his new model, was quite aware of his diminished significance in Tiger's life and was bitterly regretting his failure to take advantage of her when the opportunity and initiative had been his. Now, seeing her frequently in the company of a much younger, very attractive and obviously rich man not only made him jealous, it made him angry.

Since their weekend trip to Barbizon, and his parents' subsequent keen endorsement of Tiger, he had begun to realize that a liaison with her could be exactly the catalyst he needed, in order to achieve his full potential. She was young, beautiful, intelligent and hardworking, and he felt very sure that if she took charge of his life and work, all her natural confidence would prove immensely valuable to his quest for fame and fortune. Put less pretentiously, he thought she would make a very good public relations person.

Equally, though she had often told him that her family in Ireland was broke, he said to himself that this was probably a typical piece of wild Irish exaggeration. He could not help envisaging a great country house, and acres of valuable land, both of which, in the fullness of time, must prove to be better than a kick in the head, as far as Tiger was concerned.

She came to her class twice a week, as usual. She gave her full attention to her assignments, and Tadeusz saw that her work was developing fast, both in scope and maturity. It was becoming clear to him that there was not a great deal more that he could teach her, but he chose not to mention this, for obvious reasons. The thought of her leaving his class, of his ceasing to see her, filled him with a sense of hopelessness, almost despair, for he knew that he was in danger of letting a golden opportunity slip through his fingers.

He took himself in hand. He went to the local bath-house and had a sauna. He paid a visit to his infrequently patronized barber, who gave him a flaw-less shave, then washed his hair and cut three inches from it. Feeling extraordinarily naked, almost flayed alive, he walked back to rue St-Sulpice, put on a clean shirt recently delivered to him by his mother, and polished his boots. Finally, he examined himself in a long mirror in the ecclesiastical emporium, and saw that instead of looking like a tramp, he looked much more like the romantic figure of his wilder daydreams.

To his disappointment, Tiger seemed not to notice the extremes to which he had gone in order to impress her. She had smiled at him quite kindly. 'You've cut your hair, Tadeusz. It suits you like that,' was all she had said.

'Come and have a drink after the class, Tiger.'

'I can't tonight; I'm sorry.'

'On Thursday, then?'

'OK, Thursday.'

Accordingly, on Thursday, after the last pupil had departed, the model had been paid and the easels put away, Tadeusz and Tiger went out for a drink together.

'Where would you like to go, Tiger?'

'Oh, doesn't matter; anywhere. What about the place we went to before?'

'No, we'll go somewhere new. You choose.'

She laughed, and took his arm as they walked. 'OK, what about the *Flore*?'

'Right. The *Flore* it is.'

It was a soft, balmy night, almost warm, as it often is in Paris towards the end of February. When they reached the café they found a few tables outside on the pavement and sat down. An elderly waiter came out to take their order, with an air of disapproval, since most of the clientele were sensibly ensconced inside, in the warm, smoke-filled interior.

'What would you like, Tiger? Wine? Coffee?'

'I'm terribly thirsty, as a matter of fact. I'd like a beer, please.'

'Nothing to eat? You wouldn't like a sandwich?'

'No, no. Just beer is fine.'

The waiter departed with their order, then Tadeusz took a tin of rolling tobacco from his pocket, and began to make a cigarette. He looked across the little table and smiled. 'Can I fix you a joint, Tiger?'

'I don't do drugs, thank you,' she replied primly, slightly surprised that he had the means to indulge his occasional habit. Then her natural curiosity and hunger for new experiences kicked in, overriding her moral scruples, such as they were, and she laughed. 'I'll just have a drag of yours, to keep you company, if you like.'

'Do you really disapprove of marijuana, or is it just your elders and betters talking?'

'Don't patronize me, Tadeusz.'

'I'm sorry. I didn't intend to.'

The waiter came back with the drinks, and, casting a jaundiced eye over his client's unorthodox appearance, waited until Tadeusz had settled the bill before returning to the bar.

'Rude old sod,' said Tiger.

'They're a race apart, waiters,' Tadeusz agreed. 'Nothing but a bunch of wankers, stupid old farts.'

She laughed, and took a long pull at her beer. 'Rotten job, though. I wouldn't want to finish up like that, would you?'

'No, I wouldn't.' Carefully, Tadeusz rolled up his joint, licked the gummed edge of the paper and stuck it neatly down. He put the cigarette between his lips and lit it, inhaling the smoke slowly and voluptuously, his eyes half closed.

'It's quite a nice smell,' Tiger remarked. 'A bit like one of those herbal tea bags, don't you think?'

159

He passed her the joint. 'I wouldn't recognize the smell of a herbal tea bag if it jumped up and hit me in the face, as a matter of fact.'

Tiger took a small puff, expelling the smoke from her mouth almost at once.

'Not like that!' he exclaimed. 'What a waste! Suck it into your lungs, for heaven's sake!'

'OK, OK.' She took another drag, inhaling the smoke as she did so. She waited for a second, then breathed out, producing a tiny cloud of bluish vapour. She shook her head, and gave the roll-up back to Tadeusz. 'Thanks, but I don't think I'll bother with it. It seems a bit of a waste of time to me. Expensive, too, isn't it?'

'I suppose you think I can't afford it?'

'How you spend your money is no concern of mine, Tadeusz. You must do as you please, of course.' She leaned across the little table and took his hand. 'I'm sorry. I didn't mean to criticize you, not at all. Don't be angry, or upset, please.'

'I'm not angry, Tiger. Just sad, that's all.'

'Sad? Why?'

'Because you dumped me for that fair-haired bloke with the posh clothes. You never have time for me, now, do you?'

'I'm here now, Tadeusz.'

'Yes.' He raised her hand and kissed it gently. He gazed at her across the table, his brown eyes reproachful beneath the ragged fringe of dark hair, and attempted an ironic riposte to her disparaging comment on his spending habits. 'What you do with your time is no concern of mine, Tiger. You must do as you please, of course.'

'Idiot!' She looked at him tenderly, almost maternally, thinking what a curious mixture of maturity and childishness he was. 'Will you be offended if I offer to pay for another couple of beers, Tadeusz?'

'Not at all, although in fact I do have the means in my pocket. Would you like another drink?'

'Yes, please.'

They sat for a long time, talking far into the night, until the surly waiter came out onto the terrace and began to pile the chairs onto the tables, then, quite ostentatiously, produced a long-handled broom and started to sweep the pavement. Tiger and Tadeusz stuck it out for a few minutes, just to annoy the old man, then got up and left. As they passed *Deux-Magots*, its lights still cheerfully burning, Tiger glanced inside and saw Luc, seated at a table in the window, in earnest conversation with a young man of his own age. She very nearly exclaimed, 'Look, there's Luc!', then tore her eyes away, curiously agitated. She remained silent, telling herself not to be ridiculous, that Luc had a perfect right to have a drink with someone other than herself, especially a bloke. Another woman might have been cause for concern, she reassured herself, but this was a man, after all, and not a threat. She looked at Tadeusz, wondering whether he had seen Luc, but his face was expressionless; it was clear that he had not.

They walked slowly back to rue Monsieur, and when they reached the concierge's gate, Tiger turned to Tadeusz and thanked him for a nice evening. 'We must do it again,' she said, and kissed his cheek.

He put his arms round her, and held her close. 'I've missed you,' he said.

'What about Olga?'

'What about her, the whore?'

'I just wondered.'

'Olga,' he said stiffly, 'is no longer a part of my life, Tiger.'

'Oh? Why's that?'

'The reason's not important. She's history, that's all.'

'I see.' She touched his cheek. 'Good night, Tadeusz. Thanks again.'

'Next week? After the class, Thursday?'

'Yes, OK. Good night.'

*   *   *

Later, lying in her comfortable bed, Tiger tried to remember all the details of her evening with Tadeusz; their conversation; their occasional affectionate physical contacts; the smooth feel of his cheek beneath her hand. She was surprised, as well as rather touched, that her friendship with Luc should have provoked such a hostile reaction from Tadeusz. What happened to personal freedom; no shackles, all that? she asked herself. Where I'm coming from, it sounds like good old-fashioned jealousy. Remembering his childish, sulky face as he made a scornful reference to Luc's appearance, she grinned in the darkness. Poor old Tadeusz, she thought, he's his own worst enemy.

Suddenly, into Tiger's mind's eye came the image of Luc, drinking in *Deux-Magots*, his face close to that of his male companion as they leaned towards each other across the table, totally absorbed in each other, or so it had seemed to her at the time. I wonder what they were talking about, she asked herself. Whatever it was, it certainly looked pretty serious. 'Perhaps it's a Rimbaud and Verlaine thing,' she said aloud, and felt a small knot of disquiet flutter in her breast. 'God, I hope not.'

A few days later, in early March, two things happened that increased Tiger's vague sense of uneasiness, and seemed to suggest that unwelcome changes lurked around the corner.

In the first place, Luc left rue Monsieur and moved into his own apartment, leaving Tiger feeling ignored and rather lonely, for the house seemed dead without his presence. Then, the following week, she received a letter from Niamh. The contents were brief, and to the point: the house was full; her cookery classes were a brilliant success; she, Niamh, was run off her feet from dawn to dusk, and did not know how she could manage everything when the parties of fishermen began to arrive, especially over the Easter holiday, for which they were fully booked. *I hope I can rely on you to*

162

pitch in and help over the holiday period. I shall expect you on 27 March, at the latest. Please don't let me down, Tiger. I know you won't forget that it is me that's keeping the old place going, and looking after Mum. She concluded with a warning that Con's bedroom would, of course, be earmarked for the guests, and the expectation that Tiger would not mind returning to her old room.

Huh! said Tiger to herself, reacting angrily to her sister's strictures. I bloody do mind, so there! Niamh can get lost, if she thinks she can bend me to her will, whenever she feels like it. I'll stay here, if I can, or maybe Luc would let me move in with him, if the family are going to the country for Easter? Since the holiday was less than a fortnight away, she knew that it was vital to lose no time in making an arrangement that would allow her to remain in Paris, and avoid going to Ireland.

That evening, as usual, she took Fanny for her walk, then spent an hour with the comtesse, playing dominoes.

'The 'ouse is very quiet for you, without Luc, Tiger?'

Startled, Tiger felt herself blush. Carefully, she chose a tile and placed it on the table between them. 'Not especially,' she replied.

'I am surprise. I 'ad the idea you are friends, that you like each other?'

'Yes, we are friends, I suppose, but nothing else, I assure you, madame.'

The comtesse said nothing, but the expression on her face spoke volumes. She might just as well have said, 'Pull the other one, Tiger.'

The game came to an end, the comtesse winning, as usual, and Tiger rose to go and get ready for dinner.

'You are not going out with Luc tonight, my dear?'

'No.'

'What a pity. It amuse me to think of you together.'

Feeling rather teased and provoked by this onslaught

163

from the old woman, Tiger's temper rose to the surface. 'I regret the necessity to disappoint you, madame!' she said tersely, and left the room. Walking along the darkened terrace towards the salon, she could not fail to hear the delighted cackles of the comtesse's laughter, coming from the half-open window.

Mme de Martel-Cluny was in the salon, dressed for dinner, and writing a letter at her secretaire, a glass of champagne on the blotter before her. 'Hello, Tiger,' she said. 'Do we enjoy the pleasure of your company tonight, or are you dining with Luc?'

'Um, I'm dining in, if that's convenient,' she replied, sounding less nervous than she was beginning to feel.

'Come and sit 'ere with me, and let me give you a glass of wine.'

Tiger sat down on the satin-covered *bergère* that stood beside the writing-desk. Mme de Martel-Cluny poured a glass of champagne, handed it silently to Tiger, and sat down once again at her desk. She took a sip of her own drink, then replaced the glass carefully on the blotter. 'I think it is time we 'ave a little talk, my dear,' she said, and smiled, showing her well-preserved teeth, but her smile was far from friendly, and reminded Tiger of the wolf in *Little Red Riding Hood*.

Her heart sank, for she guessed what was coming, but she lifted her chin and looked straight at a point between her employer's eyes. 'Have I done anything to displease you, madame? If I have, I wish you would tell me what it is.'

'Not *displease* exactly, my dear, but I feel it is my duty to warn you that your attachment to my nephew 'as not gone unnotice in this 'ouse.'

Tiger lowered her eyes, and said nothing.

'For a young girl, not yet nineteen, to throw 'erself at a man of Luc's rank and future prospects is not only unwise, but degrading also.'

'Degrading for whom?'

'To yourself, of course. Can you not see that Luc 'as

164

been amusing 'imself with you, nothing more than that? I am surprise that a girl of your intelligence should fail to grasp that there is no possibility of a future alliance between you both. Perhaps it is only correct to tell you that Antoine 'as already warn Luc of the danger inherent in the situation.'

Tiger saw at once that to have a row would inevitably lead to her expulsion from rue Monsieur and a humiliating return to Ireland. She drew a deep breath, and forced herself to smile at the stern woman before her. 'I'm afraid,' she began, in as light a tone as she could produce, 'that you've all got the wrong end of the stick.'

'The stick? What are you talking about? What stick?'

'I mean that you're all under a misapprehension, madame. Luc and I are friends, nothing more, I assure you.' She leaned forward, confidentially. 'If you really want to know, I rather fancy my art master, but he's too poor to take seriously.' She laughed, delighted to have had the wit to turn the tables on her adversary. 'You have to understand that, just like Luc, I have to find a suitably wealthy candidate, if I decide to marry at all.'

'I see.'

'Well, good. Is that all? May I go now?'

If Mme de Martel-Cluny detected a note of insolence in Tiger's voice, she took care not to show it. She smiled, quite kindly. 'After all the 'ospitality we 'ave offer you, Tiger, not to mention the generosity of my 'usband regarding your salary, I am relieve that our trust in you 'as not been abuse. It seems I owe you an apology. I hope we are still friends?'

'Of course.'

Upstairs, in her room, although boiling with rage, Tiger made an enormous effort not to break down in any way, for she knew that it was vital to appear perfectly normal at dinner, if she was to succeed in retaining the moral high ground in respect of her employers' insulting behaviour. Who the hell do they think they are? she asked herself furiously, as she brushed her hair. And what's such a big deal about Luc, may I ask? He's only a provincial solicitor's son, when all's said and done, and he's got no money, he told me so.

She stared at her reflection in the glass, and wondered how Luc had reacted to the equally impertinent advice of his Uncle Antoine. Perhaps he told him to get stuffed, she thought, but deep in her heart, she knew that such a thing was quite improbable. Monsieur was a very senior figure in their mutual field, and Luc would be extremely unlikely to disregard his wishes.

Tiger waited for two days, hoping that Luc would come to rue St-Sulpice and meet her after her life class, but he failed to appear. I suppose he's busy with the apartment, and thinks it a bad idea to leave messages for me at rue Monsieur, she said to herself.

On the Saturday morning, after returning Fanny to the house, she decided to go and see Luc. I'll buy him a house-warming present, she thought; that'll be a perfectly good reason to pay him a visit, won't it? In any case, I don't care; I need to know how it is between us, and whether I can stay with him over Easter.

In rue de Buci, she bought a small pot of thyme, fashionably clipped into a ball, then made her way to Cour de Poitiers. As she approached the house, and stood at the top of the steps down to the basement, she hesitated for a few moments, asking herself whether taking such direct action in order to see Luc could be construed as 'throwing herself at him', in the offensive words of his aunt. Then she remembered their last night together, and what had passed between them. Her legs grew weak at the memory; it was impossible to believe that Luc would wish to break up with her, to dismiss her so quickly from his bed, as well as his life, whatever his Uncle Antoine's advice on the subject.

It was a cold, blustery morning, and she negotiated the slippery wooden steps with prudence. Timidly, she tapped at the door. Then, when no response was forthcoming, she rapped three times with her knuckles, quite hard. After a moment, the door opened, revealing a strange young man, wearing nothing except a towel tied round his loins. *'Bonjour, mademoiselle. Que désirez-vous?'*

It took Tiger less than ten seconds to realize that the stranger was the same young man she had seen with Luc, in *Deux-Magots*, and to draw the obvious conclusion. She held out the pot of thyme. *'S'il vous plaît, donnez celui-ci à Luc, monsieur. Merci bien.'* Then she turned, ran up the steps and hurried away across the *cour* as quickly as she could. She had got as far as the passage du Commerce-St-André when she heard running footsteps behind her, and Luc caught her up. 'Stupid girl, what the hell are you playing at?' He took her arm, forcing her to slow down.

'What the hell are *you* playing at, Luc, is more to the point?' Tiger's voice shook, her throat closed, and she could not prevent the tears of shock and misery from falling. He took her by the shoulders, turning her towards him, took his handkerchief from his coat pocket and, very tenderly, wiped her eyes. 'Don't cry, Tiger, there's no need for this, I promise.'

'There isn't?'

'No, none at all.'

'Who was that guy, Luc? The one in the towel?'

'That's Carl-Heinz. He's a very old friend of mine; he gives me German lessons, in exchange for French.'

I bet he does, said Tiger to herself, coldly. She very nearly said, 'Dressed only in a towel? I don't believe you.' Instead she chose to accept this explanation, so intense was her sudden desire for him. She ached for his kiss, for the touch his hands on her breasts, and above all, longed to feel him inside her.

'OK now?' he asked.

'OK.'

'Let's have coffee, or some lunch, shall we? What about *Le Petit Zinc*? It's just round the corner.'

Tiger drew a deep shuddering breath. 'As a matter of fact, I'd rather buy something in the market, and have lunch at the apartment, if that's not inconvenient?'

Luc, after a second's hesitation, agreed. 'Fine, if you don't mind the place being fairly untidy.'

'Of course I don't mind. Why on earth should I? I'm not your mother, Luc.'

'Right. Let's go.'

They shopped in the *marché*, then bought some wine, bread, and a bunch of papery-thin white narcissi, sharply fragrant in the wintry air. At Luc's insistence, they drank coffee in a crowded café, then walked slowly back to Cour de Poitiers.

The apartment was empty, but the faint smell of bath essence hung in the air. The studio was perfectly tidy, and several new pieces had been installed since Tiger's last visit. She sat down in the shabby old *bergère*, and looked around. In the courtyard stood a blue-painted metal table, and four matching chairs. 'They're perfect, Luc,' she said. 'Exactly right. Where did you find them?'

'Clignancourt, as a matter of fact.'

'Oh. Is that a good place for old furniture? I thought you didn't really like fleamarket tat?'

'This isn't *tat*, Tiger. Carl-Heinz has a friend who is a genius at tracking down these things. He finds them in country auctions, places like that, then sells them in his shop in Clignancourt.'

'Oh, right.'

'Can I give you a drink, while I get lunch?'

'Let me help.'

'No, it's OK; it'll only take a moment.'

Taking the shopping with him, Luc went to the kitchen. In a moment he came back, carrying a glass of a milky liquid. 'Pastis,' he said. 'It'll warm you up.'

Sensing that he did not wish her to follow him to the kitchen, Tiger remained where she was, taking small sips of the anise-flavoured drink, wondering whether she was walking straight into a trap, and was allowing Luc to make a fool of her. Why am I here? she asked herself, trying to remember what had been the purpose of her visit in the first place.

One of the new additions to the studio was a beautiful red lacquer table, long and low, standing on a sea-grass rug, in front of the daybed. When Luc returned, carrying a tray, he put it down on the red table. He took from the daybed two fat cushions made from recycled Aubusson carpets, and placed them on the floor, one either side of the table.

'Come and eat, Tiger.'

'Yes, OK. Thanks.'

They ate the mountain ham, the cheese, the bread and the soft semi-dried figs, and drank quite a lot of cold white wine. Although the wine raised her spirits and made her feel more relaxed, Tiger felt herself to be under a vague cloud, as though she had made a childish blunder by seeking Luc out in the first place, and then compounded it by insisting on having lunch at the apartment. He, too, seemed preoccupied, and disinclined to amuse her with his usual flow of jokes and chat.

When they had finished eating, Luc took the tray to the kitchen, and returned with a pot of coffee. Rather silently, they drank the coffee, and then, to Tiger's astonishment, he took her by the hand, led her to the daybed, and began to unbutton her shirt. Her strong instinct was to protest, to push him away, to tell him to get lost, but she could not, and to her shame, she allowed him to take off all her clothes and make love to her, right there in the cold light of day, both of them naked on the daybed. It was the best sex they had ever had together, and afterwards she lay in his arms, absolutely convinced that she had been mistaken to doubt him for a second.

*　　*　　*

At three o'clock, Luc looked at his watch. 'I have to go out, Tiger. I have an appointment. I hope you don't mind?'

'No, of course not. I'm sorry, Luc, I had no idea.' Quickly, she got dressed, brushed her hair, and put on her cloak, while he remained on the daybed, watching her. She picked up her bag, preparing to leave, then remembered her original reason for coming. 'By the way, Luc,' she said, 'I was wondering. The family are going to the country for Easter, and since I don't particularly want to go to Ireland, could I perhaps spend the holiday with you?'

He had not stirred from his position, but lay indolently on the daybed, his hands behind his head, smiling. 'I'm afraid that won't be possible, Tiger, though nothing would give me greater pleasure, another time.' He looked at her, his pale blue eyes gentle, candid. 'You see, I'll be away for Easter. I'm going to Hamburg with Carl-Heinz.'

For a long moment, Tiger stared at him with disbelief, then she turned on her heel and ran from the apartment.

CHAPTER NINE

It was raining hard in Cour de Poitiers. Tiger did not stop to take shelter in the covered arcade of the passage du Commerce-St-André, but ran, half blinded by her tears, all the way to rue St-Sulpice. Since it was completely out of the question that she could return to rue Monsieur in her present state, Tadeusz seemed the only refuge available to her. She tried the door to the ecclesiastical emporium, and to her relief, it opened. Quietly, sketching a tight little smile at the owner of the shop, she passed through to the studio.

Tadeusz was at work, and looked up, surprised, when she entered. 'Good heavens!' he exclaimed. 'You look like Ondine, Tiger! Half drowned. Is anything the matter?'

'Everything's the matter!' She burst into fresh, hysterical sobs.

'Shit!' exclaimed Tadeusz. He put down his brush, and crossed the room to her side. 'Come on, take off these wet things, and come by the stove. I'll make you some tea.'

'I'm not getting undressed again, Tadeusz!' she yelled angrily. 'Not for you, not for anyone!'

'Come over here and sit down, will you? And shut up, for Christ's sake! The old boy will think I'm raping you or something.'

Tadeusz pulled two chairs close to the stove. Tiger

took off her wet cloak, dropping it on the floor, then sat down, still shivering and snivelling forlornly. He picked up the sodden cloak and draped it over an easel to dry, then disappeared behind the screen. Tiger could hear him filling the kettle; rattling the tea things. In a few moments he returned, carrying two glasses, each heavily sugared and spiked with a slice of lemon. He sat down beside her and handed her a glass of tea. Then he drank his own, and waited for her to tell him why she had been so upset.

Tiger drank her tea thoughtfully. Now that she had had time to recover slightly from her initial reaction in respect of Luc's cruelty, she found herself extremely disinclined to give Tadeusz a blow-by-blow account of her recent and ill-advised sexual activities. Sitting beside the stove, the hem of her skirt gently steaming, soothed both by the tea and by Tadeusz's uninquisitive company, she began to see very clearly that to blurt out the humiliating truth would achieve nothing, and be painful to them both. So after a few minutes, she handed him her empty glass, and tried to smile. 'Sorry about that, Tadeusz. I disturbed your work. I'm OK now. Thanks for the tea.'

'My pleasure.'

'I was in a rage because my sister wants me to go to Ireland and help out over Easter, and I don't want to go. It's a pain, because I can't stay at rue Monsieur, when they go to the country. It's more than a pain, actually; it's a bloody nuisance.' Covertly, Tiger studied Tadeusz, as he bent down to pull out the ash-pan in order to increase the draught in the stove.

He straightened his back and smiled at her. 'I'm going to Przywnica for Easter, to stay with my grand-mother. You could come with me, if you'd like to. What do you say?'

Tiger smiled at him. 'I say thank you very much, Tadeusz. I'd love to, if you're sure that's all right?'

'Yes, of course. It's pretty basic there, but there's no shortage of rooms.'

'When would we go?' she asked.

'I was planning to leave on Wednesday of next week. It'll take two days to get there, on the old bike.'

'So your parents won't be going?'

'No. There'll just be us, and my granny.'

'I see.'

Tadeusz smiled. 'Is that a problem?'

Tiger felt herself growing red, and lifted her chin proudly. 'No, of course not. Why should it be?' She laughed. 'I'm sure your granny will be an excellent chaperone.'

'I've no doubt at all that she will be, more's the pity!'

Impulsively, Tiger stood up and put her hand on his shoulder. 'If you've nothing better to do, Tadeusz, let's go and buy a take-away and a bottle of wine. I'll pay, of course. I'm starving, aren't you?'

Returning to rue Monsieur that evening, late, Tiger saw that the lights were on in the salon, and would have given a great deal to have entered the room and advised Mme de Martel-Cluny that it would doubtless relieve her mind to learn that she, Tiger, would be spending the Easter holiday with her art master's family in Poland, so that any lingering fears she might have concerning Luc Marcassin would be misplaced. Instead, and prudently, she went quietly upstairs to her own room, and to bed.

Poland was a revelation to Tiger. After a long and very tiring journey on the motorbike, broken by an uncomfortable night-stop in a seedy guest-house, they arrived in Cracow in mid-morning. Tadeusz drove slowly through narrow medieval streets to the centre of town, the ancient market place, Rynek Główny. Deciding that they needed a morale-boosting treat after the rigours of the trip, he took Tiger to have breakfast at a famous art nouveau institution, the elegant Café Nóworolski, overlooking the enormous medieval square, which was

173

bathed in warm spring sunshine, and busy with market traders.

The café was a haven of velvety luxury, decorated with exuberantly patterned wallpaper and gilding, and they were shown to a marble-topped corner table, encircled by a deeply padded plush bench. A pretty waitress brought a pot of steaming hot coffee and a plate of delicious-looking cakes. As an afterthought, Tadeusz ordered two very small glasses of vodka. 'We deserve it,' he said.

After breakfast, they walked across the Rynek Główny and explored the vast former Cloth Hall, magnificently vaulted and arcaded, and now home to the workshops and boutiques of artisans of every description. Some of the stuff on sale was beautiful as well as functional, but the bulk of it seemed to Tiger in rather poor taste, and clearly aimed at the tourist trade. 'What else can they do, poor sods?' Tadeusz said. 'It's a question of making a living, isn't it? Paying the bloody rent, Tiger.'

'Yes, of course.'

'Come on, let's go home.'

They took the E40 out of Cracow, in the direction of Tarnów, and were very soon riding through an intensely cultivated valley, its upper slopes covered in dense forest, the crests of far-distant hills a pale translucent blue. On either side of the valley rose long strips of cultivated fields, some green with new spring grass, some still brown, their crops not yet showing visible growth. On the far side of the valley Tiger was surprised to see a horse-drawn harrow, driven by a young man, toiling slowly up a narrow field. On the hillside above him, a small hamlet of picturesque wooden houses clung to the steep contours of the land. They looked as though they had been there for centuries, huddled together, their open wooden galleries looking out over the valley below.

After about twenty minutes, Tadeusz turned into a

minor road, almost a lane, which followed a small stream bordered with willows, already in pale early leaf. The grass on either side of the lane and under the willows was thick with the yellow stars of celandine and windflowers. This could quite easily be Ireland, said Tiger to herself.

After a couple of kilometres, they passed a horse-drawn two-wheeled cart, travelling in the opposite direction. The driver, an elderly man with a tanned and wrinkled face, raised his hat, smiling at them as they passed. Tadeusz shouted a greeting in Polish, that sounded to Tiger like 'Jane Dobray!', and the man laughed and waved his hat in response.

The lane became steeper and narrower and soon they found themselves bumping along a bridlepath under the dappled shade of a small birch wood. The pale sun sent shafts of shimmering light through the branches, illuminating the drifting lakes of bluebells, already half open beneath the trees.

The birches began to thin out, and Tadeusz stopped the motorbike. Before them stood a pair of rusting iron gates, wide open, one of them tilted sideways on its broken hinge. Still attached to the centre of each gate was a coat of arms. A long, low building stood at the end of a poorly maintained drive, flanked on both sides by fields of emerging crops. The land had been cultivated right up to the front of the house. 'This is it, Tiger,' said Tadeusz quietly. 'Welcome to Przywnica.'

Tiger got off the pillion, and looked around her, at the fields of early peas and burgeoning maize that engulfed the house. She frowned. 'Does your grandmother grow all this stuff, Tadeusz?'

Tadeusz laughed, and shook his head. 'I wish she was in a position to do so,' he said. 'Didn't I tell you, Tiger? The land belongs to our former tenant farmers now, every last centimetre of it, and has done since the Communists grabbed it in 1945, after my grandfather was killed in the war, and my dad was just a baby boy.'

175

'Yes, of course, I remember. God, Tadeusz, how awful!'

'Not really. I expect the old feudal system was terribly unfair, if one is honest about it. It's wrong that one family should own thousands of hectares of land, and the peasants nothing at all they could feel secure about. They had the use of the land attached to their tied farmhouses, but they could be evicted without notice, if the landowner chose to exercise his rights.'

'Still, pretty tough on your poor grandmother, wasn't it? How does she manage, now?'

'She grows vegetables and fruit, and raises a few pigs and chickens in the garden. She goes to the market in Cracow to sell the surplus, just as she has done since she lost the bulk of the land.'

'Really? She must be a pretty amazing woman! How old is she, now?'

'Seventy-nine, eighty, something like that.'

'Wow!'

'Come on; we'll go and find her.'

They drove very slowly up the drive towards the house. Tiger saw that the building appeared to be constructed entirely of wood; even the roof was covered in silvery weathered shingles. Brick chimneys rose into the air at either end of the house, and on one of them a pair of storks was engaged in building an untidy nest of twiggy branches. It was the first time Tiger had seen these beautiful birds, and as Tadeusz came to rest beside the porticoed entrance, she was enchanted to hear the percussive clacking of their red beaks, breaking the profound silence that surrounded that remote and sunlit place.

The double front doors stood open. They dismounted, and Tadeusz heaved the bike onto its stand. They went into the house together, and immediately Tiger saw that in spite of the misfortunes that had overtaken its owners, their ancestral home was still beautiful, if appallingly neglected. They stood in a central hall, bare and white, with a wooden staircase leading to an upper floor. On the walls rectangular dirty lines bore witness to the occasional decision to sell a painting or a mirror. On either side of the hall, panelled pine doors, unpainted but with handsome brass fittings, stood open to reveal a long enfilade of rooms.

The floor of the hall was badly in need of cleaning, and was covered in tatters of blown straw and bits of mud tracked in on someone's dirty boots. On the back wall, another door stood open and gave onto a sunny courtyard. Through this door cohorts of swallows flew in and out, swerving to avoid the newcomers as they came and went. Tadeusz laughed. 'The old girl's off her trolley! She likes these bloody birds to make their nests in the house; it's a good luck thing with her, crazy woman!'

'Don't they make a terrible mess?'

'They do.'

They went outside, and Tiger realized that the size of the house was much greater than she had at first supposed, for in addition to the main section of the building, two further wings extended to form three sides of a courtyard. Facing them and filling the fourth side of the enclosure was a range of ugly timber sheds. According to Tadeusz, these shacks had replaced the original stable-block, destroyed by the Communists in 1945. Most of them appeared to be shut up, but two or three showed signs of occupation, housing bales of straw, garden tools and the like. One of them was being used as a tack-room, and sheltered an old-fashioned trap, some harness and a couple of mouldering saddles.

Tadeusz led the way through a narrow door at the back, which gave onto a small vegetable garden, fenced with stout chestnut paling. At one end, a wired-off muddy area was home to some chickens and a couple of black pigs. At the other end, beyond the rows of neatly tended vegetables, an elderly woman was

177

balanced on a rickety-looking stepladder. Exceptionally thin, her grey hair covered by a blue kerchief, she wore a stout sacking apron over dungarees, which were tucked into hessian boots. She was engaged in cutting back the fruiting spurs of an ancient fig tree. Tadeusz called her name softly. She turned her head and burst into an incomprehensible volley of speech at the sight of her grandson, to which he responded with equal animation.

With surprising agility, she came down from the ladder, and Tadeusz kissed first her hands and then her cheeks, in the old-fashioned courteous way of his grandmother's upbringing. Then they turned towards Tiger, switched politely into French and the introductions were made.

'It is very kind of you to allow me to come, Baroness,' said Tiger, shaking hands.

'Call me Ileana, please, my dear young lady. Here, everyone is on first-name terms. The old titles are gone now, and we are all peasants, it seems. It makes life a good deal simpler, as a matter of fact.'

'Yes, of course. I will, if that's what you like.'

'Come into the house; I've got some soup on the stove. I'll finish this later.'

She put her secateurs into the deep pocket of her rugged apron, and they followed her back to the house. In the hall, she turned left and led the way through the former dining-room, now reduced to a table and six chairs, to the kitchen.

Here, Tiger was relieved to see that the old lady was still in possession of some of the family's original domestic equipment. A magnificent stove, covered in blue glazed tiles, stood against one wall, its chimney disappearing through a large copper hood suspended from the ceiling above. Its surface was crowded with heavy old metal stockpots and stewpans, and a black iron casserole stood on a hotplate, keeping warm. The walls of the room were fitted with wooden shelves, on which were displayed dozens of mismatched eighteenth-century dinner plates, delicately patterned with flower motifs, and with scrolled rims. Rarely, if ever, used, and therefore visibly disfigured with the grime and grease of decades of cooking, it was none the less clear to Tiger that they were valuable as well as beautiful, and she silently rejoiced that they had not gone to Barbizon, in the wake of so much else from that crumbling family home.

A stone sink stood beneath a small cobwebby window, overlooking the long strips of growing crops outside. From the draining board Ileana took plates and bowls, and put them on the oilcloth-covered table that stood close to the stove. She filled the bowls with hot thick soup, instructing Tadeusz to get the loaf from the crock under the sink. This he did, bringing spoons and knives at the same time. They pulled wooden three-legged stools from beneath the table and sat down.

The soup did not look particularly appetizing, since it was of an insipid colour and appeared to consist largely of cabbage and chickpeas. However, its heavy flavouring of dill and the presence of slices of a strongly flavoured sausage called *zywiecka* turned a rather ordinary-looking dish into something delicious and filling. With the thick slices of strong rye bread, it was a complete meal in itself.

'Now you are here, Tadeusz,' said Ileana, patting his hand affectionately, 'I must make more of an effort with the food, and prepare some real Polish dishes for you and your friend.'

Tiger smiled. 'I had a wonderful dish at Barbizon,' she said. 'What was it called, Tadeusz? Big something?'

'*Bigós*,' Tadeusz replied. 'It means hunter's stew.'

'Renata is a very accomplished cook, but of course she is mostly preparing traditional kosher dishes, isn't she?' The old lady looked from one to the other of her guests, her still beautiful pale blue eyes bland, a slight smile twitching the corners of her smooth thin lips.

So that's the way the wind blows, said Tiger to

herself, not needing to be told that Ileana had never ceased to resent the fact that her daughter-in-law's Jewish background had been the cause of her son's virtual removal from Poland, and from her life.

'As a matter of fact, Baba,' said Tadeusz quietly, 'Mum cooks mostly French nowadays, and classic Polish on special days.'

'Oh, well, it seems I'm mistaken. Of course, you see much more of them than I do, so you are in a position to know, my dear boy.' She turned to Tiger. 'Can I offer you anything else, Tiger? Some ginger cake, *katarzynki*, perhaps?'

'Thank you,' Tiger said hastily, 'but no thanks, I'm absolutely full with your beautiful soup. It was quite delicious.'

'I'm glad you enjoyed it.' Ileana laughed, showing small ivory-coloured teeth, quite aware that she had ruffled Tadeusz's feathers, and not giving a damn. 'What about some coffee?' she offered.

'I'll get it.' Tadeusz got up swiftly, before she could object, and pushed the heavy kettle over the hotplate.

After the coffee, Ileana returned to her garden, leaving Tadeusz and Tiger to wash up. Tadeusz remained silent while they performed this chore, clearly embarrassed and upset by his grandmother's racist remarks concerning his mother.

Tiger hung up her damp tea towel, then stood close to Tadeusz as he rinsed out the sink, brushing away the water with a bundle of twigs. 'Forget it, Tadeusz,' she said softly. 'They're all the same.'

'Who're all the same?'

'Old people, of course. One loves them, but they're quite bad-tempered and bitchy, deep down, silly old farts!'

Tadeusz laughed. 'Do you really think so? I bet yours isn't, Tiger.'

'My granny O'Neill is dead, trampled to death by a horse, poor old thing, and I've never met my grandmother Fitzgerald. But my *mum* is a *nutcase*, absolutely. She's got something called Alzheimer's disease, which means that sometimes she gets really stroppy and violent, and scares the hell out of everyone who tries to help her. Other times, she just stares at the telly, or falls asleep in the middle of her meals, things like that. She even takes her clothes off and runs around the house naked, which is not a pretty sight, believe me.'

'My God, how ghastly,' said Tadeusz, and gazed at Tiger, his dark eyes full of sorrow. 'Terrible for her, poor woman, but probably even more terrible for the carers. Who looks after her, Tiger?'

'My sister Niamh does officially, but mostly it's a rather terrific old bloke called Liam, who's been with the O'Neills for ever. He used to be a stable-lad, but now he's Mum's nursemaid, to all intents and purposes.' Tiger touched Tadeusz's cheek, and laughed. 'So, if you think you've got problems with your family, just remind yourself of mine, OK?'

Tadeusz put his arms round Tiger and gave her a hard hug. 'You're a very good child, Tiger, and a wise one, too. Come on, let's go out, shall we?'

'Less of the child, please. Aren't you going to show me the rest of the house?'

'There's not much to see, except empty rooms.'

'There must be something. What about the mule in your great-grandfather's library? Isn't that what you told me?'

Tadeusz laughed. 'Yes, it is. Poor old Tod; let's go and check him out, shall we?'

They returned to the hall, and then approached the second enfilade of rooms. These still retained some aspects of their former glory, largely on account of the massive Biedermeier furniture that had been installed at Przywnica at the insistence of a fashionable young Hungarian bride in 1815. Chief among these acquisitions had been a large circular table made of blond

181

wood, supported by a thick single column, which stood in the centre of the second room, carrying on its surface a large oil lamp of the same period, several thick leather-bound books and an assortment of silver-framed family photographs. Milosz and Renata had, unfortunately, taken the set of matching chairs that had stood round the table for more than a hundred and fifty years, but had been unable to find a way of removing the huge and heavy table itself without special equipment.

'It's beautiful,' said Tiger. 'What lovely wood.' She touched the honey-coloured tabletop with a tentative finger, leaving a clean stripe in the dusty surface. 'Oh, shit, look what I've done! She'll think I did it on purpose, to show her up.'

'No, she won't. She won't even notice. She doesn't wear her specs, so there's a lot she doesn't see.'

'Just as well.'

'Mm.'

In the next room, there was little to be seen except a grand piano covered in a faded plum-coloured fringed cloth. The walls bore trophies of the former hunting activities of the Marylskis, in the shape of many mounted antlers, and the stuffed head of a brown bear. The guns and scimitars that had also hung on the walls had long since been sold. 'It's necessary, of course,' said Tadeusz. 'But sad, all the same. It's funny, in Paris I never think about it, or not much, but when I'm here, I regret the chucking out of everything my people stood for.'

'I'm not surprised. I'd hate it if everything had been hijacked from Neill's Court.' Suddenly, the memory of her midnight robbery of her own grandmother's emeralds smote Tiger's conscience, and she winced. Yes, well, she told herself firmly. That was for a really good reason, wasn't it? Saving Niamh's bacon. Then the gloomy truth stared her in the face. The situation here is just the same; they need the money badly. It's a question of survival, isn't it?

They continued their inspection of the plundered rooms, until, finally, they turned the corner of the house, passed through two completely empty rooms with French windows giving onto the courtyard, and entered the former library, pushing open the door with difficulty, on account of the thick bed of straw that covered the floor. The library shelves had been completely gutted and now carried nothing except a few bottles of hoof oil, some colic mixture and a curry comb. Tethered to an iron ring and gazing morosely through the French windows stood a large brown mule, resting one rear foot. As they forced their way into his extraordinary stable, the animal twitched an ear but did not even look in their direction. The place smelled pretty terrible, on account of the mule having made a recent contribution to the fetid straw in which he stood.

'Poor old bugger,' said Tadeusz. 'Not much of a life, is it? Shut in here, and only getting out once a week when Baba goes into town?'

'Why is he in here, anyway, Tadeusz? I should have thought that he'd be better off in one of the sheds. Nearer the tack-room, too?'

'Well, it's probably a question of habit with Baba. You see, after the horses were confiscated and the stables burned down to teach the Marylskis a lesson, they allowed her to keep an old pony, and I imagine at the time she chose this room as being quite a sensible place to keep him, so, over the years, the library became a stable. After the pony died, she bought a mule, cheaper than a pony, and she's had them ever since. Slowly, one by one, she put up the sheds, but I guess she reckons that Tod's better off in here. It's certainly less cold in winter.'

'Yes, that makes sense, I suppose. Poor old Tod. Perhaps we could take him out for a spin?'

'Better ask Baba.'

'Yes, of course.'

They found Ileana in the vegetable garden, still

pruning her fig. 'Good,' she said. 'You can help me gather the stuff for market. Tomorrow is my day. I have to leave at dawn, to be sure of my pitch.'

Glad to help, they obeyed Ileana's precise instructions, and filled the straw baskets with cabbages, and early salad greens from the old-fashioned glass cloches that protected the carefully tended rows of growing crops. Under her guidance, they extracted potatoes and carrots from their winter clamps of sand, and made up bunches of herbs: parsley, thyme and bay, tied with string.

When they had finished, and had carried the baskets to the hall, ready for packing into the trap, Ileana went to the kitchen to put on the kettle. As soon as she had disappeared, Tiger turned to Tadeusz. 'I'm dying for a pee,' she hissed urgently. 'You people must have bladders of steel. Where's the loo, for heaven's sake?'

'Sorry!' said Tadeusz, grinning. 'How rude of me! Come on, grab your bag, and I'll show you.'

They climbed the wooden stairs, and he pointed out the bathroom door. 'There,' he said, 'and your room is two doors further on, next to mine. I'll dump your bag for you.'

The bathroom turned out to be not only excellently functional, with running water and a proper lavatory with a wide mahogany seat, but extremely pretty, too. Frilled white curtains blew in the soft breeze that flowed through the open window, and the air was full of the scent of some unidentified blossom. A green plant grew on the window sill, and pale blue monogrammed towels were arranged on a white-painted towel horse. On a flowered soap dish stood a large cake of raspberry-coloured soap, translucent and smelling of roses, as Tiger discovered as she washed her hands, and splashed water on her dusty face.

In her bedroom, plain and white, like every other room, and furnished with an iron hospital-type bed and a small chest of drawers, she went at once to the open window, looking out over the confiscated land, to the woodland beyond. In the distance, the blue peaks of the far horizon seemed to dissolve into a rose-tinted sky. The sun was already setting behind the house, casting a long lavender-coloured shadow beneath her window. All around, the twitterings of roosting birds filled the air. The storks had ceased to clatter their beaks, and seemed to have settled down for the approaching evening. In the woods, a cuckoo called.

Feeling refreshed by her wash, but still tired and dusty after the long drive and the afternoon's toil among the vegetables, Tiger opened her bag and took out a clean white shirt, and her red *gitane* skirt. Thankfully, she pulled off her trousers, shook them out of the window, then hung them over the end of the bed. She took off the T-shirt she had been wearing for three days, and stuffed it into her grip. Then she sat on the broad window sill and brushed her hair as hard as she could, hoping to remove some of the dust that clung to it. After a few minutes, there was a tap on the door.

'Hang on a tick, Tadeusz. I'm just changing.'

Quickly, she dressed herself in the clean blouse and flounced red skirt. 'OK, you can come in,' she called, swiftly buttoning up her shirt.

Tadeusz put his head round the door, then came into the room. Tiger fastened the last button, then looked up, and what she saw gave her such a surprise that she was completely bereft of speech. Tadeusz was wearing a most beautiful fine linen shirt, its big sleeves pleated into a deep cuff, and part of the front intricately embroidered in indigo thread. With the shirt he wore wide black trousers, pleated from the waist and falling straight to his ankles, so that it looked like a skirt, until he moved. Tiger was astonished by the transformation in his appearance. Gone was the shambolic, untidy and depressed-looking creature she had become accustomed to, and in his place stood a man who looked about a foot taller, his dark head held high, and with a confident expression on his face. 'Tadeusz!' she exclaimed, breathlessly. 'You look absolutely wonderful! Where did you get these clothes?'

'They're very old, and they belonged to my great-grandfather, Baba's dad. *His* mother's family home was in the High Tatra, so these things are probably Hungarian work clothes, handed down from father to son.'

'They're beautiful, Tadeusz. Aren't you afraid of spoiling them?'

'I've got loads of them; a trunkful, in fact; some of them much grander than these. These are just everyday gear, comfortable and loose, and never seem to get worn out; I always use them when I'm staying here. They're perfect for riding, too.'

'Riding? Can you ride here?'

'There's a chap I know, who has a place quite near. He's a successful businessman, and he's got a few nice Arabs, lucky man. He's very good about letting you take them out, if he thinks you know what you're doing.'

'And do you know what you're doing, Tadeusz?'

Tadeusz smiled, and his usually sad face was transformed, as if a candle had been lit inside his skull. 'How could I not, with my little drop of Hungarian blood? What about you?'

'Well, I could ride before I could walk,' said Tiger, grinning. 'So I reckon I'd probably give you a run for your money.'

'You're on! Come on, let's go down and have tea.'

Later that night, Ileana lay in her bed, staring through the open window at the starry sky, remembering her lost youth, her magical childhood and joyful adolescence, before the horrors of war had torn apart for ever the lives of everyone who had lived through the false enchantment of the golden years of the Thirties.

As it always did, the sight of Tadeusz in her father's clothes had made her heart leap and filled her with happiness. Her own son, Milosz, seemed disinclined to take any pride in his Hungarian ancestry, frequently reminding her of that country's somewhat ignoble alignment with the Nazis during the war. He had been strongly of the opinion that ancient glories were best forgotten; that real life, the here and now, was the only thing that mattered. All very well for *him*, said Ileana to herself grimly, but it's *my* family treasures he's flogging to make a living, along with the junk he buys from the peasants, or rather, *steals*, in my opinion.

She turned her head and looked at the photo that stood on her night table, shadowy in the dim starlight. The face of her dead young husband gazed back at her, a smiling ghost. In his Polish Army uniform, he looked handsome and courageous, a man, but his light eyes and floppy blond hair were those of a boy. It's bizarre that Milosz is so much older, now, than his father was when he was killed, she thought; more than twice his age, in fact.

It had always been a source of intense regret to Ileana that Milosz had married Renata, and especially that Tadeusz should have inherited his mother's dark looks, instead of those of his Polish family. Although careful never to reveal her own sacred blood ties to strangers, and aware of the terrible fate that had overtaken the Hungarian Jews towards the end of the war, Ileana none the less refused to believe that her deepest instincts were false, entirely repulsive and incorrigibly racist. In her heart, and with passion, she lusted after the old privileged ways. To her, clinging to the ruins of Przywnica was not simply an option, it was a duty to her class. She sighed, turned on her side and closed her eyes, willing herself to sleep, for she would have to rise at dawn in order to reach Cracow in good time.

Ileana crept out of bed long before dawn, and went quietly down to the kitchen, where she put wood into the still burning stove and reheated the coffee. She swallowed a mugful when it was scarcely warm, and went at once to the courtyard. Here, she unlatched the door to the tack-room and dragged the trap out into the yard. Then she went back into the house to fetch Tod, leading him out through the French windows to the waiting trap, where she commanded him to stay. She put the harness on him, then backed him between the shafts. The mule stood motionless throughout this familiar ritual, giving no clue as to his feelings on the subject, and displaying little interest in the proceedings. The buckles all fastened tightly, Ileana led him through the double doors into the hall, where she loaded up the baskets of produce. Finally, she led the mule through the wide-open front doors, and climbed into the trap herself. She gathered up the reins, gave Tod a sharp flick on his rump and he shambled off down the drive, towards the familiar Cracow road.

Tadeusz and Tiger spent a lazy morning, delighted to have the place to themselves, and after making a telephone call to his well-heeled neighbour, and being given permission to take out the horses, they prepared to mount the bike and drive over to the stables.

'There's only one thing, Tadeusz. I can't really ride in this skirt, I'd better put on my dirty trousers.'

'I've got a better idea. I'll lend you some of mine.'

'You mean like the ones you're wearing?'

'Any problem with that?'

'No, none at all.'

They ran upstairs, Tadeusz produced the shirt and pants from his room, and gave them to Tiger. 'I'll wait for you, in the hall.'

'OK, fine.'

The shirt was baggy and big on her, but the pleated trousers were perfect, on account of her height. Delighted, she ran downstairs to join Tadeusz, as he stood waiting in the hall. 'What do you think?' she asked, spreading her arms wide, laughing.

'You look good.'

*   *   *

It took scarcely a quarter of an hour to reach their destination, and in another ten minutes they were mounted on two beautiful Arab horses, both chestnuts, one a mare and the other a gelding. They rode sedately along the bridlepath through the woods, side by side, talking quietly, taking care not to disturb the wildlife whose peaceful habitat it was. On the other side of the woods, they emerged onto a green hillside, brilliant with yellow dandelions. Quite close to them, a flock of sheep and goats grazed, tended by a solitary shepherd, who, in spite of the warm weather, wore a sheepskin coat and a flat felt hat.

Keeping their distance from the flock, Tadeusz put his heels to his horse's flanks and they broke into a trot and then a canter. Sitting well down in the saddle, and taking a firm grip with her knees, Tiger followed him up the gentle slope of the hillside, her long hair streaming out behind her, her eyes half closed, as she dodged the occasional lumps of earth thrown up by Tadeusz's horse.

When they reached the top of the hill, they came slowly to a halt at the edge of a thick pine forest, its black trees tightly packed, dark and sinister. They looked around them, down the long hill that they had climbed, over the pale green woodland to the valley where Przywnica stood, lonely, surrounded by its unglamorous market gardens. They dismounted, hitching the reins to a low branch of a tree, loosening the girths, and allowing the horses to graze at the grassy edges of the forest. Tiger lay down on her stomach, her chin resting on her hands, and Tadeusz stretched out at her side, lying on his back, his hands beneath his head.

After a moment she looked at him, smiling. 'What a beautiful country this is,' she said. 'I had no idea it was so vast, somehow, or had such a turbulent history. It's full of surprises, like you.'

'Like me?'

'Yes, like you. You're quite a different person here,

not at all like you are in Paris. Why do you suppose that is?'

'Perhaps because here I am at home, and not a stranger in a foreign land.'

'But you were born in Paris, weren't you? You're French. France is your home, isn't it?'

'I don't feel it so, Tiger. This is where I feel at home. I feel I belong here. I wish I could live here, more than anything. But how to make a living; pay the taxes; look after Przywnica and Baba, that's the problem.'

'You could always do the same thing as your parents, couldn't you?'

'No, I couldn't.'

'Why not?'

'Because.'

'Why because?'

'For Christ's sake stop nagging me, Tiger.'

'I'm sorry! I didn't know I was!'

He rolled over onto his stomach and put his hand on her cheek, very tenderly. 'Of course you didn't. It's I who should apologize, not you.'

Unexpectedly, tears filled Tiger's eyes and spilled over, making lines through the dust on her cheeks.

'Please don't cry. I didn't mean to upset you.' Carefully he wiped away the tears, then took her face in his hands and kissed her, but not at all in his former predatory fashion. His embrace was both gentle and exploratory, as if he were asking her an important question. Tiger rolled onto her back, folded her arms round his neck, and gave him the answer he sought.

In the late afternoon, as they rode quietly back to the stables, side by side, Tadeusz took her hand and pressed it to his lips. 'Are you sure about this, Tiger?' he asked quietly. 'What about your friend Luc? I had the idea that you and he were an item?'

'You're wrong, Tadeusz,' she replied, rather sharply, but she did not withdraw her hand. 'He's just my employer's nephew, that's all.'

'Really all?'

'Yes, of course. Luc's a conceited oaf; I don't even like him, much.'

'Well, good. That's a relief.'

When they got back to Przywnica, Ileana had already returned and was in the process of unhitching Tod from the trap. The two young people ran to help her, and Tadeusz took the sweating mule back to his stable, while Tiger and Ileana pushed the trap back into its shed. The old woman was in a good humour, for she had sold everything and the baskets were empty. 'Look,' she said, 'I got you both some decorated eggs for Easter. I hope you're not too grown-up for such stuff, Tiger?'

'No,' Tiger replied seriously. 'I'll never be too old for Easter eggs.'

Ileana unwrapped a paper package, and showed Tiger the pretty eggs, elaborately painted in primary colours, in the traditional patterns of the area. 'Hungarian ones are better, of course,' she said, 'but these aren't bad, are they?'

'They're lovely,' said Tiger. 'Thank you very much indeed. How kind of you.'

Ileana looked at Tiger, closely examining her clothes. 'Have you been riding with Tadeusz?' she asked.

'Yes, I have.'

'I thought so.'

They spent a happy evening together, Ileana allowing them to prepare the supper under her instructions, as she sat at the table, drinking vodka. Tiger could not help noticing that the contents of the bottle were disappearing pretty fast, although neither Ileana or Tadeusz appeared in the least drunk.

At nine o'clock, they sat down to eat the *pierogi* that Ileana had bought, ready made, in the market. These were a kind of raw dumpling, the dough having been wrapped around a filling of cheese and spinach.

Tadeusz cooked this traditional delicacy in boiling salted water, then draining them carefully, and tossing them in melted butter. They tasted wonderful; delicious.

It had been a long day for them all, and they went to bed before half past ten. Tiger lay in her bed, and thought about Tadeusz. She was amazed at the change in his entire personality that had taken place since their arrival in Poland. Her old reservations about him seemed to slip away, and she now regarded him in a much more sympathetic light, a difficult but curiously appealing man, stubbornly attached to his roots.

Briefly, she turned her attention to Luc, expecting to feel the familiar sensations of pain in respect of the humiliation she had endured at his hands, but, to her surprise, she felt nothing at all, not even anger.

She slept for a while, then was woken by the light of the moon, as it streamed through her window and made a ghostly path across her bed. She had no idea what the time was, but guessed it must be about three o'clock. She felt a sudden urgent need to feel the strong arms of Tadeusz around her again, to feel his warm body close to hers. Silently, she slipped from her bed, and stole along the corridor to his room. She closed the door very quietly behind her, and crossed the floor on bare feet until she stood, shivering slightly, beside his bed. 'May I get into bed with you, Tadeusz? I'm cold, and lonely by myself.'

She could see his that his eyes were open, and seemed like dark pools in his thin face as he lay on his pillow. He turned back the sheet. 'Get in, my darling,' he said softly.

CHAPTER TEN

On Easter Monday, Tadeusz and Tiger said goodbye to Ileana and began their slow journey back to Paris. They arrived on Wednesday evening, cold and wet, for the weather had deteriorated as soon as they crossed the German border. In rue Monsieur, Tiger dismounted stiffly from the bike, and unstrapped her grip. She smiled wanly, and thanked Tadeusz for his kindness in taking her to Przywnica. 'It was good; I really loved it,' she said.

'Me, too. See you tomorrow, for the class?'

'Sure. Good night, Tadeusz. Thanks again.'

Tiger was quite relieved to find that the family had not yet returned from the country, but Gaston was at home, looking after Fanny. 'I'd like a sandwich in about half an hour, if that's possible, Gaston?'

'Certainly, mademoiselle. In the dining-room, or upstairs?'

'In my room would be fine, thanks.'

She took a leisurely bath, and when she came back into her bedroom, she found that in addition to the sandwich, Gaston had left a covered bowl of hot soup on the table, with a half-bottle of wine. Too tired to think about anything except food and sleep, she ate her supper and went straight to bed.

*   *   *

193

Life in the Martel-Cluny household resumed its normal rhythms. Not wishing to jeopardize her job in any way, Tiger took care to carry out her duties conscientiously, and with the best possible grace, as if nothing had happened to sour her relationship with her employers. None of the family mentioned Luc's name again, and neither did she; it was as if he had never entered that orderly house, much less disturbed the inhabitants. Even the old comtesse resisted the temptation to provoke her young friend.

April passed very happily. On Tuesdays and Thursdays, after the life class, Tiger spent the rest of the evening with Tadeusz, and although it was difficult in the sordid surroundings of the studio to recapture the magic of their time together in Przywnica, they managed pretty well, and made each other happy. Any doubts Tiger might have had that, once back in Paris, Tadeusz would regress to his former difficult and unhappy persona proved to be unfounded. With Tiger by his side, and in his bed, he was able to hold on to the aura bestowed on him by Przywnica, and she had never seen him so hard-working or so happy.

Sometimes he would meet her after her French class and they would go to a movie, or visit an exhibtion. Very occasionally, they would have a meal together in a cheap bistro. If Tiger paid, it no longer seemed to be an issue with Tadeusz. All in all, they did all the things that lovers do in Paris, especially when they are young and impoverished.

From time to time, Tiger caught sight of Luc in *Deux-Magots* or the *Flore*, in the company of his friend Carl-Heinz, and once she saw him with a very beautiful blonde girl. Having no wish to speak to him ever again, she always looked away, pretending not to have seen him. After his cynical destruction of her self-esteem, she was determined to obliterate him from her memory.

Twice, Tadeusz took her to Barbizon for the weekend. His parents were welcoming, and very kind. Although clearly in favour of the alliance, they wisely said nothing, either to their son, or to Tiger herself. They were, however, anxious to see Tadeusz settled with a strong-minded and capable girl, and watched the developing relationship closely, praying for a happy outcome.

In the west of Ireland, May brought magnificent early summer weather after weeks of torrential rain. Niamh was both relieved and delighted, for every bedroom at Neill's Court was occupied, either by an amateur cook or by a fisherman, and she had been extremely concerned that the persistent rain would undermine the spirits of her guests, as well as dampen their clothes. At such times, given the extra workload of dealing with the muddy footprints tracked into the house, plus the drying out of sodden coats, hats and socks, Niamh had found herself becoming increasingly stressed.

Equally, she had failed to anticipate the need to provide indoor amusement for those lady guests who chose neither to join the cooking classes, nor to venture out in the rain, and found herself driven mad with irritation when they made it clear that a fire in the sitting-room would be nice, and a selection of board games and up-to-date magazines very welcome, too. Running between kitchen and sitting-room, doing her inadequate best to satisfy the demands of everyone, Niamh was frequently severely tempted to go out on the hill with her grandfather's gun and shoot anything that moved, just to make herself feel better. I wouldn't mind shooting a few of them, too, she said to herself.

This unplanned-for situation was not made any easier by the unavoidable presence of Alice and Liam. Occasionally, a bored and more than usually inquisitive guest, intrigued by the catcalls and mad laughter that often emanated from the orangery, would be foolish enough to investigate, in spite of the large 'Private' notice hanging on the door. The outcome of such an indiscretion was predictable. Red-faced and apologetic in the face of Alice's terrified and hysterical reaction to the intrusion, the trespasser would be evicted by Liam, kindly but firmly, with the admonishment to respect the private areas of Neill's Court. Niamh knew that after such a humiliation, few guests would wish to come again, rather naturally assuming that the place sheltered a criminal lunatic.

With Matthew's handsome addition to her working capital, she had been able to take on two young girls from the village, and they had proved an undoubted asset in the kitchen. She had invested a great deal of time and energy in their training, and had become quite fond of them, for they got on well with the cooking ladies and contributed an air of youthful enjoyment to the lessons. As well as performing the duller tasks of food preparation and cleaning up, the two girls also waited at table with deftness and Irish charm, which enabled Niamh to play the role she liked best, that of hostess in her family home. The only flaw in this happy arrangement was the nagging awareness that, in the fullness of time, both girls would leave her, taking their useful skills with them, to Dublin, or even London. She lived in daily dread of that eventuality, but did not know how to avoid it.

The organic vegetable garden, the result of enormous input on her own part and rather less on that of Billy, a fourteen-year-old village lad, had nevertheless flourished, and now supplied three quarters of their daily requirements, foodwise. Quite often, Niamh found herself out in the garden after midnight, sowing fresh rows of salads, harvesting peas and baby beans, and grubbing in the black earth for the first of the early potatoes. God, she said to herself, groaning with fatigue, what wouldn't I give for a good strong man, one with muscles?

Since Niamh's accounts in the town were once again entirely in order, the butcher, the dairyman and the baker had resumed their daily deliveries to Neill's Court, so there was little need to go shopping.

It was a good year for salmon and sea trout, and it was a rare day that a creel of splendid fish was not brought triumphantly to the kitchen, to be transformed into an addition to the menu. Surrounded by her admiring troupe of ladies, Niamh made soups, terrines, chaudfroids and even delicately flavoured fish souf-flés, all of which made a big contribution to the gourmet meals she gave them, and cost her nothing. Best of all, when a really big salmon was caught, she got down the old copper fish-kettle from its high shelf, and poached this king of fish in a *court-bouillon* of white wine, herbs, spring vegetables and slices of lemon. When it had cooled in its fragrant bath, Niamh lifted the salmon onto a suitably grand serving platter, and carefully peeled away the skin, leaving the head intact. Then, to the delight of her enthralled audience, she covered the pink exposed flesh with aspic, and, as a final touch, added transparent crescent-shaped slices of cucumber, overlapping them in order to suggest fish scales. This performance never failed to elicit an enthusiastic round of applause, and was a source of secret gratification to Niamh herself.

On red letter days such as these, sitting in her grand-father's chair at the head of the dining-room table, observing the flushed happy faces of her guests as they consumed the fruits of her labours and the contents of Dan O'Neill's cellar, she almost convinced herself that she enjoyed the daily challenge of the way of life she had chosen for herself.

Nevertheless, as one set of guests replaced another, each entirely different from its predecessor, and with an even keener expectation of obtaining value for money, Niamh was forced to admit that in reality she was allowing herself to inhabit a fool's paradise. Far from being civilized, charming and appreciative friends who graced her table, she saw them for what they so often were: a bunch of rich, spoiled and overfed people, insensitive to her own situation and out for what they could get for themselves.

At such times, late at night, or early in the morning, before dawn, Niamh would vent her frustration and anger on the black soil of her vegetable garden, as she prepared the ground for yet another sowing of the seeds that would produce the food to fill their greedy stomachs.

Towards the end of May, Alice celebrated her fifty-sixth birthday, and Liam, eager to give the woman he had loved for so long a really memorable treat, proposed that he take her for a drive in the jaunting-car.

Thrilled by the suggestion, Alice spent a good deal of time choosing an appropriately summery outfit, and, after many changes of mind, allowed herself to be persuaded into a flowery chiffon frock, green high-heeled shoes and a floppy pink straw hat.

Billy, at Liam's request, had brought the jaunting-car and pony to the door, and Alice descended the main staircase on Liam's arm, happy and smiling; looking forward to her excursion.

Niamh, waiting by the front door to see them off, was relieved to see her mother looking almost normal. Prettily dressed, pink-cheeked, her bright hazel eyes as clear and untroubled as those of a child, it was difficult to appreciate that almost nothing was going on between Alice's ears; that her current mental capacity was infinitely less acute than that of the little girl she had once been, and still so much resembled.

After a small confusion with the mounting step, Liam and Niamh succeeded in getting Alice safely onto the seat of the jaunting-car, then Liam climbed up to the driver's bench.

'By the way, Liam, would you ever do me a favour and pick up the meat parcel from McCann's? I need to marinate the lamb for tonight, and it'll be too late for today if I have to wait for him to deliver.'

'Consider it done, miss,' Liam agreed obligingly,

gathering up the reins in his strong little hands. 'Right, me lady! We'll be off then!'

Liam had intended that the drive should be a gentle and sedate affair, a quiet meander along the leafy lanes above Neill's Court, but now, in response to Niamh's request, he drove up to the main road and headed for the town, five miles away. As they bowled along in the warm sunshine, he turned round in his seat from time to time and smiled at Alice, to be sure that she was feeling secure and happy. She smiled back at him, and asked him the same question, several times. 'It *is* my birthday, isn't it, Liam? You did say it was my birthday, didn't you?'

''Tis so, me darling, and a beautiful morning it is for it, to be sure.'

'And how old am I, Liam?'

'Not a day over twenty, sweetheart.'

When they reached the town, Liam drove the mare slowly down the high street, and pulled up outside McCann's shop. The old pony was well trained, very quiet and steady, and Liam got down from the jaunting-car. He stopped a boy walking by on the pavement, and asked him to take care of the horse for a couple of minutes. 'It'll be worth half a shilling to yous?'

'OK,' said the lad, without much interest, and stood beside the mare's head, for he had nothing better to do.

Liam glanced up at Alice, sitting on her seat, as straight as an arrow, looking round with interest at the comings and goings of the street. 'I'll not be a jiff, me lady,' he said. 'I'll just get the butcher's meat, and be right back, OK?'

Alice smiled at him. 'OK,' she said.

She watched him disappear into the shop, then hopped nimbly over the barrier onto the driver's seat, gathered up the reins and slapped them smartly over the mare's rump. 'Walk on!' she ordered briskly, and laughed out loud at her own cleverness. Obediently, the mare walked on, then, in response to another sharp flick of the reins, broke into a trot.

'OY!' shouted the boy, but it was too late. Alice and the jaunting-car were well on their way, heading for the traffic lights at the bottom of the street. Completely disregarding the red lights, and to the consternation of the local motorists, Alice drove the mare at a fast trot over the crossroads, causing a fairly serious pile-up in her wake. She failed entirely to realize what she had done and proceeded joyfully down the road, until she reached the outskirts of the town and was heading for the blue hills, far away. She gazed straight ahead, through the pricked ears of the mare, taking pleasure in the cool caress of the wind against her face, the swaying motion of the jaunting-car beneath her, and the swift clopping sound of the mare's hooves on the tarmac road. Her hat flew off her head, the breeze lifting her hair from her scalp, and Alice laughed aloud, for she felt that she could fly through the air like this for ever.

Over the tops of the high hedges on either side of the road, she could see the rows of newly mown hay drying in the hot sunshine, and into her empty mind, like a clip from a black-and-white movie, came the memory of lying in just such a field, and the beautiful smell and soft feel of it. The same delicious scent wafted over the hedge now, and filled her nostrils. Was it only yesterday we did that, she asked herself, and a worm of fear crawled in her stomach. She shook her head, unable to recall what it was she was trying to remember, or who it was she had been with at that distant time.

Suddenly, a wave of despair and panic gripped Alice, and an urgent need to escape from the scent of the new-mown hay. Gritting her teeth, she snatched the long whip from its brass holder and lashed the pony's backside with all her strength. 'Ged on, you stupid bugger!' she screamed. 'Shift yer feckin' arse, will you?'

Terrified, sweating, the little mare broke into an elderly canter and flew between the hedges, dragging the careering jaunting-car behind her.

When Liam came out of the crowded butcher's shop, carrying the parcel of meat, he found the boy standing in the middle of the road with his mouth open, staring after the vanished jaunting-car. 'Bloody hell, man!' Liam yelled, aghast. 'What the hell've you done?'

'The old girl took off! So help me, she did, mister! There was no stoppin' her, sor!'

'You bloody eejit!' cried Liam. It took him ten minutes to get to the Garda and another ten to persuade an officer to take him out in a police car in pursuit of Alice.

They drove out of town, stopping frequently to ask if anyone had seen the runaway jaunting-car. Eventually, after several misdirections, they found themselves heading south, towards the Clonmel road. The officer shook his head, and frowned, for he had a deep suspicion that Mr Dainty was indulging in some bizarre foolishness of his own imagination. ''Tis twelve miles from home we are, nearly,' he said. 'I'll not believe the lady can have travelled this far, in a jaunting-car.'

'Keep going, please, just for a while.' White as a sheet, terrified that if they did succeed in finding Alice, she would be dead, or at the very least seriously injured, Liam's eyes scanned the road ahead. At last, on the crest of the rising ground before them, they saw their quarry. The jaunting-car stood on the verge of the road, with the sweat-streaked and quivering mare still between the shafts, cropping the grass beneath her feet. Alice was perched on the driver's seat, windswept and wild-eyed, her flimsy frock blown above her skinny knees.

Trembling with relief, followed immediately by fury, Liam got out of the car. 'What the hell do you think you're playing at, you stupid, stupid bitch?' he yelled at her. 'Look what you've done, you bloody lunatic!

You've had half the Garda out after you! You're a bloody menace, that's what!'

Alice looked at Liam, jumping up and down on the road below, and listened with confused dismay to his tirade of abuse. A terrible black sorrow filled her heart, and she burst into tears.

'I'm sorry, I'm *sorry*!' Distraught, filled with shame, Liam climbed up onto the seat beside Alice and attempted to take her in his arms, but she thrust him away from her, and punched him straight between the eyes with her balled-up little fist. Still screaming hysterically, like a reprimanded child, she kicked off her shoes, jumped down from the jaunting-car and began to run down the road, blundering along like a drunk, unable to see properly.

Liam, recovering from the painful blow between the eyes, and swearing ferociously, descended from the cart as fast as his tired old bones would permit and staggered after Alice, followed at a discreet distance by the police car. It did not take them very long to catch up with her. The bemused police officer remained in the car, and watched as Liam and Alice crouched together on the edge of the road, while he kissed and hugged her, murmuring words of love and reassurance, as well as apology. Eventually, she was able to respond with a watery smile, and they stood up, ready to drive home.

Liam spoke quietly to the officer, indicating the parcel of meat that still sat on the dashboard. 'I'd be eternally grateful,' he said, 'if you'd ever be a saint and take this meat to Miss Niamh at Neill's Court. It'll take me for ever to drive back with Mrs Fitzgerald, and Miss Niamh will be fretting about it.'

The policeman pursed his lips, but agreed to deliver the parcel. 'Will you be all right, now?' he asked. 'Is the vehicle still in decent working order?'

'I'm sure it'll be fine,' replied Liam, wearily. 'It's the lady's birthday. I promised her a drive.'

* * *

202

When Niamh saw the police car drive into the stable-yard, her breath stopped within her, for she was convinced there must have been an accident. She hurried through the kitchen door, just as the officer got out of his car, carrying a parcel wrapped in white blood-stained paper. 'Mother of God!' she exclaimed, her heart pounding in her breast. 'What's happened?'

'Miss Niamh Fitzgerald?'

'Yes, that's me.'

'Mr Dainty asked me to give you this, ma'am. He said to tell you he'll be a little late getting home, and he's sorry for the delay.'

'Oh.' Frowning, Niamh took the parcel. 'Is my mother all right, officer?' she asked quietly.

The young man smiled, with a faint hint of mockery in his blue eyes. 'She'll be as right as rain, ma'am; there's little doubt of that, to be sure.'

'Well, good, that's a relief. Thank you, you've been very kind,' she said, waiting for him to go. 'Thanks again,' she repeated, wondering whether he expected a tip for his trouble.

Apparently he did not, for he raised his hand in a vague salute, got back into his car and drove away.

Liam and Alice got back just before six o'clock. The sky had clouded over, the evening was still and cool, and the air was full of ferociously biting midges. Liam had not thought it wise to drive the exhausted pony at more than walking pace, and this had rendered them an easy prey to the marauding insects. By the time they reached home, every centimetre of their exposed skin was covered in swollen red lumps, painful and itchy, so that the fugitive pair presented a sorry sight indeed.

Niamh, starting her preparations for dinner, heard the pony's hooves as they clattered into the yard, and hurried to the window. She observed that although her mother appeared to be red-faced and somewhat dishevelled, she seemed otherwise all right. She chose not to go out and greet her, or to ask what had happened.

Alice waited at the stable door, scratching her midge bites, while Liam unhitched the pony, rubbed it down and gave it some nuts and a net of hay. When he had finished, they walked silently round the back of the house to the orangery door, where they let themselves in, taking care to avoid an encounter with any guests on the way.

Exhausted both physically and emotionally, Liam found it difficult to pretend that nothing had happened; that all was well; that they had had a happy time. Cautiously, he put his head round the door to the hall to be sure that the coast was clear, then took Alice upstairs to her room. There, he helped her to undress, then applied a soothing cream to her bites, and to his own. He found her a clean nightdress, and she got into her big bed.

'Is it still my birthday, Liam?'

'Yes, darling, it is.'

'Will you be coming to bed with me, then?'

The purple lump on Liam's forehead was throbbing and painful, and his feelings of anguish and exhaustion threatened to overwhelm him. 'I don't think so, darling,' he said. 'Not tonight. I'm a bit tired.' He tried to smile, but found that he could not force his lips apart, so stiff and swollen were they from the midge bites. 'You lie still,' he said, as gently as he could. 'I'll go down and get your supper, sweetheart.'

He left the room, and Alice turned onto her side. She stared at the dark red roses nodding at her bedroom window, but she did not see them. She saw nothing but a fog of uncertainty, and the bewildering awareness that Liam was still angry with her; that she had been naughty again, though what her crime had been she could not remember. She pulled a shutter over what remained of her vanishing mind, and closed her swollen eyelids. She put her thumb in her mouth, and slept.

*   *   *

Twenty minutes later, Liam came back into the room, carrying the supper tray. Tight-lipped and mono-syllabic, Niamh had made clear her feelings by slamming a glass of milk and a couple of rock cakes onto the tray, and shoving it towards Liam, as he waited by the marble-topped fitting in the kitchen. A delicious smell of roasting something came from the ovens, and Liam raised his swollen eyebrows in silent protest.

'What did you do to your forehead, Liam?' Niamh asked him, a belated curiosity getting the better of her.

'Your fucking mother hit me!' he replied, fury and resentment suddenly erupting within him. 'You're all mad, and she's the maddest of you all, Miss Niamh. For two pins, I'd walk out on the whole bloody lot of yous, here and now, considering the way you treat me.' He shoved the tray back across the marble surface. 'Here!' he shouted angrily. 'You can stick your sodding milk and rock cakes, miss, and give me a proper supper for the poor lady, for not a crust has passed her lips since breakfast. You're punishing her for some-thing she doesn't even know she's done, poor godforsaken creature. How the fuck do you think it feels to be her, getting madder and more senile every day? Have you given a moment's thought to *that*?'

Stunned, mortified, Niamh took the tray, poured the milk back into the jug and threw the rock cakes in the pig bucket. 'I'm very sorry, Liam,' she said quietly, her voice shaking. 'It's not your fault, I know, and I don't know what I'd do without you, so please don't leave us, will you?' She raised her eyes, and looked at him. 'It's just that she drives me up the wall sometimes, Liam, you must see that?'

'What do you think she does to me, miss?'

Niamh chose not to reply, but she prepared a second tray of supper for both her mother and Liam, and one rather more appropriate for a birthday celebration: an outside cut of the roasting leg of lamb, with the juices,

205

new potatoes and baby beans, the vegetables quickly prepared in the microwave oven. She got a bottle of red wine from the larder, uncorked it and put it on the tray with two glasses. 'Can you manage, Liam?'

'Yes, I can manage. Thank you.'

In the bedroom, Liam saw at once that Alice was already fast asleep, her face half buried in the pillows, and could hear her gentle snoring. He sighed, filled with remorse at the recollection of his earlier unkindness to her, and his cruel rejection of her offer of sex. He put the tray on the table and sat down, preparing to eat both the suppers, and, very likely, consume an entire bottle of wine. It had been a bloody awful day; he reckoned he deserved to get a bit pissed.

Half-term occurred in the first week of June, and Orla, seeing on the meteorological forecast that the weather in the west of Ireland looked pretty good, telephoned Niamh, proposing to bring her two boys to spend the holiday at Neill's Court.

'Sorry, Orla. It's impossible.'

'Oh? Why?'

'The house is full, that's why. This place is a *business* now, or had you forgotten?'

'What about the attics? The boys can sleep there.'

'No, Orla, that's a non-starter, too. My girls sleep there, in the season.'

'I see.'

After a pause, Niamh said, 'Why don't you take them to Paris, to see Tiger? You could go to Disneyland, couldn't you? They'd love that.'

Orla closed her eyes, and chose to ignore this suggestion. 'Well, it seems I'll have to think again, thanks to you, Niamh. I hope you're not going to deny the boys their summer break, are you? We were planning to come in August, as usual.'

Niamh hesitated. 'I'll be full, but I suppose the boys could camp, if they *really* want to come.'

'And Matthew and me?'

'The pub, I'm afraid.' Niamh smirked triumphantly to herself, knowing she had bested her older sister, for once. 'I'm surprised that you don't take them to Tuscany, or somewhere equally grand. Much more your scene, really, isn't it?'

'Actually, Niamh, it may surprise you to know that we all adore Neill's Court; it's very special to us.'

'Oh, really? I thought you wanted to sell the place.'

'Only if the situation warrants it, of course.' Hoping that she had sown a little seed of doubt in her sister's mind, Orla said goodbye very sweetly and hung up. Shit, she said to herself crossly, what a pain. I quite detest Niamh sometimes.

Going to Ireland had seemed a good way of avoiding the huge financial cost of entertaining two boys for a whole week in London. Orla was a good mother, and she loved her sons dearly. She was determined that they should receive all the material benefits available to children of their class, and that none of their peers should fare better. Of necessity, she had to be careful with the daily cash flow, and, with this in mind, had little difficulty in convincing herself that a week in her family's grand country house was infinitely preferable to several exhausting days spent flogging round all the expensive London tourist attractions.

Matthew did his best to be helpful. 'What about spending half-term with Mum and Dad, at the Rectory?'

'You can't be serious, Matthew.'

'Cheaper than the air fare to Ireland, darling.'

'Not now that the flights are rock bottom. It would be a crime not to take advantage of that, even you must see that?'

Orla's logic had been impeccable, and her husband had no response that he chose to repeat out loud.

Disappointed, and seriously annoyed with Niamh, Orla considered the problem for a couple of days and then decided that perhaps a trip to Paris might be quite a good idea, after all. Tiger liked the boys and would know all the good inexpensive places to take them, she felt sure. The train fares were pretty reasonable and a friend had told her of a really cheap small hotel, right in the centre of the city, in place Dauphine. 'It's not exactly luxurious, but it's very old and full of atmosphere, and really close to all the interesting places – you know, Notre-Dame, the *bateaux-mouches*, all that.'

'Sounds perfect,' said Orla.

It was.

At first rather put out at the prospect of Orla's proposed visit, Tiger spoke to Tadeusz about it. 'Perhaps I won't be able to see you for a bit,' she said. 'Will you mind?'

'Of course I'll bloody mind. What's the score, Tiger? Are you ashamed of me, or what?'

'No, of course not! I just assumed you'd be bored stiff to meet my family, that's all.'

'You shouldn't jump to conclusions. I'd like to meet them very much, OK?'

'OK.'

As things turned out, Orla took an immediate fancy to Tadeusz. Although in Islington she might well have felt threatened by his unconventional appearance, in Paris he seemed part of the romantic and bohemian atmosphere of that wonderful city, and she allowed herself to fall under the special enchantment of both the man and his background.

Tiger was pleased by her sister's response to Tadeusz, and found her own feelings for him greatly enhanced by Orla's obvious approbation. In view of the ultraconventional opinions normally expressed by Orla about practically everything, it seemed all the more gratifying to the younger sister that her own choices should meet with her critical approval. First, it had been her fleamarket clothes; now, it seemed that her lover had also passed the test, and evidently with flying colours.

The two boys, Edward and Charles, at first slightly intimidated by Tadeusz's rapid French, soon managed to overcome this obstacle by the simple expedient of speaking only English, loudly and clearly. Tadeusz, amused by this approach, caved in gracefully and thenceforth communicated with them in their own language, if necessary requiring them to translate a word he could not remember. 'What is the English for *catacombes*, boys?'

'Search me,' said Edward, stumped.

'Catacombs,' supplied Tiger, helpfully.

'What is it?' asked Charlie. 'Something to do with cats?'

'No, it isn't.' Tadeusz lowered his voice to a dramatic whisper. 'It's the place of the dead, where millions of skeletons are stored underground.' He looked from one boy to the other and back again. 'I thought you might like to go and see them, but maybe you'd be too scared?'

Charlie looked anxiously at his older brother, and swallowed hard.

'I'm not scared,' said Edward boldly. 'Charlie isn't either, are you?'

'No, I'm not.'

'We'd love to go, Tadeusz.'

'Good, then I'll take you, as a special treat. We won't take the women, they might be frightened. Just us, OK?'

'Brilliant!'

Tiger had thought it polite to tell Mme de Martel-Cluny that her sister and nephews were visiting Paris, and the information elicited an immediate response.

'How *lovely*, Tiger! I should like very much to meet your sister, of course. Perhaps you could invite them all to come to tea tomorrow, if that is convenient?'

'Thank you, madame. Orla would be happy to accept, I'm sure.'

The tea party duly took place, and Tiger was amused to see that the tea table in the salon was groaning with a great many more delicacies than usual, including Marmite sandwiches and a covered silver dish of hot crumpets. There were two kinds of cutting cake, one fruit and the other chocolate, as well as two kinds of tea, Indian and Earl Grey. M. de Martel-Cluny's Scottish nanny had evidently left an indelible mark on rue Monsieur, in respect of a proper teatime spread.

Orla was at her elegant best, relaxed and sociable, and did not embarrass Tiger by the slightest hint of gushing behaviour. The two little boys, their faces and hands well scrubbed, their clothes and hair immaculately brushed for the occasion, sat on either side of the old comtesse, trying not to fidget. They answered her questions politely, their identical brown eyes only occasionally straying towards the unbelievably opulent table.

'Do you 'ave a dog in London, Edward?'

'No, worse luck. I wish we did.'

'We've got a stick-insect,' offered Charlie. 'But you can't take it for a walk or anything like that. It's quite dull, really.'

The comtesse turned to Tiger. 'Stick-insect? *Qu'est-ce que ça veut dire, ma chère?*'

'Sorry, madame, I don't know.'

'*Un phasme, Maman,*' said Mme de Martel-Cluny, smiling indulgently at Charlie. 'You 'ave learn something new, little man.'

Charlie did not reply, but made a retching face at his brother, which did not go unobserved by the comtesse. She gave a cackle of delighted laughter, and squeezed his hand. 'What about some tea? We 'ave wait long enough, no?'

Tiger, who had been somewhat excluded from the conversation between Orla and Mme de Martel-Cluny, stood up in response to the comtesse's invitation, and began to hand round the teacups and plates, after seating the boys at the table. The old lady elected to sit between them, with Fanny on her lap.

After tea, Tiger took the little dog for her walk in the Luxembourg Gardens, and the boys accompanied her, glad of the opportunity to stretch their legs after their socially challenging afternoon. Leaving Tiger to follow at her own pace, and pursued by the ecstatic Fanny, they charged along the paths shouting obscenities in English, under the misapprehension that the froggies wouldn't understand them.

In rue Monsieur, after a certain amount of rather unsubtle probing from the comtesse, Orla cast both modesty and caution to the winds, and gave both her hostesses a highly colourful account of her own coming-out ball at Neill's Court, which had, in fact, taken place only in her imagination. 'Since I am the eldest child,' she said gravely, 'the place will come to me in the fullness of time, which will no doubt be a heavy responsibility.' Orla looked at the sympathetic faces of her audience, and smiled bravely. 'Of course, my chief concern is that my eldest son should be able to take over in his turn, when the time comes.'

After a suitable pause, to show proper respect for the future deceased, the comtesse proposed that they partake of a glass of sherry. In her mind's eye, Orla could already see the fluttering black veils at her mother's funeral, and accepted the proffered refreshment with dignity and pleasure.

All in all, the tea party had been an unqualified success.

In the days that followed, accompanied sometimes by Tiger and at others by Tadeusz, Orla and her children saw the sights of Paris. They inspected the cathedral of Notre Dame, followed by a visit to the interesting archaeological crypt underneath. They took a trip on a *bateau-mouche*, and visited the Conciergerie on the Ile de la Cité, which both boys found enthralling, since it was the ghastly prison where Marie-Antoinette and thousands of others awaited their execution on the guillotine. The tiny cell that had housed the unfortunate queen seemed to Orla inexpressibly sad, but her feelings were not shared by her sons. 'Imagine,' said Edward pompously. 'Fancy telling them to eat cake; what a prat.'

On the Thursday, they decided to go first to the Eiffel Tower and then, after lunch, visit the catacombs. Orla and Tiger, neither of whom wished to stand in the queue to go up the famous tower, elected to go and sit in the nearby gardens, close to the river, leaving Tadeusz in charge of the boys. It was the first time the sisters had had a chance to be alone together.

'You look happy, Tiger.'

'Yes, I am. I love it here.'

'Tadeusz is a terrific guy. That makes a difference, doesn't it? How was your trip to Poland?'

'Wonderful.'

'Tell me.'

Tiger lifted her long hair from her neck, for the day was hot, and wound it into a knot on the top of her head, fixing it with the tortoiseshell comb Tadeusz had given her. Choosing her words carefully, and avoiding any mention of her sexual relationship with Tadeusz, she told Orla everything she could remember about Przywnica and Tadeusz's extraordinary grandmother, Ileana Marylski. She described how the family's land had been confiscated by the Communists, so that all that remained was the house and a small garden.

'I thought that the Poles had thrown the Communists out, so that landowners could claim their land back, now?'

'That's true, but Tadeusz doesn't think that it would be ethical to try to reclaim his family land, when the peasants have farmed it for so long. He thinks it's best to leave things as they are.'

'More fool him. I wouldn't let them get away with it, if it was mine.'

'Tadeusz is an artist, Orla, not a businessman.'

'Yes, OK. It's nothing to do with me, of course.'

'Absolutely.' Tiger smiled at her sister. 'Or me, come to that.'

After lunch, which they ate in a tiny and very cheap café in a nearby side-street, the sisters went by Métro to the Louvre, while Tadeusz took the boys to visit the catacombs, secure in the knowledge that it would be the highlight of the trip for them.

The queue, when they reached place Denfert-Rochereau, was quite short, and soon they found themselves climbing down a steep stone staircase, horribly slippery, as well as dark and malodorous. Tadeusz produced a torch from his pocket, and told the children to hold tightly to his coat. The stairs continued down and down to an alarming depth, until they reached an iron door with an inscription carved into its stone surround.

'What does it say?' asked Charlie, trying to make out the words.

'It says, "Stop! Here is the Empire of Death!"' intoned Tadeusz, who was enjoying himself enormously.

'Oh.'

The iron door opened onto dimly lit corridors, and the boys were shattered to see before their eyes, and close enough to touch, the horrific spectacle of human bones, piled high on either side, from floor to ceiling. There were thousands upon thousands of them, the remains of eight million citizens of Paris, including the two and a half thousand victims of the guillotine. There were bones of every description and in every imaginable size, stacked in tight ghoulish layers. The skulls, especially, were a macabre sight, arranged in strange patterns, grinning horribly. Charlie, holding Tadeusz's hand, tightened his grip.

They listened to the guide's discourse on how the bones got to be there in the first place, and how this haunted place had been the headquarters of the Resistance Movement during the Second World War, a circumstance apparently never discovered by the

213

Germans. The two boys did not understand much of the lecture, but Tadeusz provided a dramatic interpretation for them, after they had left the place, and were walking to the Métro. With considerable relish, he described the nightly rumblings of carts through the cobbled streets of Paris, in the late eighteenth century, transferring the rotting contents of the overflowing city cemeteries, to the galleries of the disused underground stone quarries, the newly consecrated catacombs.

'Poor things,' said Edward, seriously. 'Didn't they have a proper funeral?'

'No, there were too many of them, but the carts were accompanied by hooded priests, bearing lighted tapers, and reciting prayers for the dead.'

'Grisly,' said Charlie, looking slightly green.

'What about an ice-cream?' Tadeusz suggested. It occurred to him that he might have gone too far.

'Yes, please,' said Edward.

'You, Charlie?'

'OK.'

The rest of the week passed equally pleasantly, with a final dinner at a Vietnamese restaurant in place Dauphine, and on Sunday afternoon the visitors took the Eurostar back to London.

'What did you like best?' Orla asked as she watched the green fields of France flash past the window.

'The Empire of Death, of course,' said Edward, and gave a lugubrious sigh. 'That was cool, wasn't it, Charlie?'

'Yes, it was OK,' said Charlie, not entirely truthfully, for he was doing his absolute best to obliterate the memory of that place from his head.

'Tadeusz is cool, too.' Edward's brown eyes shone with the admiration he felt for his new friend. 'Really, really OK. Don't you think so, Mum?'

Orla smiled, but she said nothing, and continued to stare out of the window.

CHAPTER ELEVEN

Summer in Paris was hot and airless, and even in the garden at rue Monsieur, with its shady trees and small tinkling fountain, it was difficult to imagine ever feeling cool and comfortable again. The comtesse, especially, found the heat unbearable, and her frequent outbursts of temper made it obvious that the old woman was suffering a great deal.

By the middle of July, Mme de Martel-Cluny had reached the end of her tether, and decided to take her mother-in-law to the country a couple of weeks earlier than usual. Antoine, naturally, would have to remain in Paris until the official start of the long August vacation. A prudent woman, his wife did not think it a good idea to leave her husband alone in the house with their young au pair, and took immediate steps to prevent this. When Tiger returned from her walk with Fanny, she called her into the salon.

'I 'ave been very worried about Maman, Tiger. She is not 'erself, as I'm sure you will agree?'

'Yes, poor thing. She feels the heat, of course.'

'So I 'ave decide to take 'er at once to the château. It is cool there, in all weather, and she will soon recover 'er spirit.'

'Good idea.'

'I was wondering, Tiger, whether you would wish to

come with us? My mother-in-law is very fond of you, and is use to having you near 'er.'

Tiger looked at her hands, folded in her lap, and thought furiously. She had promised Niamh that when her present contract with the Martel-Clunys expired, at the end of July, she would at once return to Neill's Court and give her sister a much needed hand with the visitors. The approach of the summer holidays had been giving her food for thought in any case, since Tadeusz had spoken of spending the summer at Przywnica with his grandmother, with the intention to looking into the possibilities of selling his paintings in Cracow, and finding out more about the artistic life of the city. 'It is time I settled down,' he said, 'and if possible, I'd like to be based in Przywnica.' Somewhat to her surprise, and consternation, he had not mentioned what part he intended Tiger to play in these plans. I suppose he just assumes I'll tag along, she thought, a little resentfully.

One thing, however, was clear. It was entirely out of the question that she should go with the Martel-Clunys to the country, if she was to honour her commitment to Niamh. On the other hand, she was anxious neither to offend her employers, nor burn her boats with them in any way. She thought it extremely likely that she would want to come back to rue Monsieur, and spend another year in Paris.

She chose her words carefully. 'I've been very happy here, madame,' she said, 'but I'm afraid I can't accept your kind invitation. You see, my sister in Ireland expects me at the end of the month, and really needs my help at home.'

'I see.' Madame smiled, but her eyes were hard. 'Yes, of course, you must go. But I shall be closing this house for the summer, and we shall be leaving on Friday. Can you be ready to return to your home before then?'

Tiger looked startled, but recovered quickly. 'Yes, of course. I'm sure that will be all right, madame.'

'So, that is settled, Tiger. I hope you will return to us in September, perhaps?'

'Thank you, madame. I will let you know, when I have spoken to my sisters.'

Excusing herself from dinner, Tiger walked to rue St-Sulpice, intending to discuss the situation with Tadeusz. On the way, she thought about her time in Paris. She smiled wryly at the memory of her early French lessons with the horrible old *professeur*, and her struggles with the complexities of the language. She had long since given up bothering to remember things like the subjunctive, particularly as she didn't even know what it really meant in English. Nowadays, she just jumped in and swam, not trying to make elegant phrases, for it seemed to her that above all communication was the important thing. To understand and be understood was the name of the linguistic game, in her opinion, and the hell with the purist approach.

Of course, her many hours spent with Tadeusz had enabled her to make rapid progress, for although his English was pretty good when he chose to use it, French was so to speak his mother tongue and the one he felt most comfortable with. What a strange chance it was, she said to herself, that he should have been pinning up that notice about his life classes, just as I was coming out of the French lesson.

As Tiger turned into rue St-Sulpice and began to walk towards Tadeusz's door, she suddenly slowed down and came to a halt. Why am I going to see him? she asked herself. What am I going to say? If I have to leave Paris on Friday, and go home, what then? Will he go to Poland? Will we make love one more time, say goodbye, and wish each other a nice summer? Is that all we mean to each other? Is that really what I want to happen?

She reached Tadeusz's door, glanced quickly through the glass, then walked on in a state of nervous indecision. Anxious not to bump into him, she crossed the road and took a short cut through the narrow back streets to place St-Germain. The cafés were packed with students and tourists, but she found room on a bench on the terrace of the *Flore*, sat down and ordered a glass of chilled wine.

She sat there for a long time, drinking her wine very slowly, and eating green olives from a little dish. She watched the sour-faced waiters coming and going, attending to the needs of the clientele. Mostly students, they congregated in animated, boisterous groups, talking over each other in loud voices. All of them seemed to be chain-smoking, and their tables were littered with overflowing ashtrays, as well as coffee cups and wine glasses.

Enviously, Tiger studied their flushed faces, reminding herself of the many convivial evenings she herself had spent in this very place, and wondering whether she would ever come here again, or be so happy.

'Hello, Tiger. Are you alone?'

Startled, she turned her head, and saw Luc Marcassin standing beside her table. He was alone. She frowned, but could not very well refuse to acknowledge him. 'Yes, I'm alone,' she said frostily. 'Is that a crime?'

'No, of course not, don't be ridiculous. May I sit down?'

'I can't very well stop you.'

Luc sat down, not on the bench beside Tiger, but on a spare chair on the other side of the table. A waiter approached and Luc ordered a beer. 'What about you, Tiger?'

'I'm OK, thanks. I'm leaving in a minute.'

Luc sat back in the cane chair, folding his arms, and studied Tiger's closed, unfriendly face. 'You're still angry with me, I suppose?'

'Certainly not! Why should I be?'

'As a matter of fact, Tiger, I think you have every reason to be.' Luc spoke very softly, so that Tiger could scarcely hear him, surrounded as they were by the roar of conversation.

She swallowed nervously, and looked at him across the table, her eyes uncertain, apprehensive. She could could not think of a suitably dignified response to this unlooked-for peace-offering, if that was what it was.

The waiter brought the beer, and Luc, pulling his chair up to the table, took a long drink. He put the glass down, then laid his hand gently on hers. She tried to pull her hand away, but he held it tightly, and smiled at her. 'I'm trying to apologize to you, Tiger, if you'll let me, please. I'm terribly sorry that I upset you. I realize now that my behaviour towards you was unforgivable, especially in view of your youth and inexperience.'

Tiger tried to smile. 'Don't worry about it,' she said. 'I expect the fault was as much mine as yours. It was naive of me to expect any sort of commitment from you, Luc, and I was probably very silly to react in the way I did.'

'No,' he said gently. 'You were never silly, darling.'

'Well, anyway, it's ancient history now, isn't it? I expect it taught me a useful lesson.' Tiger's empty stomach gave a loud, protesting growl, which rather undermined her dignified stance in respect of Luc's behaviour, and, in spite of herself, she laughed. 'I must get a sandwich or something; I'm starving, no dinner.'

'Let's have supper together. Why don't we, for old times' sake?' He was quick to seize the opportunity that presented itself. 'Please, Tiger? It would make me feel a lot better if I thought you'd forgiven me.'

'What about your other friend, Luc?' Tiger asked, coolly. 'The German chap?'

'He's on tour.'

'I see. And the elegant blonde female?'

Luc smiled. 'That's my sister, Tiger.'

'OK, I suppose we could have supper, if you really want to,' she said, for she felt extremely hungry. It occurred to her that there was an outside chance they might run into Tadeusz. 'But not anywhere round here, if you don't mind.'

'How about the *Procope*?'

'Good.'

They had a protracted and delicious dinner, and Luc chose, at huge expense, the Rhône wine that Tiger had so much enjoyed when she had first dined with him, the wonderful Château Rayas. He raised his glass to her with all his old polished chivalry: '*Salut*, darling Tiger. You have the most beautiful eyes in the world, as well as the loveliest body.'

'I bet you say that to Carl-Heinz,' she said, and laughed, for quite suddenly she didn't give a tinker's curse what Luc might have said, or to whom.

'Actually,' he replied, with mock seriousness, 'I wouldn't dream of saying that to Carl-Heinz, because it wouldn't be true, Tiger. My own body is infinitely more desirable than his, and he knows that!'

'Luc! You're absolutely gross! You really are an utter shit, aren't you?'

'Yes, I am. It's the only way to be, darling, believe me.'

'Why?' A goose walked over Tiger's grave, for she had a horrid feeling that she didn't want to hear the answer, and wished she could withdraw the question.

Luc refilled their glasses, then rested his chin on his hand and looked at Tiger, his blue eyes sombre. 'You won't laugh?' he said.

'No, I won't laugh, Luc.'

'Well, you probably will, or say something mocking, but I'll tell you anyway. I think I told you before, Tiger; I've made a serious blunder in my choice of career. I have the capacity, but not the inclination to be a career civil servant, and as each day passes I am more than ever in despair, when I see only too clearly my unbelievably boring life stretching ahead of me.'

'I understand that. But what's it got to do with you behaving like a shit in your private life?'

'Everything, that's the point. I behave as atrociously as I can get away with, in order to create energy and excitement in my life, even a sense of danger. I drink and do drugs. I screw anyone who wants to, for fun, and very occasionally I do it for money. Girls, older women, men, sometimes absolute strangers, even *clochards*, it doesn't make any difference to me, Tiger. I'm open to offers. I always will be, I expect, unless I screw up the nerve to kill myself.' Luc took off his spectacles, polished them on his napkin and put them back on his nose. 'You're not laughing,' he said. 'You don't think it's funny?'

Tiger looked at him, her eyes full of compassion, even a kind of love. 'No, I don't think it's funny,' she said quietly, and touched his hand. 'I think it's a bloody tragedy, Luc.'

'I'm so lonely, Tiger. You have no idea.'

'If you really do want to write, and feel you have the talent, why the hell don't you tell them to stick the job, and do what you really want to do?'

He shook his head. 'No, it's too late. I've no money, and I'm too spoiled and lazy. I've got used to this upmarket way of life, darling. I wouldn't have the guts to walk away from it now.'

She looked at him, her violet eyes severe under the delicate dark brows. 'But you think you'd have the courage to kill yourself, silly man?'

'That's not courage, Tiger. It's the beautiful cop-out, isn't it? The huge temptation?'

'Do you really believe that?'

'Yes, I do.'

When they left the restaurant it was nearly midnight. The sky was clear and starry, and the air cool.

'Shall I walk you home, Tiger, or would you rather take a cab?'

'A walk would be good. I'd like that.'

When they reached the corner of rue Monsieur, she stopped. 'We'd better say goodbye here. I'm not considered suitable as a friend for you, remember? I promised your aunt never to see you again, more or less.'

'Stupid old bitch, who the hell does she think she is?'

'In any case,' said Tiger, 'it's entirely academic; I'm flying home to Ireland on Friday.'

'You're not serious?'

She laughed. 'Deadly serious. Your aunt is taking the comtesse to the country, and she doesn't trust your uncle under the same roof with me. At least, that's my guess, and I'd put money on it.'

'What a pity. I was hoping we could be friends again.'

'Do you mean lovers?'

'That, too, if you wished it, darling. It was good between us, wasn't it? I've missed you quite badly, as a matter of fact.'

'It *was* good, Luc, but you're too late, I'm afraid. I'm involved with someone else, now. I think it's quite probable that I may marry him.'

'You don't mean your Polish painter? The one with long greasy hair and dirty fingernails?'

'That's him.' She smiled. 'As a matter of fact, he's quite a bit cleaner now, and better fed; not so thin.'

'I'm amazed, and sorry, too. I thought you loved me, Tiger.'

'I did. Still do, a bit.'

'But not enough to take me on?'

'I might, except for two things.'

'And they are?'

'In the first place, Tadeusz is seriously in the picture now, and I wouldn't want to hurt him.'

'And the other reason?'

'I'd find it impossible to become permanently involved with an unhappy, promiscuous and sexually ambivalent man, Luc, much less a suicidal civil servant, even if I loved him. I'd much prefer to hitch my star to a penniless artist, and live on the smell of an oily rag.'

'In that case, you've come to the wrong place, my darling. You know what they say about leopards, don't you?'

'Yes, I do.'

'May I kiss you, Tiger?'

'Yes, of course.'

Their embrace was prolonged and intense, and they clung to each other for a long time, both full of an aching regret for the way things had turned out for them, cruelly aware of the lost chance of a special happiness that could have been theirs.

Tiger was the first to break the spell, and release herself from Luc's arms. She touched his face, pale and beautiful in the starlight. 'Goodbye, darling Luc,' she said. 'Try to have a happy life.'

'Goodbye, Tiger. I love you.'

'I know.'

She turned away and ran down rue Monsieur, to the concierge's gate. She went straight in, without looking back.

Tiger woke in the very early morning, when it was still cool. She got out of bed, went to the open window, and leaned over the sill, enjoying the dewy freshness of the air on her face and bare shoulders. She thought about Luc, and the evening they had spent together, and was filled with an intense pity for him, and sadness at the fate she was convinced would be his, a barren and futile life.

Now, she thought, I must forget all that, and think about what I'm going to do now. First, I must book my flight home, then I must go and see Tadeusz, and see how he reacts to the news. I don't want him to think I'm pressurizing him in any way, but I do need to have some idea of whether he expects me to come back to Paris, or sees a future for me in his life, at all. Why did I say to Luc that I expected to marry Tadeusz? He's certainly never suggested marriage to me, that's for sure. In any case, is that what I'm really looking for, myself?

After all, I'm not even nineteen until next month; barely out of the cradle, by his standards. Why is life so bloody difficult?

There was a clattering of white wings beneath her window, as the resident fantail pigeons rose in a cloud, disturbed by the sudden appearance of Antoine de Martel-Cluny, leaving his mother's apartment and running along the terrace towards the salon doors. Tiger withdrew into her room, in case anyone should see her in her thin nightdress, but remained close to the window, listening apprehensively, for she had the distinct impression from Monsieur's manner that something was amiss, presumably with the comtesse. For several minutes Tiger stood there, waiting, but heard nothing more.

She went to the bathroom, took a shower, and began to get dressed. Then she returned to the bedroom, and was brushing her hair when she heard the sound of footsteps on the terrace. Crossing to the window, she looked discreetly out, and saw Monsieur walking back towards the comtesse's door, accompanied by a young priest, who carried his stole in his hand, and a small box. Oh God, said Tiger to herself, her heart falling into her boots, the poor old lady's dead, how dreadful!

The bereaved son did not appear at the breakfast table, and Tiger and Madame sat together in appalled and embarrassed silence, drinking coffee, and, rather guiltily, eating the delicious croissants, warm and fragrant in their silver dish. Gaston, red-eyed, moved silently in and out of the dining-room, attending to their needs, and Tiger was surprised at his obvious display of emotion. Never for one moment had it occurred to her that Gaston might actually have been attached to the old comtesse, much less loved her.

When she had finished her breakfast, Tiger waited for a few minutes, then put down her napkin and rose to her feet. 'If you will excuse me, madame, I had better take Fanny for her walk.'

Madame looked up at Tiger, her heavy-lidded unmade-up eyes dull. She smiled faintly. 'Yes, of course, that would be kind of you. Life goes on, doesn't it?'

At the door, hearing her name called again, Tiger turned back.

'You 'ave reserve your ticket 'ome, my dear?'

'No, I haven't, madame.'

'There is no necessity now, since, naturally, we shan't be going to Beauvallon until August, after all. By all means, stay until the end of the month, if you wish it. We shall, of course, be very sorry to part with you, now that my *belle-mère* 'as disappear.'

'Thank you,' said Tiger. 'I should like to attend the funeral, if I may? I feel that I have lost a friend, madame. My sister will be very sorry to hear of her death, too.'

Walking sedately along the paths of the Luxembourg Gardens with Fanny, for it seemed rather inappropriate to run in her usual way at such a time, Tiger realized that what she had said to Madame about her affection for the comtesse had been no less than the truth. She sat down on a bench, and took Fanny on her knee, for the little animal, equally, seemed subdued and in no mood for their usual games.

Tiger thought of the long, eventful life of the glamorous old lady, now brutally terminated by the hot weather, and probably in circumstances of some discomfort, if not agony. She found it hard to relate the pale corpse, now presumably lying stiff and cold in her bed, with the energetic old battleaxe who had dominated Tiger's life for nearly a year, and influenced her in so many ways, not least in teaching her to have the confidence to dress as she pleased. I'll never forget you, Tiger said to herself silently, and a tear rolled down her cheek and plopped onto Fanny's fawn head.

Sadly, she took the dog home, and then, since there was no comtesse to listen to her reading the English newspapers, she went to rue St-Sulpice, to look for Tadeusz. She found him in the studio, alone, and working, wearing only his underpants.

He looked round as she entered the room. 'Hi,' he said, turning back to his painting. 'Aren't you ministering to the old bag this morning?'

'She's dead,' said Tiger flatly.

'*What?*'

'The comtesse is dead, Tadeusz. She died in the night. It was a stroke, I understand. She'd been feeling the heat terribly lately, poor thing.'

'I'm sorry to hear it, Tiger, very. What a shame.' After a pause, he went on, 'What happens now? I imagine your job is at an end?'

'Yes, it is. Madame says I can stay until the end of the month. Then, I have to go home to Ireland.'

'Why?'

'Why? Because I must, Tadeusz. My sister expects me to be there, to help with the visitors.'

'Is that the one I met? Orla?'

'No, it's Niamh. She's the middle sister, the one who looks after my mum, and the house; keeps things on an even keel, at home.'

After a pause, Tadeusz said quietly, 'What a bloody nuisance, Tiger. I thought you'd be spending the summer with me at Przywnica.'

'You never asked me, Tadeusz.'

'Was it necessary to spell it out, darling? I thought we had an understanding?'

'I see.'

Tadeusz put down his brush, crossed the room and, pulling up a stool, sat down beside Tiger. 'Do you really see, Tiger? Don't you understand that you've become indispensable to me? I refuse to believe that this bloody Niamh is more important to you than I am. Surely she can hire the extra staff she requires, can't she? Money can't buy what you do for me, darling, so don't go away and leave me on my own again, please.'

'Tadeusz, what are you trying to say?'

'What do you think? I love you. I need you. I want you with me.'

'What, here, in the studio?'

'No, at Przywnica.'

Tiger sighed. 'This is mad, Tadeusz. What would we use for money?'

'You've got a bit saved, haven't you? That would do for the summer, in Poland.'

Tiger shook her head. 'It's no good, Tadeusz. I can't go with you. I promised Niamh I'd go home to Neill's Court. I can't let her down now.'

Surprisingly quickly, Tadeusz capitulated. 'OK, if that's how you feel, I'd better come with you, to Ireland.'

Tiger stared at him, astonished. 'Are you serious?' she said. 'It's very dull there; nothing to do, much. It's just a house and a bit of scenery.'

'I can always paint, can't I? I could even help out, too, in exchange for my meals, couldn't I?'

Tiger looked doubtful. 'I don't think I've got enough money for two airfares, Tadeusz. It's terribly expensive, flying to Dublin.'

'Train? Hitchhike? We could take the motorbike, if you like. It might be useful.'

'Oh, Tadeusz. Are you really sure about this?'

'Yes, I am. Very sure.'

Tiger looked deep into his dark eyes, and saw that he was speaking the truth. 'OK,' she said. 'I'll call Niamh this evening, and see what she says.' She stood up, put her arm round Tadeusz's bare neck and kissed him. 'I must go now, I may be needed in rue Monsieur.'

'Come back this evening. Have supper, stay the night?'

'I'll see how things go, OK?'

'OK.'

Tiger waited until after nine o'clock, in order to be sure of the cheapest rate, then called Niamh. Since she was using the phone in the hall, she kept her voice low as she gave her sister the news of the comtesse's death.

'Oh, dear,' said Niamh. 'How very sad.'

'Yes. Everyone here is very upset, as you can imagine.'

'Indeed. Please give them my condolences, Tiger.'

'I will.'

'Does this mean you'll be coming home right away? I certainly hope so.'

'Um, no; not exactly, Niamh. There's the funeral, of course, and Madame needs me here to help her sort things out. Clothes and stuff, you know how it is. Sending things to charities, all that.'

'Yes, I see. When will you come, then?'

'The end of the month, as we planned.'

'Well, OK. That'll have to do, I suppose.'

'Actually, Niamh, I've got good news on that front. I'm bringing an extra pair of hands with me, if that's OK with you?'

'Oh?'

'My friend Tadeusz Marylski wants to come, too. He's the one whose family I stayed with at Easter, remember? He's a hard worker; I'm sure he'll get through a mountain of work in the vegetables for you. He's good at mending things, too.'

'I see. Will he want paying, Tiger?'

'No,' said Tiger, gently. 'Just his food, Niamh. I think we could manage that, don't you?'

'Well, OK. As long as I'm not out of pocket, he can come.'

The mortal remains of Madame la Comtesse de Martel-Cluny were carried from the house, and transported by refrigerated hearse to the family chapel at Beauvallon. Here, the coffin would rest until the entire clan had gathered for the obsequies, scheduled to take place at the end of the week.

In the village cemetery, the stone tabletop tomb of the comtesse's long-dead husband was already being prepared to receive a second occupant, and at the gateway to the château, a book of condolence lay open upon a small folding table. From time to time, a car stopped and a local worthy signed the book, and when the sun went down, the housekeeper walked down the drive in the cool of the evening and carried both book and table back to the house.

In rue Monsieur, Tiger and Madame, aided by Gaston, sorted through the old lady's clothes and divided them into separate lots, according to their seasonal function. Some of her things, like furs, were set aside on account of their value. Like her jewels, they were not intended for charitable disposal.

Monsieur had taken compassionate leave from his ministry and spent his days going through his mother's papers, emerging from her apartment only at meal-times. Tiger noticed that he ate very little, and took this as a sure sign of his genuine grief, for he was a man of normally hearty appetite.

One evening, returning from her walk with Fanny, Tiger heard angry voices in the salon, and realized that Monsieur and Madame were having a row.

'Certainly not, my dear Céline! To start using the title now would be hypocrisy of the worst kind.'

'But surely, now that Maman has gone, why not?'

'As you very well know, I could have assumed the title when my father died. I chose not to do so then, on account of my political beliefs, and I am not going to change my mind now.'

'But I have already ordered the new writing paper, Antoine! I can't cancel it now!'

'You must, Céline. I insist. It is not for you to tell me how to order my affairs. I would be obliged if you would respect my decision in the matter.'

There was silence, followed by the unmistakable sound of weeping. Two at a time, Tiger took the stairs to her own room, and stayed there until Gaston knocked on her door and told her that dinner was ready.

*   *   *

The Requiem Mass took place on the following Friday evening, in the little chapel, which had been filled with late-flowering roses, the elderly gardener at the château having stripped his most beautiful bushes in order to give his comtesse an appropriate send-off.

After the service, the entire population of the village followed the funeral cortège to the cemetery for the interment, the procession led by the captain of the local dustbin men, wearing his leather hat and badge of office.

The weather was still stifling hot, and Tiger, dressed in her black coat and skirt as a mark of respect, thought that she would die of heat. She stood at the outer fringe of the crowd, for she had no wish to intrude on the grief of the close family members, and since she could not hear the words of the priest, quietly intoned as the coffin was put into the tomb, she was able to look around at the assembled relations and friends. On the far side of the tomb, half hidden by several rows of mourners, she saw Luc, his fair head clearly visible in the black-clad crowd. He was with an equally fair-haired woman, and Tiger at once recognized the sister she had assumed to be his lover.

When the formalities were over, the crowd began to drift slowly away, and Tiger followed them, walking along the stony lane back to the village, under the merciful shade of the plane trees that bordered the road. She had reached the gates of the château when Luc caught up with her, and together they walked up the drive towards the house.

'We're the first to arrive, I think,' he said. 'Shall we go in, or would you rather have a walk round the garden, and join the boozing millions a bit later?'

Tiger laughed. 'Good idea. I'd hate to be first in the thirsty queue.'

In the garden, the sun had already slipped behind the tall bulk of the building, and long shadows had crept across the sun-baked grass, turning its colour to a dusky, luminous lavender. Great banks of gallica roses grew against the limestone walls of the house, as well as those that enclosed the flower garden. In spite of the gardener's determination to pay his last respects to the old comtesse in the way that he knew best, the remaining roses were still magnificent, and their scent in the cooling air sublime.

Following Luc's example, Tiger slipped off her coat thankfully. They hung their jackets on the beak of a lead gryphon, and walked together, silently, along the beautiful, sweet-smelling border.

At the bottom of the walk, they turned and retraced their steps, not hurrying, enjoying the solitude of that peaceful place. Tiger glanced at Luc, with a shadow of a smile. 'It's sad, death, isn't it, Luc? But at least, here, she's at home; she knows where she is, among her own people. I liked her so much; I shall miss her.'

'Don't be sad, Tiger. She would have hated that, I'm sure. The last years of her life were pretty good hell, you know. She suffered a lot with arthritis, things like that, and she absolutely *detested* the uglinesses of old age; sagging flesh, wrinkles, all that horror.'

'How do you know that, Luc?'

'She told me how she felt, many times.' He laughed. 'She had the death-wish, just like me. She had a few goes with pills and booze, but she always came round. The life-force was too strong with her, poor old thing.'

'I don't believe you! You're making it up!'

He shook his head. 'I'm not, I promise.'

Tiger stared at him, aghast. 'You don't think . . .?'

'Yes, I do. If it had been a simple matter of old age, do you really think Uncle Antoine would have been so shattered?' He turned towards her, and touched her cheek. 'Don't be upset. She's happy now, and free, isn't she? That's to say, she is if you believe in all that stuff.'

'Do *you*, Luc?'

'Yes, I do.'

*　　*　　*

They walked back to the house together, putting their coats back on before entering the crowded salon. A young waitress offered them champagne, and they stood together by a tall window overlooking the park.

Tiger looked down at the billowing folds of the silk curtains that hung at the windows. 'This must be where poor Fanny blotted her copybook last Christmas,' she said.

'Why, what happened?'

'It was too cold for her to go out, so she peed on the curtains, naughty thing.'

Luc laughed. 'Good for her. I always liked that little dog. She's a natural rebel. I wonder what will happen to her now?'

'I wonder.' She turned towards him and smiled. 'We'd better circulate, Luc, don't you think? It's been lovely to see you again. I won't forget you.'

'Tiger?'

'Yes?'

'If you ever need me, you know where to find me, don't you?'

'Yes, I do.'

The Martel-Clunys were very kind to Tiger during the rest of her time with them, and as a leaving present they gave her a green velvet evening dress that had belonged to the old comtesse and a cheque for a thousand francs, in addition to her salary. Surprised and touched, Tiger embraced them both warmly, and said she hoped very much they might meet again, some day.

Armed with this substantial boost to her finances, Tiger felt entirely justified in buying two Eurostar tickets to London, and she and Tadeusz arrived at Waterloo on the evening of 31 July. When Orla had heard from Niamh that Tadeusz was coming with Tiger to stay at Neill's Court, she had immediately invited them to break their journey in London, and spend a night in Islington. This they did, and received an enthusiastic welcome from the two little boys, who lost no time in hijacking Tadeusz, and taking him to their room.

Orla, watching as the children dragged their victim upstairs, smiled indulgently. 'He's adorable, Tiger; the boys really love him. You're a lucky girl, to have him.'

Tiger accepted a glass of wine from Matthew, and gave him a kiss. 'I think you're pretty lucky to have Matthew, as a matter of fact, Orla.'

The next day, Tiger and Tadeusz travelled by coach and ferry to Dublin, and thence by another coach to Neill's Court, arriving in the late evening, tired and extremely hungry.

CHAPTER TWELVE

If Tadeusz was surprised, and slightly shattered, by the room to which he was escorted by Colleen, one of Niamh's young domestic helpers, he took good care not to show his feelings, and thanked her for showing him the way there.

The room in question was, in fact, the tiny loft over the stables, formerly occupied by Liam Dainty and the scene of his early trysts with the young Alice O'Neill. Tadeusz sat down on the hard, narrow bed and listened to the solid clumps of Colleen's hefty platform shoes as she stumbled down the wooden steps that provided the solitary means of access to the room. He gazed around him, at the cobwebs that festooned the roof timbers above his head, at the bare boards underfoot and at the rough, rather dirty blanket that covered the bed. Nervously, he pulled down the blanket a little, and was relieved to see that the sheets and single pillowcase were clean, though not ironed.

He unzipped his bag, and unpacked the few things he had brought with him: a couple of shirts, plus two of his embroidered Polish ones; a pair of clean jeans and some underpants. His luggage consisted mostly of painting materials: some small sheets of primed board and his box of pigments. Brushes and charcoal were in a black-enamelled tube, along with small bottles of oil and turpentine. He unscrewed the tube to make sure that nothing had been broken during the journey from Paris, and was relieved to find that all was well.

He looked around more carefully, wondering where he was supposed to store his possessions, but could see nothing except a row of tarnished brass hooks screwed into the planks that lined the low wall. OK, he said to himself, if that's how it is here, that's how it'll have to be, I suppose. He hung his spare clothing on the hooks and slid his painting gear and his grip underneath the bed. He looked at his watch: seven forty-two. He frowned, aware that he needed a shower, or at the very least a wash, and having no idea at all how to access the means of these necessary functions.

There was a renewed clatter of shoes on the stairs, and Tiger's head emerged through the trapdoor, her face flushed with annoyance. She was looking exceptionally beautiful, in spite of the fatigue of a long journey, and had already changed into one of her frilly white blouses and her red *gitane* skirt. 'Bloody Niamh!' she exclaimed, climbing into the room. 'She really is the pits, and frankly, I don't know why we've bothered to come, if it's going to be like this, Tadeusz.' She looked around the shabby loft with distaste. 'Fancy putting you up here, the cow! It's disgusting, and where I am isn't much better. She's making me share my old attic with one of her skivvies.'

'Perhaps you'd better share with me, then?'

Tiger slid an arm round Tadeusz's neck. 'I wish, but I've got the distinct feeling it's not on. Niamh has always been a bit screwed up about sex, you know. I expect she's put you here quite deliberately; out of bounds, so to speak.'

'I didn't get those sort of messages from your other sister. Quite the reverse, in fact. I thought she approved of us, Tiger.'

Tiger looked at him thoughtfully. 'You're right, she does. And it's pretty surprising, because she definitely intended me to find a rich husband, preferably a classy French job.' She smiled gently. 'Perhaps she thinks a

Polish count isn't someone to be sneezed at, Tadeusz?'

'Huh! I'm not a count!'

'No, but your father is.'

'No way, Tiger. He thinks that's all a load of outdated crap, and I agree with him. He dropped all that sort of pretension when he left Poland, just as my grandmother has.'

'So, how come that you're so keen on Przywnica? I thought you loved that place better than anywhere on earth, Tadeusz?'

'I love the *place*, Tiger, not the privileges it used to carry with it, a long time ago. Times have changed; we all know that.'

'Oh, well. If it gives Orla a buzz to imagine that they haven't really, what's the harm?'

Tadeusz laughed, and kissed her. He glanced towards the bed. 'What about it, darling? Is there time, before supper?'

'Shit! No, there isn't! I've been sent to fetch you! Come on, the dinner's ready. Aren't you hungry?'

'Why don't we go and have supper at the pub, and then come back here for a while?'

'Don't tempt me, Tadeusz! Come on, we must behave, or there'll be trouble, for sure.'

'Right! Whatever you say. But first, I badly need a wash, as you've probably noticed.'

Tiger put her arms round him and laid her head against his chest. 'I had noticed, but you smell terrific to me, as a matter of fact.'

'I still need a wash.'

'OK. I'll show you where it is.'

Niamh sat in front of her dressing-table, and thought about the evening of Tiger's homecoming. She's nearly nineteen, she said to herself, as she rubbed Pond's cold cream into her face. It's about time she grew up and took life seriously, instead of floating about in those ridiculous old-fashioned clothes, looking romantic. Actually, she thought bitterly, Tiger would probably look romantic in a plastic bin-liner; she's always been much the best-looking of us all, in spite of the handicap of Dad's nose. She seems to have grown into it, somehow, or maybe it's just the way she does her hair now.

Niamh wiped the surplus grease from her face, then sat idly, staring at her reflection in the mirror. God, she thought, I look bloody old, I really do; much older than twenty-nine; nearly as old as Orla, God forbid. She began to brush her hair, soft and curly like her mother's but much darker, and already slightly speckled with grey. Looking into her own wide-apart eyes, exactly like Alice's but a cool blue-grey, she knew that she looked more like her mother every day, and the knowledge gave her little pleasure. Will I go mad in the end, too? she wondered apprehensively. It runs in families, doesn't it?

The evening had passed pleasantly enough, and the dinner had been excellent. The artichoke hearts vinaigrette were perfect; the sea-trout baked with fennel a miracle of subtlety, and the chocolate sorbet with its sharp raspberry coulis a triumphant end to a superb meal. Afterwards, as they drank their coffee in the drawing-room, the guests had gone out of their way to express their appreciation of Niamh's culinary skills, and to remark on the charm and beauty of her younger sister.

As she unwillingly admitted to herself, it had been rather perverse of her to feel irritated by Tiger's display of social competence, as she sparkled away at the far end of the table, effortlessly amusing the middle-aged guests whose presence was the key to the survival of Neill's Court. As the company had assembled for dinner, Niamh had sought to upstage Tiger by inviting Tadeusz to sit on her right hand side. 'Be an angel and hold the fort at the bottom of the table, darling,' she had said to her sister. 'The old boys will love to have you to flirt with.' She had been entirely right in this

237

supposition, and Tiger's end of the table seemed to be in a continual roar of jokes and laughter.

Tadeusz, on the other hand, had been much less inclined to pitch in and help in this way, and he did the unforgivable thing. He put his right elbow on the table, and pointedly addressed himself entirely to Niamh throughout the meal, totally ignoring the unfortunate woman on his other side. After one or two feeble attempts to include all her neighbours in the conversation, Niamh gave up and allowed him to monopolize her, an experience she found far from unpleasant.

'This is a beautiful house,' he said. 'Has your family lived here for a long time?'

'Not particularly, by comparison with some. The O'Neills bought the place just after the First World War. My mother is the third generation; my sisters and I are the fourth to live here.'

'Not like the Marylskis.'

'Oh, really?'

'My people have been at Przywnica for three hundred years, though you'd hardly think so, to look at the place now.' He smiled. 'You're doing a much better damage limitation job here; I congratulate you.'

Niamh looked at him speculatively, wondering whether this little tribute to her efforts was rather patronizing, then decided that it was not. A soft pink bloomed in her cheeks. 'Thank you,' she said quietly. 'Very few people actually notice what a huge amount of work and organization such an undertaking entails, and if they do, I don't think they give a toss, actually.'

'It's the same with painting,' he replied. 'Par for the course, I'm afraid.' Tadeusz put his fork carefully at the side of his plate, and looked his hostess straight in the eye. 'How is it that a young woman as impressive as you has not a husband to shoulder some of the burdens?'

Taken by surprise, Niamh spoke without thinking: 'No-one asked me, that's why.' She frowned, lowering her eyes to her plate. 'I suppose you find that pathetic?'

'Not at all. I find it absolutely incredible. Are there no redblooded men left in Ireland, or have they all run away to England, perhaps?'

'The States, more likely.' Niamh laughed, secretly delighted that Tiger's boyfriend should have lost so little time in making a mild pass at herself, albeit rather a predictable one. 'Anyhow, now that you and Tiger are here, I hope you'll both be able to shoulder some of the burdens, as you put it.'

'But, of course. Isn't that what we're here for?'

Aware of his dark intense gaze upon her, Niamh raised doubtful grey eyes to his. 'Is it?' she asked, quietly. 'Or are you both here just to have a free holiday, and piss me off?'

'Oh, dear,' he replied, and took her hand in his. 'You *have* been taken for granted, and abused, haven't you? And for far too long, it seems.' He raised her hand briefly to his lips. 'As for your rather insulting remark about free holidays, let's wait for a couple of weeks, and then you can answer the question for yourself, my dear Miss Fitzgerald.'

'Niamh.'

'OK. Niamh.'

Was he just winding me up? she asked herself, staring grimly at her pale shiny face in the mirror, or did he really mean what he said about me being impressive? Perhaps it's just the way Poles behave as a matter of course, all that old-fashioned gallantry thing? Kissing hands and stuff? Anyway, he hardly spoke to me for the rest of the evening, he was far too taken up with bloody Tiger. He didn't even have the courtesy to ask me to dance, not once, when they put on Granny's old Thirties records and rolled back the rugs.

With an emotion close to revulsion, Niamh recalled the faces of the elderly audience, full of wistful admiration for the two young dancers, tinged with a certain nostalgic regret. Silly old farts, she thought. Not one of those ridiculous women would ever have looked anything like as beautiful as Tiger; they're kidding themselves if they think they once did. As for the men, if any of *them* imagine they looked like Tadeusz when they were young, or danced like him, they're away with the fairies.

And what about *you*, Niamh? she asked herself bleakly. You're much the same age as Tadeusz, or even younger, perhaps. There's no reason why he shouldn't fancy me, is there? Is there? He's not *engaged* to Tiger, is he? Niamh made a face in the mirror. 'In your dreams, you silly cow,' she said crossly, and switched off the dressing-table lamp. She opened the window wide, then lingered for a moment, breathing in the scented night air, and watching the night mists rise over the trees. Then she got into her bed, and turned on the little transistor that sat on her night table. Listening to the radio helped her blot out the irritations and disappointments of each day, and would, eventually, allow her to fall into an exhausted and uneasy sleep.

Breakfast was a running buffet, served on the dining-room table. Several of the fishermen, anxious to take advantage of the low light and tranquil waters of early morning, walked down to the lake soon after sunrise to try their luck. Niamh, too, rose before dawn, to be sure that Colleen and Siobhan had laid out the cold ham and rolls, and brewed the coffee for the early risers. On the whole, the system worked smoothly, particularly as Niamh found the men on their own much easier to get along with, since they seemed far less inclined to complain than their wives. Sometimes they even thanked her for her efforts in sending them to their morning's angling with a mug of hot coffee inside them. 'A packet of sandwiches would be perfectly all right, you know,' one of them had said, though not with a great deal of conviction. 'I hate the idea of you having to get up, just for us.'

*   *   *

On the morning after Tiger's arrival, Niamh got out of bed at five twenty as usual, and went down to the kitchen. There, to her huge surprise, she found Tadeusz, leaning against the stove drinking coffee, and chatting to the girls.

'Good heavens!' exclaimed Niamh. 'What on earth are you doing up at this hour?'

He grinned at her. 'You said you needed extra help, Niamh. I asked Colleen what time you started in the morning. She said about half past five, so here I am, at your service.'

'Well, OK. Thanks.'

'Tell me what to do, and if I can, I'll do it.'

'Right.' She poured herself some coffee, and took a few scalding sips. 'Don't you want anything to eat?' she asked.

'No, I'd rather work first, and have something later, if that's OK?'

'Any good at gardening?'

'Depends what you mean by "gardening". I can do digging, humping muck, weeding, but nothing fancy, you understand?'

'Weeding is just what I need doing. Come on, I'll show you.'

They left the house and walked across the stableyard towards the high brick wall that concealed the kitchen garden. Niamh glanced towards the stables as they passed. 'I hope you weren't too uncomfortable in Liam's old room, Tadeusz? I'm afraid it's a question of completely running out of places to put people. I'm dreading the arrival of Orla with her brood.'

'What will you do?'

'Matthew and Orla will have to put up at the pub, though they'll eat here, of course.'

'And the boys?'

'Tents in the orchard.'

'Sounds like fun.'

Niamh laughed. 'Clearly, you've never spent August

241

in Ireland. Almost always, it rains. Great for fishing; lousy for camping.'

'Oh.'

She pushed opened the door to the kitchen garden, and led the way through. They walked together down the broad central path that divided the beds of growing fruit and vegetables. Compared to his grandmother's garden at Przywnica, the place seemed to Tadeusz enormous, and he whistled incredulously. 'My God, there's enough stuff here to feed an army.'

'That's the general idea,' replied Niamh crisply.

In the farthest corner, next to several wooden compost bins, was a large netted cage, and inside Tadeusz saw a boy of about fourteen feeding chickens. 'Is that your gardener?' he asked.

'Yes, it is, and a fat lot of good he is at the job. If I wasn't chasing him every hour the Lord sends, he'd be mooning around wasting time doing the jobs he likes: collecting eggs; picking raspberries, stuff like that. He's an absolute moron.'

'Why don't you sack him?'

'Because I've no bloody alternative to him, that's why. It's so frustrating, I could scream. But there's no-one else will take the wages I can afford, so I'm stuck with stupid Billy.'

'I see.'

They reached the end of the path, and turned to survey the garden. 'Well, what do you think?' Niamh said, crossing her arms defensively.

'I think,' began Tadeusz slowly, then paused, letting his eyes drift over the abundant and really very beautiful garden. 'I think that this is a most romantic and wonderful place, Niamh, and has enormous potential. Your problem is that you've had to work so hard and single-handedly to bring it to life that you can't see the rewards of your labours, only the continuing struggle to maintain it. Right?'

Niamh looked at him, her eyes wary. 'Do you really think so?'

'I do.'

'So, what do you suggest?'

'All you need here, my dear girl, is some organization, and someone with muscles.'

'Oh, really? And where will I get them, Tadeusz?'

'Here. This is just the sort of vacation job I love. I'll do it, if you like, in exchange for bed and board.' He looked at Niamh, and laughed. 'Though, I have to say, a better mattress on the bed might be quite an incentive.'

'Are you serious?'

'I am.'

'I thought you'd come here to paint, Tadeusz? What about that?'

Tadeusz looked around him, speculatively. 'I reckon if I work here from six to twelve every day, and manage to motivate young Billy as well, I'll have plenty of time to paint in the afternoons.'

'Oh, dear. You make it sound so easy.'

'It is easy.' He took her arm. 'Come on, introduce me to Billy, then show me where you keep all the tools and things. By the end of the week I promise you'll see a big improvement.'

Back in the kitchen, Niamh found the girls doing the fishermen's breakfasts and Liam making tea and toast, to take up to Alice in bed. 'Did my mother not sleep very well, Liam?' she asked, for he did not usually appear in the kitchen much before seven.

'Indeed she did not, I'm sorry to say, Miss Niamh.' He shot a reproving glance in her direction. ''Twas all the loud music wound her up, miss, so it did. She was all for coming down and joining in the fun, so she was. I had the devil's own job, getting her to settle.'

'Well, I'm sorry she was disturbed,' said Niamh. 'I'll tell Tiger to keep the sound down in future. The young are so thoughtless, aren't they?'

'Ah, no! She should have all the fun she can get. After all, a lot's changed hereabouts since your mother

243

was a girl, hasn't it?' Liam's eyes grew soft. 'There was plenty of good crack then, for sure, and no need for pennypinching, either.' He picked up his tray, and smiled at Niamh. 'Of course, you're too young to remember all that, miss, but they were fine times, indeed they were.'

'Tiger's nearly nineteen,' said Niamh brusquely. 'It's high time she grew up; got a grip on real life.'

Liam offered no response to this, but left the kitchen. Irritated at herself for discussing her sister's behaviour with a servant, Niamh turned to Colleen. 'Where is Tiger, anyway? Isn't she up yet?'

'I don't think so, miss. She was still asleep when I came down.'

'Is that so?' Niamh turned to Siobhan. 'Is everything ready for the dining-room? Can you two manage on your own for a few minutes?'

'Sure.'

Up in the attic, Tiger lay on her lumpy old mattress. She was deeply asleep, her limbs spread-eagled across the bed, her entire body profoundly relaxed. In her dreams a kaleidoscope of fleeting images passed seamlessly through her unconsciousness: the funeral cortège at Beauvallon, led by the village dustman; the despairing wrinkled face of the old comtesse, her skin the colour of parchment, surrounded by a coquettish frill of starched lace; the pale blond hair of Luc, and his blurred blue eyes, red-rimmed, suddenly obscured by a pair of black sunglasses; Orla's little boys, Charlie and Edward, dragging Tadeusz upstairs to their room, and the sentimental smile and lustful eyes of their mother as she watched them. In her dream, Tiger frowned uneasily. Does Orla fancy Tadeusz? She couldn't, surely? She's far too old for him, for a start, not to mention being already married. The dream began to drift away, and desperately, Tiger clung to it, willing herself to stay asleep, but the sound of a door being slammed, the thunder of heavy shoes on bare floorboards and the imperious voice of her sister, calling her name, forced her to open her eyes. Niamh stood at the side of the bed, arms crossed, implacable.

'What?' said Tiger, blinking and passing her tongue over her dry lips.

'Get up, you lazy cow! What the hell do you think you're doing?'

'What's the time?'

'Bloody six o'clock!'

'*Six o'clock!*' Tiger squeaked. 'That's the middle of the night, Niamh! I'm knackered! I need to sleep!'

'Like hell you do, my girl!' Niamh caught hold of the thin blanket and sheet that covered her sister, ripped them off and flung them on the floor. 'THERE!' she yelled. 'NOW! GET OUT OF THE BLOODY BED!'

Tiger sat up, wide awake and very, very angry. She got out of bed, squared up to her sister, raised her arm and whacked Niamh across the side of her head as hard as she could. Niamh recoiled, clutching her ear, then reacted equally violently to the assault. She took hold of the bodice of Tiger's nightdress, and tore the fragile garment from top to bottom in one viciously comprehensive movement.

Tiger stood there, trembling, half naked, and stared at her sister with total disbelief. 'What's got into you, Niamh?' she asked, her voice choked, on the edge of tears. 'You always were a bit of a control freak, but as far as I remember, you were never a sadistic fascist dictator.'

Niamh, red-faced, eyes blazing, stared back. When she spoke, it was in a sarcastic tone of controlled anger. 'Someone has to get things organized in this fucking place, Tiger, and up to now it's had to be me. You've spent the last year frolicking about in Paris, wearing your flash unsuitable clothes, behaving like a fully paid-up member of the stupid upper crust, but now it's got to stop, my girl.' Niamh crossed her arms, and blinked, for she, too, felt the pressure of tears behind her eyes. 'If you had come back to us with a rich husband, Tiger, as Orla confidently expected you to do, things might be different. As it is, all you have managed to acquire is an impoverished Polish artist. Hardly a triumph for you, is it?' She swallowed, then laughed vindictively. 'It might interest you to know that your *artist* has been up since five thirty, and is even now labouring in the vegetable garden.'

'Really?'

'Yes, *really*! So bloody get a move on, or you'll get no breakfast. I'll expect you in the kitchen in five minutes.'

Tiger stared at the door through which Niamh had departed, and slowly let out her breath. Sadly, she examined the wreckage of torn lace and lawn that had been her beautiful antique nightgown, and let it fall to the ground with a regretful sigh. Naked, she went to the tiny dormer window of the attic, and looked down over the stable-block and into the kitchen garden, far below. There, she saw that Tadeusz was indeed hard at work, his shirt off, his pale torso exposed to the already hot sun, guiding the mechanical hoe between the crowded rows of vegetables. The formerly idle Billy, scarlet with exertion, staggered up the central path, trying to control the unwieldy Victorian wooden wheelbarrow, as he delivered huge loads of weeds to the compost bins.

If she had not felt so angry, confused and miserable, Tiger would have laughed at the sight of such feverish activity. As it was, her instinct told her to find some way of escaping from the situation in which she perceived herself and Tadeusz to be trapped. She still had quite a lot of money. They could return to Paris, couldn't they? Go to Przywnica? It couldn't possibly be as unpleasant as being here, and at least she would have a decent room all to herself, wouldn't she?

Taking some confidence and comfort from these positive thoughts, Tiger pulled on her old jeans and a T-shirt, and ran downstairs. In the kitchen, she spoke to no-one, poured herself a mug of tea from the pot stewing on the stove, and left the room, carrying the mug with her. She crossed the yard, and went straight to the kitchen garden. She closed the door carefully behind her, and marched up the path to Tadeusz's side, taking slurps of cold tea as she went.

'Hi,' said Tadeusz, straightening his back, wiping the sweat from his brow. 'Have you come to help?'

'Certainly not!'

'Oh? What brings you here, then?'

Billy stood on the path close by, his eyes round with interest. Tiger stared at him pointedly, until he got the message and applied himself once more to his task, trundling slowly away with his barrow. She turned back to Tadeusz. 'You're not really intending to get up at dawn every day and do this sort of back-breaking work, are you, Tadeusz? It's a joke, you must realize that?'

'I'm perfectly happy to do it, Tiger. It's good for the soul, manual labour, or hadn't you noticed?'

'You're not serious?'

'I am, perfectly.'

'Well, if that's so, you're a prat, and have less backbone than I gave you credit for.'

Tadeusz smiled, and his teeth looked very white in his face, already darkened with a three-day growth of beard. 'I'm sorry if you think that, Tiger, but you don't own me, you know, and you don't form all of my opinions, either. As it happens, I find it rather liberating, pitting my body against the forces of nature, and I intend to continue doing so, with or without your permission.'

After a brief pause, during which they stared at each other with ill-concealed hostility, Tiger drew breath and returned to the attack. 'So your intention to do some painting is up the spout, is it, Tadeusz? You'd rather be an unpaid minion to my sister, would you?'

'No,' he replied evenly. 'The arrangement is that I

247

work from six to twelve. My afternoons are free, to do as I please.'

He advanced towards her and put a sweaty hand on her neck. 'I rather hoped we might spend our free time together.'

'Doing what?'

'What do you think, you silly girl?'

In spite of herself, Tiger's anger melted, and she laughed. 'Well, I'll think about it,' she said and marched off down the garden path.

She returned to the house, and sought out Niamh, who was writing out menus in the library. 'OK,' she said without preamble, or apology. 'What do you want me to do?'

'I've made a list of your daily tasks, Tiger,' Niamh replied quietly. 'It's easier than you having to ask me all the time.'

'Oh, right.' Tight-lipped, Tiger took the proffered list, and left the room.

Niamh looked after her with a small, triumphant smile.

In the orangery, Liam was reading the *Sporting Life* aloud. Dreamily, listening to Liam but not taking much in, Alice let her gaze drift through the tall open French windows, across the wide uncut flower-sprinkled lawns and down to the distant lakeside. In the rushy shallows stood two figures in waders, casting their big rods out over the water, its surface slightly rippled by the summer breeze. Closer to the house, a party of three women sat idly at a garden table, drinking coffee. One of them was turning the pages of a magazine, and snatches of conversation drifted towards the orangery from time to time.

I don't remember seeing those women at my party, said Alice to herself. Perhaps Niamh invited them? I do wish she'd ask my permission before she brings strangers to the house. She's so bossy these days, any-one might think the place was hers, but she could at least oblige me in that respect. What am I talking about? What respect am I talking about? What do I mean? As the lapse into amnesia took hold, the familiar panic clutched at Alice's soul. She gripped the arms of her rattan chair, as her breathing became deep and laboured, and a cold sweat broke out on her brow. Her eyes filled with terror, she looked mutely towards Liam, but he went on reading. Making an enormous effort, she uttered a faint mewing sound, like a half-drowned kitten, and immediately Liam looked up. 'Is it you, Con?' she whispered.

At once Liam put his paper on the floor, got up from his chair and knelt at her side, taking care not to frighten her by touching her. ''Tis me, darlin'; Liam. Who else is it loves you and looks after you?'

'Not Con?'

Liam shook his head. 'No, not Con.'

'Liam?'

'As ever is, me darlin' girl.'

The relief on her small face was palpable, and they both laughed, as at a shared joke. 'It was a lovely party, wasn't it, Liam? The music and the dancing. The band played "Cheek to Cheek", didn't they? Do you remember that one, Liam?'

'I do. You were as light as a feather; beautiful.'

'Did I wear the spangly white one, and Mummy's emeralds?'

'You did; you did.'

'Can we go again, Liam?'

'Yes, any time.'

'Soon, Liam?'

'Yes, very soon, darlin'.'

'Is it breakfast time, Liam? I'm hungry again.'

'Nearly lunchtime, sweetheart. Will I go and bring it now, if you're OK for a minute?'

'All right.'

He got to his feet, and carefully closed the doors to the garden and locked them, in case Alice should take it into her head to wander off. He picked the pages of the *Sporting Life* off the floor and rearranged them carefully to reveal a page of pictures of horses at a recent race meeting. 'There,' he said. 'Will you look at this, while I go for our lunches? I'll be gone only a minute.'

'Good man,' said Alice, with all her father Dan's cool authority, and turned her attention to the horses.

Niamh's cookery class had gone well, and the eight women clustered round her marble worktop felt well pleased with their part in the preparation of the delicious lunch which was now almost ready. Last-minute attention was paid to matters of presentation, for as Niamh herself told her pupils in her kind, unassuming manner: 'However fundamentally perfectly you prepare the food, the final touches are what transforms the dish into a work of art.'

With this end in view, the ladies busied themselves chopping parsley; making a gremolata of finely chopped garlic, parsley and grated lemon rind to sprinkle over dishes of fresh trout-stuffed tortellini; patiently slicing up pan-roasted almonds for a last-minute addition to a crisp salad of rocket, broad beans and lamb's lettuce, and, finally, sieving icing sugar over the miraculous little cold chocolate soufflés that were to be the highlight of the meal.

The lesson over, the ladies departed to wash their hands, then join the men for a drink before lunch. The guests safely out of sight and earshot, the staff, as Niamh rather grandly called her paid help, transferred the dishes to the dining-room, while she herself checked every little detail of the table. At one o'clock precisely, Niamh opened the drawing-room door and announced that lunch was ready, and invited her guests to join her in the dining-room.

In the kitchen, a rather less elegant lunch awaited the rest of the household, including Tadeusz and Tiger. As Niamh had pointed out to Tiger, it would be rather a waste of time for them to stop work early in order to make themselves presentable enough to appear in the dining-room for lunch with the guests. When Tiger opened her mouth to protest, Niamh broke in swiftly, assuring her that at dinner they were both more than welcome, and would prove to be a positive asset to the civilized atmosphere of the occasion, she was sure.

'You really are a bitch, Niamh,' said Tiger through clenched teeth, but she knew that there was nothing she could do; Niamh had her over a barrel.

The kitchen lunch had been roughly thrown together from the unused pieces of trout, the less attractive bits of salad, and, fortunately, a large freshly baked loaf of farmhouse bread. The two girls, Billy, Tadeusz and Tiger sat down without ceremony, and hungrily attacked the food before them.

'What about something to drink?' suggested Tiger.

'There's only water allowed, miss,' said Siobhan, grinning nervously.

'We'll see about that.' Tiger went to the larder and fetched a bottle of cider, deliciously cold from its sojourn on the slate shelf. She unscrewed the stopper, and an apple-scented aroma drifted over the table. Silently, the lunchers pushed their tumblers towards Tiger, and she filled them with the russet-coloured liquid, the fragrant bubbles winking at the rim of each glass.

When the fish and salad had been despatched, Tiger looked at Colleen. 'No pudding for us?'

'No, miss, only for the guests.'

'Right. What about some cheese?'

'Not allowed.'

'Oh, bollocks! Go and get some, Colleen!'

'If you say so, miss.'

Colleen went to the larder and came back with a large piece of what looked like Cheddar cheese. 'I think we'd better just have a bit of this, miss. We'd best not to open the posh stuff Miss Niamh keeps for the visitors.'

'OK,' agreed Tiger. 'You're probably right.'

The company had eaten nothing since six o'clock that morning and were understandably still quite hungry. They made short work of both bread and cheese.

After lunch, the two girls and Billy remained in the kitchen, to deal with the clearing of the dining-room and the washing-up. This chore was not on Tiger's list, so she went up to her attic room, lay down on her bed and went at once to sleep.

Tadeusz, after a moment's hesitation, decided that he, too, could do with a rest, and made his way to the stables. After his long morning in the sun, his shoulders felt scorched and tender, and he wished he'd had the sense to keep his shirt on. He climbed the ladder, took off all his clothes, and lay down rather carefully on the still unmade bed. The sheet felt cool and soothing against his hot skin, and he closed his eyes and stretched his arms above his head, feeling the sweat prickle in his armpits. I wonder where this rain is, that Niamh seems so confident about, he said to himself, and smiled, recollecting her militant posture, crossed arms and aggressive attitude during their early morning discussion about his terms of employment. She's a silly bitch, he thought, but admirable, in her way, too. She's got a lot of energy and determination, the will to succeed, and no-one in the family appreciates her at all, as far as I can see, except perhaps that funny old fellow, Liam, the mother-care man. No wonder Niamh's so bloody prickly and sour; I reckon she needs a man about the place, in more ways than one. He laughed out loud at the improbable idea of Niamh succumbing to the advances of a randy lover, and the sound of his own laughter made him jump. He opened his eyes and looked warily round, his ears pricked, in case he had been overheard. But there was no sound except the liquid burblings of pigeons, on the roof above his head.

He closed his eyes again, and felt his whole body grow limp and relaxed. What a lovely place this is, he said to himself; peaceful, beautiful and sad; full of ghosts, too. What Niamh is doing is completely mad; ridiculous, but heroic none the less. She's desperate to maintain a lifestyle that ceased to exist all over Europe in 1939, to all intents and purposes. She can't subscribe to the idea of modern democracy; the level playing field for everyone; no privileged people at all; but she's prepared to work her arse off in a way that today's meritocrats would consider entirely pointless, just to save a crumbling house and a few acres of land.

He thought of his grandmother, toiling away in her tiny garden at Przywnica; driving to the weekly market in Cracow; keeping the memory as well as the home of her dead husband alive, in the mistaken belief that her son, Milosz, would wish to live in the old house after her death. Wild horses wouldn't drag Dad back there now, Tadeusz thought. For him Poland's an alien country; the Marylskis don't live there any more.

At four thirty, Tiger woke. She lay for a moment, wondering where she was, for the cider had caused her to fall into a deep, dreamless sleep. After a while she got out of bed, wrapped herself in a towel and made her way to the servants' bathroom, where she took a cool bath.

She went down to the kitchen by the back stairs, feeling increasingly like a second-class citizen in her own home, and put the kettle on to make some tea. The kitchen was empty, and she stood patiently waiting for the kettle to boil, half expecting the door to be flung open by a vengeful Niamh, hell-bent on reprimanding her sister for eating the cheese at lunch, not to mention drinking the cider. If she does any such thing, I'll really let her have it, Tiger said to herself. Who does she think she is? I rather hope Orla will come soon. She wouldn't put up with this sort of bullying for a second. Or would she take Niamh's side, perhaps? God, I don't really understand either of them, not at all.

The kettle boiled and Tiger made two mugs of tea. Carefully, she carried them across the courtyard to the stables, and, slowly, she climbed the ladder, holding the handles of both mugs in one hand. At the top of the ladder she paused, and put the mugs on the floor of the loft. She looked across the room at the sleeping body of Tadeusz, naked and relaxed, like a piece of Greek sculpture, beautiful in the golden afternoon light. Very quietly, she crossed the room, slipped out of her clothes, and sat down on the side of the bed. After a moment, Tadeusz opened his dark eyes and gazed at her sleepily, smiling. 'Hello, beautiful,' he said.

'Hi,' Tiger said. 'I brought you some tea.'

'Wonderful, just what I was hoping for.'

'Only that?'

'No, not only that, my darling.'

CHAPTER THIRTEEN

The Cleoburys arrived at Neill's Court in the first week of August, and Matthew, from the start of the holiday, devoted himself entirely to his children. He took them out in the dinghy, fishing. He taught them to swim, and how to use a snorkel. When Niamh did not require the jaunting-car, he took them for drives along the lanes around Neill's Court, and from time to time they drove into the town to buy ice-cream. All in all, he made sure that his sons had the kind of traditional British holiday he himself had enjoyed as a boy, the only difference being that his own had been spent at home, and alone with his parents.

Orla, exhausted from her summer in London; the committees she sat on; the ferrying to and from school of her children; the shopping and cooking; and the organization of their social life, was determined to do as little as humanly possible. She got up late, missing the pub breakfast, and walked slowly up to Neill's Court. There, she spent the early part of her day in the orangery, chatting to her mother, having despatched Liam to the kitchen in search of coffee and toast. Liam was, in fact, extremely glad of Orla's daily visits, for it enabled him to have a bit of time to himself, as well as providing stimulating company for Alice. Since she was now unlikely to recognize anyone other than Liam, Niamh and Orla, and often confused even them, these small breaks seemed heaven-sent to Liam and he made the most of them.

There was more than a touch of disingenuousness in Orla's attentions towards her mother, for in spite of the improved financial situation at Neill's Court, she had not entirely abandoned her plan to sell the house and put Alice in a home. Her morning visits were more than a loving daughter's kindness; they were a cool, ongoing assessment of Alice's degenerative condition. It did not take Orla very long to be pretty sure, with a certain grim satisfaction, that the crunch was not far off.

None the less, when Orla had handed over to Liam and gone out into the garden to find a quiet spot in which to read her current novel, she found that her old home still had a powerful grip on her soul, and although she longed to get her hands on the money that she considered rightly hers, she hated the idea that her sons should not continue to enjoy the inherited advantages of the place. Often, as she ploughed her way through *Tristram Shandy*, she found herself staring through the page at the vivid memories of her childhood. In those far-off days, Alice had been in good health, albeit a little dreamy and vague; her father Con had been a glamorous if fleeting entity in their lives, and Dan and Tara had been a living, breathing, cheerful and above all constant presence. Those were good times, thought Orla. What happened to make it all go wrong? No money left to keep it all going, when Grandpa died; that's what happened, more's the pity, she said to herself, sadly.

Tadeusz, having explained quite firmly to Edward and Charlie that he could not spend much time with them, particularly in the mornings, was taking an enormous pleasure in restoring the kitchen garden to a model of perfection that even the Victorians would have admired. As he worked, aided by the moronic but malleable Billy, he speculated on the enormous potential of Neill's Court. Niamh's ideas had been perfectly sound, and her houseful of paying customers was proof of her success, but in Tadeusz's fertile imagination, she had barely scratched the surface.

As he hoed, dug, and raked the black earth, he visualized rows of ever more exotic fruit and vegetables. As he uncovered the beautiful blemish-free pink potatoes, and picked basketfuls of purple artichokes, he saw in his mind's eye the glass peach houses restored to productive use, and new raised beds, deep in steaming manure, overflowing with courgettes, cucumbers and melons. He straightened his back and looked around him, at the high walls of the sheltered garden, at the roofs of the stable-block, at the chimneys and turrets of the beautiful Georgian house beyond. It's bloody paradise here, he said to himself, or could be.

He carried the baskets of produce to the house, passing the stables on the way. All those empty spaces doing nothing, he thought; what a terrible waste. In the kitchen, Niamh was fully occupied with her morning class, so he took a glass of water from the tap, drank it swiftly and returned to the yard. There, he made a quick inspection of the empty buildings, and became increasingly convinced that a good and profitable use could be made of them. I could run a painting school here, easily, he said to himself. Why not? All these partitions for the loose-boxes could be ripped out, and that would give us two or three really big spaces. We could have at least sixty people here, at any one time. We'd make a fortune. If Niamh wanted to continue with her cooking lessons, that'd be OK, but just catering for the art students would be less of a hassle for her, I should have thought. We could just have the fishermen and the amateur painters; it would be great.

Tadeusz did not realize it, but he was already beginning to think of himself and Niamh as a team. He went back to the garden, gave Billy a bollocking for eating the raspberries and set about preparing a new bed for a sowing of perpetual spinach.

* * *

Tiger, meanwhile, was not enjoying her holiday. She felt bored to tears, and fed up with her tedious household duties. Worse still, she was beginning to be uneasily aware that it was hardly ever possible to spend much time alone with Tadeusz. Sometimes, after lunch, he went back to the garden, making the less than convincing excuse that he had a job to finish. Quite often, he silently disappeared with Edward and Charlie on some secret ploy, deliberately excluding Tiger from their plans, or so it seemed to her.

On one such afternoon, Tiger sought out Orla's company, to complain bitterly about Tadeusz's change of attitude towards her, but her sister failed to offer any comfort, or even sympathy. Perfectly happy herself to sit alone under her tree with a book, while other people amused her children, Orla thought Tiger was being childish and a bad sport, and told her so. 'You can't be jealous of Tadeusz's having fun with the boys, surely?'

'Not *jealous*, Orla; of course not. Just pissed off with them for dumping me.' Tiger looked at her sister, through her half-closed, black-fringed eyes, hurt and resentful. 'It's all Niamh's fault. I'm beginning to hate her, I really am. She's nothing but a sodding slave-driver, and now she's even got Tadeusz eating out of her hand, the cow.'

'I'm sure you're wrong, darling.'

'I'm sure I'm *right*! Niamh could get blood out of a stone, if she wanted to.'

Orla laughed. 'Don't be absurd, Tiger. Tadeusz is enjoying himself, one can tell. He's doing a terrific job; it's making such a difference to Niamh to have his help. No wonder she's pleased with him. You should be, too, darling, instead of whingeing all the time.'

'Huh!' said Tiger crossly. 'It's just the great house thing that appeals to him; he's such a pathetic little snob. Knowing him, he'll soon get hacked off, and want to leave.'

'Do you really think so?'

'Yes, I do.'

'And where would you go, Tiger?'

'To Przywnica, probably. It's lovely there, and one's not expected to work one's bloody fingers to the bone, either.'

'Are there servants at Przywnica?'

Tiger laughed. 'Are you kidding? Of course not. Ileana does it all; it's her thing.'

'Ileana?'

'Tadeusz's granny.'

'Yes, of course, I remember. You told me about her.' Orla looked at Tiger, frowning. 'And how old is the grandmother, or is that an officious question?'

'Oh, she's seventy-something; I can't remember.' Tiger stared at her sister defiantly. 'It's *her* choice, Orla. No-one *makes* her do what she does. She's a control freak; quite like Niamh in some ways, actually. Just as nasty, sometimes, too.'

'I see.'

While Tiger was sitting under the walnut tree, unburdening herself to Orla, Niamh was upstairs, taking a well-earned break. It was an unusually warm day, and the kitchen had been stiflingly hot during the morning class. After lunch, she had gone quietly up to her room, and slowly removed every stitch of her clothing. Wrapping herself in a cotton robe, she had gone to the bathroom and taken a long, near-cold bath, at the same time washing her lank, greasy hair.

Outside, on the landing, she heard the long-case clock strike three and got regretfully out of the water. Slowly, she blotted the moisture from her body, then, wrapping her head in a towel, she slipped on her robe and went back to her room. Here, she sat down in front of her dressing-table, and dried her hair, scrunching it with her fingers, so that it stood out round her head in a curly halo. She let her robe fall to the floor, and stared at her reflection in the glass. I look like a nun,

259

she said to herself with a grim little smile, all tanned face and arms, and creepy snow-white body, really disgusting. Her slender waist, flat stomach and well-developed muscles did nothing to diminish the unattractive appearance of her anatomy, and she sighed. She raised her hands, easily cupping her small pointed breasts. Even my tits are like a nun's, she thought. What's the word? Virginal, that's it. Even my stupid thing with that idiotic Michael didn't make much impact on me, did it? To all intents and purposes, I'm still pretty much intact, in mind as well as body.

She crossed the room to the window, and looked out towards the kitchen garden. There, as she had subconsciously hoped, she saw Tadeusz standing on a ladder, stripped to the waist, his bronzed back gleaming in the sun. He appeared to be nailing vine wires to the wall, as far as she could see at that distance. It was some time since Niamh had studied a near-naked and beautiful male torso, and a long-suppressed sensation, warm and tingling, filled her breasts, causing the nipples to harden. She turned away from the window, despising herself for her own easily roused sexuality, and went at once to her wardrobe, where she chose the first thing that came to hand, a faded, rose-printed frock.

In the garden, Tadeusz, perched on his ladder, driving vine-eyes into the crumbling brickwork, did not hear Niamh's footsteps as she approached.

'You're busy, Tadeusz,' she said. 'I thought the deal was that you worked in the morning, and did your own work in the afternoon?'

At the sound of her voice, he slewed round on the ladder, still holding three vine-eyes between his teeth. He looked down at her, his dark eyes alert. He removed the nails from his mouth and put them in his pocket. 'Sorry,' he said, grinning. 'Is overtime forbidden? I wasn't planning to charge you for it, in case you're worried.'

Niamh flushed, annoyed with herself, and with him. 'It would be too bad if you had been,' she said tartly. 'I wouldn't have paid you!'

'It was just a joke, Niamh!' He smiled slowly, displaying even white teeth. 'As a matter of fact, I'm enjoying myself doing this; I find it rather creative. It's a shame I won't be here to see the vines ripen, next year.'

'You could be, if you wanted.'

'What?'

'You could have a job here, if you wanted. In my opinion, you'd be a good investment, Tadeusz. You're just what I need here.' She looked up at him, unsmiling, stern. 'Of course, it's a non-starter, I know.'

'Why?'

'Why? Because of Tiger, of course. She'll want to go back to Paris, I expect.'

Tadeusz did not immediately reply. He finished driving in his vine-eye, then slowly descended the ladder and stood close to Niamh. A powerful male smell came from his sweating body. Her composure disturbed, she lowered her eyes, but stood her ground, determined not to take a step back.

'It's odd that you should mention my staying here, Niamh. I've been having similar thoughts myself.'

She shot a suspicious glance at him, and their eyes locked. 'What sort of thoughts, Tadeusz? And what about Tiger?'

'Tiger's her own woman, Niamh. She'll do what she wants.' Tadeusz looked deep into Niamh's distrustful grey eyes. 'I'm not the first man in Tiger's life, you know,' he said quietly, and put a hand on her hot cheek.

Niamh took a step back, and crossed her arms defensively, in the gesture Tadeusz was beginning to expect from her. 'Let's leave Tiger out of this,' she replied. 'Her private life is nothing to do with me.'

'Why don't we sit down,' suggested Tadeusz calmly, 'and I'll tell you what I have in mind.' He took her by the arm and led her to the wooden bench, where his shirt lay waiting. He looked at the shirt, became aware of his nakedness and said: 'Do you mind me being like this, Niamh? Would you rather I put my shirt on?'

'Of course not. You're fine as you are.' She sat down on the bench, and Tadeusz, moving his shirt out of the way, sat beside her.

'Fire away,' she said. 'Tell me what you have in mind.'

Carefully, and without persuasiveness or over-enthusiasm, he told her about his exploration of the empty stables, his ideas about running courses in painting, and the possibility that Niamh herself could give up her own classes, and concentrate on feeding the resident fishermen and art students with her wonderful food.

'What makes you think I'd want to give up my cookery classes?' Niamh gazed at Tadeusz, her eyes hard.

'I just thought that it would make life a bit easier for you. You look so knackered most of the time, poor girl.'

'Well, I'm not so knackered when you're doing the gardening, am I? At least, now, I do get to bed at a reasonable hour.'

'Well, sorry. It was just an idea, Niamh. I didn't mean to denigrate your achievements, in any way.'

'Yes, well, as long as you're not trying to patronize me, Tadeusz, or take over.'

'Why would I do that?'

'Because you're a man, that's why.' The bitterness in Niamh's voice was palpable, and Tadeusz flinched visibly.

He got up from the bench, and put on his shirt. 'If that's how you feel, there's nothing more to be discussed, is there?' He turned away, and began to gather his tools together.

'Hang on, Tadeusz,' Niamh said. 'I didn't reject your suggestion out of hand, did I? The painting school might be a very good idea, properly thought out.'

'Really?'

'Yes, really.'

'So, where do we go from here?'

'Work out a business plan, and then we can discuss it in detail, formally, in my office, OK?'

If Tadeusz had harboured the expectation that Niamh would fall on his neck with gratitude when he told her about his scheme, he was utterly mistaken. Thoughtfully, he finished fixing his row of vine-eyes, then carried the ladder to the shed, and put away all the tools. He went up to his room, pulled his drawing materials from under the bed, and began to work.

Tiger did not come to visit him, as she usually did, and for this he was thankful, for he had no wish to be disturbed as he wrestled with the economics of a scheme that could be the means of transforming his life. Although shocked by Niamh's poor opinion of the male sex in general, he did not really believe that he would have too much trouble in softening her attitudes, once she had come to depend on him. Tadeusz had yet to envisage precisely what he expected such dependence on Niamh's part to encompass, but whatever it was, he knew that he wanted it, and badly.

For three days, Tadeusz fulfilled his contracted hours in the garden, and spent the afternoons in his room, working on his scheme. On the fourth afternoon, he put his papers into a folder, changed into a clean shirt and went in search of Niamh. She was in the kitchen, icing cakes, but when she saw him, she handed the icing-bag to Colleen and led the way to the library.

She sat down behind the desk, and indicated that Tadeusz should take the chair facing her. He laid his folder on the desk, and opened it. Silently, he arranged his drawings in front of Niamh and she studied them carefully. After a while, she smiled. 'Very nice, Tadeusz,' she said. 'But how much will it all cost?'

'If we got in outside labour to demolish the redundant stalls, and all the other paraphernalia, it would

263

cost a lot, obviously. If I carried out the work, it would cost nothing, and we could sell quite a lot of those good mahogany partitions for a tidy sum, I imagine. Then, it would be a question of limewashing the walls, and building storage units, so I've included a price for the raw materials for all that. The only really big outlay would be for painting materials. We'd need easels, drawing boards, canvas and stretchers, and, of course, paper. I reckon a couple of thousand would cover all that, easily.'

'Did you work out what we could expect as profit, assuming that you have a fifty per cent take-up in the first year?'

'Yes, I did. I did it for a hundred per cent occupancy, but you can divide it by two, if you like.'

He pointed out his figures on the page, and Niamh's eyes widened, and she whistled. 'You're not serious, Tadeusz? Is that what people are prepared to pay for art classes?'

'It's what I charge in Paris, for a mature amateur, on an hourly basis.'

'I see. Of course, that doesn't include their board and lodging, does it?'

'Certainly not. It would be for you to decide what you charge them for that, Niamh.'

'They might prefer to stay in the pub.'

Tadeusz shook his head. 'I rather doubt it, when they've seen the impressive brochure I have in mind.'

For the first time, Niamh relaxed. She sat back in her chair, and smiled at Tadeusz. 'I must say, it does look quite promising,' she said. 'Would you mind if I showed your drawings to Matthew? He advises me about such things.'

'By all means; why not? You would be foolish not to get a second opinion.' Tadeusz got to his feet. 'I'll leave the drawings with you, Niamh. Thank you for looking at them.'

'Don't rush away,' said Niamh. 'There are lots of things I want to ask you. Let's have some tea, shall we?'

She went to the fireplace, took the speaking-tube from its hook on the wall, blew into it and said: 'Colleen?'

It was evident that Colleen was quite accustomed to using this antique means of communication, for after a short pause, Niamh asked her to bring a tea tray to the library. Amused by the expression of astonishment on Tadeusz's face, Niamh returned to the table. 'Mad, isn't it?' she said, and laughed.

'But efficient, it seems,' replied Tadeusz, laughing too. It was the first time he had heard Niamh really laughing, as though she were happy to be alive, in spite of everything.

After dinner, Niamh asked Matthew to come to the library with her, showed him Tadeusz's drawings, and outlined his proposals for the summer painting project. With his usual cautiousness, Matthew studied the figures carefully, then expressed the opinion that the scheme might be worth a try. 'After all,' he said, 'you have very little to lose, if Tadeusz is prepared to work for nothing until the thing is established.'

'Yes, that's exactly my feeling.'

Matthew, who had drunk more than his self-prescribed two glasses of excellent claret that evening, looked at Niamh speculatively, and did something he normally avoided like the plague: he posed an interfering question. 'What about Tiger?' he asked. 'I take it she approves of all this, Niamh?'

'What the hell's it got to do with her, Matthew?'

'Everything, I would have thought, my dear.'

'Don't "my dear" me, Matthew. What I choose to do in the way of business, with or without Tadeusz, is no concern of Tiger's, and I'll thank you to remember that.'

Recalling the business with the emeralds, Matthew very nearly said something he might later have regretted, but stopped himself in time. 'I have no wish to offend you, Niamh,' he said quietly, with a touch of pomposity, 'but I must express some concern at your

265

involving yourself with the man assumed to be the close friend of your sister, particularly as it seems she is unaware of your plans.'

'Is that all?'

'Yes.'

'Good.' Niamh gathered Tadeusz's plans together and put them carefully back in the folder. She sat back in her chair, crossed her arms and looked at Matthew, her expression revealing nothing. 'Apart from any considerations of a personal nature you may have, Matthew, I assume that in principle you approve of my scheme?'

Reluctantly, and truthfully, Matthew agreed that he did.

Later that night, Niamh lay in her bed, rejoicing in the fact that Matthew believed her capable of poaching Tadeusz from under the nose of the younger, and much more attractive, Tiger. Never in her entire life had she believed such a thing to be possible, and the sensation of power that now filled her deprived heart was extraordinary, and wonderful.

In the darkness of the night, a series of amazing projections flashed before her, and she saw herself and Tadeusz, rich, successful, living at Neill's Court as of right, certainly married, possibly with children to bind them securely together. She had observed how good Tadeusz was with Charlie and Edward, and how much they adored him. I can't see Tiger sharing her man with a bunch of kids, she said to herself smugly; she's far too obsessed with herself, silly child. Somehow, as Niamh planned her own bright future and Tadeusz's, this philosophical thought allowed her to dismiss any doubts she might otherwise have harboured, in respect of the necessary betrayal of her sister.

Too excited to sleep, Niamh got out of bed and went to the window. The waning moon had risen, and a million stars filled the sky. The night air was cool and dew-drenched, and she took deep voluptuous breaths of it, stretching her arms above her head. Then she leaned on the sill, and let her gaze wander over the lake, the hills and woods, then back again to the gardens and outbuildings below. All at once, she noticed that a dim light was burning in the tiny little window in Liam's old room above the stables, and her heart leapt within her. What's he doing, awake at this hour? she asked herself. Is he alone, painting maybe? Or perhaps he's got someone with him?

Her heart pounding, Niamh slipped on her robe and left the room. On bare feet, she crept down the staircase and let herself out by the garden door. She closed it noiselessly, then put on her slippers. Keeping close to the walls of the house, she walked quickly round to the stableyard. The door to the stables was standing ajar, and she went in. At the foot of the ladder to Tadeusz's room, she paused, listening intently, but could hear nothing at all, not even the sound of breathing. She waited for several minutes more, then stepped out of her slippers and began to climb the ladder. She had nearly reached the top when Tadeusz spoke. 'Who's that?' he said, sounding slightly alarmed.

For a moment, thinking that she might find Tiger in Tadeusz's bed, Niamh very nearly bolted down the ladder. Then, with clenched teeth, she poked her head through the hole in the floor. Tadeusz, alone, and resting on one elbow, almost laughed at her belligerent, accusing posture. 'Hello,' he said. 'This is a pleasant surprise.'

Relieved, gratified, feeling a little foolish, Niamh gathered what remained of her dignity about her, and climbed into the room. Fastening her robe more tightly around her waist, she advanced towards the bed. 'I saw your light on, Tadeusz. I just thought I'd let you know that Matthew approves of our scheme, in principle.'

Tadeusz closed his book and put it carefully on the crate that served as a night table. He looked at Niamh, as she stood uncertainly beside the bed, and smiled at her, his dark eyes full of comprehension. 'That's not the only reason you came, is it, Niamh?'

She swallowed, her pulses racing, so that she felt slightly light-headed. She took a deep breath. 'No, it isn't,' she said, and her voice shook.

Tadeusz turned back the sheet, and she saw that he was entirely naked. 'Come here,' he said quietly. 'There's nothing to be afraid of.'

She sat down on the side of the bed, and he took her in his arms and kissed her. Her response was electrifying, and for a second Tadeusz felt repelled by her rapacity and hunger, but in spite of this, it took very little time indeed for their encounter to reach its natural conclusion.

Afterwards, they slept for a while, then woke as the sun streamed through the window. 'Stay for a bit,' said Tadeusz, gently, sliding his hands down Niamh's responsive body.

'I'll stay for ever, if you like,' said Niamh. She wound her arms round his neck, and laughed. 'This is a bloody uncomfortable bed,' she said. 'It might be better if you came to me, in future. What do you think?'

'It'll have to be late, when everyone's asleep. I wouldn't want Tiger to find out about us.'

'She'll have to know, sooner or later, won't she?'

'Yes, she will; but not yet, please.'

'OK.' She pulled his face down to hers, and kissed him, slowly and languorously. 'I'll leave the garden door open for you. You can come whenever you like, darling.' She laughed softly, and looked at her watch. 'Shit! I must go! It's nearly time for the early breakfasts!'

She leapt out of bed, pulled on her night things and hurled herself down the ladder. Tadeusz stared after her in astonishment, then folded his hands behind his head, leaned back against the lumpy pillows, and laughed triumphantly, loud and long.

Tiger's nineteenth birthday, in the latter part of August, dawned bright and clear, for the prophesied rain had still not appeared and the summer weather continued, day after perfect day.

Matthew, disturbed by the suspected plotting against his dearly loved little sister-in-law, took an unusually firm stand with his indolent wife, and insisted that she accompany himself, the children and Tiger on a surprise birthday picnic, to be held on the tiny island in the middle of the lake.

'Oh, Matthew, sweetheart, must I? I really hate going out in that leaky old boat, you know that.'

'Ridiculous woman! You're quite happy for Ed and Charlie to go out in it, aren't you?'

'Well, they've got you to save them, if the boat sinks.'

'What makes you think I wouldn't save you? The boys are wearing life-jackets, in any case.' Matthew took his wife's hand, and adopted his special-pleading stance. '*Please*, my darling. Oblige me just this once, won't you? I have a very good reason for needing a bit of family solidarity, especially today.'

Orla frowned. 'Why? And why especially on Tiger's birthday? Niamh's giving her a party tonight, isn't that enough for her?'

'I can't believe you haven't noticed how miserable Tiger is, darling. It's clear to me she's anxious and upset, and quite tense. I'd have thought it only human to make sure that she has a good day today, poor little thing.'

Orla recalled her recent conversation with Tiger, and gave a sigh of resignation. 'Oh, bugger. I suppose you might be right, Matthew. OK, I'll come, if you insist.'

'That's my girl.' Matthew kissed his wife's hand, and then, remarkably for him in broad daylight, her lips.

Edward and Charlie, crouched in the rhododendrons close by, listening to this exchange between their parents, squirmed with embarrassment and giggled, their hands clapped over their mouths. 'Ugh!' whispered Edward hoarsely. 'Wet kissing! Disgusting!'

* * *

The day passed happily enough, and in the late afternoon a slight breeze ruffled the waters of the lake as Matthew pointed the boat towards home, and sparks and flashes of sunlight bounced off the shallow waves. Seated in the prow, staring into the emerald-green depths, Tiger thought she had never known the lake to be so glorious, and almost tropical in its beauty. 'Why don't we stop the boat, and go for a swim?' she suggested.

'Too jolly cold, out here, and too deep,' said Orla firmly.

Tiger leaned over and trailed her hand in the water, as it flowed swiftly past the gunwale. 'You're right,' she said. 'It's freezing.'

The dinner party was a celebration fit for a queen, as a few of the guests remarked afterwards, not once, but several times. At Tiger's request, Edward and Charles were allowed to stay up, and she sat between them at the festive table.

Niamh had excelled herself, and all Tiger's favourite dishes appeared, including, strictly against the house rules concerning the closed season, a magnificent lobster bisque, served in a silver tureen. Niamh was able to indulge this special request, owing to her well-stocked freezer cabinet. After this masterpiece came another, a truffle-studded loin of pork and its *jus*, with a mousseline of potatoes, and a salad of romaine lettuce and rocket. A selection of Irish cheeses followed, and then came the pudding. This was a huge *bombe surprise*, a moulded ice-cream packed with glazed fruits, candied peel and nuts, crowned with nineteen birthday candles.

After dinner, the entire party removed to the drawing-room, where Colleen and Siobhan had already put coffee, beside the bottles of liqueurs.

Edward and Charlie, stuffed with food but determined to stay up long enough to take part in the dancing, rolled back the rugs and advised their father, as he chose the gramophone records. Tiger, her violet eyes alight, beautiful in her frilly white shirt and red *gitane* skirt, put her arms round Tadeusz and asked him to be the first to dance with her. 'Please, Tadeusz?'

'NO!' shouted Edward, his cheeks flushed, his brown eyes bright with over-excitement, and he tugged at Tiger's skirt. '*I* want to be the first to dance with you, Tiger, *please.*'

'And after Edward, ME!' cried Charlie.

Tiger laughed, and then, realizing that they were both exhausted, and not wishing to spoil the day for them by provoking a tearful scene, she allowed Edward to lead her out onto the floor, and they performed an Irish jig together, without any mistakes. When the music stopped, there was a spontaneous burst of applause, and Charlie ran up to take his brother's place. Tadeusz turned to Niamh, and asked her to dance, and Matthew and Orla, too, walked onto the floor, along with two other couples. They all trundled round the floor in a stately slow waltz, which was just as well, for Charlie was by no means as nimble of foot as his brother. Tiger smiled kindly at the little boy as he clung to her forearms, his eyes on his own feet. No question, she thought; a jig would have been his undoing.

Orla took her boys up to bed, and the party began to break up at midnight, the guests drifting off to their rooms. On balance, Tiger had spent a happy day, and had danced with Tadeusz for the rest of the evening, her resentment in respect of his recent neglect forgotten. When the last guest had gone, she said good night to Tadeusz, and to Niamh, who was dowsing the lamps, and went to bed.

Lying in her attic room, listening to the heavy breathing of Colleen in the other bed, Tiger thought about the day, and about the evening. It was a lovely dinner, she said to herself, really lovely; I'll never forget it, never. She frowned uneasily, realizing that she

271

had forgotten to thank Niamh properly for going to so much trouble. I wonder if she's still awake? she asked herself.

She got quietly out of bed, then leaned out of the little window, craning her neck to see whether there was a light on in Niamh's room, and saw that indeed there was. Good, she thought, I'll go straight down and thank her, now. It will be a good chance to make things OK between us.

She went quietly down the attic stairs, and along the corridor to Niamh's room. She opened the door, and went in. In the lamplight, she recognized all too clearly the naked body and dark hair of Tadeusz, as he straddled the supine form of her sister. A sudden and violent rush of bile filled Tiger's throat, and she covered her mouth with her hand, but not quickly enough to prevent herself vomiting all over Niamh's carpet.

CHAPTER FOURTEEN

Horrified, Niamh and Tadeusz stared at Tiger, as she bent over the carpet, retching spasmodically, until she had brought up her entire birthday dinner. When nothing remained in her stomach, she straightened her back and pushed her long black hair away from her damp forehead. Ashen-faced, trembling, but composed, she looked coldly at her former lover. 'How *could* you, Tadeusz?' she asked in a small, almost polite voice. 'It's only quite recently that you were screwing *me*, or had you forgotten?' Without waiting for an answer, she turned on her heel and left the room.

She stumbled along the corridor to her mother's bathroom, and washed; first herself and then her sick-smelling hair. She took Alice's silk robe from its peg on the door, and wrapped herself in it. Although still trembling with shock, her mind felt curiously calm and lucid, but in spite of this seeming self-possession, Tiger felt unwilling to return to the attic. After a slight hesitation, she went along the corridor and tapped on Liam's door. There was an immediate response from inside the room, and Liam appeared in the doorway, wearing striped pyjamas, an alarmed expression on his face. 'Is it herself?' he asked. 'Is something wrong?'

'It's not Mum, Liam,' said Tiger, her teeth chattering. 'It's me.'

'Holy Mother! Come in at once, darlin'. For the love of Jesus, what's the matter, my lamb?'

At these words of love and sympathy Tiger dissolved into a flood of tears, and swiftly, Liam pulled her into his room and closed the door. 'There, there,' he murmured, holding her close to his chest. 'You have a good cry, me darlin' child. You'll be all the better for it, after. It'll be the reaction that's got to you, that's for sure. Will I ever get you a drink, now?'

'What sort of a drink?' Tiger made an attempt at swallowing her tears, and hiccupped.

'Tea? Brandy, if you'd rather?'

Tiger drew breath, and pulled away from Liam's embrace. 'Thanks, darling Liam, you're a star. A brandy would be great.'

'Here,' he said briskly, 'put this on; you're frozen stiff.' He took a folded blanket off the small sofa at the foot of his bed and wrapped it round Tiger's shoulders. 'Hop into my bed, and get warm.'

Obediently, Tiger hopped, and Liam fetched two glasses of brandy from his private supply. He handed one to Tiger, and sat down on the rocking chair beside the bed. He took a swig of his drink, and looked thoughtfully at the hunched shoulders and pale wistful face of the young woman he had known for nineteen years, and adored. Wisely, he said nothing, but waited until she might decide to talk to him, or not.

Tiger sipped her drink, feeling the fire of the brandy trickling slowly down her throat and into her battered stomach. When the glass was empty, she handed it to her old ally, with a tremulous smile. 'Sorry I've involved you in this, Liam,' she said. 'But I didn't have anyone else to turn to, as it happens.'

'Oh? Why's that, sweetheart? The place is awash with your sisters, isn't that so?'

'Yes, it is. And that's entirely the trouble, Liam.'

'So, tell me about it, if you want to.'

'I do, please.'

'Go on, then.'

Tiger hung her head, and he could see the tears, trembling once again on the spiked tips of her dark lashes. 'It's Niamh, Liam. She's got Tadeusz in bed with her. I found them, just now.'

'Was it sleeping they were?'

'No, they weren't asleep. They were screwing.'

'Shit! I don't believe it!'

'It's true, Liam. I went into Niamh's room, to thank her for the party, and there they both were, banging away.' Tiger tried hard to laugh, but failed. She put the heels of her hands against her eyes and wiped away the angry tears, furiously. 'Bloody shits and *fucking bastards*, so they are, the two of them!'

'Well, 'twas indeed a rotten trick to pull on your birthday, Miss Tiger darlin', but better find him out now than later, wouldn't you think?'

'What do you mean, later?'

'Was it marrying you had in mind with him, sweetheart?'

'Certainly not!' said Tiger crossly. 'Well, maybe; possibly; eventually. I don't know.'

'So, 'tis a lucky escape you've had, then?'

'Do you think so, Liam, honestly?'

'I do. Lie down and go to sleep now. You'll feel better in the morning. Then we can talk about it, and decide what to do.'

Tiger yawned, suddenly exhausted. 'Where will you sleep?' she asked, not really caring. She pulled the blanket over her shoulders, and closed her eyes.

'Here,' said Liam, his eyes full of tenderness. 'Where else?'

'Don't go,' whispered Niamh, locking her hands in a vice-like grip around Tadeusz's neck to prevent him leaving. 'It doesn't matter about Tiger; she'll get over it.'

With difficulty, Tadeusz prised himself away from Niamh, his face stony. He pulled his trousers on, picked up his shoes, took his beautiful shirt from the

275

back of the chair on which it hung, and went to the door.

'Where are you going?'

'Where do you think? To my room, of course.'

'You're being silly, Tadeusz; the damage is already done, and if you want to know, I'm glad. The sooner Tiger understands that everything's changed, the better for everyone. Come back to bed, it's only half past two.'

'Don't you care at all how shattered she must be feeling, Niamh?'

'No, I don't give a shit, and neither should you.' He said nothing, but turned towards the door. 'Tadeusz?'

'What?'

'It's a simple matter of decision-making, isn't it? You can either stay here with me, as we planned, or wander about in an ineffectual way with Tiger, being artistic. Which is it to be?'

Tadeusz stared at the ruined, sour-smelling carpet beneath his feet, his face dark with shame and his heart full of a hopeless grief. He remembered the lightness of Tiger's slender body, as she danced with him, and her kindness to her little nephews. Most of all he remembered Tiger's joyful radiance in bed, quite unlike the near-brutal ardour of her sister. It had not occurred to him that the loss of Tiger would give him so much pain.

Slowly, unhappily, he raised his eyes, and stared across the room at Niamh, as she lay unperturbed on her rumpled bed, her limbs relaxed, her smile insolent. 'Which is it to be, Tadeusz?' she repeated softly.

'Stay here with you, of course,' he replied, so quietly that she could hardly hear him. He put on his shirt, buttoning it carefully, and opened the door, checking that the corridor outside was empty. 'I'll see you later,' he said, and left.

At half past five Niamh got out of bed, dressed quickly and went down to the kitchen. There she found Liam, making a tray of tea and toast. She saw at once that he had put three cups on the tray. She raised her eyebrows, and looked pointedly at the tray. 'Have you a visitor, Liam?' she asked, sarcastically.

'I have, Miss Niamh, and since you've raised the subject your own self, I must say I'm surprised at you.'

'Really? It's lucky that your opinions are not of any consequence to me, isn't it?'

Liam put his slices of toast into the curly silver toast rack. He looked carefully at Niamh as she stood at the stove, pouring boiling water into a mug. Her brown hair was newly washed and wavy, her cheeks unusually pink for her; she looked almost pretty, and that had never been a word he would have used to describe his employer. She flicked the tea bag expertly into the sink, and turned towards him, her grey eyes shining and confident. 'Whose side are you on, Liam, when all's said and done?' She took a noisy gulp of her tea. 'Do you want this place to be a success, or don't you? If Mr Marylski goes, everything here will go on much as before; dodgy; hand-to-mouth, don't you realize that? If he stays, the place will be transformed, totally. We need a man here, Liam. Not an old bloke like you, but someone young and fit, with energy and ideas. I've found him now, and if you think I'm going to let him slip through my fingers on account of Tiger, you're a bloody sight stupider than I thought.'

It did not take Liam more than a few seconds to see the wisdom of Niamh's reasoning, and the undoubted good effect the presence of Tadeusz could have on all the residents at Neill's Court, including Alice and himself. In his heart, he grieved for Tiger; in his head, he bowed to the inevitable. He sighed, and picked up his tray. 'I'm sure you're right, Miss Niamh,' he said.

'I knew you'd see sense, Liam. We understand each other pretty well, don't we?' She smiled at him, but her eyes were cool. 'Please ask Tiger to come and see me at half past nine, in the library, will you? Tell her not to be late; I'm very busy this morning.'

'Very good, miss, I'll do that.'

*　*　*

The interview between Tiger and Niamh was brief, and to the point.

Niamh had always taken the view that, in difficult circumstances, attack was the best method of defence, and she lost no time in applying this principle. Before Tiger had time to get through the library door and give vent to the flow of angry accusations that hovered on the tip of her tongue, Niamh spoke, with brusque assertiveness. 'Sit down, Tiger.'

'I'd rather stand.'

'Don't be ridiculous. Sit down, and we can discuss this like grown-ups, not like a pair of silly girls.'

'I don't think of you as a silly girl, Niamh. I think of you as a thief; a bloody cheat and an adulterous whore!'

Niamh laughed scornfully. 'I wasn't aware that you and Tadeusz were married. When did the happy event take place, or was it a secret?'

Tiger flushed angrily. 'You know what I mean. You've been behaving like a cheat and a whore, and you can't deny it.'

'In that case, my dear, the same prissy strictures must apply to Tadeusz, mustn't they? As you so clearly saw last night, he was a willing participant in the act you found so disturbing.'

Tiger looked at her sister, her violet eyes blazing with contempt. 'I thought you looked like a desperate old tart, if you really want to know, Niamh. I hadn't realized you were so ugly, before.'

'And Tadeusz?'

Tiger could find no words to express her humiliation and cruel disappointment that her lover should have preferred her sister's unlovely body to her own. She hung her head, and was silent.

'Right. Good. We've got that straight, at least.' Niamh regarded her younger sister with a vengeful smile. 'I take it you won't want to hang around here for the rest of the holidays, Tiger. I don't imagine you can take

278

much comfort in the present situation. Why don't you push off?'

'Push off?' Tiger's eyes were round with alarm. 'What do you mean, "push off"? Where to, for Christ's sake?'

Niamh played her trump card. 'We thought it might be a good idea for you to spend the rest of the summer with your father, in Italy.'

Tiger, speechless with surprise, stared at Niamh's smug and implacable face, unable to think clearly, or make any response to this suggestion.

'Think about it, Tiger. I expect you would have rather a good time. I don't suppose you would have to do housework, or all the other things that seem to bore you rigid. I expect you could paint pictures all day long, if you wanted to.'

'What about money?'

'I've no doubt Orla and Matthew would see to that for you, if you asked them. They'll have to know about Tadeusz and me, sooner or later, so it's probably best if you speak to them yourself.'

The day crawled past with unbearable slowness for Tiger. Matthew and the boys had gone out for the day, and Orla spent a longer time than usual with Alice, in the orangery. In any case, Tiger had the feeling that Matthew would be much more sympathetic towards her unhappy predicament than Orla, whose view would probably be much like Liam's; namely, that she was well shot of Tadeusz.

She searched everywhere for Tadeusz, determined to force him to tell her himself that he no longer loved her, but he was nowhere to be found. In the kitchen garden, Billy told her that Miss Niamh had sent Mr Tadeusz to town, and that he would very likely be away all day. I bet he will, said Tiger to herself angrily; he's a coward, as well as a two-timing shit.

By the time Matthew and the boys came home, she had come to the reluctant conclusion that there was very little she could do to alter the state of affairs between Tadeusz and Niamh, and that her best option was, in fact, the one suggested by her sister. All afternoon, she walked along the shore of the lake and thought about her father. All she knew about him was that he looked very like herself; that he was a writer; that he had taken one look at herself as a newborn baby, and removed himself to Italy without delay.

In spite of the fact that her father had not shown the slightest interest in her so far, a tiny worm of curiosity stirred in Tiger's heart. If Matthew would pay the fare for me, she thought, it might not be such a bad idea, after all. If I go away, perhaps Tadeusz will realize what a fool he's been. Who knows what might happen, then? I can always leave him my address, can't I?

After dinner, she asked Matthew to walk with her in the garden. Quietly, for he had already sensed that some mischief was afoot, he excused himself to Orla, and followed Tiger through the French windows and onto the lawn.

'What's up, darling?' he asked, without preamble.

'A lot, Matthew.' Tiger glanced up at him, her eyes full of pain. 'I expect you've noticed that Niamh's been throwing herself at Tadeusz, since we came here?'

'I had noticed, yes.'

'Well, she's managed to get him where she wants him, Matthew; in her bed, as a matter of fact.'

'Really? How do you know that, Tiger? Did he tell you so himself?'

'No, he didn't have to. I went down to Niamh's room last night, to say thank you for the party, and found them in bed together.'

'God, you poor girl! I'm so sorry.' Matthew sighed. 'Niamh really is appallingly behaved, when it suits her, I'm afraid.'

'The thing is, she's told me to bugger off; that I'm in her way here.'

'She has no right to do that, Tiger, none at all, if you want to stay. This is your home as much as hers or Orla's.'

'I know that, but I don't particularly want to *be* here, Matthew, when she's screwing my lover.'

'Yes, I see.'

'Niamh suggested that I ask you for the fare, to visit my father in Italy.'

Matthew put his arm round Tiger's shoulders, and gave her an affectionate hug. 'Is that what you'd like to do, yourself, darling?'

'Yes, I think it probably is. I've had all day to think it over, and I think it might be best.'

'Of course I'll give you the money; as much as you need. We'll go into town, and sort it out tomorrow.'

Tiger put her arms round Matthew's waist and hugged him, glad that they were safely hidden by the darkness of the garden. 'Darling Matthew, I do so wish that I had an adorable husband like you,' she said.

Gently, Matthew kissed her. 'You're not the only one with dreams like that, Tiger,' he said. 'The trouble is, I'm not like Tadeusz and never will be, I know. I gave my hand and heart to Orla, and they're hers till one of us dies.'

'She's a lucky woman,' said Tiger. 'Will you kiss me again, Matthew? Just once?'

He kissed her again, and they walked back to the house together, hand in hand.

Three days later, Tiger arrived in Bari in the full roasting heat of late August, and was met at the airport by her father. She recognized him, tall, towering over the Italian crowd, black-haired and handsome, as soon as she passed into the arrivals hall. Con, too, spotted his daughter at once, and raised a tentative hand in greeting.

'Mr Fitzgerald? Dad? It is you, isn't it?'

'It is, but don't call me that, for Christ's sake. Call me Con, if you like.'

'Oh, right.'

Con Fitzgerald smiled for the first time, pleased that the young woman in front of him was so beautiful, gratified that she looked so much like himself, and had nothing of the O'Neills about her. 'You're still called Tiger, then, according to your sister's fax?'

Tiger laughed. 'Yes, I am. Do you mind?'

'Not at all. It rather suits you.' He took her suitcase from her and they went out to the car park, in search of Con's elderly and battered Fiat. 'It's a longish drive in this old heap,' he said, 'but with luck, we should get home before dark.'

They drove south, along the coast road. Tiger sat beside her father, observing the sea on her left-hand side and the parched countryside on the other.

Con drove in silence, as fast as the car would permit. Although fairly curious as to the reason for the sudden appearance of a daughter in his life, he was not much given to prying into the affairs of his fellow men, and had already decided that it would be more civilized to wait until Tiger herself should decide to confide in him.

Tired after the long journey from Dublin, still feeling incredibly hurt and bruised by the events of the past few days, Tiger was relieved not to be asked probing questions or expected to give an account of her life story. She sat back in her seat, her eyes half closed against the fierce glare of the sun, scarcely taking in the passing landscape of vineyards and silvery olive groves, trembling in the heat haze. She did notice, from time to time, curious conical stone roofs, perched incongruously on simple whitewashed buildings, standing alone or in groups, surrounded by their vines or olives. 'Are those roofs a traditional thing here?' she asked. 'The pointed stone ones?'

'They are,' replied Con, giving her a swift glance. 'They're called *trulli*. What do you think of them?'

'They're amazing. They look as though they've been here for ever.'

282

'They have, as a matter of fact. Since around 1500, maybe even earlier, some of them.'

'Oh.'

They had been driving for a little over two hours and the sun was beginning to sink low in the western sky, when Con pointed ahead to the spires of a city, its stone buildings a warm honeyed gold in the evening light. 'There you are,' he said. 'Lecce. It's the capital of the Salento region, and arguably the most beautiful place in Italy, after Florence.'

Tiger sat up, suddenly wide awake. 'Is that where you live?'

'No, but it's not far away. We won't go into town today. It's getting late and you must be tired. There'll be plenty of good reasons for a visit, later.'

They skirted the city limits, then headed east, towards the sea again. In a quarter of an hour they had almost reached their destination, and Con turned the car into a rough track, switching on his headlights. Slowly, they approached what appeared to be a large ruin; a sprawl of limewashed stone buildings clustered round a low circular tower. Isolated on a little hill, the place stood marooned in a sea of olives and vines, which grew right up to the walls.

Con stopped the car beside a shabby blue-painted door, and they got out. 'This is it, Tiger,' he said. '*La Commanderia*, which makes the place sound a good deal grander than it actually is. Let's go in, shall we?'

She turned towards him. 'Con?'

'Mm?'

'Thank you for letting me come.'

'Don't thank me yet, Tiger. You may hate it here. It's hot in the day, cold at night, and bloody primitive, by most people's standards.' He took her suitcase from the boot, opened the blue door and went in.

She followed him. 'I don't think I'll hate it,' she said, but he did not seem to hear her. The door opened straight into a long vaulted rough stone corridor, a sort of covered terrace, pierced by arches giving onto an open courtyard. There, the lamps had already been lit, so that Tiger could see the dark shapes of several massive, bizarrely shaped fig trees, growing straight out of the unplastered stone walls. Under one of them stood a solid wooden table, and some plain kitchen chairs.

'Enzo!' Con shouted. 'We're here!' He turned to Tiger. 'He's a bit deaf, so you'll have to speak up a bit. It's frustrating for him when people mumble.'

From the far side of the courtyard came a booming response, and an old man with a deeply wrinkled face, black eyes and a shining domed head above a fringe of grey hair hurried towards them, his arms extended in an extravagant gesture of welcome.

'This is my daughter, Tiger Fitzgerald,' said Con. 'Tiger, meet Enzo Molini, my friend and landlord.'

Tiger smiled, extending her hand, and the extraordinary old man clasped it between his massive paws, and raised it to his lips. '*Bellissima!*' he exclaimed. 'You did not tell me that your daughter is a beauty, Con!'

'I didn't know that she was,' replied Con, and laughed.

'Some wine, something to eat?' On the table, already laid out, they could see a flask of wine, glasses, a dish of small ripe tomatoes and one of glossy black olives.

'I'd love a drink, but I really need a wash first, Con,' said Tiger, turning anxiously towards her father. 'I'd like to change into something cooler, too, if that's OK?'

'Yes, of course.' Con said something in Italian to Enzo, who said '*si*' several times, nodding his head, and hurried away across the courtyard.

'Come, I'll show you,' said Con, and picking up Tiger's suitcase, he led the way along the vaulted covered terrace, turning into another corridor at the corner. She followed him, until he stopped beside a dark-stained door. 'Bathroom,' he said. 'Your door is two further on, OK?'

'Thank God,' she exclaimed, opening the bathroom door. 'Actually, what I'm desperately needing is a pee, but I didn't quite like to say so in front of Mr Molini.'

Con laughed. 'I thought so,' he said. 'You had that slightly fidgety air about you, poor old thing. Go on, in you go.'

Tiger's room, whitewashed, sparsely furnished, almost monastic in its simplicity, seemed to her a place of peaceful refuge, and she felt welcome there, as well as strangely comforted.

There was only one quite small window, which looked towards the sea, across an ocean of vines. The window had no curtains, but was shaded from the sun by a delicately carved wooden grille, through which the evening breeze now flowed, scented with thyme and curry-plant, cooling the air.

A narrow bed, of painted tin, inlaid with mother-of-pearl, was the only furniture in the room, apart from a baroque-looking mirror hung above a plain wooden table. She looked around, wondering where to put her clothes, and saw that the door had been equipped with a double row of stout wooden pegs. From these pegs dangled several wire coat-hangers, of the type provided by dry cleaners.

'Good,' she said, and opened her suitcase.

Ten minutes later, washed, her hair brushed, wearing jeans and one of her frilly shirts, Tiger found her way back to the courtyard on bare, silent feet. Seated at the table she saw her father and Mr Molini, glasses of wine before them, their faces rosy in the light of the lantern hung in the fig tree above. She stood for a moment, observing them, and it seemed to her that she was watching a movie, in which the characters were two old and very close friends, their mutual affection palpable. They look exactly like father and son, she said to herself. You can tell that they love each other.

Gazing at them, Tiger felt a stab of envy, or possibly, fear. When the old man dies, she thought, Con will miss him terribly. I wonder whether anybody would miss me, if I died? Tadeusz and Niamh wouldn't, that's for sure. Oh shit, don't be so bloody wet, get a grip, she silently reproached herself; you're just being tired and pathetic. Taking a deep breath, she crossed the courtyard to join the others at the table.

'Here she is, at last!' Con stood up as Tiger approached, and the old man waved his enormous hands expressively, smiling a welcome.

'Sorry,' said Tiger, sitting down. 'I hope I haven't held things up at all?'

'Certainly not,' replied Enzo at once, and turned to Con. 'Would you mind telling Giuliana we are ready to eat, and I will give our guest a glass of wine, while we wait?'

'Right.' Con disappeared under the arches of the vaulted corridor, which Tiger now realized ran round all four sides of the courtyard. She turned to the old man. 'What a lovely place this is, Mr Molini,' she said shyly. 'It's so quiet and peaceful; it's like a dream.'

'Call me Enzo,' he said, pouring wine into Tiger's glass. 'I don't like to be an old man to whom great respect and politeness are obligatory, as of right.'

'Thank you,' said Tiger. 'I will.' She took a sip of the wine, which was scented and powerful.

'Eat something, my dear. The wine will taste better.'

Obediently, she took an olive with an anchovy wrapped round it, and put it in her mouth. She looked at her host with admiration. 'You speak extremely good English, Enzo,' she ventured. 'I'm ashamed to admit it, but I scarcely know one word of Italian.'

'You soon would, if you had the need to,' he said, and laughed his big booming laugh. 'You forget, I've had many years of instruction in English, at the didactic hands of your father.'

Tiger smiled. 'I suppose.'

'You are exactly like he was, when we first met. It is like looking back down the years, a long, long way. Incredible, and a little disturbing, to say the truth.'

Tiger put down her glass, looking anxious. 'I don't

want to be disturbing to you, in any way. I would hate it if I thought you felt you had to entertain me, so you must please tell me exactly how your working day is planned, and I can make myself invisible.'

Enzo raised a protesting hand. 'You won't have to make yourself invisible, Tiger. We are both very happy to have you here.'

'Well, thank you, it's very kind of you both.' She took another sip of her wine, and tried to smile, finding it difficult to do so. 'My father tells me you're a sculptor; that you're still working full time?'

'That's right. Just as he is a full-time writer. When you feel like it, I will show you the studio, and my work. Tonight we will all enjoy being together, and take a holiday from work, or whatever is worrying us, no?'

Tiger, aware of the old man's dark watchful eyes upon her, guessed that he was interested in knowing the reason for her sudden intrusion into his life and Con's, and gazed into the ruby depths of her glass, saying nothing. She was relieved when Con returned to the courtyard, carrying a large platter of steaming pasta. In his wake came Giuliana, a short, swarthy, middle-aged woman with a big toothy smile, bringing plates, a dish of shredded cheese and a bowl of salad, all precariously balanced on a tray.

Giuliana put the tray on the table, and a brief conversation ensued between herself and Enzo, in a dialect that sound like machine-gun fire to Tiger's ears. 'OK. *Buona notte, Giuliana. Grazie!*' The old man waved her away impatiently, his eye on his cooling supper.

'*Prego!*' Giuliana gave the company an all-encompassing smile, with a sharp look at Tiger, then took herself off without further ado.

The meal was simple and delicious. Within the golden mound of hot pasta lurked tiny meatballs, spiked with fiery little peppers and scented with torn leaves of basil. A fragrant tomato *sughetto* bound the elements of the dish together, and it seemed to Tiger that she was really tasting tomatoes for the first time in her life. Rich, thick, fruity and powerfully perfumed, the sauce was a revelation to her. 'Is there a secret ingredient?' she asked. 'Do you put in something special, like sugar, to make it so luscious and sweet?'

Con shook his head, smiling. 'Nothing except the tomatoes, some herbs and a bit of garlic,' he said. 'The way tomatoes grow here, that's all that's needed. At the end of summer we make them into a sort of jam, for winter use. That's good, too.'

'And the meat?' she asked.

'Goat, probably.'

'*Really?* It's delicious. I'd never have guessed it was goat.'

Enzo laughed, and took another helping. 'We Apulians are a frugal lot,' he said. 'We don't drown delicate meats like lamb or chicken in *sughetto*. We usually grill them on the spit with lemon and a drop of olive oil, brushed on with a faggot of thyme.'

'Sounds wonderful.'

'You shall judge for yourself, Tiger. Do you like to cook?'

'I haven't done much so far, but with food like this, I'd certainly like to learn.'

After they had finished eating, Con and Tiger took everything to the kitchen and stacked the dirty dishes in the sink, to be dealt with by Giuliana in the morning. Con filled the sink with cold water. 'You should always do this,' he said, 'or there'll be scorpions in the sink by dawn. It's a pain if they sting you, so take care.'

'Don't worry. I will.'

'Look in your shoes, too, before you put them on.'

'Right.'

They made coffee, and carried the tray out to the courtyard, where Enzo was smoking a short black cigar, and reading the evening paper that Con had brought from Bari. As they approached, he flung the paper on the ground, with a snort of derision. 'It's nothing but robberies and murders around here,' he exclaimed crossly. 'At least, that's all that's reported in the papers, isn't it? What kind of an impression does that give to our visitors? A very frightening one, I should have thought.'

'I was in Bari for at least half an hour,' said Tiger, seriously. 'I can't say I noticed any murders happening, or even a bag being snatched.' She picked up the pot, and poured the coffee, very carefully, in view of the fact that she felt extremely tired, as well as slightly drunk. She handed their cups to the two men, sat down herself, and drank her own.

'Hadn't you better phone home, Tiger? Shouldn't you let Orla know you've arrived safely?' Con spoke very quietly, as though he were thinking aloud.

Tiger choked on her coffee, and hastily put down her cup, as she fought to regain both her breath and her composure. She shook her head, vehemently. 'No, I'd much rather not, if you don't mind, Con,' she said, sounding agitated. 'No-one there gives a toss how I am; they're all thankful to see the back of me, if you want to know.'

'Oh, well, never mind. You know best, of course.'

Enzo looked from father to daughter, and back again. Then, very smoothly, he made an announcement, and one he hoped would steer the conversation away from such an obviously sensitive area. 'In a week or two,' he said, 'it will be the beginning of the *vendemmia*, and the pickers will come. We shall be busy, and everyone must help.' He looked at Tiger, with a teasing little smile. 'I am keeping all the fingers crossed that Sandro will come and stay with us for the *vendemmia*. He usually does.'

'Sandro?' asked Tiger.

Con laughed. 'Alessandro is Enzo's famous grandson, Tiger. He is quite a hero in these parts, I can tell you. I dare say a few girls would tell you so, too.'

'Don't be absurd, Con!' protested Enzo. 'You make my grandson sound *ottuso*!'

'What's *ottuso*?' Tiger asked, with a tight little smile.

'It means he's a prat,' said Con, with a malicious grin at his old friend.

'*Diavolo!* Sandro is very nice boy. You will like him, I promise, Tiger.'

Tiger did not respond to this recommendation, but rose to her feet, explaining that she was very tired and must go to bed. She said good night politely, and thanked Enzo for allowing her to visit them at such short notice.

Con accompanied his daughter to her room. As they walked together along the vaulted stone terrace, cool in the night air, he took her arm. 'Are you all right, Tiger? All these silly jokes aren't a bore for you, just now? You don't mind Enzo, making his sly remarks?'

Tiger shook her head. 'It's OK, I don't really mind. At least, I'll be better at handling it when I've had a good sleep, I expect.' At her door, she turned towards her father. 'Is he really a prat, this Sandro? I've had a belly-ful of prats, recently, as a matter of fact.'

Con laughed. 'No, of course he isn't; that's just me pulling Enzo's leg. Sandro's a perfectly ordinary guy; perfectly nice. He's a student in Rome. He's about your age, or maybe a few years older; he's been at university for a couple of years, now.'

'Oh. He's a clever-clogs, then?'

Con smiled, and kissed her on the cheek, gently. 'Go to bed, Tiger, you're exhausted. Good night, my dear. Sleep well.'

'Good night, Con. Thanks.'

In the safety of her room, Tiger looked at the painted bed with weary longing. Then, unable to stop herself, she lay down on the coverlet, closed her eyes and fell at once into a deep, dream-filled sleep. She woke just before dawn, chilled by the cold draught that blew through the window. Still half asleep, she got undressed, and got properly into bed, pulling the sheet and blanket over herself. She turned onto her stomach, and slept once more, undisturbed by the light of the rising sun, as it streamed through the grille of her window, casting a beautiful pattern across her bed.

CHAPTER FIFTEEN

'The little *ragazza* is very sad, Con, one can tell.' Enzo sighed, and peered over the rim of his breakfast coffee cup at his friend. 'We must rouse ourselves, to amuse her.'

'I get the feeling that she just wants to be left alone, poor kid,' said Con, dunking bread in his coffee and transferring the soggy lump perilously to his mouth. 'Something pretty humiliating must have happened, by the sound of things. No doubt she'll tell us about it, when she's ready. Well, I hope so, anyway.'

'You're right, of course. We must wait; *pazienza* is the thing.'

Con laughed. 'Since when was it the thing with you, Enzo? Like never?'

'OK, OK. But this time I will be, you'll see!'

Inside the covered terrace, Con saw Giuliana carrying a tray in the direction of Tiger's room, and he called out to her not to disturb the signorina, that she must be allowed to sleep. With a look of astonishment, even disapproval, and without stopping, Giuliana did a smooth U-turn and carried the tray back to the kitchen.

On the third day, Tiger, to the enormous relief of her two mentors, got up early and had breakfast with them in the courtyard. She remarked on the gloriousness of the day, told them she had seen a Sardinian warbler in the olive tree outside her window and asked Enzo whether she might see his studio. Surprised and delighted, the old man expressed his pleasure in the only way he knew, by silently kissing Tiger's hand.

After breakfast, Con, with visible relief on his handsome face, took himself off to his study and settled to a normal morning's work. Enzo led the way to his studio, which was in the former watchtower. It was a whitewashed, airy space, and full of light; pierced by openings introduced by himself, in order to obtain both ventilation and illumination in his workspace.

Tiger looked around the circular room. 'It's beautiful,' she said. 'Tell me about the tower. Is it old?'

'Very. A lot of these towers were built five hundred years ago, in the reign of Carlo Quinto. He erected them all along the coast, to guard against pirates.' He smiled, pleased at Tiger's interest. 'There's a splended view from the top, if you like to go up and see.'

'I believe you,' said Tiger. 'But, if it's OK, I'd really like to look at your work.'

'*Prego!* Take your time; look around. Ask any question you like.' He went to his worktable, removing his shirt to reveal a rather tatty old string vest, picked up a chisel and a mallet, and applied himself to the carving in which he was currently engaged. A tall slender block of the local limestone, beautiful in itself, and the colour of honey, stood on its plinth, waiting. On its sides, the sculptor had drawn a series of mysterious marks with charcoal, and was now in the process of removing the superfluous areas of stone. Unhurriedly, he began to chip away, seemingly undisturbed by Tiger's presence.

She walked slowly round the studio, examining each piece in turn. Some of them were simple blocks of stone, one face incised with bas-relief images, almost like fossils: wings of birds; shells; skeletal leaf-forms; serpents. There were in addition several powerful three-dimensional and near-abstract studies of the human torso, which reminded Tiger of her life classes in Paris, and brought a bitter taste to her mouth.

Beside the tallest of the window slits stood an extra-ordinary stone statue in the baroque manner, a florid vision of the Virgin and Child. It was over life-sized and bathed in the bright shafts of sunlight that caressed the swirls and scrolls of its elaborately carved surface. Tiger laid a tentative finger on the undulating folds of the Virgin's hem, and wondered how it was possible to achieve such a technically flawless work from a block of stone. 'May I ask you something, Enzo?'

'Anything.'

'How is it that you can do this delicate work on such hard stone, without it cracking or chipping?'

'It's a confidence trick, *cara*. When the stone comes out of the ground, it is very soft; very easy to work. It is only with time and exposure to air that it becomes hardened.'

'I see.' She came and stood beside him, watching as he continued to work his stone, along a sinuously curving contour. 'Is that fun to do?'

'Try it.' He offered her the chisel and mallet.

'Oh, I couldn't! I might damage it! What a horrible thought!'

Enzo laughed. 'It wouldn't matter if you did. I'd just make a little adjustment.'

Tiger shook her head. 'No, really, I'd rather not.' She looked across the studio at the Virgin, standing in her pool of light. 'Is it a commission, the Virgin?' she asked.

'Why do you ask?'

'Because it's quite unlike all your other things, isn't it?'

'You're right, it is. Yes, she's a copy of one in Lecce, done for a private client.'

'Really? Did she take for ever to do?'

'Two years, and I'm still making small refinements.'

'Wow!'

'I used to do that sort of thing full time, for a living. Restoration; stuff like that. It's not a bad life. Now I

294

work to please myself, it's not like work at all, you understand, it's a pleasure.'

'Yes,' said Tiger. 'One can tell.' She looked at him shyly. 'I was in Paris for a year, being an au pair, you know. I used to go to life classes in the evenings, twice a week. Drawing was the only thing I was any good at, at school.'

'Did you enjoy your life classes?'

'Yes, I did. A lot.'

'Good. So you can continue, now, can't you?' Enzo put down his chisel, went to a plan chest, pulled out a drawer and took from it a block of paper. 'Here is paper, and over here is charcoal.' Mesmerized, Tiger followed him to his worktable, where he selected three sticks of charcoal and gave them to her. 'If you would enjoy a change from the human body, go outside, look at the trees, at the lizards on the rocks, at the *cicala* with her scarlet wings. Even a *pagghiaru* is interesting to draw.'

'What's a *pagghiaru*?'

'It's the little stone hut you often see in the olive groves, with only one small hole to go in and out. They're like beehives.'

'Oh. Well, good, I'll go and find one.' She smiled, her beautiful violet eyes full of gratitude for the unspoken sympathy and support of her new friend. 'Thank you very much, Enzo,' she said.

'Nothing to thank,' he replied. '*Sta bene!* Watch out for the vipers!'

Wistfully, the old man watched her go, slender and graceful in her jeans and loose white shirt, her black hair hanging down her narrow, youthful back. He sighed, remembering the lovely women of his distant past, then picked up his chisel and resumed his work.

Seated in the dappled shade of a centenarian olive tree, Tiger studied her *pagghiaru* with intense concentration, before allowing the thin stick of charcoal to mark the pristine whiteness of the paper. All around her, the air was alive with the sound of insects, and full of the smell of sun-kissed myrtle, lentisk and rosemary, whose wind-sculpted and stunted bushes grew everywhere in the stony red earth.

The time passed swiftly, and at the end of two hours she had made a fairly good drawing of the small stone hut, with its tiny opening, overhung by the silvery fronds of an olive, its ripening green fruit clearly visible.

Critically, Tiger looked at her work, and frowned. I'm not actually mad about charcoal, she said to herself. It's too tricky, and smudges so easily. I wonder if Enzo has any watercolours? I'd get on better with something more fluid and impressionistic, I think.

Suddenly, into her mind came the memory of her trip to the Louvre, and her afternoon studying the wonderful Giorgione painting, the *Fête Champêtre*. She thought of the beautiful black-haired young lute-player, gazing at his male companion, in spite of the close proximity of two lovely, and alluringly naked girls. Why was I so enchanted by that picture? she asked herself. What on earth possessed me to be taken in by those two rotten little shits? They were behaving just like Tadeusz, and even Luc; they didn't give a toss for the girls, did they? They'd screw you, and then drop you in it when they got bored, one can tell. *Bastards!* she thought; I hate them all! I'd much rather be with a kind old man, like Enzo, any day. Or Con, come to that. At least they wouldn't try to get into my knickers, and then betray me with my bloody sister, would they?

She sat there for some time, angrily brooding on the imperfections of the men in her life. Then, feeling quite hungry, she looked at her watch, and wandered back to *La Commanderia*.

After lunch, she showed her drawing to Enzo. 'It's not very good, is it?' she admitted, humbly. 'I found it rather difficult working outside, in the wind and the hot sun. It's quite different from working in a studio, where everything keeps still. I was wondering if I'd get on better with watercolours. What do you think?'

'You have to try everything, and find the medium that suits you best, *cara*. I do have some very old colours, but it's likely they are all hardened and dried out by now.'

Con interrupted, quietly. 'I have to go into Lecce later this week, Tiger. Perhaps we can find what you need, there?'

'Could we, really? That would be brilliant, Con; thank you.'

'My pleasure, darling.'

It was the first time Con had used such a term of endearment towards her, and Tiger looked at him shyly, her bruised psyche comforted. 'Mine, too,' she said.

Matthew had returned to London, leaving Orla and the boys to stay on at Neill's Court until the end of the month. Since one of the double guest rooms was now temporarily free, Orla moved into it, and, as the long-awaited rain arrived, the boys dismantled their tent and brought their sleeping-bags up to their mother's room.

In a perverse way, the very fact of spending her whole day in the house brought home to Orla the disagreeable realities of day-to-day existence in the company of strangers. It's all very well for Niamh, she said to herself bitterly; she's seven years younger than I am. She can't really remember how terrific it was here, in the old days, when the place was full of servants, and there were parties all the time.

Lying in her bed, reluctant to get up and face yet another day avoiding the paying guests, Orla stared at the ceiling, thinking about her gregarious and very hospitable grandparents. It was fun then, she said to herself, remembering the horses, the shooting parties and the hunt balls. Curiously, she did not have a very clear picture of her mother, Alice, during the happy time of her own girlhood. If she remembered her at all, it was on the hill, riding out with Liam. He was always with her, she thought. How strange that no-one thought it odd, at the time.

Now that Matthew had gone back to work, and Tiger had gone away, Charlie and Edward seemed at a loose end, and were growing more impossible and whingeing as each day passed. Niamh, in her bossy way, was forever telling them to shut up, or get lost, or run to the village on an errand, which did nothing to improve their quarrelsome and resentful mood. For two pins, I'd take them home for the last few days of the holidays, Orla said to herself, frowning unhappily. It'd be more fun for them there, especially now it's raining here, nearly all the time. They've got the computer at home, to amuse them, as well as all their friends.

Feeling exhausted, although she had been in bed for nearly ten hours, Orla got up and went to the bathroom, where she was forced to take a tepid bath, the bulk of the hot water having already been drained from the inadequate tank. Bloody hell, she said to herself, angrily, this place is little better than a common lodging-house, and not a very posh one either, except for Niamh's cooking. I don't know why I insisted on bringing the boys here at all. It's not as if Neill's Court is such a big deal nowadays, when all's said and done. I sure as hell wouldn't want the boys to tell their friends that we take in bloody paying guests.

In spite of her snobbish dislike of the current state of affairs Orla was doing her best to be fair to Niamh, and reminded herself how great had been her sister's achievement in turning the place into a successful business, especially now that she appeared to have acquired Tadeusz as a working partner. Sleeping partner, too, I don't doubt, she said to herself, sourly. Poor old Tiger, what a shitty thing to happen. I wonder how she's getting on with Dad?

As she made her way down to the orangery, steadfastly refusing to meet the eye of any stray guest lurking in the hall, Orla sighed dispiritedly. I think I'll ring up Matthew tonight, she promised herself, and tell him I've had enough. We're coming home.

After dinner, Orla made her call to Matthew, but was disappointed to find that he was not at home. She left a message on the answering-machine, asking him to call her. Feeling put out and depressed, she chased the children up to bed, and then, reminding herself what a boring time they were having, offered to play Racing Demon with them.

At ten o'clock, Orla saw that both boys seemed tired, their concentration slipping, and she gathered up the cards, while they got into their sleeping-bags.

'Bother,' said Edward sleepily. 'We haven't cleaned our teeth, Mum.'

'Don't worry about it, just this once,' said Orla. 'The bathroom's probably full of grockles, anyway. Best keep a low profile, really. Give your teeth an extra scrub in the morning.'

Charlie sniggered. 'You shouldn't call them grockles, Mum,' he whispered. 'It's rude, you know.'

'It's only rude if you say it. It's OK if I do, or Dad.'

'It's boring here without Dad,' said Edward, fixing his serious brown eyes on his mother's face.

'And Tiger,' said Charlie. 'I really love her. I wish she was still here, don't you?'

'And Tadeusz isn't fun, like he was in Paris. I wish we could go home.'

'Do you really? Are you sure, both of you?'

'Yes!' Their response was instant, and enthusiastic.

'OK, we'll see. I'll ring Dad tonight. I tried earlier, but he was out. I'll try again now, and see if he can meet us at Fishguard.'

'Cool!'

Feeling more lighthearted than she had done since Tiger's birthday party, Orla went downstairs and called her husband. He answered at once. 'I've just come in,' he said. 'I was wondering whether it was too late to ring you back. How's it going?'

'Bloody awful,' said Orla. As quietly as possible, in case she should be overheard, she explained about the bad weather, the boys' frustration and lack of amusement, and her own boredom. 'I'm sure I can get a booking on the ferry, darling,' she said. 'But it would be lovely if you came to Fishguard to meet us.'

'Of course I will, sweetheart.'

'Great. I'll fix it all tomorrow, then ring you in the evening, OK?'

'Wonderful. I can't wait.'

'Me, too.'

In the early hours of the morning Alice woke, sweating, in the grip of a terrifying nightmare. She lay for a long time, her heart pounding, while fragments of the dream that had frightened her so much slipped in and out of her unreliable consciousness. On waking, she had thrown off the bedcovers, for her legs and feet had been burning hot. Now, as her body cooled rapidly in the night air, she began to shiver violently, and became dimly aware that she was drenched in a cold and disagreeable-smelling sweat.

Alice raised her head, and called out several times, and waited for Liam to come. But Liam, feeling unbearably guilty, blaming himself for his complicity in respect of the cruel expulsion of Tiger from Neill's Court, had taken a few comforting brandies before going to his own bed, and was even now sleeping the drugged sleep of the tormented.

Alice sat up, put her bare feet to the floor, and took off her cold and clammy nightdress. She crossed the room to the wardrobe and opened the door. Staring at the limply hanging clothes in its dark interior, Alice gave an angry little snort of derision and turned away, quite sure that she did not want to wear any of those dreary old frocks, and equally sure that she could find a new one if she really tried. Slyly, silently, she opened her bedroom door and stepped out into the corridor. She looked carefully up and down its length, saw that it was empty, and began to run along the passage, keeping close to the wall, and giggling like a child. Just before she got to the landing that surrounded the staircase, Alice came to a halt, put her hand firmly on the brass knob of the door on her left, and went in.

The curtains were drawn, so that the room was dark, but Alice saw that the cold light of dawn was already visible at the edges of the windows. She stole across the carpet, and pulled back one of the curtains. She looked towards the bed, and saw two humps, like beached whales, motionless and silent. She smiled, pleased that they had not heard her. She went to the wardrobe, pulled open one of the doors, and took out the first thing that came to hand, a long evening gown. Lovely, she thought, and began to drag it over her head, neglecting to remove the hanger before she did so. This frock's no fucking good, she said to herself, as she struggled to get it either on, or off, with equal difficulty. There was a ripping sound, as the closed zip gave way, and Alice was able to rid herself of the offending article. She flung it on the floor, and went back to the wardrobe, rummaging among the contents, dragging out first one garment and then another, until the carpet was strewn with rejected clothing, and Alice, still naked, opened her mouth and let out a loud and frustrated bellow of rage and disappointment.

The uproar that ensued was frightening to hear, and worse to behold, as a mortified Liam could hardly fail to observe as he rushed to the scene in answer to Alice's shrieks, and turned on the light at the door. Seeing Alice, stark naked, cavorting about on a pile of someone else's clothes, clutching her head and screaming like a banshee, he immediately turned it off again, and blundered across the floor, in an attempt to capture his escaped charge. 'Come on, me darlin',' he cajoled. 'Liam's here. It's all right; come along, like a good girl.'

Alice resisted his encircling arms, and thrust him away. 'Get off, you bloody eejit, Liam. I'm not dressed, can't you bloody see that? I'm looking for a fucking frock! I need a FROCK!'

Desperately, and apologetically, Liam turned towards the bed, and addressed himself to the shattered couple who sat there, speechless with surprise and horror. 'I can only beg your pardon, sir, madam,' he said, with an attempt at dignity. 'My lady's not herself, I'm afraid.'

Suddenly, Tadeusz appeared in the open doorway, with a poker in his hand, and Niamh at his elbow. Alice took one look at the angry face of her daughter and a terrible recognition of her crime came over her. She turned to Liam, in a flood of frightened tears. He took off his pyjama jacket, wrapped it round her, and led her from the room, leaving Niamh to deal with the situation as best she could.

For Orla, her mother's disgraceful behaviour was exactly the evidence she needed to convince herself that the sooner Alice was put away the better, for all concerned. Angry and publicly humiliated, or so she thought, she left Neill's Court with no regrets at all, determined that Matthew should insist that her mother be institutionalized without delay, and the house sold.

Alessandro Molini arrived at *La Commanderia* in the middle of September, two days after the start of the *vendemmia*. He had driven all the way from Rome in his Toyota, a noisy souped-up four-wheel-drive affair, and came bouncing along the dusty track through the heavily laden vines, pulling up by the blue front door with a scrunch of loose stones.

Enzo, Con and Tiger were already in the courtyard, enjoying an iced aperitif under the fig tree, when the outer door banged, and Alessandro appeared in their midst, hot, dusty and smiling.

'Sandro! *Ragazzo mio! Ciao!*' Enzo lumbered to his

feet and clasped his grandson to his heart, kissing him firmly on both cheeks, and thumping his back with an enormous hand.

Alessandro responded with equal affection, and turned to Con, who greeted him with a flurry of rapid Italian. Then, politely, the young man approached Tiger, who sat regarding him coolly, determined not to be over-impressed by his extravagantly beautiful looks, and polished manners.

Enzo introduced them in his impeccable English, and to her relief Alessandro, too, switched to a fluent but less perfect English at once. 'How do you do,' he said, with a slight inclination of his dark curly head.

'Hi,' said Tiger, holding out a firm bronzed hand.

Alessandro shook hands, then went immediately to the kitchen, to inform Giuliana of his arrival. The others heard the exclamation of joy that his visit provoked, and Enzo and Con smiled at each other, indulgently.

'Doesn't Giuliana mind him appearing out of the blue like this, with no warning?' asked Tiger.

Enzo shook his head. 'Never in this world, or the next,' he assured her. 'Giuliana worships the ground Sandro walks on, and has from his nativity. She adores him, and he loves her, too.'

'That's nice,' said Tiger, though privately she thought Alessandro sounded like a spoiled brat.

'Good-looking, isn't he?' Con smiled at his daughter, ironically.

'Yes, he is.' Blandly, Tiger returned her father's smile, refusing to allow him the pleasure of annoying her.

Alessandro returned from the kitchen, poured himself a glass of water and drank it without sitting down. 'I need a shower, *Nonno*,' he said. 'I'll just get my bag from the car, and then clean up a bit. Shan't be long.'

Tiger observed that Alessandro appeared to have a permanent room on Enzo's side of the courtyard, for he fetched his bag and disappeared along the terrace in

303

that direction. Good, she said to herself, that means he won't find it easy to creep into my room in the middle of the night. She almost laughed at the idea of such an eventuality, and then composed herself, staring seriously into her glass. I quite wish he hadn't come, she thought; it won't be the same now. It was lovely, being here alone with Enzo and Con.

Father and daughter paid their first visit to Lecce in the late afternoon, after the siesta hours were over and shops and historic monuments were open again.

They had gone first to the bookshop where Con hoped to find that the books he had ordered had arrived, and was pleased to discover that indeed they had. Afterwards, they had walked along narrow stone streets, luminescent with golden reflected light, a strip of brilliant blue sky above, in search of the small shop that sold artists' materials. They found it without difficulty, and Con, with touching kindness, bought Tiger a beautiful, old-fashioned, black tin paint box, fitted with twenty-four separate little blocks of solid water-colours. He also bought her a pack of hand-made paper, some brushes and pencils, and a small fold-up easel. The proprietor of the shop made an exquisite parcel of these purchases, and handed it to Tiger with a friendly smile, and some Italian good wishes. Outside, in the street, Tiger turned to her father, reached up and kissed him on his cheek. 'That was so lovely of you, Con! Thank you very much; you're a star, you really are!'

'Well, good.' Con laughed, pleased that his generosity had brought a smile to Tiger's face. 'I'm glad someone thinks so. What shall we do now? Have some tea, or visit one of Lecce's treasures?'

'Both, perhaps?'

As they walked through Lecce to Con's favourite café, Tiger was astonished at the richness of the baroque architecture that seemed to embellish each little piazza, not only the churches built in the seven-

304

teenth century, but the many beautiful houses of the same period that graced the streets of the city.

They had tea under a shady umbrella on the terrace of the café, and then made their way to the Basilica di Santa Croce. In spite of the proliferation of such work throughout the city, nothing had prepared Tiger for the splendour of this masterpiece of the Leccian baroque style, or the exuberance of its façade. It was covered with the most incredibly rich stone carvings, and seemed to Tiger a miracle of intricate beauty. The interior was light and airy, and far less ornate, and they sat for a while, enjoying the peace and tranquillity of the place.

On the way back to the car park, they bumped into a friend of Con's, a middle-aged woman, grey-haired, slender, with dark eyes and a long nose. Con introduced the two women, and they smiled warily at each other, both shy, both inquisitive to know more about the other. 'We must go,' said Con. '*Ciao, Maria. A presto!*'

On the drive home, Tiger asked herself whether Maria was more than just a friend to Con, and was on the point of asking him, in a roundabout way, when he partially answered her question.

'Maria's a very nice woman, Tiger, and a painter; a very good one too, in my opinion.'

'Have you known her a long time?'

'Ten years or so, I suppose. Why?'

'Oh, nothing. I just wondered, that's all.'

Con laughed. 'You want to know if we go to bed together?'

'No, no, of course not.'

'Well, the answer is yes, we do, but she's not the only one.'

'I see.'

'Actually, darling, you probably don't. From the outset of each relationship I make a point of making it clear that I'm married, with three daughters. I find a certain safety in not allowing myself to become too involved with any one of them, and it's convenient to blame my married status for my behaviour.'

Tiger laughed. 'Sounds terribly cruel, but I can see your point, as a matter of fact.' She looked sideways, studying his profile, with its strong hooked nose and dark straight hair, untidy, just like her own. 'I think we're quite alike, you and I,' she said. 'And not just to look at. I'm beginning to agree with you that it's a mistake to get too involved with people. They always let you down, in the end, don't they?'

'Is that what happened to you, darling?'

'Yes, it did, twice.' Sudden tears spilled over, and Con stopped the car at the side of the road, mortified that he had made her cry. He produced a folded handkerchief from his jacket pocket, and Tiger mopped her eyes. Then very quietly, and looking steadily through the windscreen, she told him all about her time in Paris; about Luc; about Przywnica and Tadeusz; and the trip to Ireland. Last of all, she told him about Niamh, and exactly how she had stolen Tadeusz from her.

When she had finished, and was silent, Con reached over and took her hand. 'Life's a bitch, Tiger, and I should know, because the bitch has frequently been me.' He squeezed her hand, gently. 'But it doesn't necessarily follow that there aren't *any* good bits, does it? Life's a challenge. You have to make things happen yourself, and call the shots, too. You'll learn not to trust people too much, and that's good.'

'Don't you trust anyone at all, Con?'

'Yes, I do. I trust Enzo, absolutely, and above all I trust my work. In the end it's the only reality, the fundamental centre of one's life, unless you're content to be a moron and be led by the nose.' He touched the tip of Tiger's nose, and laughed. 'With one like yours, darling, I think that's extremely unlikely to happen.'

'Do you really?'

'Yes, I do.'

He switched on the ignition, and they drove slowly

home, both knowing they had learned a great deal about each other, and happy that it was so.

The *vendemmia* was in full swing, and it was hot and tiring, working under the blazing sun all day, snipping the bunches of ripe black grapes and putting them carefully into the plastic buckets that had replaced the traditional heavy vine baskets. From time to time, a small tractor came slowly past, and the pickers emptied their full buckets into the trailer attached to its back bumper.

Tiger, wearing one of her father's old shirts and a wide straw hat, did her best to keep up with the other pickers, but found the long hours in the heat incredibly exhausting. Rarely used muscles in her shoulders and the calves of her legs felt agonizingly stiff and painful, making each step she took a torment. There were times when she longed to admit defeat to her father, and ask to go back to doing what she enjoyed most, spending her solitary mornings under the comforting shade of the olives, teaching herself how to use the water-colours he had given her.

The local pickers, whose annual job it was to harvest most of the vineyards of the area, were all old friends, and this, added to the language difficulty, made it almost impossible for Tiger to be other than a visiting guest of *La Commanderia*, as far as they were concerned. She could not help feeling a little excluded.

When Alessandro appeared, on the morning after his arrival, he was greeted as an old friend by the team, and a lot of good-natured banter was exchanged between him and the younger male Apulians. What its subject was Tiger had no way of knowing, but had little difficulty in guessing that women and sex were uppermost in their minds. Nevertheless, when Alessandro chose to work alongside her, Tiger's loneliness and isolation weakened her resolve and she did not discourage him.

*   *   *

At noon, a long trestle table was erected in the olive grove, and Giuliana and two women helpers brought out platters of food for the pickers' midday meal. Pasta with tomato sauce, bread, cheese, olives and salami were the staples provided, as well as a generous quantity of wine. A long siesta followed the meal, and everyone found himself a comfortable and shady spot in which to sleep.

Tiger, deciding that it would be rude and unfriendly to return to the house and take a nap on her bed, looked for a lone tree and sat down, leaning against its gnarled grey trunk, stretching out her tired legs, trying to make herself comfortable. She took from her jeans pocket the paperback novel she had borrowed from Con, found her place and began to read. Presently, Alessandro came and sat down at a little distance. 'Is it a good book, Tiger?' he asked.

'Very,' she replied, without looking up.

'I wish I could read English for pleasure.'

'I'm sure you could, if you tried.'

'No, I don't think so. It's too complex and difficult for me to understand the hidden meanings.'

Tiger looked up, leaving a finger in her book, to mark the place. 'Do you want to talk, Alessandro?'

'Don't you?'

'Not particularly.' She closed her book. 'I will, if you insist. What do you want to talk about? Yourself, by any chance?'

Alessandro smiled, and lay down on the hard ground, closing his eyes. 'It's too hot to quarrel, isn't it? I was going to suggest that it might be nice to go for a swim, but if you'd rather not, that's OK, I'll go by myself.'

'I didn't know there was a pool here.'

'There isn't, unfortunately. But there's the sea, only fifteen minutes away in the car. I thought we might go there, after work.'

'Perhaps. I'll think about it.'

* * *

All afternoon, the tempting thought of a cooling swim in the sea filled Tiger's head, and at six o'clock, when the day's work ended, she turned casually to Alessandro. 'Right,' she said. 'Let's get our things and get going, shall we?'

As they rattled cheerfully along in Alessandro's jazzy little Toyota, Tiger felt that the effort of maintaining her abrasive attitude towards him was becoming pretty boring, and as they drew near the sea she could not prevent her spirits from rising.

He parked the car beside a tall, grass-tufted sand dune, and they walked down to a long, white, and completely empty beach. Tiger, having had the foresight to get into her bikini before they set out, pulled off her shirt and ran straight into the water, diving over the first big wave that broke on the beach. She headed out to sea, then swam under the water for as long as she could hold her breath, enjoying the glorious coldness on her sun-scorched body. When her lungs gave out, and she broke the surface, she was surprised to find Sandro just beside her, treading water, grinning. 'What kept you?' he asked.

'*Ottuso!*' she replied, and putting her hands on his shoulders, pushed him under the water.

CHAPTER SIXTEEN

The *vendemmia* lasted for ten days, since every bunch of grapes had to be picked by hand, before being taken to the estate's cool cellars for pressing, and subsequent transfer to the fermenting vats. Enzo did not belong to one of the comparatively new co-operatives of the area, for the bulk of his wine was for his own consumption, and he took a justifiable pride in its originality and special character. Any surplus was sold in the village shop, and provided a small but useful income, sufficient to cover the costs of the chemicals required for the healthy maintenance of his vines.

Tiger and Sandro, toiling together under the hot sun, could hardly fail to develop a working relationship, and under more normal circumstances Tiger would have taken much greater pleasure in his company. But she was still missing Tadeusz badly, in spite of the fact that he had not written to her, or done anything at all to excuse his treachery. She did not again discuss her feelings of humiliation with Con, but he found little difficulty in drawing the inference that all was still not well with her. If he and Enzo had seen the advent of Sandro as a cure for Tiger's broken heart, they were sadly mistaken.

Each afternoon, after the day's work was finished, and they had taken a cup of tea with Con, Sandro would propose a trip to the beach; a drive into Lecce to browse around the shops and eat ice-cream; even, once, an expedition right across the peninsula to Taranto, to visit the National Archaeological Museum. Housed in a former monastery of the Alcantarini Fathers, they found a collection of astonishing objects dug up from the graves of the rich residents of the area, put to death in 209 BC, when Quinto Fabio Massimo conquered the city of Taranto. In addition to the vases, toiletry objects and amphorae on display was an impressive collection of gold jewellery – the famous Gold of Taranto – the earrings, bracelets, necklaces, diadems and rings with which the dead had been adorned before burial.

'Bit of a waste to bury it, don't you think?' Sandro shook his head in disbelief at such profligacy.

'I don't know,' said Tiger. 'It's lovely, of course, but I'm not much into jewellery, really. It must have looked pretty grisly when they dug it up, all this shiny gold hanging on skeletons, mustn't it? A bit like that Donne poem, you know?'

'Tiger, what the hell are you talking about?'

'Oh, nothing. It's just a poem by John Donne, about a bracelet made of hair, on the wrist of a dead woman.'

'Sounds disgusting.'

'It's not; it's beautiful, as a matter of fact.'

They drove back to *La Commanderia* in the cool of the evening, stopping to eat supper in a village trattoria on the way. Sitting at a table on the tiny terrace, inhaling the fumes of passing cars and motorbikes, they ate the only dish on offer, chargrilled tender little birds, with roasted peppers. The food came with a bowl of spicy tomato sauce, and was delicious.

'What are these poor little birds, Sandro?' asked Tiger suspiciously.

'*Tordo*, I think. I don't know the English word. It's a brown sort of bird, with a spotted front.'

'I don't *believe* it! Are you telling me we're eating defenceless little *thrushes*?'

'Is that a problem for you, Tiger?'

'Not really.' She laughed. 'The poor thing's dead anyway, so I might as well eat it.'

Sandro observed that she ate every scrap of the tender meat, holding the little drumsticks in her fingers and sucking off the last delicious morsels. 'I'm glad to see that your delicate feelings haven't spoiled your appetite,' he remarked drily, pouring wine into her glass.

She looked at him, her eyes mocking. 'Life's full of compromises, Sandro,' she said. 'Or are you too inexperienced to have reached that conclusion yet?'

If she expected to get a rise out of him, she was disappointed. 'As a matter of fact, my work is a daily reminder of the fragility of the human condition, and the consequences of failure to make *compromessi*,' he said, mysteriously, if a little pompously.

'Really? What is your work?'

'I'm a forensic pathologist; or, more accurately, I'm training to be one.'

'Isn't that rather a depressing way to spend your life, cutting up bodies? That *is* what you do, isn't it?'

'Yes, that's what I do, and no, it's not depressing, once you get used to frequent physical contact with the dead. You can feel the coldness of the flesh, even with gloves on. It's a bit like being a butcher, I imagine.'

'Whatever made you decide to do such a grim job?'

'Probably because I used to enjoy dissecting frogs, lizards, rabbits, things like that, when I was a boy.' He smiled. 'What I do now is a sort of grown-up version of that, I suppose.'

'How old are you, Sandro?'

'Twenty-four. And you?'

'Nineteen.'

'And what are *you* studying?'

Tiger sighed. 'I'd like to study painting, and the history of art, but I don't know if I'll ever be able to. It's a question of money, isn't it? Not enough, in my case.'

'And a question of talent, too, wouldn't you say?'

'Yes, of course.'

'And you have the talent, I imagine?'

'I think I do. I hope so, anyway.'

They drove back to *La Commanderia* through the narrow, dusty back-roads, skirting the long half-stripped vineyards, the unfolding lanes dappled with the flickering shadows of olive trees, their leaves silvery in the moonlight. Sandro drove in silence, until they had almost reached their destination. 'Tell me about this poem; the one you mentioned when we were in the museum.'

Tiger frowned, staring through the widescreen. Then she began to recite the only bit of the poem that she remembered:

'When my grave is broke up again
Some second guest to entertain,
(For graves have learnt that woman-head
To be to more than one a bed)
   And he that digs it spies
   A bracelet of bright hair about the bone,
     Will he not let us alone?'

'Is that all?'

'No, there's more, but I can't remember it.'

'Who did you say the poet was?'

'John Donne. He was a seventeenth-century priest, and rather a sexy one, so I'm told.'

Sandro laughed. 'Did they teach you that sort of thing at school?'

'No way! At the sort of school I went to, the poems of passionate priests don't form part of the curriculum.'

'Who told you about him, then?'

'A chap I used to know, in Paris. He was French, but he thought it the most tragic and beautiful poem in the English language, as a matter of fact. I expect your take on it would be different, being a pathologist?'

313

Sandro drew up at the blue door, and turned off the engine. 'That bit about a bracelet of bright hair about the bone might have been written by a pathologist. Equally, it might have been a bit of bright hair clinging to the skull. Either way, you never get used to that. You know something terrible must have happened to the victim; just like the bodies in Taranto, buried in their gold.' He turned towards her, his face stern. 'Just because I dissect dead people, Tiger, doesn't mean that I am without feelings.'

'I'm sorry. I didn't mean to seem to be criticizing you.'

'It's OK.'

They got out of the car, and went into the house. It was late, and the courtyard was empty, the lights extinguished, the fig trees throwing their grotesque shadows across the paved floor.

'Good night,' said Tiger, 'and thank you for a lovely evening.'

'Not at all. Thank you for telling me the poem of the sexy priest.'

Tiger smiled. 'I expect Con's got the complete poems in his study. I'll ask him tomorrow.'

'Tiger?'

'What?'

'May I kiss you?'

'How boringly predictable you are, Sandro! Are you sure it's only a kiss you expect, in exchange for paying for my dinner?'

He flushed angrily. 'Of course not! What kind of a bastard do you take me for? Why do you always spoil everything by being so suspicious, Tiger? If you want to know, I wanted to kiss you because I think you're a beautiful girl, and worth kissing, that's all. Now I'm not so sure.'

'Bollocks!' said Tiger coldly. 'You're like all bloody men; you just want to get into my knickers!' She turned on her heel, and ran down the corridor to her room.

Confused, and curiously hurt, Sandro stared after her, his dark eyes perplexed and sad.

At the end of the *vendemmia*, Enzo gave the traditional feast, a celebration of the successful harvesting of the grapes, and a reward for the labours of the pickers. For two days the kitchen had been full of the smell of a richly flavoured stew; a huge metal covered pot containing several kilos of horsemeat, which simmered gently on the stove in its *gran ragu*, a sauce of red wine, onion and ripe tomatoes. This festive dish was to be served to the guests in two parts. First, pasta would be brought to the table, and eaten with a ladleful of the sauce, and grated pecorino cheese. After this would come the tender meat, cut into thick slices and accompanied by vegetables, and more of the wonderful dark sauce.

On the day of the party, Tiger did not go to the vineyard with Sandro, but remained at home, to help prepare for the meal, counting out knives and forks, polishing glasses and plates, and making garlands of vine leaves to decorate the long tables. Her knowledge of Italian had improved sufficiently for her to understand a good many words connected with food, and had become necessary on account of Giuliana's professed ignorance of English.

When the laying of the tables had been completed, and approved, Tiger went with Giuliana to the kitchen and helped prepare the *dolce*. This was to be roast peaches, and she was instructed to halve the peaches horizontally, removing the stone. The fruit was then packed snugly into baking dishes, cut side up, and sprinkled with caster sugar, with a lump of butter added to each cavity. After twenty minutes the dishes emerged from the oven, the peaches covered in a crisp, golden glaze and smelling of summer orchards. Tiger, who had until that moment regarded cooking as a boring but necessary prelude to eating, clapped her hands in astonishment and delight. When the dishes were cool enough to handle, she carried them to the larder to get ice-cold.

At six o'clock, a dozen massive loaves were delivered to the house, and laid out on the festive tables, along with jars of olives, aubergines, dried tomatoes and peppers preserved in oil. These, with dishes of ham and salami, were the raw materials for serve-yourself *antipasti*. Earthenware jugs of wine were placed at strategic intervals along the tables.

At seven, the pickers arrived and were welcomed by Enzo with an aperitif, which was despatched with surprising speed, before the guests adjourned to the waiting tables and prepared to do justice to their host's renowned hospitality.

Tiger ran backwards and forwards between olive grove and kitchen, ferrying plates and dishes, carrying out Giuliana's incomprehensible instructions to the best of her ability, aided by Sandro, who cut bread, poured wine and removed dirty plates as though he had spent his life in a restaurant. When the last peach had been swallowed, and the coffee and *grappa* placed upon the tables, Tiger slipped away, suddenly exhausted by the noise of the party, and needing to be by herself.

She lay under the olive trees, her eyes closed, listening to the distant roar of the party, glad of the slight breeze that flowed between the trees.

Since the trip to Taranto, her relationship with Sandro had been fairly cool, and she was aware that this was a matter of concern to both her father and Enzo, for they had begun to treat her with exaggerated solicitude, as though she were ill. Sandro himself had avoided being alone with her, and this she had found frustrating, for it meant that her chances of a swim had been put on hold. Annoyingly, Sandro himself had several times gone to the beach, alone. It's my own silly fault, she said to herself. I really didn't need to jump down his throat like that.

She became aware of the slight, slippery sound of

quiet footsteps walking over the carpet of brittle, dried olive leaves, and realized that they were approaching her personal tree. She sat up quickly, peering into the darkness, trying to see who it was.

'It's OK, Tiger, it's only me.' Sandro sat down beside her, brushed aside a few of the withered leaves to make a level space, and put a bottle and two glasses on the ground. '*Nonno* thought you might like a drink, after all the racket back there. I hope you don't mind me bringing it?'

'No, of course not. Thank you.'

Sandro poured the wine, and handed her a glass. 'Chin-chin!' he said.

Tiger burst into laughter. '*Sandro! Nobody* says chin-chin nowadays! It's dreadfully corny and old-fashioned.'

'Really? You surprise me. I saw a terrific English movie a few months ago, and there was this guy who said chin-chin all the time. I thought he was cool.'

Tiger frowned. 'What was the name of the movie, Sandro? It must have been a very old one.'

'I don't think so. It was called *Withnail and I.* It was brilliant; very funny and very sad. I'm surprised you've never seen it.'

'Never heard of it,' said Tiger shortly, feeling vaguely caught out, and irritated.

After a while, Sandro said quietly: 'It would be good if you were here for the *raccolta* of the olives, Tiger. It's a sort of medieval winter time-warp. The pickers crawl around, just as they have for centuries, gathering the ripe fruit from the frozen ground, their poor numb fingers stiff with cold.'

'Tell me about it,' said Tiger, relieved that Sandro seemed inclined to ignore her harshness. 'When does it happen?'

'In November. At the end of October, they clear away all the weeds and rubbish round each tree; flattening the ground; beating it to make it hard. Then, when the time is right, they come to strip the crop, first

317

spreading nets under the trees. The men climb into the trees and shake down the olives, and the women collect them as they fall, throwing them into buckets.' Sandro looked at Tiger, with a teasing smile. '*Come d'abitudine*, the women do the lousiest part of the job, and the most back-breaking. It's horrible work, bent double all day long, picking up the olives, throwing out all the twigs and *scarto*.'

'Why don't *they* climb the tree and tell the men to do the picking?'

'Two reasons. One, it's *tradizione* and that's almost impossible to ignore around here. Two, the girls are far more nimble-fingered and a lot quicker than the guys. They can gather twice as fast as the men, so there's no contest, really.'

'And do they get well paid for their skills?'

'What do you think? They get the rate for the job.'

'I see. It's not very fair, is it?'

'Of course not, but then nothing's fair for country women, Tiger. They work like dogs all their lives, and think themselves lucky to have a husband, bear his children, look after him, and not mind if he gets drunk on Saturdays. Not much of a life, is it?'

'What about women in the city? Do they get a better deal?'

'Yes, they do, but even there, in many ways, there's still a lot of *discriminazione* against them.'

Tiger stared at Sandro, and thought how sensitive he really was, and how good-looking, with his dark, glowing skin and black curly hair. 'It's strange,' she said. 'The women don't appear to mind being exploited, do they? They seem very attached to their men, as far as one can tell.'

Sandro turned his head, and looked at her seriously. 'That's because the women around here are exceptionally tolerant, and the men are exceptionally lucky.'

'Do you really believe that?'

'Yes, I do.'

'And do you approve of it, Sandro?'

He laughed. 'No, of course not.'

'I'm relieved to hear it.'

Through the trees, they could hear the departing guests, revving up their engines prior to their erratic journeys home along the lanes. Tiger got to her feet. 'Come on, we'd better be getting back.'

Sandro picked up the bottle and glasses, and they strolled slowly home together. Tiger, walking beside him, glad of his comforting presence, told herself that she had been idiotically swift to write him off as a typical Italian *machismo*, and predator of defenceless girls. As they drew near the house, she stopped and turned towards him. 'I'm sorry that I mistook your motives the other night, Sandro. It was silly of me, I realize that now.' She put a hand on his arm and smiled at him, slightly nervously. 'If you still want to kiss me, I won't mind.'

'No, thanks.' Gently but firmly, he removed her hand from his arm.

'Why not? I thought you fancied me?'

'I did, I do, especially under the influence of alcohol.' He turned his eyes on her, cool and detached. 'I've been dumped by two girls so far, Tiger, and frankly, I don't want to go down that road again for the moment. Sex is OK, I expect it can be wonderful, but in the end, without real commitment, there's something degrading about casual screwing, in my view. These days, it's become like having a glass of wine, pleasant but meaningless.'

Touched, amazed that a mere man should betray such emotions, she could only offer him a banal form of consolation. 'I'm sorry if the others gave you a hard time,' she said. 'I hope you find someone, some day.'

'Me, too.'

'I agree with you about the promiscuity thing, Sandro, but a kiss between friends is OK, don't you think?'

'Are we friends, Tiger?'

'I hope we are.'

He put his arm round her shoulders, and they exchanged a very gentle, very chaste kiss. They smiled at each other. 'Shall we go to the beach tomorrow?' he said.

'Yes, let's.'

September drew to a close, and at Neill's Court, Niamh allowed herself to wind down a little, for the guests were departing one by one, and the cooking demonstrations had been discontinued for the season. Since most of the remaining guests were fishermen, and out of the house for the greater part of the day, they did not present the same problems as the student cooks, or require so much of her attention.

Tadeusz had now moved into her bedroom, and whether anyone knew or cared about this was a matter of indifference to Niamh. In fact, as far as her suspicious nature allowed, she was feeling both happy and successful for the first time in her life. Tadeusz seemed to her a very perfect lover, both for the colossal amount of work he achieved during the working day, and for the enchantment he brought to their nights together. Quite often, and especially in bed, she was tempted to tell him how wonderful he was, and how essential he had become to her, but wisdom prevailed, and she kept all such thoughts to herself. She had no wish to allow him to assume that he had the slightest influence or control over herself or her authority.

Alice, too, had entered a period of comparative tranquillity, and spent her days in the orangery with Liam, giving little trouble, give or take the occasional maniacal laugh.

It was, therefore, all the more aggravating that Orla should have chosen to revive her ill-thought-out but determined campaign to have their mother consigned to a nursing home. She had taken it upon herself to write to the reverend mother at the local convent, asking her to quote a price for accepting Alice as a patient in their infirmary, and had received an offer which she felt they would be foolish not to accept. Triumphantly, she wrote to Niamh, informing her of this new development.

When Niamh received this letter, she was both distressed and angered by it. Her distress was entirely for her mother, for in spite of the difficulties involved in caring for her, Niamh felt very strongly that Alice had an inalienable right to remain at Neill's Court until such time as her condition required real professional nursing; until, for example, she became doubly incontinent. Orla seemed to have forgotten that it had been largely the question of their mother's well-being that had been the original motivation for turning their home into a hotel. Rereading the letter, Niamh found it infuriating as well as deeply insulting to realize that her sister appeared to disregard the hard work involved in achieving this goal. It was not hard to guess that if the house were to be sold, Orla would insist that the spoils be divided equally between the three sisters. Niamh's enormous input into the rehabilitation of the house and garden would count as nothing.

Now that the vegetables were in immaculate order, and the growing season slowing down, Tadeusz was able to turn his attention to the conversion of the stables into the studios in which he intended not only to earn his living as a tutor, but resuscitate his own creative work, during the quiet winter months. As he ripped out rotting partitions, and heaved the splintered wood onto a huge bonfire in the stableyard, his head was filled with ambitious dreams. He saw a rosy future for himself, and, of course, Niamh, for without her his scheme would never see the light of day. Without her behind him, he knew it would be back to the drawing-board in Paris. He was beginning to recognize his own weaknesses, and submit to the humiliating awareness that he needed a strong, tough woman like Niamh, to help him reach his potential.

Occasionally, though less and less as the weeks passed, he thought about Tiger, faintly regretting her loss. It was better that it ended, really, he told himself firmly. Tiger's like me, a drifter; we'd have been a disaster as a permanent thing. She's not exactly into the work ethic, either, is she? Niamh may not be everyone's ideal woman, one wouldn't want to paint her, but she sure as hell knows how to get things done. She's not a bad shag, either, even if it is a bit like making love to an octopus.

One afternoon, as she drove the jaunting-car back from town with the weekend groceries, Niamh saw two village women leaving the church, presumably after making their confessions.

She had discussed Orla's disturbing letter with no-one, but it occurred to her that a chat with the Catholic priest might bring forth his strong condemnation of her sister's wicked intent, and maybe, even prompt him to write to Orla, telling her so. Although not, of course, a Catholic herself, Niamh knew the priest to be a powerful force in village opinion, and wished to procure his comforting confirmation that she alone was behaving in a responsible, almost saintly manner towards her poor, benighted mother.

She tied the reins to the graveyard railings, and entered the dark, incense-smelling church. There was one other person waiting her turn to enter the confessional box, so Niamh sat down in a pew behind her, and composed her thoughts. After a few minutes, a black-clad figure emerged from the confessional, red-faced, dabbing at her eyes with a handkerchief. As she hurried past the waiting penitents, the woman stopped for a second, staring at Niamh with a look of contemptuous disbelief. Niamh glanced up at her, and realized with horror that it was Mrs Keen, the wife of her ex-lover.

The woman in the pew in front got up and made her way to the confessional. Mrs Keen, with a snake-like, slithering movement, sat down beside Niamh and thrust her unattractive face close to hers. 'What a surprise!' she hissed. '*Miss* Fitzgerald, the heretic as ever is, come to confession! So it's not content you are with stealing a respectable married man, *Miss* Fitzgerald? It's after breaking the heart of your poor little sister you are, too, or so I'm told on very good authority. Is it saying you're sorry and absolution you're looking for, you evil bitch? I dare say Father O'Reilly will tell you to burn in hell, for he knows all about you, and it's what you deserve!' With her characteristic slippery sideways movement, Mrs Keen withdrew from the pew and walked briskly away, her heels clacking on the tiled floor.

Stunned, Niamh stayed where she was for a few seconds, then she got up, left the church and drove thoughtfully home.

In October, Sandro returned to Rome, and his studies. Tiger missed his company and the daily outings to the beach, and knew that soon she would have to talk to Con about her future. It must be a pain for him and Enzo having me mooning around when they're trying to work, she thought. I really must get my act together, and make decisions. As it turned out, she had no need to bring up the subject herself, for one evening, at supper, it was Enzo who raised the subject. 'What about art college, Tiger?'

'Art college?' repeated Tiger. 'Is there one, here?'

'Probably, but I was assuming Rome. So much to see in Rome, so much to do. Many interesting peoples.'

Tiger rolled her tagliatelle round her fork with precision, considering Enzo's suggestion. 'Wouldn't I need qualifications?'

'Haven't you got any?'

'Pretty basic. Bad, actually, except for art.'

'That's OK then, since it's art we have in mind?'

'But is my work good enough, Enzo?'

'Yes, I think so.' He smiled. 'I used to teach at the

college. I expect they will find a place for you, if I request it.'

'Great! Could you really?' She turned anxiously to her father. 'But what about money? Fees and stuff like that?'

'The fees I'm sure we could manage, but you'd have to work to pay for your lodgings, and food.'

'What could I do?'

'Cleaning? Bar work? Walking dogs?'

'Not walking dogs *again*!' Tiger laughed. 'Actually, walking dogs isn't so bad. At least you get some exercise, while you're doing it.'

Two weeks later, Tiger found herself alone in Rome, and enrolled in the art college. She had a tiny apartment on the third floor of a dilapidated townhouse belonging to an expatriate Englishwoman, a friend of Con's, and in order to support this independent lifestyle, she had obtained two jobs, one in the early morning, the other in the evening. Enzo's suggestion that she contact Sandro she had chosen to ignore for the present, preferring to settle down and learn to stand on her own two feet. After all, she said to herself, I coped with Paris perfectly well, didn't I?

The college of art was situated in a narrow street off the Via del Corso, and occupied the formal rooms of a beautiful classical *palazzo*, the former property of an impoverished aristocratic Roman family. The administrators had managed to find suitable spaces for every discipline, however contemporary, and classical painting and modern sculpture were studied side by side within the marble columns and frescoed walls of the palace.

The former *salone* was now equipped with an interesting collection of plaster casts of well-known sculptures, some Roman and Florentine, some Greek, and it was in this room that Tiger began her formal studies. She loved the long silent mornings, seated in front of a delightfully immobile Greek, drawing his beautiful plaster torso. Illuminated by streams of brilliant autumn sunlight, flooding through deep windows overlooking an internal courtyard, the cast room was filled with an intensity of feeling and purpose that Tiger had never before experienced, and she absorbed it like a sponge. It was always a matter of huge surprise to her when the session came to an end, and the morning's work was finished.

Her private life was less of an enchantment to her, for her two jobs entailed cleaning the apartments of two women, twice a week. The first employer was an elderly writer, evidently a well-known poet, and she lived on the top floor of a building close to the house where Tiger had her own apartment. She had been instructed that on no account should she disturb this important personage, and the cleaning had to be carried out before the poet rose from her bed. This condition meant that Tiger had to get up at six on those particular mornings, climb the many stairs to the poet's apartment, and carry out her duties as silently as a mouse, leaving the flat at five minutes to eight, having prepared the breakfast coffee and warmed a *cornetto*, bought at a *pasticceria* on her way to work.

The second woman, by comparison, was only too visible and audible, for she worked from home. Tiger's hours with her were from four to six, two afternoons a week, and when she arrived, she always found Signora Grazioli ensconced in the *salon*, telephones ringing, the fax machine spewing out reams of untidy paper, and, frequently, in the company of two or three wildly gesticulating and voluble Italians. Usually, on catching sight of Tiger, the signora would order her to bring tea, or cocktails, or to run out for a pack of cigarettes. Although her Italian was rapidly improving, Tiger was sometimes completely foxed by these instructions, and frequently misinterpreted them. She did not find it pleasant to be treated like a moron when these unfortunate lapses occurred. Equally, she found it quite humiliating to try to carry out her domestic duties under the critical eyes of the smartly dressed colleagues of the signora. Often, as she performed her monotonous and distasteful tasks, she remembered the kindness of the Martel-Clunys, and compared her present employers very unfavourably with them.

Between classes and jobs, Tiger found time to explore those parts of Rome that were significant to her, and frequently visited the Vatican. She gazed with awe at the roof of the Sistine Chapel, astonished that Michelangelo could have completed it alone in four years, not surprised that he should have complained of developing a crick in his neck. She ventured into the Room of the Chancery to study Raphael's frescoes; went to the *Pinocoteca Vaticana,* to see Caravaggio's *The Laying in the Tomb,* and was stunned by its drama and sense of bereavement. Walking across the huge Piazza San Pietro, turning to look back at the great church and its spectacular Bernini colonnade, Tiger marvelled at the numbers of faithful pilgrims, their presence in the piazza rendered insignificant by the vastness of the place. We might as well be ants, she thought.

She rarely saw her landlady, and spent her evenings alone, reading, writing her essays. Although lonely, she nevertheless felt happy and alive; conscious that she was lucky to be doing what she wanted to do with her life; grateful that her father and Enzo had been prepared to help her realize her dreams.

CHAPTER SEVENTEEN

At half-term, feeling exhausted by the double pressures of her jobs and her studies, Tiger telephoned her father and asked if she could spend a few days with them at *La Commanderia*.

'Of course; delighted,' said Con, and they arranged that he should meet her at the bus station in Lecce on the following evening.

'I hope I'm not being a nuisance, Con?'

'No, of course not. I usually go to Lecce on Friday afternoons, anyway. It's not a problem.'

'Great. See you tomorrow.'

'*A domani, cara.*'

Con was a little late at the bus station, and when he came roaring up in his battered old car, Tiger had little difficulty in guessing the reason for his delayed arrival, for not only was his face flushed, but his smile was extremely complacent. She threw her bag and her portfolio onto the rear seat and got into the car, suppressing a conspiratorial grin, then planted a kiss on his cheek. 'Hi,' she said.

On the way to *La Commanderia* she sat silently, listening to her father's account of local happenings; the olive harvest; a concert in Lecce; the satisfactory delivery of his manuscript to his publishers, and an invitation to do a book promotion tour in the States.

'Sounds exciting?'

'Sounds ghastly. I'll probably refuse.'

'It'd be good for sales, though, wouldn't it?'

'So they tell me; I'm not convinced, though.' Con swerved to avoid a minute rodent scurrying across the road. 'I love it here, Tiger. I hate leaving the place, even for a week. I have this nightmare that if I go away, I'll never write another word, ever again.'

'Oh.'

'Anyway, what about you, darling? Is it going well?'

'Yes, it's terrific at the college; I love it. The jobs are a slight pain, though. I must see if I can find something less gross to do than skivvying for boring old tarts.'

Con turned into the lane, and Tiger gazed with rapture at the jagged outlines of the farmhouse, half submerged in its surrounding olives, misty in the lavender dusk, a few small yellow squares of light piercing its battered old walls. 'I'm not surprised you love it here, Con. I do, too.'

As the car came slowly to a halt, Tiger saw Sandro's Toyota parked beside the blue door. 'You didn't tell me Sandro was coming,' she said. 'I could have got a lift with him.'

'We didn't know that he *was* coming. He pitched up at lunchtime, today. He never bothers to call us, rude bugger.'

Since the winter winds and rain had set in, the courtyard had been abandoned in favour of the winter sitting-room. For the greater part of the year this large vaulted space was used exclusively by Con as his workroom. Now, his computer, bookshelves and filing cabinets were temporarily concealed behind a beautiful Florentine leather screen, its panels depicting a Tuscan landscape with a pack of thin white greyhounds pursuing a frightened-looking wild boar across the foreground. They found Enzo and Sandro seated in front of a roaring log fire, playing chess. At their entrance, Enzo tipped up the board, and got to his feet, holding out welcoming arms. '*Finalmente!*'

'Oh!' exclaimed Tiger. 'You shouldn't have spoiled the game! What a shame!'

'*Mi e indifferente!* I am losing, anyway!' He folded Tiger in his arms and kissed her cold cheeks and forehead. 'You're frozen, *cara*; come by the fire.'

Sandro, picking up the chessmen and putting them away in their box, smiled at her. 'Why didn't you call me, Tiger? We could have come down together.'

'Yes, we could. I was a prat, not to think of it.'

After tea, Tiger went with Enzo to his studio and showed him her portfolio. Although pleased with her own progress at the college, she was none the less slightly nervous of hearing Enzo's judgement of her work. Silently, he turned the plastic sleeves containing her drawings, occasionally turning back the pages to take another look at something of particular interest to him. Leaving the portfolio open at a drawing of a detail of Michelangelo's David, showing the huge hand holding a sling, he turned to Tiger, and embraced her tenderly. '*Benissimo!*' he said. 'It's a big pleasure to see the first work of an artist; to guess what will be his or her future true voice.'

Tiger smiled. 'And what is your guess for me?'

'It's too soon to say, *cara*, but I *hope* for you. Very much.'

'Well, good.'

After her weeks of cheap pizza suppers, dinner seemed like a gastronomic heaven to Tiger. Giuliana had made a richly flavoured dish of breast of lamb, stuffed with garlic, raisins, pinenuts, pecorino, chopped herbs and soft white breadcrumbs, bound together with eggs and heavily seasoned. Baked in the bread oven, the meat came to the table as a golden brown pillow. Con carved it into thick slices, and it filled the air with the aromatic scent of its meltingly moist stuffing, redolent of garlic, rosemary and thyme. Eaten with hunks of Giuliana's home-made bread, and a salad of rocket, chicory and radicchio, the wonderful dish was complemented by Enzo's new wine, his *vino sincero*, dark red and delicious, tasting of wild strawberries and a hint of manure. They finished the meal with some ewe's milk cheese, a pear, and a glass of *grappa*. Full of food, even fuller of happiness, Tiger was never to forget that festive dinner. It was the first time in her life that she had experienced a real sense of homecoming; a strong feeling of belonging to that place, and of being loved and valued by its inhabitants.

The next day dawned bright and mild, with a warm wintry sun and very little wind. Sandro and Tiger drove to the beach, and walked together along the hard, clean, white sand, with banks of dry seaweed, beige-coloured and smelling of iodine, piled up along the highest tideline. In her happiness at being back at *La Commanderia*, Tiger had chosen not to enlarge on the indignities of her paid employment or the discomforts of her apartment, fearing that Enzo and Con might think her ungrateful and complaining. Alone with Sandro, any such inhibitions were quickly forgotten and she lost no time in giving him a lurid account of her life as an impoverished art student.

'Poor old thing,' said Sandro. 'Sounds horrible.'

Tiger sat down on the bank of dried seaweed and watched as he searched for flat stones to skim over the waves. 'It is, a bit,' she said.

'What?' He turned towards her. 'Sorry, I didn't hear what you said.'

'I said, it is a bit horrible, my life in Rome. Apart from the college, that is.'

Sandro threw another pebble, then sat down beside her, stretching out his long legs, digging his heels into the hard-packed sand. 'My apartment is big. I have a spare room. You could rent that, if you like.'

Tiger laughed. 'Is this what I think it is, Sandro?

Another thinly disguised attempt to get into my knickers?'

'No, it isn't, not at all. The truth is, I need a third person to share the flat.' He took her hand in his. 'Don't worry, Tiger, you'd be quite safe. You're like a sister to me now, I promise.'

'Oh, right.' Paradoxically, Tiger found herself not entirely delighted at Sandro's altered attitude towards her powers of attraction. She frowned, then looked at him uncertainly. 'I suppose if three of us are sharing, it would be less of a drain on my non-existent resources, wouldn't it?'

'And more fun, perhaps?'

Tiger laughed. 'That, too,' she said.

The rest of the weekend passed happily for them all, and on Monday afternoon Tiger and Sandro drove back to Rome. As it turned out, the narrow street where Sandro lived was not far from the house where Tiger had been lodging, so that collecting her belongings and paying two weeks' rent in lieu of notice was swiftly accomplished, and twenty minutes later they were humping the suitcases and boxes up the four flights of stairs to Sandro's apartment. The walls of the stairwell were damp and flaking, and the threadbare stair carpet was held in place by tarnished brass rods, so that it came as a huge surprise to Tiger that the apartment, when they entered it, was stunningly beautiful.

Occupying the greater part of the original attics of a Renaissance mansion, the main room seemed to crouch beneath the exposed beams of the heavy timbers that continued to support the roof. Sea-grass matting covered the floor and was augmented by several gloriously patterned Persian rugs, whose predominant colour was raspberry. The walls, washed with a warm ochre, were covered with a great many paintings and drawings, evidently the collection of someone of eclectic tastes and an excellent eye. The furniture, too, seemed to have been haphazardly assembled, and appeared to Tiger to be the probable consequence of family inheritance and judicious forays into long-forgotten lofts.

At the far end of the room was the only window, framed by a low arch, and opening onto a little balcony. Tiger put down her baggage, went to the window and gazed silently at the panoramic view of the city, across rooftops blue in the early evening light.

In the distance, the dome of a church rose majestically above the roofs. Confused, Tiger frowned. 'That's not St Peter's, surely?'

'No, it's the Gesù, the Jesuits' mother church.'

'What a wonderful view, Sandro.'

'Yes, it is.'

Tiger turned from the window, and surveyed the room. She found it very difficult to understand how a mere student could afford such luxurious surroundings, and watching her, Sandro guessed what was in her mind. 'It belongs to my mother,' he said quietly.

'What?'

'The apartment belongs to my mother. I rent it from her.'

'I see. So, why doesn't she live here herself?'

'She went to live in Tuscany, after my father died. It was too sad and lonely for her, here in Rome. She has family and quite a few old friends, in Siena.'

'Oh, I'm sorry, Sandro. I didn't know that your father was dead. He must have been quite young?'

'Fifty-four. He had cancer, poor guy.'

Tiger frowned. 'He was Enzo's son, then?'

'That's right.'

'He didn't tell me.'

'No. He can't speak about it, except to me, sometimes. It's lucky that he has Con living down there with him. He's like a second son to him.' Sandro smiled. 'Come on, let's not talk about it. I'll show you where everything is, or shall we have a drink?'

'I'd love a drink, but I'd better get unpacked first, hadn't I?'

*   *   *

Tiger's room was small, with the walls and ceiling beams painted white, the floor covered in terracotta tiles. The bed was a long, narrow rattan sofa, with a white canvas buttoned mattress and a pile of indigo-patterned cushions, square and fat. Across the foot of the bed was an indigo-and-white knitted blanket, and two white sheets and pillowcases, folded neatly. In a corner of the room, radiating warmth, and with its slender chimney disappearing through the ceiling, stood a white porcelain stove, embellished with bands of indigo. Against one wall stood a bamboo, glass-topped table, on which stood a collection of ferns in terracotta pots. A group of small bamboo-framed botanical prints hung on the wall above the table, ghostly dried versions of the living ferns below.

On the opposite wall was a pair of beautiful cedar doors, and behind them Tiger found a deep cupboard, complete with clothes hangers, and a set of built-in shelves. 'This is bliss,' she said to herself, and opened her suitcase.

When she returned to the sitting-room, she found that Sandro was not alone. At first sight, she thought that the cool blond creature relaxing on the sofa beneath the window was a young woman. Wearing a softly tailored pale-grey trouser suit, legs elegantly crossed, a wine glass in one pale, long-fingered hand, the stranger looked in her direction, and Tiger realized with a small shock of surprise that the newcomer was a man.

Sandro got to his feet, and introduced them to each other. 'Tiger, meet Luigi. Luigi, this is Tiger, our new flat-mate.'

Luigi held out a languid hand. '*Ciao*, Tiger,' he said softly.

'Hi.'

'What would you like, Tiger? Campari? Punt è Mes?'

'A Campari would be fine, thanks.'

The three of them sat for a while, in a curiously

constrained atmosphere, as though none of them could think of anything to say. Then Sandro put down his glass. 'It's a bit late to start cooking tonight, and there's not a lot in the fridge anyway, so I'm taking Tiger out to eat, Luigi. Do you want to come with us?'

'No thanks. I have a date, actually.'

'Oh, fine. *Andiamo*, Tiger; let's go.'

They walked around the corner into a tiny, darkly lit cul-de-sac, its pavements shining in the cold thin rain that had been falling all evening. On the left hand side of the little street was a small restaurant, with several deep woven-willow baskets standing outside the door, in the fresh air. They were piled high with oysters, resting on beds of slippery brown seaweed, and garnished with enormous gnarled yellow lemons, complete with their shiny green leaves. Inside, the little place was empty, for it was still early in the evening for normal Roman dining. In the centre of the room stood a single long table, covered with a white cloth, and surrounded by simple country chairs. Above the table was a long black iron rod, and from it hung cooking pots and pans; bunches of herbs, onions and garlic; and a large antique oil lamp, which cast its soft yellow light on the tablecloth below.

A fat, smiling woman appeared from the dark rear of the room, and greeted Sandro in an affectionate manner, for she had known him from his childhood. Tiger watched indulgently as the customary lengthy enquiries into the health of their respective families took place. '*E la mamma?*'

'*Bene, grazie.*'

They sat down at the table, and the *padrona* brought glasses, carafes of both red and white wine, knives, forks and plates. Swiftly she set two covers. After a short consultation with Tiger, Sandro ordered oysters, to be followed by pasta, with the sauce of the day.

The oysters were selected from the baskets in the street, brought to the table and opened with impressive dexterity. Although ravenously hungry, Tiger tried hard to spin out the treat of the exquisite oysters, to prolong the enjoyment of the delicious shellfish with careful squeezings of lemon juice, and sips of cool white wine. She turned to Sandro, her eyes bright with greed and happiness, and smiled. 'This is heaven,' she said. 'It's my very first proper dinner out in Rome. I hope it's not going to cost us too much?'

'It won't, but don't worry. It's my party, today.'

'Don't be silly. If anyone's going to pay, it'll be me. Con gave me some money, so I'm temporarily solvent.'

'OK; whatever.'

If Tiger was a little surprised that Sandro gave in without more of a struggle, she took care not to show it, and surrendered to the pleasures of the table, so abundantly set out before her.

A dish of pasta was presented with a flourish, and in a cloud of steam. It was a huge bowl of absolutely plain and very hot tagliatelle, tossed in oil, butter and grated parmesan cheese and almost green in colour, so great was the quantity of fresh herbs folded into it. 'My God,' said Tiger faintly. 'Is all this for us?'

Sandro smiled. 'I expect we'll manage to eat it.' He was right; they did, and he looked regretfully at the flecks of cheese and herbs still clinging to the sides of the bowl. 'When I was a little boy, I was always allowed to scrape out the dish with a finger,' he said. 'I suppose that's not allowed, now?'

'You suppose right; it's not,' replied Tiger, and laughed. She leaned back in her chair, and undid the top button of her jeans. 'In any case, how could you, Sandro? Aren't you stuffed with food already?'

'Don't you want a steak, or some fish?'

'You're mad! I couldn't eat another thing, honestly!'

'Coffee?'

'Yes, lovely.'

The coffee came, with a dish of crisp almond biscuits and a glass of *grappa*. 'Is every meal in Italy a kind of celebration, Sandro?'

335

'That's the general idea. Don't you approve?'

'I could get used to it, that's for sure.'

A few more customers began to arrive, but the place was still uncrowded and Sandro and Tiger remained at the table for another hour, relaxed and happy, comfortable in each other's company. 'Tell me about Luigi. Is he like us, or does he have a job? He looks too well dressed to be a student, don't you think?'

'In Italy, appearances don't tell you the whole story. Very often, the most expensively turned-out people come from poor backgrounds, though in Luigi's case, this isn't so. His old man is rich, rather famous, something grand in the museum world; Luigi did tell me what, but I forget the exact details. Luigi himself is a post-graduate student; he's doing a master's degree in anthropology.'

'How interesting.' Tiger took a sip of coffee, then looked up at Sandro, her violet eyes perplexed beneath the heavy fringe of black hair. 'Tell me if I'm wrong, but I had the distinct impression that he wasn't all that thrilled about me sharing the apartment. I felt like an intruder.'

'If that's how he feels, he can always leave, can't he? No-one is forcing him to stay.'

'Isn't that a bit tough? After all, he was there before me, wasn't he?'

'*E vero*, but the apartment has to have three people sharing to make it affordable. Luigi thinks the third person should be a bloke, and I disagree with him.'

'But *why*?'

'Why do you think? Because, to use your horrible expression, *he* is pretty keen to get into *my* knickers!'

'Holy Mother! And does he succeed?'

'No, he bloody *doesn't*!' Sandro grinned. 'So that's why I've brought you into the picture. You're my — *come si dice?* – I don't know the English word.'

'Chaperone?' suggested Tiger, and began to laugh.

'That's it, chaperone. I hope you don't mind?'

'No, I don't *mind*, but what a weird set-up! How

336

come you took him on as a tenant in the first place? Didn't you have any clue about him?'

'Strangely enough, no, I didn't. It never occurred to me. One lives and learns, as they say.'

Sandro asked for the bill, and paid without Tiger's making a fuss about it. They said good night to the *padrona*, and walked slowly home together.

'Tomorrow,' said Tiger sleepily, as they climbed the stairs, 'I'll cook supper at home, OK?'

'*Benissimo!*'

November slid unobtrusively into December, and the weather became a little colder. By now, Tiger had found a more congenial job, working on Saturday mornings for a local florist. At the college, she had moved on from the cast room, and was now studying painting with egg tempera on wooden panels, making copies of the works of the early masters.

In the apartment, after an initial period of thinly disguised hostility on Luigi's part, life had become much more relaxed, even happy. Luigi was a kind and sensible man at heart, and he soon got bored with the negative atmosphere he was creating. If you can't beat them, better join them, he said to himself, and invited Sandro and Tiger to the theatre. After this highly successful evening, things between them became a great deal easier, and they went about together as a threesome. Luigi became very fond of Tiger, and frequently gave her small gifts of flowers or scent; even a beautiful antique coat. Life, for all of them, was interesting, and good.

Christmas came, and Tiger and Sandro went home to *La Commanderia* for the holiday. Living with Sandro and Luigi, both of whom were more than competent cooks, Tiger had greatly expanded her culinary repertoire, and she and Sandro elected to cook the Christmas Eve dinner, in order that Giuliana could be with her own family for a change. At half past eleven, they all walked along the lanes to the little church for

Midnight Mass. The church was packed, boiling hot, the air thick with the fumes of alcohol and incense. At the far end of the church, Tiger could see the blue-robed plaster statue of the Virgin and Child. The heads of both figures were surrounded by bright haloes of electric light bulbs. Not for the first time, she thought how curious it was that these tawdry, sentimental representations could inspire such intense, unquestioning religious fervour in so many people.

When the moment came for the people to get in line, and file slowly towards the statue in order to kiss the baby's foot, Con stood up, gathering his long tweed coat about himself. He looked down at Tiger, with a small, crooked smile. 'This is where I put my new-found faith to the test,' he said, and made his way towards the shuffling queue. Tiger stared after him, absolutely astonished.

In the wooden gallery, above the main entrance, the choir of local teenage girls burst into loud song, with a sound reminiscent of tearing lino. To her amazement, tears filled Tiger's eyes, and into her head came the image of the angel musicians in Piero della Francesca's *Nativity*, five sturdy country girls, joyfully welcoming their Saviour into the world.

Walking back to *La Commanderia* after the Mass, Enzo and Con went ahead, together but separately, each wrapped in his own preferred solitude. Tiger and Sandro followed them at a little distance, their moon-cast shadows black on the white dusty track. The contorted stumps of the ancient vines, black and hairy, seemed to hold out brittle stunted hands in an anguished appeal for the signal to put out new green leaves with which to cover their withered old limbs. The moon sailed overhead in a brilliant clear sky, and a shooting star raced across the firmament.

Tiger slipped her hand through Sandro's arm, glad of his proximity and warmth. 'Did you notice that Con went up and kissed the baby's foot?' she asked.

338

'I did.'

'Isn't that sort of thing a bit late in the day, for him?'

Sandro smiled. 'No, I don't think so, Tiger. I reckon it happens quite often.'

'Oh. You mean fire insurance?'

Sandro laughed, and the sound of his laughter echoed across the fields, so that the two older men turned round to look back at them. 'No, *of course* I don't mean fire insurance, you crazy girl!'

At Neill's Court, Christmas passed almost unobserved, for Tadeusz was working flat out to get the conversion of the stable-block finished, in order to allow him a useful period of private working time before the start of the new season. By the end of December, the job was almost complete, and Niamh decided that they should celebrate by opening a couple of bottles of champagne to welcome in the New Year, and their new partnership.

On New Year's Eve she cooked a goose for dinner, and invited Liam to join them, for he had been caring for Alice without a break for weeks on end. Happy to accept the invitation, Liam gave Alice her bath and put her to bed, bringing her supper to her on a tray. When she had finished, which was soon, for she was in a tetchy mood and unwilling to eat, Liam tucked her up and kissed her good night. 'Shan't be long, sweetheart,' he said. 'I'll be up presently.'

In winter, when the house was without guests, they maintained only minimal heating, and lived almost exclusively in the kitchen. It was here that they were to celebrate the turn of the year, and Niamh set the table in a suitably festive manner, with candles and a garland of apples, tangerines, dried figs and nuts. She brought out the family glass and silver, and her grandmother's beautiful table linen. Tadeusz, as he would have done in Poland, changed into his finest embroidered shirt and his wide trousers, and looked his romantic and handsome best. Niamh, drizzling honey over the golden, sizzling skin of her goose, glanced at him as he skilfully pulled the corks of the wine, and thought how lucky she was to have him as a lover. Everything will be fine, she told herself. All will be well with us; I know it will; I'm sure. She returned the goose to the slow oven, then put the first course, smoked trout, on the table. As if on cue, Liam entered the kitchen, carrying Alice's tray. Niamh took off her apron and they all sat down to eat.

At midnight, all the clocks in the formal rooms of the dark and silent house chimed, in poorly regulated sequence, some tinkly and shrill, the long-case clocks with a deeper resonance. In the kitchen, the radio was tuned to the BBC and the booming voice of Big Ben filled the air.

Smiling, happy, full of the bonhomie induced by the excellent food and copious wine, the three revellers raised their glasses and wished each other a happy New Year.

In her sleep, Alice heard the chiming of the clocks, and opened her eyes, for in a corner of her mind she was aware that it was a special day of some kind. I must ask Liam what it is, she said to herself; he did tell me, but I forgot. She got out of bed, and wrapped herself in her dressing gown. In the passage, the light was on and she made her way to Liam's room without difficulty, but found it empty. She frowned nervously, and began to whimper unhappily. She left the room, and went downstairs to the darkened hall, intending to look for Liam in the orangery. In the dimness, she mistook the doors and found herself in the drawing-room. The shutters and curtains were half closed, but enough light came through the windows to enable Alice to see quite clearly the room she had not sat in since her father's death, or so it seemed to her.

All at once, the fumbling grey fingers of her lost memory dissolved, and Alice recalled with extra-ordinary clarity the morning of the birth of her youngest daughter: Tiger, blue-eyed and black-haired, and hideously ugly. She remembered lying on the sofa, and saw Tara, her mother, holding the towel-swaddled baby before the boozy old priest, come to baptize the newborn child. I remember it all quite clearly, she said to herself confidently; there's nothing wrong with me, nothing at all. She crossed the room to the fireplace, brushing her fingers across the lid of the piano as she passed. The fire was laid, with paper, sticks and coal, topped by a big pile of logs, all ready for lighting.

Alice looked carefully round, and found a box of matches on the chimneypiece. She took a match from the box and struck it, squatting down in order to apply the flame to the paper. But the paper was damp and refused to ignite. Match after match Alice struck without success, burning her fingers in the process. She stood up, and, losing patience, began to strike the matches in rapid succession, hurling them angrily towards the uncooperative fire. She failed to notice when first one, then a second match landed on the hem of her nightgown. In seconds, she was engulfed in a sheet of flame, and, terrified, began to scream. She rushed to the windows and tried to wrap herself in one of the long heavy curtains, but the flames were so intense that the curtain caught fire as she pulled its frayed fabric from its wooden rings, and it fell on top of her, a great blazing torch.

It was only a matter of seconds before the smoke alarm sounded in the kitchen, but by the time they had succeeded in locating the source of the fire, it was too late. Tadeusz put out the flames with the extinguishers the law had compelled them to install, but when Liam tried to lift Alice's blackened body from the sea of foam, he knew that she was dead. Weeping, distraught, he cradled to his chest the charred remains of the woman he had loved for so long, and could not be persuaded to let her go until forced to do so by the arrival of the doctor, the police and the coroner.

*   *   *

Orla and Matthew, followed by Tiger and Con, arrived for Alice's funeral, in response to Niamh's brief but tearful telephone calls. The funeral took place in the local town, and after the burial, the family drove back to Neill's Court in the hired cars. They got out in the courtyard, and walked round the side of the house to the formal entrance. Matthew waited until Con and Tiger drew level with him. 'Could I have a word, Tiger?'

'Yes, of course.' She detached herself from her father's side, and looked up at Matthew enquiringly. 'What is it?'

'I thought I'd better let you know. I've put the emeralds back where they belong.' He smiled, rather self-mockingly. 'As a matter of fact, I got them valued, and it seems they're fakes.'

'Oh, God, Matthew! How awful! What about your money?'

'Least said, soonest mended, darling.' He looked ahead, and saw that his wife was waiting for him. 'I must go. Orla needs me.'

'Yes, of course. Thanks for telling me, Matthew.'

Niamh had turned up the heating for the benefit of the mourners, and Tadeusz had lit the fire in the hall, since the drawing-room was out of bounds for the time being.

It was, therefore, in the hall, under the watchful gaze of antlered stags' heads and Edwardian family portraits, that the company, having drunk a warming glass of sherry, were invited by the family lawyer to hear him read Alice's will. He had travelled all the way from Dublin expressly for this purpose, and was anxious to get back as quickly as he decently could.

The three sisters sat solemnly down at the head of the old rent table, with the men in their lives in a slightly embarrassed huddle at the other end. Liam, naturally, was in the kitchen, awaiting instructions. So intense was his grief at the loss of Alice that he hardly gave a thought to the inevitability of his being given notice by Niamh, now that his usefulness to her had come to its natural conclusion.

The lawyer opened the file containing Alice Fitzgerald's will, unfolded the document and began to read, his voice gravelly with self-importance.

'I, Alice Mary O'Neill Fitzgerald, do give and bequeath my entire estate to my beloved friend, Liam Dainty, to have and to hold, or to dispose of as he thinks fit. In the event of his predeceasing me, my estate shall pass after my death to his daughter, Orla Fitzgerald.'

The lawyer looked up, and his cynical little eyes swept round the astonished faces of the assembled company. 'The will was signed, dated and witnessed, in accordance with normal procedure, on 18 October 1963,' he said silkily.

After several frigid seconds, Orla, white-faced, spoke. 'Did you say "*his* daughter, Orla Fitzgerald", Mr Quinn?'

'Yes, Mrs Cleobury, I did. Those are the very words written here.' He cleared his throat. 'There's also a letter, dated 21 May 1981,' he added. 'Shall I read it?'

'Please do,' said Matthew clearly, from the end of the table.

Mr Quinn broke the seal of the envelope, and unfolded the single sheet of paper it contained. He laid the letter flat on the blotter before him, and began to read aloud.

'My dear daughters,

No doubt it will come as a shock to you to learn that the blood of Con Fitzgerald does not run in the veins of all three of you. In fact, only Tiger is his child for sure, and you only have to see them together to realize that.

'Orla, my firstborn, is Liam's child and no-one else's, and I only agreed to marry Con to save my parents the humiliation of finding out that I was pregnant by the stable-lad.

343

'*Darling Liam, he is and always will be the only man I ever loved. Orla is his child, and for all I know, so is Niamh, but you'd have to get the tests done to be quite sure of that, I suppose.*

'*Considering that you two girls are the daughters of a stable-lad, I reckon you've had a pretty good crack of the whip so far. Now, you'll have to look to Liam for favours, won't you?*

'*As for Tiger, she's her father's daughter, and he can take care of her.*

'*Ever your mother, Alice Fitzgerald.*'

Horrified, deeply shaken, Orla and Niamh, white-knuckled, kept their eyes fixed on the table, and said nothing. Tiger pushed back her chair, her face flushed, and stood up. 'Hadn't we better fetch Liam?' she asked.

'Hang on a minute, Tiger,' said Matthew. Calmly, he addressed the lawyer. 'Are you quite sure the will is valid, Quinn? Was it made before Mrs Fitzgerald became a victim of Alzheimer's disease?'

'Absolutely. It was written in my father's office, and witnessed by two members of his staff, shortly after the birth of Mrs Cleobury. Mrs Fitzgerald sent us the letter much later, in 1981, to be kept with her will, and remain unopened until after her death.' Mr Quinn stared frostily at the younger lawyer. 'Even at that later date, sir, Mrs Fitzgerald was still in her right mind. It was not until after the death of her parents some years later that her distressing illness began to manifest itself, as I'm sure you're all quite aware.' He looked sternly round the table. 'At that time, as far as I remember,' he remarked coldly, 'none of you seemed inclined to challenge Mrs Fitzgerald's legal right to her inheritance, or her competence to administer it.'

'Right,' said Matthew. 'That all seems perfectly clear, Mr Quinn. You can proceed in the usual way, of course?'

'Of course.'

Silently, Orla got to her feet, and equally silently left

the room, followed by her husband. In less than half an hour, a taxi had been summoned and they were on their way to the airport.

Liam was fetched from the kitchen and apprised by the lawyer of his good fortune. 'It will take a while for the will to be proved, but to all intents and purposes, Mr Dainty, the place is yours, for what it's worth.'

'I see,' said Liam, doubtfully.

'You stupid old fool!' exclaimed Niamh spitefully. 'Don't you understand? You can chuck us all out if you want to.'

Liam raised his sad and rheumy blue eyes to hers. 'Why would I want to do that, Miss Niamh?' he asked, his voice blurred with tears.

Tiger, refusing to meet the angry eyes of her sister, went to Liam and hugged him hard. 'I'll never forget you, darling Liam,' she said. 'You were always a good friend to me, as well as a terrific one to my mother, poor sad creature.' She kissed his tearstained old cheek, then, ignoring both Tadeusz and Niamh, took her father's arm and left the room. Half an hour later, they too had driven away from Neill's Court, never to return.

After supper that night, when Liam had recovered himself a little, he made the suggestion to Niamh that after all her hard work in making a success of the place, he would be quite happy for her to go on living and working at Neill's Court. 'You can carry on with the business, just as before, if that suits you and Mr Tadeusz,' he said, without too much conviction.

For the greater part of the night, she and Tadeusz discussed the pros and cons of Liam's proposal, and in the end decided to turn it down. 'After all, when Liam dies, Orla will want her pound of flesh, won't she? And it's not even certain that he's *my* father, too, is it? And if he's not, where will that leave us, Tadeusz?'

'In the shit, where else?'

*　　*　　*

At the end of the week, they transferred all Niamh's savings to Tadeusz's account in Paris, and left Neill's Court together, with the vaguely formulated plan of undertaking a similar scheme, comprising cookery and art classes, at Przywnica.

Liam stood on the steps and watched their cab disappear across the hill. Then he turned and went back into the house. From the drawing-room came the unmistakable sound of the old gramophone playing, and he hurried to switch it off, assuming that someone had been fooling around with it. As soon as he opened the door, he saw Alice, her beautiful body entirely visible through her gauzy pink night-gown, dancing in wide sweeping circles. He took her in his skinny old arms and kissed her eager lips, as they danced together. 'You always were a little whore, me darlin' girl,' he whispered, and they laughed delightedly.

Con and Tiger arrived in Rome, and, unexpectedly, were met at the airport by Sandro, come to drive them home. After supper, Sandro and Tiger took a walk under the olive trees. The same brilliant Christmas moon, although quite a lot smaller, still shone upon them, and Tiger found it difficult to believe that so much had happened between then and now.

'I hardly knew my mother, but it still feels awful, her being dead. Please God, Con lives for ever,' she said. 'I couldn't bear it without him.'

'I hardly ever see *my* mother, these days, but I feel exactly the same about her.'

'Why don't you see her, Sandro?'

'Inertia; idleness; stupidity. It's a lovely place, where she lives. We could visit her and see some of the churches, where the Giottos and the Piero della Francescas are, if you'd be interested in that?'

'*Interested?* Are you mad? I'd love to see them, more than anything.'

'OK, we'll arrange it, soon.' They began to walk back

346

to the house. 'I forgot to tell you,' he said. 'Luigi's leaving the apartment.'

'Oh, why?'

'He's found someone, at last. He's moving in with him.'

'Oh, well, that's good, isn't it?'

'So that just leaves us, now.'

'Won't we look for another tenant?'

'Personally, I'd rather not, if that's OK with you.'

Tiger turned towards him, frowning. She put a hand on his arm. 'What are you trying to say, Sandro?'

'I'm trying to tell you that I love you.'

'Well, *tell* me, then!'

'I love you, Tiger.'

'I thought you said I was like a sister to you, crazy man?'

'Well, I wasn't telling the strict truth, was I?'

'That's a relief, because as a matter of fact, I think I love you, too.'

'Only *think*, Tiger?'

'Won't that do?'

Sandro laughed, and kissed her. 'Yes,' he said. 'It'll do, for the moment.'

THE END

A BAREFOOT WEDDING

Elizabeth Falconer

Two families, both with secrets in their pasts . . .

Phyllida loved the magical Channel Isle of Florizel, where she had been spending summers since she was a small child. But this year she was in disgrace – expelled from school in the middle of her A Levels – and not looking forward to the family holiday at all. But then she met Andras, a handsome young fisherman whose family was hiding a secret from the wartime occupation of the islands, memories of which still divided the tiny community.

Meanwhile Rachel, trapped in a loveless marriage with a tyrannical Oxford academic, decided to make a sudden bid for freedom. She travelled to Italy and discovered passion for the first time; she also, inadvertently, stumbled on the clue to an old wartime tragedy. A clue which led Andras and Phyllida to Tuscany – and to the discovery which would change their lives.

'FALCONER'S BOOK IS OPTIMISTIC ABOUT THE HUMAN SPIRIT'
Woman and Home

0 552 99756 0

BLACK SWAN

WINGS OF THE MORNING

Elizabeth Falconer

Christian and his younger sister Emma, children of
a wealthy but spectacularly ill-matched couple,
had been brought up by their mother Flavia in the
hope that one of them, at least, would find a
vocation to the religious life. Their father Ludovic,
meanwhile, was absent from their lives for a great
deal of the time – an absence which, as they grew
up, became all too readily understandable. But
while Christian lived in London and
Gloucestershire with his wife Phoebe and their two
small children – a shamefully irreligious life,
according to Flavia – Emma followed her heart's
desire by training to be a fresco painter in Italy and
then, bowing to the incessant pressure from her
mother, became a nun in an enclosed order.

A tragedy in the family brought them all to crisis
point. Flavia fell apart, becoming increasingly and
fanatically religious. Phoebe and Christian had to
rebuild their family life, while Emma became
gloriously, unexpectedly free – finding love of a
more earthly kind in the glorious countryside of
Provence.

0 552 99755 2

BLACK SWAN

THE GOLDEN YEAR

Elizabeth Falconer

One enchanted summer in Provence and its
aftermath.

Summers, to Anna, had always meant the
Presbytery, the mellow old stone house in
Provence where her mother, the formidable
Domenica, lived. Now that Anna's marriage to
Jeffrey was all but over, she thought that she had
herself well organized, dividing her time between
her riverside home in London, her two teenage
children and her career as a gilder and restorer of
antiques. And then there were her summers in
France – a chance to eat and drink magnificently,
to sit in the sun and to recharge the batteries. She
hardly realised how narrow and lonely her life
had really become.

But one summer her brother Giò, an antiques
dealer in Paris, brought down a new friend to the
Presbytery. Patrick, a handsome television director,
suddenly opened up Anna's life in a new and
wonderful way, offering her a wholly unexpected
chance of happiness. But she did not immediately
see that others might not share her joy, and that her
beloved brother Giò could have quite different
ideas about Patrick and the future.

'A DELIGHTFUL EVOCATION OF THE SIGHTS,
SOUNDS AND FLAVOURS OF LIFE IN
PROVENCE'
Family Circle

0 552 99622 X

BLACK SWAN

THE LOVE OF WOMEN

Elizabeth Falconer

Nelly and Hugo lived a seemingly enviable life, with their three adorable little girls, their holidays at the beautiful family home in the Channel Islands, and their large, if disorganized, London house. Why, then, did Hugo feel increasingly inadequate? He began to wonder why Nelly had married him instead of Basil, their close ally from Cambridge days. Basil had instead become an indispensable family friend, and Nelly's demanding job as a hospital doctor seemed to overshadow Hugo's own successful but unremunerative career as a writer – Hugo felt as though his only function in Nelly's life nowadays was to babysit the children and keep an eye on the erratic au pair. One day, in a fit of rebellion, he packed his bags and went to stay with Basil's mother in her peaceful Paris flat on the lovely Ile St-Louis.

Basil, meanwhile, was facing an uncertain future. Tied by loyalty to Nelly and Hugo, and with a muddled and ambivalent series of past relationships, he was at first reluctant to commit himself when he met Olivia, the self-confident young English art student living in Paris who was interested in the work of Basil's late father, a much-admired Russian painter. While Hugo discovered how hard it was to escape from family ties, Basil was to find that friendship and love do not easily mingle.

'AN UNHURRIED, LUXURIOUS STORY OF RESOLUTION AND DISCOVERY . . . THE NOVEL'S CHARM LIES IN ITS UNPRETENTIOUSNESS AND THE AUTHOR'S AFFECTION FOR CHARACTERS'
Elizabeth Buchan, *Mail on Sunday*

0 552 99623 8

BLACK SWAN

A SELECTED LIST OF FINE WRITING
AVAILABLE FROM BLACK SWAN

THE PRICES SHOWN BELOW WERE CORRECT AT THE TIME OF GOING TO PRESS. HOWEVER TRANSWORLD PUBLISHERS RESERVE THE RIGHT TO SHOW NEW RETAIL PRICES ON COVERS WHICH MAY DIFFER FROM THOSE PREVIOUSLY ADVERTISED IN THE TEXT OR ELSEWHERE.

99822 2	A CLASS APART	Diana Appleyard	£6.99
14764 8	NO PLACE FOR A MAN	Judy Astley	£6.99
99854 0	LESSONS FOR A SUNDAY FATHER	Claire Calman	£5.99
99687 4	THE PURVEYOR OF ENCHANTMENT	Marika Cobbold	£6.99
99622 X	THE GOLDEN YEAR	Elizabeth Falconer	£6.99
99623 8	THE LOVE OF WOMEN	Elizabeth Falconer	£6.99
99755 2	WINGS OF THE MORNING	Elizabeth Falconer	£6.99
99756 0	A BAREFOOT WEDDING	Elizabeth Falconer	£6.99
99839 7	FROST AT MIDNIGHT	Elizabeth Falconer	£6.99
99795 1	LIAR BIRDS	Lucy Fitzgerald	£5.99
99759 5	DOG DAYS, GLENN MILLER NIGHTS	Laurie Graham	£6.99
99801 X	THE SHORT HISTORY OF A PRINCE	Jane Hamilton	£6.99
99848 6	CHOCOLAT	Joanne Harris	£6.99
99887 7	THE SECRET DREAMWORLD OF A SHOPAHOLIC		
		Sophie Kinsella	£5.99
99737 4	GOLDEN LADS AND GIRLS	Angela Lambert	£6.99
99909 1	LA CUCINA	Lily Prior	£6.99
99697 1	FOUR WAYS TO BE A WOMAN	Sue Reidy	£5.99
99747 1	M FOR MOTHER	Marjorie Riddell	£6.99
99814 1	AN INNOCENT DIVERSION	Kathleen Rowntree	£6.99
99753 6	AN ACCIDENTAL LIFE	Titia Sutherland	£6.99
99872 9	MARRYING THE MISTRESS	Joanna Trollope	£6.99
99780 3	KNOWLEDGE OF ANGELS	Jill Paton Walsh	£6.99
99673 4	DINA'S BOOK	Herbjørg Wassmo	£6.99
99723 4	PART OF THE FURNITURE	Mary Wesley	£6.99
99835 4	SLEEPING ARRANGEMENTS	Madeleine Wickham	£6.99
99651 3	AFTER THE UNICORN	Joyce Windsor	£6.99

All Transworld titles are available by post from:

Bookpost, P.O. Box 29, Douglas, Isle of Man IM99 1BQ

Credit cards accepted. Please telephone 01624 836000,
fax 01624 837033 or Internet http://www.bookpost.co.uk.
or e-mail: bookshop@enterprise.net for details

Free postage and packing in the UK. Overseas customers: allow
£1 per book (paperbacks) and £3 per book (hardbacks).